# THE
# THIEF'S
# RELIC

**The *Son of Avaria* Trilogy**
*The Thief's Relic*
*The Bloodstone's Curse*

# THE THIEF'S RELIC

ANGELA KNOTTS MORSE

AN ENCOURAGING THOUGHT PUBLISHERS

The Thief's Relic

www.angelamorse.com

The story, all names, characters, and incidents portrayed in this production are fictitious. No identification with actual persons (living or deceased), places, buildings, and products is intended or should be inferred.

ISBN 978-1-73-788092-9 (Paperback)

ISBN 978-1-73-788093-6 (Hardcover)

Edited by Sara Jean Englert

Book Cover by Etheric Tales

Chapter Headers and Breaks by Etheric Tales

Portrait Illustrations and Pendant Art by Laura Parker

Map Art by Angela Knotts Morse

2nd Edition 2023

An Encouraging Thought Publishers

Birmingham, AL

11 10 9 8 7 6 5 4 3 2

*To Mrs. Smart,*
*Who lit within me the fire to write*
*twenty years ago*

## Praise for *The Thief's Relic*

"Adventurous, exciting, and thrilling. A fantastic start to a promising trilogy! I can't wait for more!"

-H.C. Newell, author of the *Fallen Light* series

"Wow, *The Thief's Relic* really blew me away. I had goosebumps at the end!"

-Jen Woodrum, author of *When Death is Coming*

# PRONUNCIATION GUIDE

## PEOPLE

| | |
|---|---|
| **Eamonn** | AY-mun |
| **Hadli** | HAD-lee |
| **Dorylss** | DOR-ulss |
| **Leyna** | LAY-nuh |
| **Marielle** | mair-ee-ELL |
| **Melwyn** | MEL-winn |
| **Noriden** | NOR-ih-dinn |
| **Kinrid** | KIN-rid |
| **Gilleth** | GILL-eth |
| **Taran** | TAIR-an |
| **Teiyn** | TAYN |
| **Imrilieth** | im-RILL-ee-eth |
| **Rothgard** | ROTH-gard |

## PLACES

| | |
|---|---|
| **Sarieth** | SAH-ree-eth |
| **Erai** | AIR-eye |
| **Idyrria** | ih-DEER-ee-uh |
| **Nos Illni** | NOHS ILL-nee |
| **Teravale** | TAIR-uh-VAIL |
| **Caen** | CAYN |
| **Avaria** | uh-VAH-ree-uh |
| **Holoreath** | hu-LOR-ee-ath |
| **Nidet** | NIY-dett |
| **Rifillion** | ri-FILL-ee-un |
| **Braedel** | bray-DELL |

## OTHER

| | |
|---|---|
| **Kaethiri** | kuh-THEER-ee |
| **Réalta** | RAYL-tuh |
| **Rovis** | ROH-viss |
| **Bardan** | BAR-dun |

ONE

THE NIGHT SKY COVERED the world like a heavy curtain, black as tar, with no moon to cast light on Eamonn as he skulked along the street's edge. Three-story buildings stood close together on the tight street, the wood and stone shops quiet in the shadow of the mountains.

Dogs barked in the distance, trying to assert their dominance over each other with no concern for the sleeping residents of Erai. Deep into the night, Eamonn could count on meeting no one in the sleeping city. In recent years, he had become skilled in the art of thievery—rather, the art of not getting caught.

A soft breeze played with Eamonn's fair curls and tickled his ear. He brushed the hair away and checked over his shoulder to make sure no one followed him. No, the way was clear. Only an empty street and silent shop faces lay behind him.

He headed in the direction of Mirab's shop, hoping to get a little coin out of the moneybox and perhaps a parchment or two, if he could stash them. Eamonn hadn't stolen from Mirab in a few weeks, putting his shop at the top of his rotation.

Eamonn's destination awaited him around the corner, a few paces away. His heart began to jump, the way it always did when he was about to commit a theft. In all his time stealing, he'd never been able to determine whether it stemmed from guilt or the fear of being caught. Maybe both.

He ignored the fluttering of his heart and focused on steadying his hands. At the door of the shop, Eamonn pulled two long, slender tools out of his belt pouch and gently slid them into the lock together. As his left hand held one tool steady and his right began to work the lock, a strong hand gripped his shoulder.

Eamonn froze, all his muscles tensing in a mix of surprise and regret.

"What do we have here?" a male voice hissed behind him. "You look as though you've done this before."

Not good. Really not good. The nervous fluttering of Eamonn's heart escalated to panicked pounding. Where did this person come from and how did he catch him? He'd heard no footsteps or rustlings of movement. Eamonn's mind raced with the possibilities of what his next move should be. Try to run? Plead for mercy?

He had never even come close to being caught before and hadn't fully thought out what he would do if it ever happened. Even the minimal punishment for stealing—a short jail sentence—frightened him. Eamonn couldn't let anything get in the way of his education and plans for the future. If he ran and didn't escape, though, and his captor discovered his history of thefts... well, even his age wouldn't keep him from the gallows.

In that moment, he decided his best chance would be to beg for any kind of pardon he might receive. If he surrendered and asked for forgiveness, he might be shown a little mercy.

Eamonn pulled his tools out of the lock, hands shaking. The metal tools clattered to the ground as he turned to face his accuser. His eyes had adjusted to the pitch-black night well enough to distinguish a group of lads, only a few years older than himself, smiling down at him.

"Go on, show us."

Eamonn narrowed his eyes, confused, trying to better read the boy's face. Was this a trick? It might be a set-up, hoping to catch him in the act, but they were teenage boys. What could they do?

Best to do as they say, he figured. Eamonn picked up his tools and inserted them into the lock as before, now intensely aware of his audience. His heart slowed a little but still beat like a rock in his chest. He zeroed in on his task, moving the picks back and forth in a delicate dance, feeling the gears of the lock through the tools as if they were his own hands. In seconds, the lock clicked quietly and Eamonn turned the knob. The door pushed open. Stashing his picks, he stared back up at the faces watching him. The boys grinned with approval, the one in front simply nodding his head as he spoke.

"You have skill. You must be the one we've been looking for."

Drawing his eyebrows together, Eamonn stood up and crossed his arms. "What do you mean you've been looking for me?"

With a single chuckle, the lad replied, "Someone has been beating us to a lot of the best spots in recent months, and we can't go in right after. Wrecks our strategy. So, we watched you, learned your pattern, and planned to look for you at your next location."

"But why?"

A subtle jerk of the speaker's head signaled for the other boys to go into the shop, ready to steal. "What's your name?"

Flashing his eyes to the boys passing him into his target, he warily answered, "Eamonn."

"And how long have you been doing this, Eamonn?"

"A year or two, my father—"

"You see no reason that you will stop anytime soon, do you?"

Eamonn shifted on his feet. "No."

A grin spread across the boy's face. "Then you're just like us. Thieving is our way of life. We would love to have someone with your skill set and ingenuity join us."

Then it clicked. Eamonn knew these boys. Well, not personally, but their band was infamous. They had a legendary reputation in Erai, living and stealing in the city but never being seen. They might as well have been ghosts. He couldn't believe he now stood with them, saw them in the flesh. "You're the Thieves' Guild," he breathed.

The boy nodded. "So, you've heard of us."

"Everyone has."

"But you never see us. And we never get caught. You must be doing this as a way to sustain yourself; it's why we do it too."

Eamonn glanced over his shoulder at the pillaging happening in the shop he had broken into. The boys of the Thieves' Guild were strategic, meticulous—only taking enough to be worthwhile but not too much to be missed right away. Perhaps he could still manage to take the parchments, but he would have to settle with less coin, and it was the coin he needed most. He was down to his last loaf of bread.

"Think it over," the boy said, drawing Eamonn's attention away from the shop. "But I know you have nothing to lose by joining us, or else you wouldn't do this at all."

Their loot in tow, the boys left the shop with almost no indication they had robbed it, propping the door open for Eamonn as if giving it back to him. A show. A sliver of anger rose in Eamonn's chest. Part of how they recruited, he supposed. A "join-us-or-we'll-beat-you-to-all-your-spots" tactic.

The group turned away from Eamonn to slink like shadows through the night. Before their leader had gotten far, though, Eamonn let out a sharp whisper.

"Wait!"

The leader turned back around, his face triumphant. He must have already predicted this outcome.

"I'll join."

The boy held out his hand for Eamonn to shake. "Good choice. My name is Hadli, and this is my band. You'll fit in quite well here."

Eamonn grinned a little, but his stomach turned for it. He was glad to belong somewhere, even if it was to the Thieves' Guild.

Hadli and the thieves led Eamonn to their hideout on the outskirts of Erai, where they concocted all their schemes and convened before thefts. Outside the city, they followed the edge of the mountains where the river cut through, with a rocky, tree covered bank on either side. They trekked far from any habitation, losing all sight of the city behind them, and finally turned from the river at a face of inconspicuous rock no different from the rest.

Each boy disappeared behind the rock face, but where were they going? The small outcropping came to an end almost as soon as it began. Hadli flashed a smile at the bewilderment on Eamonn's face.

"We have a pretty secret hideaway," he said, answering the questions in Eamonn's head. "If you're not looking hard enough, it just looks like the side of the mountain. But you'll see," he continued, stepping around a jutting rock and slipping his body through a crevice, "there's a whole cave in here."

Eamonn copied exactly what Hadli did, threading his slim frame through the small opening in the rock, surprised to come out on the other side. Never in his life had he been inside a mountain before—never till this moment. He and Hadli stood in a natural tunnel, spacious given the opening but still narrow. Eamonn had thought the night especially black, but here he found a new level of darkness. He heard Hadli breathing, confirming the lad's presence in front of him, but otherwise, Eamonn wouldn't have even known he was there.

"It's dark, for sure, but you'll learn it just as we have," Hadli explained, taking Eamonn by the wrist and delving further into the mountain's depths on a slight incline. "It opens up as you go on through."

Eamonn stuck close to Hadli while he navigated through the tunnels, as Hadli clearly knew each twist and curve like the back of his hand. A faint orange glow ahead of them, indicating they must be close to the hideaway, gave Eamonn a little more clarity to his surroundings. Hadli turned a corner and released

Eamonn's wrist, and lantern light welcomed them into a rugged, dank lair.

The end of the tunnel opened both wider and taller, making for a spacious hideout. Eamonn looked up in awe at the cave's ceiling, studded with pointed stalactites. A narrow opening high in the cave drew the smoke away from the fire that filled the room with light. Hadli joined the rest of the boys, and Eamonn took two staggering steps forward, studying the rest of the space.

In the center of the cave, a fire pit had been built into the ground, edged with stones from the rocky bank outside the mountain and circled with halved logs as seats. A single large, rectangular table stood to its right, and Eamonn couldn't help but wonder how the boys fit that through the cave's entrance. They had to have brought the lumber in and constructed it themselves. Several maps of the city covered the table top, each one marked in places with different symbols. A few shelves stood at the left wall, housing their stores of loot, and farther back sat some cots with simple bedclothes: more construction they must have done inside the cave.

Hadli turned back to Eamonn while helping the other boys unload their latest acquisitions onto the shelves. With light shining on them for the first time since they'd met, Hadli looked Eamonn up and down and took in his features.

"You know, you hardly look Idyrrian," he said, and he spoke the truth. Eamonn's sandy locks, light skin, and green eyes had always made him stand out in the crowd in his home province of Idyrria. Hadli, on the other hand, represented the typical Idyrrian man, with tawny skin, dark brown hair and eyes, and a dark stubble of facial hair that grew along his jaw.

Eamonn shrugged at Hadli's comment. He had heard it all his life. "My mother was Mirish," he answered.

Hadli chuckled and emptied the last bit of loot into the pile. "You must look nothing like your father."

Another truth. There was no speck of resemblance tying Eamonn to his father, the strong, broad, dark, handsome soldier. Without a doubt, the man could have denied fathering Eamonn, and Eamonn always thought it curious he never had.

"Why don't I show you around?" Hadli suggested, tearing Eamonn from his thoughts. "Introduce you?"

Eamonn gave Hadli a weak smile in agreement. "Oh, uh... sure."

Beaming, Hadli turned to the crowd of thieves organizing the loot on the shelves. "Lads," he announced, "let's officially welcome our newest member, Eamonn!"

A round of applause echoed off the stone walls of the cave. The boys in the Guild smiled at him, their faces as young and innocent as his own. Not one of them looked like a hardened criminal, the kind of person you'd be afraid to cross. No, just a bunch of downtrodden boys who had found each other. Eamonn saw his own reflection in this crew—unfortunate, hungry, driven to stealing just to eat.

The applause died down and the boys returned to their tasks. Hadli directed Eamonn to the table covered with maps, notebooks, and papers.

"Here is where we plan our... operations, if you will," Hadli told him, a corner of his mouth raised. "We've taken notes on how easy it is to get in a place, what kind of loot is there, if they have any security, if it's worth going back, things like that. We're particular about only taking a little at a time to not be easily noticed. Like I said before, we've never been caught."

"That's really impressive, especially considering the City Guard is keeping an eye out for you." Eamonn said, eyebrows raised.

Hadli lifted his hands, palms up, in a shrug. "Maybe. We try to keep a low profile. We'd prefer to be seen as a menace rather than organized crime. I think we accomplish that. Anyway, we meet here every three nights. Sometimes we're just planning, sometimes we have an operation. It just depends."

Eamonn nodded slowly as he absorbed this information. In only a few hours on a night as ordinary as any other, he'd managed to find a whole secret world full of people so much like him. And now, he was a part of it.

"You can stay here if you like, or you can return home," Hadli told him, gesturing to the line of pallets in the back of the cave. "Several of us don't have a home to go back to, so there will always be someone here if you need to get away."

Eamonn cleared his throat. "Thanks, but, um... I should probably go back home. My father might wonder where I am."

Hadli's head bobbed in understanding, and he clasped a hand onto Eamonn's shoulder. "Well, the offer stands. And, uh, for your trouble—" Hadli dug into a pouch at his waist and held his hand out to Eamonn, giving him a small pile of coins. "Since we took your target." He grinned again, a little apologetically. "See you in three days."

With a small smile to Hadli, Eamonn turned toward the tunnel and trekked back the length of the cave. The oppressive darkness that shrouded him inside the mountain now gave way to the gray-black of night in a stark contrast.

Outside, Eamonn could at least make out his surroundings, even though he still had a few more hours till dawn. Millions of stars twinkled above him, glittering specks that decorated the night sky. Only the slightest tinge of coolness hung on the air, summer not yet having given way to autumn. Eamonn breathed in deeply, enjoying the mild weather and trying to push away the nagging tug in the back of his mind. It was bad enough that he had resorted to thievery to survive, but now to actually be a member of the Thieves' Guild? His father would disown him. No, actually, his father wouldn't care.

He arrived home with darkness to spare and climbed into his small bed in the spare room of his father's provided quarters in the military district. Florin's loud snoring passed through the wall, assuring Eamonn that he was entirely unaware of his son's nighttime disappearance, as usual.

The bed felt especially lumpy as Eamonn tried to fall asleep, and he tossed and turned on the thin mattress, trying to get comfortable. Perhaps his lack of sleep—and load of guilt—kept him from finding a soft spot in the bed. In a few short hours, he would have to be back up and ready for school, and he made it a point to never be late.

Eamonn reached under the neck of his tunic and pulled out the pendant that always hung on a chain around his neck. The necklace previously belonged to his mother and Eamonn had grown up with it, never knowing a day without it. He held the pendant between his fingers, running his thumb over the familiar shape. Its intricate swirls of silver met in four points that surrounded a central green stone. He always kept it close, the sole connection he had to his mother.

Eamonn often wondered what she would think of him, having resorted to the life of a thief. He knew he never would have started to steal if she still lived. His father rarely spoke of her, but on the uncommon occasion that he did, he revealed some attribute of her that likened her to an angel. Eamonn hoped she was in fact an angel, staying close to him and keeping him from harm. With thoughts of the mother he never knew filling his mind, Eamonn relaxed and closed his eyes, and the exhaustion that plagued his body finally overcame him and he fell asleep.

The sounds and smells of sizzling meat wafted through the door to Eamonn's room. His rumbling stomach woke him up, and he ached for the taste of the meat. Still worn out from the previous night's adventures, Eamonn forced himself to get out of his bed and put on his threadbare clothes for school. They swallowed him, even when he put a belt around his hips to hold up his trousers and tied a rope around the waist of his tunic. The clothes came from his father's training days when he was young, a fresh recruit for the military. Clearly, they had seen better days.

Eamonn picked up his last loaf of bread out of the box in the corner where he stashed his stolen food, tore off a bit to munch on, then stuffed it into his school bag. He grabbed his canteen, planning to fill it up at the nearby water pump, and entered the main room of the house.

Florin crouched over the fire, turning the screaming sausages over in the frying pan that hung above the flames. He glanced up at Eamonn's appearance in the room, then returned his eyes to the sausage he was cooking.

"Good morning, Father," Eamonn greeted with only a little cheer. Despite his father's distance, Eamonn still attempted a relationship.

"Hello, Son," Florin replied. He poked a sausage, decided it was done, and put it on a plate.

Eamonn didn't remember a day when his father treated him with anything more than apathy. The strong, silent soldier didn't hurt Eamonn, he didn't yell or belittle him, but neither did he provide him with more than basic necessities. Eamonn grew up as the burden Florin was forced to bear.

As a soldier in the Idyrrian army, Florin didn't earn much money, and what he did, he spent primarily on himself. He fed Eamonn less than half of what he ate, clothed him in his old garments, and sent him to school with worn out materials.

Eamonn could get by with less food—he had grown accustomed to his stomach's constant rumble—and he made do with his father's oversized clothes, but his lack of good school books and proper materials drove him to start stealing. He found joy in school, in learning, unlike anywhere else, and he refused to let his father take that from him. Going to school and gaining knowledge felt like acquiring power to Eamonn, the only power he had.

Eamonn lingered in the doorway, drinking in the scent of the sausage, daring to hope his father might have made some for him. "I'm about to leave for school."

"Very good," Florin responded, looking up at his son once again. His dark eyes reflected the fire before him, his black eyebrows knitted together in thought. "Have you always been so thin?" he asked.

Eamonn stopped short. He had only taken his first step toward the door, but his father's question surprised him so much it caused him to stop mid-step, and he nearly toppled over.

"Um, uh—" He tried to find his answer. "Well, yes, I have."

"Here." Florin stuck one of the sausages with a fork and held it out before Eamonn. "You won't be of much use as a man if you don't have some meat on those bones."

Eamonn hesitated to stretch out his hand and take the offering, trying to decipher his father's motives. It could be a nasty trick, taunting Eamonn with kindness only to pull it back and laugh in his face. No, that wasn't like him. Florin was distant and apathetic, but never cruel. Maybe he was finally changing. Maybe Eamonn would no longer have to steal.

But he had just promised his allegiance to the Thieves' Guild.

The sausage hung in midair until finally Eamonn reached out and took it from the fork. With one bite, savory flavors he seldom tasted flooded his mouth. He relished every morsel of hot, cooked food. After the small portions his father gave him, he tried to fill his belly with bread, fruit, and raw vegetables; that is, food that was easy to steal.

Eamonn must have closed his eyes to better taste his food, because when his father spoke again, he realized he had to open them.

"You're almost to training age now. You'll need some muscle on you if you're going to make a good soldier."

Eamonn's heart sank. Of course. Florin wanted him to be a soldier, just like him. Eamonn didn't have the heart to admit to his father that his love was for learning, that he longed to go to the prestigious College at Nos Illni one day and further his education. This morning, his father showed kindness, showed an interest in his son; that conversation could wait.

Taking another bite of the sausage, Eamonn simply nodded in response and headed for the door, stopping at the threshold. He turned, his heart fluttering as he said over his shoulder, "Thank you."

Instead of waiting for words from his father that would never come, he shut the door behind him and began his journey to school.

Dust kicked up around his heels as he trod through the military residences toward the path that would lead him into the city. What little joy he found in his father's moment of kindness was held hostage by the confirmation of what Florin wished for Eamonn's future.

Had Florin paid any attention to Eamonn through the years, he would have noticed his son excelling in school. Idyrria boasted the best schools of all provinces in Sarieth, valuing the education of future generations as a core value of their culture, and Eamonn grew up with access to the finest education. Each advancing year of classes displayed his brightness, his talent, and his continual thirst for more.

He made an ideal candidate for the college at Nos Illni, the greatest institution of higher education in the whole country. Only the most dedicated students continued on to the college after finishing the standard education, pursuing futures as physicians, apothecaries, scholars, philosophers, alchemists, or justices, to name a few. The advisors and council of the kings had all been educated at Nos Illni. Graduates of the college boasted the finest opportunities.

At fourteen years old, only two more years remained until Eamonn would come of age and complete his schooling. When he turned sixteen, he would be expected to either become an apprentice of a trade, continue to the college, or train for the military. Truth be told, he had lost hope of going to the college years ago; they charged fees. Eamonn knew his father would never supply the funds.

He sighed as he trudged to his free standard education. He could go through with Florin's wish for his future, or he could remove himself from his father's authority entirely. *Works out*, he thought, *now that there's another place for me to go.*

As he approached the inner city, buildings stood closer together, the streets narrowed, and more people surrounded him.

Though not the largest city in Idyrria, Erai came close. The school loomed in the distance on a hill, the central feature of the city and their most prized one. Eamonn pushed toward it, falling into the same path of other students who smiled and waved at him. No one knew the life he lived after dark. His teachers all loved him. He licked his lips and tasted the sausage his father had given him.

Nothing had changed, not really. His father knew no true love. Florin only saw in Eamonn another recruit for the inactive, useless, brawny military that spent their time frequenting pubs and occasionally settling disputes.

Resolute, Eamonn set his jaw and pulled open the heavy wooden door to the school. He would not become a soldier to please his father.

# TWO

THE THIRD NIGHT ARRIVED. Eamonn left for the cave two hours after sunset, waiting for the cover of night to keep him veiled during his journey to the Guild's headquarters for his first operation.

A shiver ran through his body despite the warmth of the night. What if the Thieves' Guild didn't accept him? His newfound determination to strike out on his own would be shattered. Or what if he wasn't as good a thief as they imagined him to be? He knew nothing about these boys, not really. They seemed kind enough the other night, taking him into their company, but had they shown their true character?

Eamonn shook his head at himself as he trod on the dry grass. Best not to make assumptions. Tonight would show him a better picture of this crew. Tonight, he had to prove himself to them, secure his place among them. Among thieves.

He followed the river though the mountains with sharp eyes, dragging his left hand along the rough rock face as he walked. The entrance to the cave could be easily missed even though he was looking for it, and the moon only offered a little light, so feeling the mountainside should help him find where the rock separated.

Eamonn trekked for a while down the riverbank. Had it taken this long to reach the cave the other night?

He took a few more steps, convinced he'd gone too far, when his hand slid off the rocky side of the mountain into an opening. He peered into the crevice behind the rock face. Yes, he'd made it. His eyes darted around the riverbank and back over the way he came to make sure no one watched him, then he slipped his body through the opening and into the cave.

Pitch black darkness hit him. Even though his eyes could see in the night, the bit of moonlight outside made a remarkable difference to the complete absence of light in the cave. He reached out his hand again to feel the cave wall, following it as his eyes strained to make out any kind of shape. A dim light appeared around a corner as he continued down the black tunnel. He must be close. The musty scent of the cave grew stronger, and Eamonn turned up his nose. He figured he would get used to the smell over time, but that didn't make it pleasant.

Rounding the last corner, he blinked at the sudden light of the innermost room. Hadli stood over a table and pointed at a map, plotting with two of the others. Eamonn moved like a shadow in his worn shoes; no one noticed he'd entered the cave until the firelight illuminated his face.

"Crow's feathers, Eamonn, no wonder you make such an ex-cellent thief!" Hadli exclaimed, gripping the cloth at his chest in surprise. "I didn't know anyone could move so quietly."

Eamonn swelled at Hadli's praise, one corner of his mouth lifting for an instant. A good start. This was only his second encounter with the group and he already felt more welcome there than he did in his own home.

Eamon cleared his throat and stepped forward to get a better look at the map on the table. "What's our plan for tonight?" he asked, hoping he gave the impression of assertiveness. He figured that would be the fastest way to prove he belonged there.

Hadli laid a finger on a marked area. "We were thinking of going into the fishing district, over on the river. Tonight's primarily a food night."

Eamonn nodded, scratching behind his ear. "How do we carry that much fish?"

"Well, first of all, we don't get that much," Hadli explained, facing Eamonn. The firelight glowed on the right half of his face, casting the other side in shadow, making him appear more sinister than he sounded. "We may be thieves, but we know our limits. We take enough to sustain ourselves until we can go again."

Eamonn deflated. The fraction of pride he felt vanished with Hadli's clear, but gentle, reminder that he was still new.

"But to answer your question, we have bags." Hadli gestured over his shoulder to a spot by the shelves where burlap sacks lay in a pile. "We don't take them every night, and not all of us go out every time. It just depends on what the haul is. But for something like fish, we'll need all hands and bags in them."

Eamonn glanced at the sacks and then at the boys who lounged on their cots or sat around the fire, playing games and laughing, and his heart ached to be one of them.

"When do we leave?" he asked, eager to fit in and show his commitment to their way of life.

"Oh, not for a while yet," Hadli answered, leaning against the table. "People in the city need to be sound asleep. But you know that." He chuckled once. "You're probably better at this than some of these guys on their own."

Cries of "Hey!" and "Who are you talking about?" flew from the gatherings at the fire and the makeshift beds, and Hadli threw his head back with a laugh. A full, rich sound that bounced off the walls of the cave, the laugh encompassed everyone around.

Eamonn didn't know how Hadli had taken charge of the band, but he possessed such a natural charisma and undeniable leadership quality that made him the obvious leader of the group. Hadli was easy to like and easy to follow. His charm and congeniality filled Eamonn with an intense curiosity—what background led Hadli to this life?

Hadli sauntered over to the bed and motioned for Eamonn to follow. "You can sleep some, if you like. A few of us try to rest before an operation. Don't worry," he added, grinning at Eamonn, "we'll make sure to wake you before we leave."

Smiling back in thanks, Eamonn sat on one of the empty cots as Hadli joined the boys by the fire. The lads near him on the other cots introduced themselves before lying down to rest.

Eamonn stretched out on one of the simple beds, but adrenaline pulsed through his body and kept his mind buzzing. The anticipation of his first theft as part of the Thieves' Guild had him wired. But Eamonn needed the sleep to do his best job on their operation, so he forced his eyes shut and begged his brain to turn off, to ignore his mixed feelings about being part of such a group. He took a deep breath of the damp cave air and released it slowly. This would be all right, this would work out, he had nothing to worry about. Everything would be fine.

Hadli shook Eamonn awake minutes later. At least, it felt like minutes to Eamonn. He rubbed his eyes fiercely, pushing out any remnants of sleep. Other boys stretched and stood up, some of them changing out of heavy boots into leather slippers. Hadli picked up the sacks and tossed them out individually, one nearly landing on Eamonn's head.

"Careful where you toss, there," Eamonn said, trying to keep his attitude light. Hadli chuckled at him and passed out the remaining sacks.

"All right, lads, gather 'round," Hadli called, and the boys all convened at the candlelit table, some of them jostling elbows while others threw their arms over their friends' shoulders. "We're going to the fishing district, so we don't have far to travel. Now here—" he pointed to a spot close to the river's edge, "is where they keep their freshest catches, what they haven't yet salted or put in the cold cellar. It means more work for us in the end, but it would be easier to acquire. It's also only a barrel or two, the last catches of the day. Here—" his finger moved in toward the fishing district, "is the cold cellar for fish that has been processed, packed in barrels of salt, and is ready for market. It's the majority of the supply." He tapped his finger on the map. "This is our target."

Hadli looked at Eamonn. "We've taken from the barrels near the river before, and it wasn't too difficult, but risky. Very open, easy to be seen. They shouldn't have anyone guarding—at least, they haven't in the past. But anyone outside could see us."

Eamonn nodded, giving Hadli his rapt attention. He didn't want to miss a single syllable.

Turning back to the group, Hadli continued. "We'll scout out and see if they have anyone patrolling, but put our focus on the cellar. The entrance is at ground level and locked with a padlock, but that should be easy enough to pick, right Eamonn?"

All eyes turned to him. Eamonn shifted his eyes over the whole gang, finally landing on Hadli. "Easy enough," he replied, shrugging off the question. He'd rarely had a problem with a lock before, but the expectations of the group added an extra pressure that made him doubt. He couldn't let them down on his very first mission.

"Excellent. Everyone will take ten fish, pulling from different barrels. They don't need to know they have been stolen from, understood?"

The boys around the table all nodded in acknowledgment. Eamonn studied their faces, finding them all ready, all willing, with no trace of fear or hesitation.

The Guild consisted of twelve thieves, whom Eamonn assumed to be in an age range of about fifteen to eighteen. Why the older ones remained with the group, he could not fathom. At sixteen, they could take apprenticeships or at least become soldiers. Some tradesmen might have a hard time taking on an apprentice with little formal education or background, but the military took anyone willing.

As Eamonn stood there considering, though, the realization fell to the bottom of his gut like a rock. This must be the only life they knew. The older boys could have been doing this for years, maybe even quitting school and functioning as a member of honest society. The Guild was possibly all they had left.

While Eamonn saw his membership in this group as a means to an end, for others, it *was* their end.

"All right then," Hadli announced, "let's head out."

Two boys at a time left the cave. They could slip through the night more deftly that way, not to mention if a pair ever got caught, they wouldn't implicate the entire group in their crime. Although Hadli assured them that no one would get caught as long as he was in charge.

Hadli paired himself with Eamonn to give him "the best first-hand experience" as Hadli put it. In other words, he intended to oversee Eamonn's "training." They left the cave third, keeping close to the ground and quiet as shadows as they skimmed through the fragrant grass that grew along the riverbed.

A sliver of moon shone above them, just beginning its waxing phase. Thin clouds passed overhead and diffused the light, casting the night in a dark gray rather than black. Soft winds rustled the reeds that grew at the river's edge. Eamonn heard the movement of the reeds and almost looked, but his instincts kicked in before he betrayed himself by checking for followers. He needed to show his courage tonight, his aptitude, and his stealth.

The fishing district lay at the edge of city limits, where the river ended and the city began. The distinctive smell of recently caught fish permeated the air, and Eamonn wrinkled his nose.

Piers and boat docks built into the river signaled to the boys that they were nearing their target. Hadli and Eamonn kept as far away from the riverbank as they could as outlines of buildings took shape before them. Hadli pointed in front of Eamonn, and Eamonn turned in the direction of his finger, spotting the entrance to the cellar he had described.

Eamonn didn't often come to this side of the city, far away from his home in the military district on the south side and not on his way to the school in the city center. A tingling of nerves started in his stomach and threatened to move upward. Eamonn wished they hadn't come to a part of the city so foreign to him. He could really showcase his talents in an area he felt comfortable, but unfamiliar territory put him on edge.

Hadli guided Eamonn to a spot in the grass still several meters away from the cellar, and they crouched down. A low form slithered up to them, silent as a snake.

"No patrols spotted," one of the boys in the Guild, Joris, whispered to them. "Alithir scouted the opposite direction as me, and he didn't see any either."

"Good," Hadli whispered. "Now lay low until we get the doors open, then hurry inside."

Joris nodded and slinked off to pass the information along.

Could they really pull this off so effortlessly? Alone, yes, but in such numbers? It seemed like nothing to them. Eamonn knew four members of the Guild hid here in the tall grass already, and another two followed close behind, yet aside from Hadli right next to him, Eamonn had only seen any sign of Joris. Somehow, the boys had become invisible. No wonder they never got caught.

Hadli turned his face toward Eamonn in the dark, his black eyes catching the starlight. The twinkle it created in his eyes looked vibrant, mischievous... cunning. Perhaps his eyes reflected his soul.

"Ready?" he murmured. Eamonn nodded, and Hadli shot off like a dart. Eamonn kept close on his heels, both staying low to the ground as they crossed from grass to paved road. They flung their bodies in the shadows cast by the cellar entrance, an awning over the doors helping to keep them concealed.

Eamonn knelt down at the double door entry of the cellar, examining the chain and padlock that held them together. Internally, he released most of his nerves and replaced them with relief. He knew this lock mechanism well, a pretty standard mechanism for a padlock. Getting the padlock open would not be an issue, he determined, but the rattling of the chain might be.

"Hold it steady," he said to Hadli in a low whisper, tapping the lock with one of his picks. Hadli took the lock in one gentle hand and held the chain in the other. Eamonn inhaled a slow breath to steady his hands, needing his movements to be exact. He slid his picks into the lock and began to move the gears slowly and delicately.

*This is no different than what you always do*, he reminded himself as his heart started to beat faster. He stole this food because otherwise he would go hungry, and so would the other boys. Being an official member of the Thieves' Guild made him no more a thief than he already was. He had no reason to feel any additional pressure. Or guilt.

A soft click indicated he almost had it. Exhaling, he lifted his right hand a little higher, pushing the mechanism inside the lock, while he kept his left hand in place, allowing the mechanism to turn. The padlock fell open, and Hadli counteracted the fall by holding tightly to the lock and the chain it unclasped. The boys eased the chain out of the metal door handles, trying to keep the soft *tink-tink* of metal hitting metal to a minimum, and laid it quietly on the ground. They eased the doors open, careful to avoid creaking, and descended the staircase to the cellar.

The strong smell of fish hung in the air. Eamonn shivered from the cold, a sharp contrast to the mild night. He remembered learning of underground cellars filled with ice that kept food cool year-round, but he'd never gone inside one before. He squinted to examine his surroundings, the only light coming from the moon outside the cellar doors. Chunks of ice carved from Idyrria's mountains edged the room full of barrels, the earthen walls insulating the room and keeping the ice solid even in late summer.

Hadli rushed to a barrel and lifted its lid, and he signaled for Eamonn to follow suit. Eamonn picked a barrel and pulled the lid off, the pungent odor of raw fish streaming out. The barrel held cleaned raw trout buried in salt up to the brim, each fish about the length of his elbow to his fingertips. He pulled out the sack tucked into his waistband and opened it, then dove a hand into the barrel. Salt fell off the trout as he picked it up, so he pressed the mouth of the sack up to the barrel to avoid leaving a trail. Dumping the salty fish into his sack, he took two more from the barrel and replaced the lid.

Eamonn looked up, noticing that several of the other boys had slipped inside without so much as a murmur, bagging fish in quiet haste. Claiming an untouched barrel, he took out two fish and wiped his hands to clean off some of the salt that stung cuts in his skin. He split his next five fish between two more barrels and nearly dropped the lid onto the last one, losing his grip because of the salt that clung to his fingertips.

Two or three of the boys had finished bagging their loot and left the cellar, already on their way back to the cave. Eamonn searched for Hadli in the darkness and found him at the door, full bag in hand, supervising the rest of the operation.

Four more boys returned lids to the barrels, leaving them as though they hadn't been touched, and made for the cave. The last three to arrive grabbed their final couple of fish, all particular about not making a mess but still swift in their movements—precision they gained with discipline and practice. Eamonn watched them, stunned at the deftness of the whole operation. Within minutes, the crew was in and out and hadn't left a trace.

"All right, let's go," Hadli whispered, hanging back in the corner of the room to let Eamonn observe the Guild's skill. He led the way up the stairs and out of the cellar into the warmth of the summer night. Bringing up the rear, Eamonn closed the double doors to the cellar behind him without a sound. Eamonn picked up the chain and looped it through the handles, but before he grabbed the padlock, a sound pricked his ears and he froze.

"Listen," he breathed.

Hadli stopped dead in his tracks and listened along with Eamonn. Horses' hooves. And they were getting closer.

Instinct urged Eamonn to refasten the chain and padlock as quickly as possible and dive into the night. But Hadli remained still, hand extended to tell Eamonn to do the same. The hooves clacking on the road sounded closer. Eamonn dared only to move his eyes to watch Hadli, ready to take off in a split second if Hadli signaled. His limbs warmed as his heart pumped faster, shooting adrenaline through his veins.

A road ran beside the cellar and ended at the river, just a stone's throw away from where Hadli and Eamonn stood. If the rider took this path, he would come right next to them.

The sound of the hooves continued to approach them; the river must have been the rider's goal. As they heard the horse reach the rear of the cellar entrance, Hadli pointed at the ground and mouthed *down*. He and Eamonn dropped, flattening themselves against the stone path and keeping their bodies pressed against the unlocked doors. Eamonn rolled his lips together and tried to control his trembling hands.

A horse trotted down the road, passing the cellar entrance and coming to a halt where the road met the main dock. An uncomfortably small distance separated Eamonn and Hadli from the horse and rider—they could hear the horse huff and snort, catching its breath. The horse's rider sat tall and alert atop it, the soft moonlight reflecting off his rounded metal helmet. A night sentry.

In all the time Eamonn had been thieving, he had never run into a night sentry, a soldier in the City Guard who patrolled the city overnight. Occasionally, he'd heard their horses' hooves in the distance, but he always managed to finish the job and get out in enough time to miss them. Their presence had almost kept Eamonn from starting his life of thievery, because he knew their purpose was to catch criminals like him. He soon learned, though, that being small and quiet gave him an advantage; the sentries only caught thieves less skilled than himself.

Until now.

Eamonn willed himself to be as small and inconspicuous as possible, and he could tell Hadli had similar thoughts based on the nervous gleam in his eye. It was almost imperceptible, but it was there all the same.

The shadow of the building and the sparse moonlight worked in their favor. Eamonn begged the Lady of the Stars that it would be enough. He watched the sentry out of the corner of his eye, praying he would keep his gaze in the direction of the river.

The horse flicked its tail and shook its head, enjoying the respite.

Eamonn realized he hadn't been breathing and struggled for a short, quiet breath. His heart thumped in his ears, every inch of his body on edge. He glanced at Hadli, whose eyes were fixed on the horse and rider, waiting to see what the sentry would do.

Only now did Eamonn notice Hadli's hands gripping the padlock and chain. Ready to make a swift move out of locking the door, he figured. Hiding in the cellar wasn't an option since Eamonn had already threaded the chain through the handles, and pulling it back out might make too much noise.

Seconds ticked by in slow motion, each one feeling like an age. The longer the sentry remained, the more convinced Eamonn grew that his first theft with the Guild would be his last, that he would be caught and flogged and imprisoned or worse, never returning to his beloved school.

He pressed his body deeper into the shadows, wishing he was invisible.

Without warning, the rider jerked at the reins and gave a quick, short whistle to his horse—either ready to return to his patrol or unable to find what he searched for. He turned the horse's head around and led it back up the road. Eamonn's heart threatened to burst as the sentry rode past them a second time, this time even slower than before.

Eamonn squeezed his eyes shut—probably not what he needed to do, but he couldn't bear to witness the moment they were discovered, to see the sentry's eyes on them and know what lay ahead.

But the moment didn't come. The sound of the hooves moved past them and grew distant as they picked up speed. When the horse was out of earshot, Eamonn let out a breath that threatened to release his entire soul. Only then did he open his eyes and see Hadli's face inches away in the dark, watching him.

"You going to make it?" Hadli teased, the hint of a smirk on his lips.

Eamonn laughed in relief and nodded. The boys stood up, lifting the chain and padlock back into place around the door handles. They clicked it shut and gently allowed it to fall into its weight. Hadli double and triple checked their surroundings as they eased out of the shadow of the cellar entrance, then they dashed away, hunched over into the grass.

Hadli and Eamonn met the rest of the anxious boys as they ran into the cave, tightly clutching their bags of fish and catching their breath. The Guild let out a triumphant cheer on their entry.

"We thought something had happened!" Joris exclaimed, relief flooding his features as he grabbed Hadli by the top of his arm.

"Nearly, but no," Hadli explained, smiling victoriously at them all. "A night sentry came to the river just as we were about to leave, but we hid until he went on his way."

"Oh, Blessed Lady!" one of the boys cried out.

"Eamonn must bring good luck," Alithir said, coming to him and clapping him on the back. "Do you have some magic you haven't told us about?"

The boys all laughed, and Eamonn's mouth lifted at the corners as he tried to read their reactions. They didn't seem to take Alithir seriously.

He wondered if they actually believed in magic—some people did, but Eamonn always thought it must be more wishful thinking than true belief. He liked the idea of magic, of course: the stories and fables from his childhood. He'd love to have magic at his disposal to get him out of sticky situations, or to keep him from having to steal in the first place, but he never believed that magic existed in their world centuries ago.

If any of the other thieves believed magic was history rather than myth, they didn't make it known. They made a few more comments about Eamonn bringing them good fortune, and a smile spread across his face, warmth rising to his cheeks.

"It was a successful night!" Hadli announced, setting his bag down in front of him. "Now let's get these fish smoked!"

The boys set to building up the fire and preparing smoking racks. Jittery and abuzz with excitement, Eamonn helped the boys hang the trout from the racks.

His heart still thumped from his encounter with the sentry and his sprint back to the cave. They'd had a close call, too close for his own comfort, but their stealth and skill saved them. Eamonn knew he had talent as a thief, that he moved silently and picked locks with ease, but now he began to realize how much he could gain from being part of such a group. He'd learn to be part of a team, to share plunder, and how to handle trouble when it arose.

Yes, he could imagine himself doing this for two years until he finished at the standard school, saving a part of what he stole for his education and hopefully making it to the college one day.

He set himself a goal. He wouldn't let thieving become his life's work, just a way to achieve his dreams. Maybe by then, the guilt of it all would sit a little better on his heart.

# THREE

NOTHING ABOUT THE NEXT several weeks at home convinced Eamonn his father's attitude toward him had dramatically changed, regardless of the additional food Florin offered him. Eamonn got the impression his father was hoping to avoid humiliation more than anything else. He must be trying to beef up his slim son so the military recruiters wouldn't laugh and shake their heads when Florin presented him.

Thankfully, though, Florin's continued apathy meant he didn't notice Eamonn yawning all the time, taking uncharacteristic naps during the day, and disappearing after supper. Florin occupied his free time frequenting pubs with his fellow soldiers, uninterested in Eamonn's comings and goings, as always.

As Eamonn returned to the cave several times and participated in a few more of the Guild's operations, any last smoldering embers of desire to have a relationship with his father were snuffed out. He felt more at home in the cave with the Thieves' Guild than he did where he'd lived all his life.

Eamonn packed his few belongings and his small stash of food into his school bag. Looking over his shoulder at the bare room, he chuckled once at the irony. It didn't look much different. He adjusted the bag on his shoulder before entering the living area where his father sat in an armchair, smoking a pipe. As usual, Florin didn't look up at Eamonn's entrance, pensively puffing away.

After clearing his throat to make sure he spoke confidently, Eamonn announced, "I'm leaving, Father."

Florin took in a long breath through his pipe and let out a slow stream of smoke. "Why?" he asked, his dark eyes finally meeting Eamonn's.

"I don't want to be a soldier," Eamonn said, stumbling over his words, trying to get them out before he could talk himself out of his decision. "I know it's what you wish, but it's wrong for me. But you've never paid enough attention to know that."

Eamonn had sworn to himself that he wouldn't get emotional while addressing the man who had merely fathered him, but all the pain he'd carried his entire life rushed to the surface. Finally, he would speak the words he'd rehearsed for years. Finally, he would express to his father how he felt.

"I'm excellent at school, and one day I want to go to the College at Nos Illni. I'm at the top of my class, and I know I'll get in. I was never meant to be a soldier. I want to do something where I use my mind." Eamonn stifled a sob, willing himself to get the rest of his speech out before his feelings overcame him. "I've never known what it was like to have a parent who cared.

I don't understand what I've done to make you barely feed me, barely provide for me, but I think as your son, I at least deserved your love."

His voice ripe with emotion, he chose his final words to cut. "I'd hoped that maybe one day you would recognize me as something to be valued, but I was a fool. I'm leaving, and I'm not coming back."

There. He'd said it. Maybe he didn't cover everything he'd hoped to say to his father, but he'd said enough to feel the weight fall. With his thoughts off his chest, Eamonn waited, feet planted, to see if his father might say anything in response. Deep in his heart, he hoped he might get some sort of explanation or apology from his father, but he knew better. Eamonn blinked away the stinging in his eyes. This man was not worth his tears.

Florin puffed thoughtfully on his pipe for several moments. Eamonn's heart sank. So, his father would give him no reply at all. He took a few steps toward the door but stopped upon hearing his father's voice behind him.

"Do what you think is best."

Eamonn's chest rose and fell heavily, tears threatening to spill over. He couldn't lose control, not here, not now—at the end. He grasped the handle of the door and let himself out, not looking back.

A faint chill hung in the air, the first hint of autumn's imminent arrival. Eamonn wished he could blame the slight change in temperature for the wetness in his eyes as he stormed through the night.

*Do what you think is best.*

The most unbiased, unattached response. No anger at Eamonn's sudden decision to leave his father and his home. No desire for him to stay. No curiosity about where he planned to go next. Florin essentially told Eamonn he could do whatever he pleased, as long as it did not involve him.

Eamonn's heartache surprised him a little. He could have guessed such a response from Florin, but this hit a nerve. Eamonn resolved not to let his father's detachment get in the way of his new life. Instead, he used it to steel himself, to erase any lingering doubts about his decision.

The road leading outside the city from the military district headed west, eventually reaching the river that defined the border between Idyrria and Miren, but Eamonn turned north toward the smaller river that branched off in the mountains, making his own path.

Stars twinkled in the navy-blue sky, with not a cloud to cover them. Eamonn threw his head back to admire them in their multitude. He loved nights like this: crisp and clear and beautiful. They filled him with a sense of peace, that there was more out there for him than the life he lived.

The wind picked up just as he caught the reflection of moonlight on the river before him. Eamonn gripped his worn wool outer shirt tighter, the sudden winds trying hard to blow summer away. He took careful steps as he followed the rocky riverbank along the mountains, the ground sloping more toward the river as he went. Loose pebbles slid down the bank into the river as he walked, creating a little more noise than he felt comfortable with. Every so often, he stole a quick glance over his shoulder to make sure he wasn't being followed.

As he got closer to the outcrop that hid the cave's entrance, Eamonn wondered how the boys would take his sudden appearance at the hideout. Did they have some kind of lookout or defense plan in case of intruders? They'd never mentioned anything about it before. Only the boys who lived in the cave would be there tonight, as it was not a night for a meeting or operation, and they wouldn't be expecting anyone to show up.

Eamonn found the outcropping and stopped at the entrance to the cave. A knot formed in his stomach, heavy like lead. Maybe this wasn't a good idea after all. Maybe he had made a mistake, leaving his home and coming here.

He took a deep breath, hoping it might settle his stomach. There was only one way to find out for sure.

Eamonn slipped through the crevice, but even in the utter darkness, he didn't feel as lost in the mountain anymore. He let his instincts take over, the twists and turns of the tunnel now much more familiar to him after sneaking down there for the past couple of weeks. He delved deeper into the mountain, into the depths that held the boys' headquarters. As he got closer, the dark, damp cavern began to come to life, soft firelight illuminating the walls and chatter ringing off the stone. He turned the final corner into the den, catching the attention of a couple of the boys sitting around the fire.

"Eamonn!" Joris cried, leaping to his feet. "What brings you here tonight?"

His abrupt arrival extinguished all conversation. Eamonn scanned over the faces staring up at him in surprise from around the fire. These were the boys who lived here in the cave, with nowhere else to go and no one missing them. Just like Eamonn.

Hadli stood as well, a pleasant smirk playing on his lips. He crossed his arms in front of him in his well-meaning manner, a motion that subtly signified his authority without making him seem cocky.

"I want to stay here," Eamonn announced, his voice echoing through the cave. His eyes widened at the unexpected reverberation of his voice. Lowering his volume, he added, "That is, I want to live here. Permanently."

Hadli's smile grew, and he stepped toward Eamonn, clasping a hand on his shoulder in comradery—a common symbol of brotherhood in the Guild. "And you are welcome here." He turned and held out his arm in the direction of the cots at the back of the cavern. "We'll get you a bed."

Showing Eamonn to an unoccupied cot, Hadli helped him unload his few things and make the small space his own.

"I'm glad you've decided to stay with us," he said with a grin, unfolding a blanket over Eamonn's new bed. "We have a good life here; an orderly but enjoyable life. The members of the Guild who live here are expected to abide by certain guidelines, but nothing too outlandish."

He stopped, getting Eamonn's attention. "Mostly, they involve respect for others' personal belongings and to not abuse our supplies, along with equal distribution of loot among all members. Just because this is our home doesn't mean we are entitled to more than the members of the Guild who don't live here." Hadli ran his hand over the blanket to smooth it out, Eamonn's space complete. "Come on, join us by the fire."

Hadli returned to his spot by the fire, and Joris scooted over to make room for Eamonn between them. "I still want to go to school," Eamonn told Hadli once they sat down. "I'd like to complete my education, and I only have a year and a half to go."

"Of course!" Hadli replied, full of assurance. "Just because you live here now doesn't mean you can't have a life outside. What you have to learn is how to manage two lives, a life of crime and a life of honor. But it can be done. Melkris lived with us in his last year of school, and he kept up with his studies while working for us in the black market."

"You did?" Eamonn asked Melkris across the fire, thankful to learn that another Guild member had finished his education.

Melkris nodded in confirmation. "I found what I needed in the Guild, but I still felt an obligation to finish my schooling. My mother always wanted me to, and I thought it would honor her memory if I did." A sad smile appeared on his face, and his eyes lowered to the fire for a moment. "It was a little tricky, though. If a schoolmate ever wanted to study together, I suggested meeting at the library or the hall. I figured out how to manage."

"That's great to hear! I'll probably be coming to you for advice about it," Eamonn said with a smile, taking off his outer shirt as the heat of the fire warmed him.

His pendant, usually hidden under his clothes, fell from behind his tunic. Eamonn felt all eyes turn to him as the pendant caught the firelight, and he stiffened. Only the crackling of the fire could be heard. The atmosphere in the cave changed in an instant.

Hadli's dark eyes widened, blazing with the reflection of the fire. He leaned in closer to Eamonn, studying the intricate swirls of silver and translucent light green stone. "Where did you get that?" he breathed, enraptured, as his demeanor transformed. "I've never seen anything like it. Did you find it in Idyrria? Rare jewelry is nearly impossible to steal, always tightly guarded."

Eamonn released a nervous breath, a little amused that Hadli—and all the other lads, probably—assumed he had stolen it. He knew that living with a group of thieves would require absolute trust, and at some point, one or more of them would see his pendant. The awe in Hadli's eyes, though, caused a pit to form in Eamonn's stomach, and he swallowed hard. Something about it gave an impression of more than just wonder. His eyes shone of desire, of avarice.

"I didn't steal it," Eamonn responded, his voice deeper than usual. He touched the pendant in a delicate motion, an old habit. He swallowed again, his throat dry. "It belonged to my mother. She died when I was born, and my father gave it to me. I've never known a day without it. It's like..." He paused, thoughtful, his gaze passing through the walls of the cave. "It's like having my mother with me all the time. It's all I know of her."

Hadli tilted back his head in a mixture of understanding and curiosity, and possibly something like admiration. "On your first night here, you said your mother was Mirish."

"So my father told me."

"I've never seen the treasures of Miren, but I know the Mirish people take pride in crafting beauty," he murmured, lowering his eyes back to the pendant, his hands in loose fists at his lap. "They won't trade their most prized and beautiful creations; they keep them for themselves." His eyes examined every detail of the pendant, drinking it in as though it was able to finally satisfy a thirsty part of his soul. "This speaks truth to the tales of the Mirish beauty. You're fortunate to have it."

Hadli finally pulled his eyes away and looked back up at Eamonn's own, as if the firelight that glinted off the pendant had cast a spell on Hadli and he'd just broken free. He smiled at his friend jovially, like nothing strange had happened, but Eamonn didn't share his ease.

"I'd be more fortunate to have my mother."

Sympathizing grunts from the other lads around the fire put his heart at ease. Many of the Guild knew the same kind of loss.

Hadli shifted back into the charismatic, kind-hearted leader of the group that one could not help but like. "Yes, you would." His lashes fell over his eyes in a manner that spoke of sorrow and compassion. When he lifted his gaze, he addressed the entire group. "It's gotten late now; we should probably make our way to bed."

Eamonn and Hadli stood simultaneously, and Hadli gripped Eamonn's shoulder. "I'm sorry you've lived life without your mother. I'm sure things would be much different now if you'd had her." His mouth turned up at the corners. "But don't worry. Tomorrow, I'll start showing you how we do things around here, and you'll come to see this place as your home, as we do. You've made the right choice, Eamonn."

Eamonn gave Hadli a small, thankful smile, all uncertainties from moments ago brushed aside. Hadli was a thief—of course, he was bound to be attracted to beautiful, extravagant objects. But Eamonn had come to know him better in the past couple of weeks. He'd seen Hadli plot, learned his methods, knew the kind of loot he chose to steal. The Thieves' Guild promoted survival, not indulgence.

"Can I ask you a question?" Eamonn murmured to Hadli as the other boys moved over to their beds.

Hadli's cheek lifted in a curious half smile. "Of course."

"How did you come into this way of life?"

Hadli's smile fell a little and became nostalgic. "It's nothing too surprising, much like the other lads here. My father was killed in the War with Cardune before I was born, and my mother died from the disease survalet when I was young. Her sister took me in, and I lived with her for a while, but after she married, her husband pushed her to put me in an orphanage. That's where I met Joris and Alithir. We hated the orphanage, so we ran away. We came away from the city down the river until we found the cave, and that's when the three of us started stealing to survive."

"And how did the other boys come to join you?" Eamonn asked, whispering now since the others had gone to bed.

Hadli shrugged. "Different ways. Some found us. We found some, like you. We wanted to help as many of those like us as we could, be a family to those who didn't have one." The weight in Hadli's voice and the earnestness in his eyes convinced Eamonn that he spoke the truth. "But it looks like we're the last ones up, now. Let's go to bed."

Hadli and Eamonn parted to climb into their beds, and Eamonn found it easy to relax this time around. Thieves they may be, but not entirely by choice. Eamonn knew he belonged with them, and even with the strange incident earlier, nothing worried him about living with the Guild. Hadli was first his leader, but second his friend, and Eamonn felt comfortable trusting him.

# FOUR

EAMONN STOOD TALL, HEAD held high, waiting for his name to be called. Snow floated down in soft swirls outside, but a broad, blazing fire in the hearth kept the stone room warm. Long wooden benches in two rows filled the hall, full of graduates' family and friends. At the front of the room, Eamonn stood in a line with his graduating classmates, every one of them beaming.

Eamonn had succeeded in all his classes, finished his exams with high marks, and was about to receive his certificate of completion from the Standard School of Erai. He swelled with pride at his accomplishments, more pleased with himself than he had ever been before. No part of him cared that his father knew nothing of his achievements. Eamonn rarely thought of the man these days, certain that Florin never wondered about his son. Eammon only wished that his mother could bear witness to this glorious moment. Maybe she looked down on him from the Land of Light, smiling at her son. Eamonn's eyes pricked with tears at the thought.

There *was* one person in attendance for him. Hadli had slipped in the back after the ceremony had begun and leaned against a pillar. Eamonn caught his eyes and grinned. Hadli rarely came into Erai during daylight hours, especially not to be part of such a deliberate crowd.

The headmaster called out Eamonn's name, and he stepped forward to receive his certificate as the audience applauded. Hadli pushed himself off the pillar and clapped, smiling at his friend.

At long last, Eamonn had completed the first step of his journey to the College at Nos Illni.

Working with the Thieves' Guild for the past two years, he had acquired a comfortable sum of money to go toward his college fees. In a few months, he would have enough for his first term. He thought about staying with the Guild as long as he needed the money to continue his education, but after he had achieved all he could at the college, he planned to take an honest job.

The Guild had become his family, but even after two years of regular operations, Eamonn could not entirely get rid of the twinge of guilt that hung in his heart. He reminded himself every night that the Guild was only ever a means to an end, and nothing more.

At the end of the ceremony, Eamonn exited the hall while his classmates hugged their families, coming into the white-blanketed courtyard and lifting his face to the snow. Soft, fragile flakes fell on his cheeks and nose, and he closed his eyes and smiled. He felt weightless, invigorated, like any door he wished to open stood there before him and he only had to push. A world of opportunity waited at his fingertips. Nothing could stop him.

Eamonn took a deep breath of the sharp, frigid air and opened his eyes. He saw Hadli approaching him, and his mouth spread wide across his face. Hadli reflected the smile, lines popping out around the corners of his mouth. He threw an arm around Eamonn's shoulders, patting him on the chest with his other hand.

"Well done, Eamonn," he said, his voice as light as air as they walked out of the courtyard. "I have to say, I'm really proud of you."

A laugh escaped Eamonn's lips as Eamonn realized how much he appreciated those words. "Thanks," he replied, snow crunching under his boots. "It doesn't feel completely real yet."

"That's because it's such a huge accomplishment!" Hadli pulled his arm from Eamonn's shoulders and turned to face him, walking backward along the road. "You've wanted this your whole life, and you worked so hard." He lowered his voice and slowed his steps down, letting Eamonn come closer to him. "Very few of us in the Guild have completed a Standard Education. It's a big deal."

Eamonn's smile never left his face. It might be plastered there forever, but that would be all right with him. He'd never felt as overjoyed about something in his entire life.

Hadli returned to Eamonn's side, and they both pulled their coats tighter as a bitterly cold wind swept through the street. They kept silent the rest of the way out of the city, reaching the river's edge before Hadli spoke again.

"So, does this mean you'll be leaving us?"

Eamonn wondered how long he'd been trying to ask the question. He'd been trying to figure out how to bring it up himself. He lifted his face to the biting air and let out a breath.

"Eventually," he admitted. "Not yet. I don't have quite enough money yet." He looked over at Hadli and found a smile on his friend's face. "Oh, what, you don't want me to pursue my dreams?"

"Of course I do!" Hadli replied, dropping his smile and lifting his eyebrows. "You know we all want you to accomplish your dreams." A corner of his mouth lifted in a sad smirk. "Most of us don't have dreams."

Eamonn clapped a reassuring hand on Hadli's back. "We've got some time. I'll help you find a dream."

Hadli grinned back at Eamonn before he slipped through the crevice in the rock and ducked into the cave. Eamonn followed him, kicking snow off his boots and shaking it from his coat. Once he turned the corner into the warm lair, the other boys cheered on his arrival.

"Hail the alumnus! He's done it!" Alithir shouted, and the other lads applauded.

The smile still on his lips, Eamonn lowered his head in humble appreciation as they all patted him on the back and gave him their congratulations.

The Guild had prepared a feast in his honor—a typical meal for most other residents of Erai, but a feast for thieves. Rather than being covered with maps, papers, and notes, the table where they planned their thefts was laden with smoked fish, roasted potatoes and carrots, steaming beans and rice, and even some frosted cakes they'd nicked from the bakery the night before.

"Go on, Eamonn, you go first!" Joris insisted, and the other boys agreed. Alithir even pushed him toward the table and handed him a wooden plate.

The College at Nos Illni would be there. Eamonn didn't have to leave the Guild any time soon. He finally had a family.

# FIVE

Trees dripped from their last snow of the season. Frozen earth started to thaw. Ice on the river cracked and floated away. Green buds dared to poke out their delicate heads toward the sun, its growing warmth drawing them out. Spring teased its arrival, and the citizens of Erai rejoiced.

Since finishing school, Eamonn had tossed back and forth the idea of taking up an apprenticeship and leaving the Guild. Some of the other boys had done that after they turned sixteen, but they didn't stay in Erai. Melkris left to seek work somewhere in Farneth the year before, and Ryerdin took a smithing apprenticeship in Gaulmiri soon after Eamonn had joined the Guild.

Eamonn's good records from school would help him get any apprenticeship he wanted, and he could earn money honestly to pay college fees, but in Erai he would be expected to stay and work. He would give his life over to a chosen trade. While Idyrria valued education and seeking knowledge, one was not expected to change paths. Although unlikely, it might be possible for him to learn a trade, work, and then go to Nos Illni, but what really held him back was leaving his brotherhood. Some members had left and new ones had joined, but Eamonn still saw them as his family. As much as his conscience plagued him about stealing, he couldn't leave his brothers. Not yet.

With nothing to occupy his time now that he'd graduated, Eamonn started to get restless. He'd never realized just how mundane his day-to-day life would be in the Guild without his studies to keep him busy during the day.

Since the Guild only had meetings every three days and operations less than that, Eamonn felt too idle sitting around in the cave the rest of the time. The boys made sure to go outside, to walk and get some fresh air, but they always had to mind their surroundings and not linger. Even so, Eamonn needed more time outside the cave, so he started going to the Erai library every now and then. Old classmates or teachers who saw him there would speak to him, questioning him about his life after school. His excuse for being in the library was to study for the entrance exam at Nos Illni, but he knew he couldn't keep it up forever.

Eamonn returned to the cave one evening after spending his day at the library and found Hadli at the table with the other boys who lived there. They were deep in discussion, papers laid out before them, glancing from one to the next. Hadli looked up at Eamonn's entrance and then cast his gaze back down to the table.

"Good, you're back. We have a lot to discuss," he said, motioning for Eamonn to join them. Eamonn dropped his bag on his bed and stood by Hadli at the table.

"Our next operation?" Eamonn asked.

"Yes, and it's big." Hadli pointed to the headline of a flyer from town: *Merchant Caravan Coming to Erai*

Eamonn picked up the flyer and skimmed over the few lines, reading them aloud. "'Teravalen caravan will be in Erai the eighth of this month, bringing goods from all across Sarieth. The caravan will set up in the city square for two days only.'" He dropped the paper and turned to face Hadli, his brow furrowed. "How do we steal from a caravan?"

Hadli inhaled through his nose and released the breath in a sharp puff, expressing that he understood the perils already. "It'll be tricky. We'll have to do everything perfectly. But we can't pass up a caravan with goods from the entire country. The last time they came was shortly before you joined us."

"So, you've stolen from the caravan before?"

Hadli opened his mouth only to close it in an apologetic smile. "Ah, not exactly."

Eamonn locked eyes with Hadli, expecting a better answer.

"Well, we were a lot less experienced than we are now," Hadli explained, earnest in his response but with an edge to his voice as though he had to justify their actions. "We made a plan, but we got there and found a pretty heavy City Guard presence, more than we expected. So, we came back—didn't attempt the operation. But now we know about them and we can plan accordingly."

Eamonn heard only excuses. Hadli knew the dangers of such a theft but tried to brush them off. "What do we expect to gain from it that we can't get here? We do well enough with our regular operations." A touch of irritation rose in Eamonn's voice. Did Hadli not see the greater than usual peril involved?

"They'll have lots of money," Hadli answered, calm and nonchalant about putting every member of the Guild at risk. "And I'm sure there will be other expensive goods, exotic goods—ones that can get us a great deal on the black market. We'd be able to trade for so many things we need."

Eamonn placed his hands on the table top and leaned over, shaking his head. "Maybe so, but I just don't see how we can do this safely. We know the shops and things in the city, but this," he waved his hand over the papers, "is completely foreign."

"Then we go to the caravan beforehand," Hadli countered, his frustration mounting. "We can send Ramin and Gareth, and even you. The three of you can go to the city during the day without drawing too much attention. You can map it out for us, learn what we need to know to do it safely."

Eamonn stood back from the table and crossed his arms, considering Hadli's suggestion. With enough research, they might be able to try it. They'd only had some scrapes and close calls a handful of times since Eamonn had joined the Guild, so he knew they had enough skill. They'd just never done anything quite like it before.

The heavy presence of the City Guard worried Eamonn the most. Hadli had never proposed an operation with more security, so every detail had to be planned out. Just one day to case the caravan market didn't seem like enough time to do everything properly.

"Have you determined where the merchants will be housed overnight?" he asked Hadli, almost trying to catch him out.

"Sometimes merchants of valuable goods like to sleep with their wagons, or right nearby. They won't abandon them at night. And you came across the Guard last time. You said we can make plans around them this time, but it's still a lot of watchful eyes for us to try to get around. On our normal operations here, we make sure to avoid them completely." He shook his head. "This might be too much for us."

"But Eamonn," Hadli pleaded, his eyes lit with passion, "we can't miss this caravan. Opportunities like this rarely ever come our way. I know the caravan will be guarded, but we're good! We can slip in and slip out. We won't send everyone to the wagons, just our best. They can haul loot to designated spots away from the caravan, where the others can take it back to the cave. We'll make it work."

Eamonn cocked his head and narrowed his eyes a little, holding his gaze on Hadli as if it would sway him, but Hadli stood his ground. He tipped his chin up and looked down his nose at Eamonn with crossed arms, a subtle reminder that Hadli was the one in charge.

"I still don't like it," Eamonn said, relenting. He wouldn't fight Hadli about it, but a nagging in the back of Eamonn's mind cautioned him. Something about the look in Hadli's eyes reminded Eamonn of the night Hadli had first caught sight of his mother's necklace. Even as a survivalist thief, Hadli wasn't exempt from greed.

"We'll be smart," Hadli continued, trying to assuage Eamonn's apprehension. "Tomorrow is another meeting, and we'll tell Ramin and Gareth to learn everything they can about the caravan since they still live in town. We'll find out what kind of security presence will be there, where the merchants will be set up, everything. Don't worry." He leaned closer to Eamonn, his dark eyes earnest. "We can pull this off."

Eamonn swallowed, reluctant to accept Hadli's word. Glancing around the table, he could tell that a few members shared his viewpoint, but they kept silent. Others seemed ready to follow Hadli into anything. Maybe, if Hadli didn't let greed cloud his vision, he would see clearly enough to plan a safe operation.

The caravan arrived in Erai the evening before the eighth and set up in the main city square. Hadli, Eamonn, and Joris crept into the city well after midnight to scout out the configuration of Guard around the wagons.

Simple three-story buildings surrounded the square, three or four individual shops connected as one unit and separated by the next only by a small alleyway. Eamonn broke them into a shop facing the square that they knew would be empty overnight. The third story of the shop was a single room for storage with two windows, giving the boys an excellent vantage point. Not to mention, they could steal some money and a few goods from the shop, making the most of the night.

Twelve guards surrounded the fifty wagons in the square, three on each side, taking turns patrolling through the rows. A hand might as well have reached into Eamonn's chest and gripped his heart. Every single fear and concern he had about the danger of this operation came surging up.

"There are too many," he whispered, standing by Hadli at one window while Joris looked out the other. "We'll never be able to get in and out unseen."

"We just need to learn their pattern," Hadli argued, his gaze locked down below. "See, when a guard finishes his patrol, the one closest to him on his right takes his turn." Hadli pointed into the square, tracing a pattern in the air with his finger. "If we keep track of which guard is on his patrol and when they swap out, we should have a solid idea of where they are at every moment. We'll plan out which wagons to steal from accordingly to make sure we're on the opposite side as them."

Hadli's collected and rational demeanor let the hand loosen its hold on Eamonn's heart a little. It sounded like Hadli still approached this operation with a mostly level head. Maybe they *could* pull this off.

They took the information and goods back to the cave, getting a little sleep before starting to finalize their plans. Ramin and Gareth arrived late in the afternoon, bringing descriptions and placements of the vendors and suggestions about which wagons looked simplest to break into. Hadli scratched notes and scribbled drawings as they spoke, every now and then stopping to rub his hand over the scruff along his jaw. He drew on maps of the city square where the caravan would set up, made a list of expected vendors, and wrote out who in the Guild would steal from which wagons. By nightfall, he gathered all the thieves around the table to debrief them.

"All right, this is the plan. Only four of us will be breaking into wagons to get the loot: Joris, Eamonn, Listrik, and me. Everyone else will set up at these four locations just outside the square." He pointed to spots on the perimeter of their target.

"We're going to keep our loot from each wagon small. For the four of us in the wagons, we'll rendezvous at our designated points outside the square to hand off our loot after going to two wagons. For those of you at the perimeter, run back once you get your drop-off. The four of us will leave with the last loads. We have to be quick and quiet. If you come upon trouble, don't risk getting caught. Go back to the cave. Everyone understand?"

The boys nodded around the table. Eamonn's stomach twisted, still uneasy about their plans. There was too much room for error. But he wouldn't back out now. This was his team, his family, and he owed it to them to give it everything he could.

Hadli looked each lad in the eye as he always would before an operation.

"Let's get ready."

Late into the night, Hadli gathered up his band of criminals and handed them each a sack. To Eamonn, it seemed like Hadli tried to treat this just like any other theft, but the heavy atmosphere in the cave told a different story. In the preceding hours, their usual fun and games had been replaced with isolated quiet conversations. Even though they were all going along with it, the members of the Guild knew the danger facing them.

Hadli and Eamonn left the mountain first, the rest of the crew leaving in pairs after them. They ran low to the ground, keeping their bodies as out of sight as possible. The moon shone above them, almost full, threatening to betray them on their mission. At a checkpoint to pause and look for signs of life, Eamonn glanced up at the sky and huffed. Of all nights, this one needed the deepest darkness, and yet the moon flooded the night with its solemn silvery light.

Once in the city, the pair hid in a narrow alley at the perimeter of the city square, bags in hand. From there, they could only see four guards, three on one side of the square and one on another nearest them. Some faced into the caravan while others faced away. While Hadli and Eamonn waited for the next pair to join them, they watched the guards in their line of sight to see when one of them made his rounds patrolling.

"When the guard in front of us goes through, that's our opening," Hadli whispered to Eamonn.

Eamonn nodded as soft footfalls came upon them and two dark figures emerged—the next pair from the cave. The boys crouched close together to hear Hadli's quiet instructions.

"All right, Joris, Listrik, we're waiting for this guard here to go on his patrol," Hadli said. "We know his route, and you each know your first intended targets. When we're on our second run, the next guard should have started his patrol, so don't forget to come out at his post and meet at the second rendezvous. If we dash to and from the wagons, the nearest guards shouldn't see us. One at a time. We are shadows."

The boys nodded. Eamonn's heart rate accelerated and he hoped the others couldn't hear the thumping in his chest. He could feel the blood warming in his arms already and fought against the trembling that accompanied his nerves.

The guard in front of them turned and entered the maze of wagons. Hadli lifted his hand, allowing a few beats for the guard to get out of the first row. He dropped his hand and Joris shot off like a bolt into the wagons without a sound. None of the guards they could see appeared to notice the movement.

As Eamonn's heart caught in his throat, he cursed the moon. Any good luck wouldn't last under such an illuminated night. Hadli signaled again and Listrik raced off, the ten feet of distance between the alley and the wagons looking like miles. Blood pounded in Eamonn's ears, now his turn to make the sprint, and he flashed his eyes up to the sky, asking the Lady of the Stars to cast a cloud over the moon in a last-ditch effort. Nights like this, he wished magic did exist—he'd darken the moon, or at least create a shadow to shroud himself.

When he looked back down, Hadli gave him a subtle nod, and he ran.

In a second, Eamonn made it to the wagons and dipped this way and that among the rows, following his planned pattern. Only when he reached his first target did he stop and take a breath. He listened for any sound in response, but he heard no call to act or heavy footsteps hurrying toward him. The guards must be half asleep.

*Right, time to get to work.* Eamonn inhaled deeply and released his breath with control to slow down his heart and steady his hands. He pulled his lockpicks from his belt pouch and climbed the wooden steps to the door at the back of his first wagon.

The enclosed merchant wagons worked a little more like carriages than traditional wagons, with windows on the sides and a locked door at the back. Many of them had front rooms where the merchants could sleep, and they would convert to a stand for the market. Eamonn unlocked the back door in one swift motion and slipped his body into the wagon.

Inside, Eamonn realized they needed the moonlight after all. They had no way to bring candles or torches to illuminate the interiors of the wagons, and without the moonlight streaming through the windows, they wouldn't be able to see anything inside. Even with the nearly full moon, Eamonn squinted and strained to make out the contents.

Based on Ramin and Gareth's report, this should be a wagon of Mirish treasures. Eamonn couldn't deny he'd actually been looking forward to breaking inside this wagon in particular. He felt connected to the Mirish goods, wondering how much a part of his life these items might have been if his mother had lived. Would that vase sit on their mantel? Would that painting hang on their wall?

Eamonn knew he had to hurry, but the treasures of a culture lost to him drew him in. The people of Miren excelled as craftsmen, artists, musicians, writers, and the like, and the beauty of their goods could not be rivaled in Sarieth.

He found a collection of jewelry—his primary target from this wagon since it could be pocketed so easily—and picked up various pieces, examining them for similarities to his mother's necklace. Nothing stuck out to him, though, as being in the same design or craft as the pendant around his neck. Where his mother's necklace had wisp-like silver swirls surrounding the central gemstone, these necklaces often had crossing curves or interlocking strands of metal. The Mirish jewelry often hearkened back to something from the earth: flowers, leaves, branches, and the like. He found nothing that resembled the four-cornered pendant he wore, with a stone as clear as pure water touched with green.

He didn't have time to sit down and ponder the differences, though. He stashed two necklaces, two rings, a brooch, and a headpiece in his sack and glanced around for a money container. His eyes landed on a small box with a lock on the front. *Gotcha.*

Eamonn crouched down in front of the box, setting his bag at his feet and pulling his lockpicks out again, but he immediately noticed a problem. His sturdy lockpicks wouldn't work on such a miniscule lock.

He couldn't take the whole box; the merchant would notice the theft first thing the next day and alert the City Guard, who might start to hunt for the perpetrator and even increase regular night sentries and patrols. Neither could Eamonn leave without taking any money at all. They could obtain supplies easier with money, having the members who lived in the city purchase things they needed and bring them to the cave.

The sound of soft footsteps shot past his wagon. No clamoring of pursuit or shouts from the guards. Someone must have finished with his first two wagons and now raced back to the rendezvous to drop off his haul. Eamonn hadn't even made it to his second wagon. He took a quick breath to reorient him to his task and glanced around the wagon for anything he could use to open the moneybox. His eyes landed on a collection of hairpins adorned with flower-shaped jewel clusters and his heart leapt. He should have no problem getting into the box using the thin metal arms of the hairpins.

Choosing a hairpin with the smallest decoration—the least likely to get in the way—Eamonn pinched it together and inserted the slender metal into the lock. He'd never used such a tiny lockpick before, nor anything that was all one piece. He bit his lip, finding it much more of a challenge to locate the mechanism of the lock this way. He'd spent too much time here already, but he wouldn't leave this wagon without some coin.

Eamonn felt some resistance in his fingers and drew in a sharp breath. There. He'd found it. But he couldn't lose it. Blood pulsed through his body as his heart rate shot up. He manipulated his fingers carefully, pushing against the resistance. If he could just hold on...

*Click.*

Eamonn released a loud sigh and instantly clapped his free hand over his mouth. This wagon had a front room, and the merchant might be asleep in it. Waiting a few seconds and hearing nothing, Eamonn opened the box. Gold and silver coins nearly spilled out when he lifted the lid. He took as much as he thought he could without being too obvious, then used the hairpin to move the gears of the lock back out of place so that it would lock again when he closed the lid.

He pulled the hairpin out of the lock and put it in his bag, not wanting to leave behind any evidence that might point to a moneybox break-in, and replaced the box in its original spot.

So far, so good. No one had attracted the attention of the guards yet and Eamonn felt better about their chances. Maybe they *could* actually pull this off.

He left the wagon with loot in tow, looking and listening for a guard on patrol. His coast was clear. Locking the door behind him with his picks, he bolted the short distance to his second wagon.

Any nerves he'd felt before had dissipated now. This could be like any other theft after all. He unlocked the door to the next wagon in seconds and hurried to grab his predetermined items, along with some more money. Here he found a money bag rather than a box, and he added a handful to the bag he carried and rushed back out. He couldn't afford to get distracted.

Eamonn waited at the steps of the wagon, heard nothing, and dashed back the way he came to the edge of the caravan market. He peeked around the corner of the wagon that separated him from the alleyway and his first drop-off. Good, the guard hadn't returned from his patrol. He stuck his head farther around the wagon to see the next guard, some twenty or so feet away. Eamonn saw the guard's drooped head and a corner of his mouth lifted. Some security. No wonder they were managing to get away with this.

Crossing the distance from the edge of the market to the alley, Eamonn met Alithir, waiting on him in the darkness, and handed him the bag.

"Well done, keep it up," Alithir whispered, swapping out Eamonn's sack for another empty one, then turned to slink through the city back to the cave.

The guards still appeared to doze as Eamonn turned and raced back into the market. The one who had been opposite the alleyway when they arrived would be finishing his patrol soon and would return to his post. Eamonn listened out for the steady thud of boots even more than before as he found his next target, picked the lock, and disappeared into the wagon.

The rich scent of leather hit his nostrils. This merchant clearly sold leather goods, and a lot of them: shoes, belts, tunics, gloves, pelts, anything. If it could be made out of leather, this merchant had it.

Eamonn opened his new bag, dropping a pair of shoes and a pair of gloves into it first. He leaned over to grab a leather coin purse, his necklace falling out from behind his shirt, when a nearby *creak* stopped him on the spot.

His eyes darted around the dark wagon as he held his breath, his body frozen in place. None of the other lads had a wagon close enough for him to hear the wood creak with their weight. Had the guard made it back? Was he investigating a wagon? No further noise came, so Eamonn continued the job. He grabbed the coin purse and stuffed it into his sack, then reached for a belt when a sharp object jabbed him in the back.

# SIX

"DON'T MOVE AGAIN," A gruff voice murmured behind Eamonn, so quiet that no one outside the wagon would hear.

Eamonn's body turned to ice and his heart fell to his stomach. This was it—it was over, he was finished. His lungs constricted and he could barely draw breath. He wished he could warn the others before they were found out, but shouting out for them to flee would only put every single guard in the square in pursuit.

More than that, though, he wished he'd never agreed to do this at all. This moment dashed any hopes he had of attending Nos Illni. The thought of what faced him now threatened to send up the contents of his stomach—he would hang, or if any mercy at all existed in the world, he'd be flogged and sentenced to a jail cell for the rest of his life. Eamonn swallowed hard and dropped his bag.

"You think you can steal from me and get away with it?" the man asked, his voice rough and low. "I'll have you tried and hanged, thief."

Eamonn pressed his eyelids shut and tightened his jaw. Everything he'd done to get closer to Nos Illni—his hard work in school, leaving his father, joining the Thieves' Guild—had all been in vain. Nothing mattered now. One bad night, one risky operation, and all was lost.

"Turn around and look me in the eye," the man ordered, his accent distinctly Teravalen.

Peeling his eyelids apart, Eamonn obeyed, albeit reluctant to face his captor.

The man's size drew Eamonn's gaze upward, his dark, looming figure larger and more intimidating than Eamonn expected. Eamonn's mouth fell open and sweat formed on his palms. The last type of person Eamonn would want to be caught by was someone who looked like he could break bone with his bare hands, yet here he was. Darkness obscured most of the man's features, but it couldn't hide his untamed hair or bushy beard. The man held a slender silver dagger low, pointed right at Eamonn's gut.

Eamonn tried to hold himself together, clenching his teeth to keep emotion at bay and fighting to hold the water in his eyes. Even in defeat, he wanted to appear strong and composed, but any confidence or courage he'd managed up until this point vanished. He felt like a child again, reverting to the days of his youth when he first stole, sick to his stomach with guilt. Back then, the queasiness of his stomach had been overpowered by its emptiness, but now, nothing could ease the ache.

"I'm so sorry," Eamonn whispered when his eyes met the man's, desperate for mercy. After all these years, his reaction to getting caught had not changed since the night Hadli and the crew found him breaking into Mirab's shop. "Please, forgive me. I know it's foolish to ask, but I have to. I wish I'd never come tonight."

"Of course not," the man continued, keeping his voice low. "You got caught. No one would steal if they knew they would be caught."

Eamonn dropped his head and shook it. "I never wanted *any* of this." Swallowing, he found his throat dry and rough like sandpaper. He felt filthy and stained inside. "This is who I've become, but it isn't who I am."

"Then who are you?"

Eamonn lifted his head, tears stinging his eyes. He didn't have a good answer—in truth, his identity lay in the Thieves' Guild. "I'm Eamonn."

The man sheathed his weapon, the anger in his expression transformed, but to what? Curiosity? Or perhaps disbelief? Eamonn couldn't quite tell. "And why do you steal, Eamonn?"

"To eat," Eamonn replied, shrugging. Why try to make himself into something he wasn't? Honesty seemed the right call over bravado now. "To achieve my education. To survive."

"You've done this since you were young?"

Something about the man's voice changed too, quickening Eamonn's pulse. Might he show mercy? Eamonn dared to hope.

"I chose this life a long time ago," he answered, one hand reaching up to his necklace and clutching it out of habit.

The man leaned over and put his hands on his knees, coming to Eamonn's level. Eamonn fought the urge to step back, instead locking eyes with the man inches away from him. Kindness—not wrath—pervaded his features.

"Sometimes our circumstances make our choices for us," he murmured, his eyes catching the smattering of moonlight in the wagon. "What if circumstance was removed from the equation? If the choice was yours alone, what would you decide?"

A sob caught in Eamonn's throat, and he tried to swallow it. "I wanted an honest life, but it's impossible now." He choked on the words. "I don't have a way out, at least until I have enough money to go to the College at Nos Illni."

"Yes, you do," the man said, standing up straight again. "Come back tomorrow and find me."

Eamonn drew his eyebrows together, not sure he heard the man right. "What?"

"If you mean what you said, if you really are willing to put this life behind you, meet me here tomorrow morning."

Eamonn searched for words. "I—I don't understand."

"Everyone deserves second chances, don't they?"

Had he passed out and slipped into a dream? This couldn't be real. He should be in the clutches of the city guards and on his way to jail right now. Instead, this merchant who caught him in the act of stealing from his wagon not only showed him mercy but seemed to be helping him. He probably should question it—what sane person helps the thief stealing from him?—but he wouldn't, not yet. For the moment, he would just take the opportunity to escape.

"Keep what you stole from me. It will be my gift to you. Now I am going to call the guards and run your band out of here. Yes, I know you're not alone. I may not have you hanged, but I won't allow you to continue."

A corner of Eamonn's mouth tipped up and he nearly stumbled backward before picking up his sack and running from the wagon. He might as well have floated on air, still in disbelief he had been let go. Not only that, but it also seemed he had a way out of his life of crime. Eamonn had to get his wits about him, trying to remember which way to go to avoid the guards and make it out of there in one piece. He picked a route and ran, nearly colliding with Hadli as he turned a corner.

"We've been found out!" Eamonn warned his friend in a rough whisper. "Get everyone out of here!"

At that moment, Eamonn's liberator opened the door of his wagon. "Guards!"

"Oh, *fikes*," Hadli cursed. "You get everyone at this drop point; I'll get the other."

Footsteps started pounding all around them and guards called to each other as Eamonn raced to the drop point where only two lads remained. "Let's go!"

Like lightning, the thieves shot off from the alleyway. The sounds of the guards behind them began to die out, but they still ran like their lives depended on it. The boys tore through the quiet city, making more noise than they ever did on an operation, but until they put some distance between themselves and the guards, they needed speed more than they needed to stay quiet and stealthy.

Eamonn brought up the rear of the group, glancing over his shoulder every few seconds to make sure they weren't pursued. He let out a low whistle to stop the other boys after several blocks.

"What?" Gareth asked, coming to a halt as the leader of their group.

"Listen," Eamonn commanded, and the boys hid in the shadows of the building beside them as they caught their breath. Eamonn strained his ears for any sound over their panting, but he heard nothing. "I think we're in the clear," he whispered, leaning close to the others. "We should be careful the rest of the way. We don't know where any other night sentries are."

Gareth and Kanan nodded, and for the rest of their route through the city to the river, they kept to the shadows, staying light on their feet and watching out for guards. They crossed paths with no one, breaking back into a run at the riverbank until they arrived at the cave.

Eamonn let out a relieved sigh once he'd slipped through the crevice of the mountain, the adrenaline of the run catching up with him and leaving him shaking. The merchant may have spared him, but he didn't make it easy on them. Eamonn heard a murmur of voices coming from their hideout before he'd turned the corner that opened into the cave. Joris stood right at the opening, his hands on his knees and his head hanging, catching his breath. Eamonn hadn't seen Joris anywhere ahead of them, but he must have just arrived.

"What happened?" Alithir cried, helping Joris to the fire and sitting him down.

"We were discovered," Joris answered, still heaving. "A merchant. He called the guards."

"Where are Hadli and the rest of the group?"

Eamonn's eyes darted over every face in the cave as he tried to steady his breathing. "They're not back yet?"

Alithir shook his head.

"They went another way. I didn't see them behind us, but..." Eamonn gulped for air. "I'm sure they made it out."

Gareth and Kanan heaved and huffed, easing down to the floor of the cave. Some of the lads who had returned earlier brought them flasks of water. Eamonn took the flask offered to him and gulped it down, his pulse throbbing in his ears. Hadli and the others should be back by now. Could they have been caught?

Eamonn gave the flask back and wiped the sweat off his hairline with the back of his hand. What if the reason his group hadn't been pursued by any guards was because the guards had picked up another trail? They didn't know how many boys were out there. Maybe they found some and all followed them, not realizing there were more elsewhere.

A rumbling like an earthquake sounded in the mountain, growing louder until Hadli and the last of the Guild came to a halt inside the cavern, covered in sweat and struggling for breath as the others had.

The cave erupted with a cheer from the entire Guild upon their entrance, but Hadli simply waved a hand in the air before leaning forward and clutching his knees with his hands. Questions bounced around the walls of the cavern, but Hadli and the other boys didn't have the breath to answer. They drank the water offered to them and sat down where they stood, too spent to even make it to the fire.

"There were a few guards on our tail," Hadli explained when he could finally speak. "We had to lose them, so we split up. Joris and Listrik went on ahead, but a guard caught on and Listrik had to duck under a cart sitting in the street. The rest of us hid in an alley until they'd gone; then we got Listrik and bolted."

"Blessed Lady!" Alithir exclaimed.

Hadli glanced around the room. "Everyone's here. Good. No one was captured." He released a heavy breath and lowered his head into his right hand, rubbing his fingers along his forehead. "This wrecks us for a while, though. We'll have to lay low now, get them off our scent."

Eamonn collapsed to the floor and held his head in his hands. The man who'd caught him had been so compassionate, so merciful... if he'd run into anyone else, it wouldn't have ended the same way. Eamonn could be in a jail cell right now, awaiting trial that most likely led to the noose. He knew going in that the mission was too risky, that Hadli put all of their lives on the line for a big haul, and he was right.

"We can't do that again," Eamonn murmured, shaking his head as he held it. "It was reckless and foolish. We never should have even planned it."

Hadli stood up from his seat on the cave floor, crossing his arms and taking a few steps toward Eamonn. "What did you say?" he asked, almost daring him to repeat it again.

"You heard me," Eamonn responded, whipping his head up to meet Hadli's gaze, finally willing to thoroughly defy his leader. "It was stupid of us to attempt that. I knew it from the start, but you wouldn't listen."

Hadli tilted his head down, drawing his eyebrows low over his eyes. "We all made it out. We're all here. Sometimes we have brushes with the law, but we always make it out."

"But we almost didn't!" Eamonn cried, jumping to his feet so that he could meet Hadli at eye level. "This was *too* close, Hadli! You risked our lives."

"What? That's nonsense!" Hadli exclaimed. His eyes pierced right through Eamonn's, rising to his challenge. "Those guards weren't worth their salt!"

"Maybe the guards weren't, but you don't know how we got caught. The third wagon I went to, the merchant was inside!" Eamonn paused for a moment, adjusting his story. He hadn't decided if he wanted to let Hadli know everything about his encounter with the man. "I heard him stir and jumped out just in time. But he was on my heels! He called the guards just after I got away. A second too late and I'd have been caught!"

"Now you're really exaggerating!" Hadli fumed, throwing his hands in the air. "Sometimes we cut it close, but we're *never* caught!"

"I could have gone to the *gallows!*"

"But you didn't!"

"It was pure luck that I didn't!"

"Just be more careful from now on!"

"More care—" Eamonn lost the end of the word. He swallowed down what he wanted to say and bowed his head. Hadli couldn't be serious. He actually had the nerve to defend his stupid decision—all to stay in power, all for some better-than-average loot. *Goes to show what he prioritizes.*

Collecting himself, Eamonn lifted his gaze to Hadli and said, "I can't do any more missions like that. I'm not going to heedlessly risk my life for you."

Hadli narrowed his dark eyes, crossing his arms again. His chest heaved and his nostrils flared, and he stepped closer to Eamonn. "So does that mean you're leaving the Guild?"

After taking slow, steady breaths, Eamonn unclenched the fists that had formed at his sides. Finally breaking his stare with Hadli, he said, "I'm going to bed."

Hadli relaxed his brow as Eamonn trod to the back of the cave, took off his belt and shoes, and climbed into his bed. Hadli inhaled deeply, regaining some of his usual composure, before announcing to the rest of the Guild, "We all should go to bed. It's been a long night. We'll organize our loot tomorrow, but for now, we'll sleep."

The other members obeyed, giving each other inconspicuous glances and getting ready to go to sleep without saying a word. Hadli had never let control of the Guild get to his head before—at least he hadn't shown it—but no one had ever defied Hadli like that either.

Eamonn lay in his bed, eyes closed but mind spinning. His encounter with the merchant played over and over in his head, and the more he thought about taking the man up on his offer, the more torn he felt. The Thieves' Guild had become his family, the cave in the mountainside his home. He couldn't imagine leaving them.

*But I never planned on staying forever.*

This wasn't exactly how he had pictured leaving the Guild, though. Throw in with a traveling merchant he didn't know, trusting him blindly with his future, with his life? Giving up everything he knew just like that? He would have to take a monumental leap of faith.

Eamonn may not know the merchant, but he'd seen his character: showing him and the rest of the Guild mercy, giving him the items he stole, offering him a second chance. He could lead an honest life with this man. Otherwise, Hadli would keep Eamonn at his beck and call, running him all around Erai, stealing and risking his neck without a second thought. Eamonn may have had a home with the Guild, but if he didn't accept this proposal, he was a fool.

Eamonn rolled around in bed, pinched himself, tapped his fingers on his face—whatever he could do to keep himself awake as he waited for the other lads to fall fast asleep. Dawn approached quickly, and he needed to leave the cave before it was light outside, while the rest of the Guild slept.

He couldn't try to explain this to Hadli—he would never understand. Regardless of their fight, they were brothers, and Hadli would do or say whatever it took to keep Eamonn from leaving. Other boys had left the Guild before, and Hadli had let them, but they hadn't had the same bond as Hadli and Eamonn did.

Heavy breathing and rhythmic snores filled the cavern. Eamonn sat up on his cot, careful not to make it squeak and creak too much, and slipped his boots onto his feet. He laced them up, strapped his belt around his waist, then tiptoed around the cave as he gathered up his few belongings in his old school bag. After slinging his coat over his shoulders, Eamonn picked up the sack that held the leather goods he'd stolen and added the contents to his own bag.

The fire had burned down to embers. A lantern sitting on the table provided the only remaining light in the cavern. Eamonn closed the distance between the sleeping lads and the way out, but before he turned the corner, he looked back over his shoulder. The most important people in the world to him—the closest thing he'd ever had to brothers—slept peacefully behind him.

He lifted his hand in a silent wave goodbye, then turned toward his new path in life.

At the intersection of rock and dewy grass, Eamonn stopped and breathed in the cool fresh air. It smelled sweeter than usual. Cleaner. The soft rush of water played on his ears; the river had grown with the recent thaw. A gray haze hung on the horizon in the east, hinting that the sun was near.

He needed to get moving, needed to be far away from the cave before dawn, but he couldn't pick up his feet. The river, the pebbly bank, the skinny trees, the mountain wall—he imprinted everything in his mind. How long would it be before he saw them again, if he ever did? But new landscapes lay before him, a whole world he'd dreamed of seeing, so he moved his feet and didn't look back.

Eamonn had tried to put Hadli and the Guild in the back of his mind the whole time he walked to the city, imagining what they might do or say when they woke up and discovered him gone. He felt a pang in his gut every time he pictured Hadli's expected reaction. Eamonn wished he could have explained to Hadli that he wasn't leaving as a result of their fight, but Hadli wouldn't have believed him.

When Eamonn arrived in the square where the caravan market had begun to come to life, he came to a stop just past the line of wagons. The whole scene looked different in the growing daylight, so it took him a minute to remember his route from the night before and figure out where this merchant's wagon could be found. He started wandering through the wagons, piecing his way together. Customers approached wagons and made purchases while some merchants still set out their goods. Strange that he'd been here just hours before with the Guild.

His eyes flitted from wagon to wagon until he spotted the leather vendor. How could Eamonn have even though he might miss such a behemoth of a man? The man laughed at a comment a customer made, the deep sound reaching Eamonn several wagons away. The muscles in Eamonn's right cheek lifted. The merchant's size made him intimidating, but it seemed deceptive. Everything about the man screamed of a good nature and soft heart, from his contagious laugh to his rosy cheeks and kind eyes. Eamonn hoped he could trust him, but his heart still pounded against his ribcage as he came toward his wagon.

The merchant didn't notice Eamonn's approach, still engaged in a conversation with his customer. When the customer gathered his purchases and left, the man turned his attention to his inventory, his back to Eamonn. Eamonn reached out to tap the man's shoulder but changed his mind before he touched him, drawing his arm back and clearing his throat instead. The man glanced over his shoulder at the sound, and catching sight of Eamonn, he turned around and smirked.

"You look different in the light," he said, leaning his elbow against the vendor stand and resting his weight into it.

"So do you."

The man let out another merry laugh, pushing off the stand. "I'm glad you've come. Here, let's go inside for a moment," he said, motioning with his head for Eamonn to step up into the wagon. Several lanterns assisted the light from the windows in illuminating the wagon's roomy interior, revealing a door at the front of the wagon that Eamonn hadn't noticed the night before.

"Do you sleep in here?" he asked.

"When I travel, yes," the merchant responded, a glimmer in his eyes. "Keeps away the thieves."

Eamonn wasn't sure if he should take the wisecrack as a dig, but his mouth turned up at the corners nonetheless.

"My name is Dorylss," the man told him, sitting on a stool near the front of the wagon. "And you're Eamonn, yes?"

Eamonn nodded, taking a seat on the stool that Dorylss offered across from him.

"Are you hungry?"

Eamonn's jaw fell. How generous could one man be?

He half-expected the food to be a tactic. Maybe Dorylss would go find a guard while Eamonn conveniently waited in the wagon. But the rumble of his stomach argued with him.

"Yes, actually."

Dorylss grabbed a box beside him holding bread, cheese, and cooked ham. "Just my leftovers from yesterday. Here," he said, handing Eamonn a portion of the food on a wooden plate.

Eamonn accepted the plate, staring down at it for a moment as if he was waiting for some kind of catch. Why did he deserve this man's goodwill, especially since they met as he stole from him? Eamonn looked up and locked eyes with the man. "Thank you," he said, then picked up the bread and took a massive bite.

Dorylss hopped out to assist a customer while Eamonn ate, returning just as Eamonn set down the empty plate. He sat down again, resting his elbows on his knees and leaning his chin on his hands.

"So Eamonn, tell me—you say you must steal to survive. Why is that?"

Eamonn dropped his eyes and focused on his boots, ashamed of the life he'd been leading. "My mother died when I was little;

I'm not exactly sure when, but I don't remember anything about her. My father barely took care of me. I started stealing because I was so hungry, and when I got better at it, I took money and school supplies too." Eamonn met Dorylss's eyes again. "School made life worth living for me. But my father didn't provide me with everything I needed, so I stole it instead. I never liked doing it, but... I felt like I had to."

Dorylss nodded slowly as he listened, his hand stroking his unruly red beard. "And when did you join up with this group of lads? Did you meet them at school?"

Eamonn puffed out an ironic chuckle. "No, they—they found me. It was a couple of years ago." He propped his chin in his hand and dropped his eyes, his gaze distant with memory. "They caught me stealing one night and asked me to join. I didn't really have a reason not to, so..." He shrugged.

When Eamonn looked back up to read Dorylss's expression, he didn't find a stern or disapproving stare. Dorylss's features only spoke of understanding and compassion.

"You might be surprised to learn that our stories are not so different, young Eamonn."

Eamonn lifted his eyebrows and his forehead wrinkled, taken aback by the turn in the conversation.

"Yes, I started stealing at a young age. I spent my younger years in the orphanage of Hale in Teravale. Those were different times, and the orphanage was cold and unloving. I ran away after a while, stealing food and taking shelter wherever I could find it. For a short time, I squatted in the barn on the outskirts of Hale, but one day the farmer there found me." Dorylss paused. He clasped his hands together and sat up straighter on the stool. "Instead of punishing me, which would have been just and well within his rights, he took pity on me, raising me in his house with his own children. When I came of age, he found me an apprenticeship with a merchant, and this has been my life ever since."

Realizing his mouth had fallen open, Eamonn snapped it shut and rolled his lips together. "Is that why you pardoned me?"

The rise in Dorylss's cheeks sprouted wrinkles at the corners of his eyes. "I chose to show you the mercy I was shown myself. I see much of my younger self in you. Your circumstances sent you down a path you were not meant for." He shook his head, tenderness in his voice. "I could see last night that you are not meant for the life of a thief. I want to help guide you to the life that is meant for you."

The tears that stung Eamonn's eyes surprised him. Dorylss's kindness, the prospect of a new life, leaving behind his family in the Guild—all the emotions from the past day welled up at the same time, catching him off guard. He let a tear fall, wiping it from his cheek just as it fell.

"I won't ever be able to thank you enough," Eamonn murmured, considering pinching himself to make sure it wasn't a dream.

"You can," Dorylss countered, a smile still softening his features. "Prove to me that you're truly the person you say you are, and not the person circumstance had formed. That will be all the thanks I need."

A grin spread across Eamonn's face and he nodded twice. "I will."

"In the meantime," Dorylss said, reaching beside him for a large jug, "here's some water. I'll set you up a pallet in here—you

can sleep while I'm working the market today. Our work together starts tomorrow."

Dorylss handed Eamonn a mug of ale and held his own in the
air. "To a new start."

Eamonn's eyes lit up and he lifted his mug as well. "To a new
life."

## SEVEN

THE WAGON APPROACHED ERAI under the hot summer sun, and Eamonn was anxious to see how the city might have changed. After coming through the provinces of Farneth and Wolstead, where the kings had either died or been deposed and the restless dissenters rioted in the streets, Eamonn and Dorylss wondered how much the unrest had spread to Idyrria.

Over three years had passed with Eamonn as Dorylss's charge. They traveled all over Sarieth together, Dorylss teaching Eamonn the trade and Eamonn soaking everything up. He had learned so much working side by side with the man who started as his mentor, but soon treated him as a father would—a proper father, at least. The closest bond he'd had with anyone before had been with Hadli, but the brotherhood they'd shared didn't compare with Dorylss's fatherly support and guidance.

It wouldn't be long before Eamonn had saved up the necessary funds to go to the college at Nos Illni. Something important he'd learned as Dorylss's apprentice was that he definitely did not want to stay a merchant, so he still planned to go to the college. Something else he'd discovered, though, was that he didn't think he could bear to leave the man who had taken him in and offered him a new life.

The caravan rode below the mountain ridge to the west of Erai, the same mountain ridge that contained the cave where Eamonn had lived with the Thieves' Guild. His eyes lingered on it as they passed, wondering about Hadli and the other lads. Maybe by this point, there wasn't a Thieves' Guild anymore.

With Eamonn nineteen, that would make Hadli twenty-one, and Eamonn couldn't imagine Hadli still planning thefts the way they used to as a fully grown man. But if the Guild had disbanded, what would Hadli be doing now? He had no formal education and no training. Maybe he'd gone into black market dealing, doing shady business with unsavory characters. Eamonn hoped he'd found some kind of honest work, maybe as a fisherman or ice harvester or some other laborer.

"Are you looking forward to being back in Erai?" Dorylss asked, breaking the silence that had accompanied them almost since Miren.

"I am," Eamonn replied, his head leaning against the wagon's wall from where he sat beside Dorylss at the front. "It's a little strange, though." He said, crossing his arms loosely in front of him. "It was such a different life. I'm not sure I want to see anyone I know."

"No one?" Dorylss wondered, looking over at Eamonn with a crease in between his eyebrows. "I understand why you don't want to see certain people, but were there not people from school you might like to see? Professors? Classmates?"

Eamonn shrugged. "I'd feel like I'd have to explain to them what I'm doing now, how I got here."

"Why, you're a merchant, lad!" Dorylss said, straightening in his seat and holding the horses' reins higher in front of him. "There's nothing to explain about that."

Maybe not. It might be nice to see some people he associated with Erai in a good way. Yes, professors and classmates knew he had hoped to go to the College at Nos Illni after graduating, but many of them also knew of his family dynamic. They would understand that he had to earn money before he could go to the college, so he shouldn't have to worry about them questioning the details of how he met Dorylss.

"Could I go to the library after we get settled?" Eamonn asked, rolling his head against the wagon to look at Dorylss. He could say hello to the old librarians who guarded the volumes as though they were gold; he knew they would be happy to see him. And Eamonn, too, would be happy to spend some time in one of the places in Erai that he missed.

Dorylss grinned. "Of course you can. Just don't stay too late."

"Thanks." Eamonn closed his eyes with a smile on his lips, his head swaying back and forth against the wagon as they rumbled along the rough road to the city. He could already smell the library, the scents of the old books and scrolls that filled polished wooden shelves. Eamonn would likely run into people he knew there, but it wouldn't be so bad. In truth, he'd much rather see someone he knew from the school than anyone in the Guild or even his father. How he might handle those encounters, he had no idea.

Without warning, Dorylss pulled back on the reins and Eamonn jerked forward.

"What are you—" he began, but cut himself off as soon as he opened his eyes. The line of wagons in the caravan had come to a halt. Eamonn stepped onto the seat to get a better view of what was going on, shielding his eyes from the harsh sun. The road curved ahead past a rocky outcropping that partially blocked their view, where what looked like a military outpost had been set up outside the city.

"Looks like it might be a checkpoint of some kind," Eamonn said, squinting his eyes to see better. "That wasn't here the last time we returned to Idyrria, was it?"

"No," Dorylss replied. His forehead wrinkled between his unruly auburn eyebrows as they drew together. "No, it was not."

Eamonn and Dorylss moved little by little down the road as each wagon ahead of them passed through the checkpoint. When they'd cleared the outcropping, they could spot Idyrrian soldiers at the wagons ahead of them, speaking to the merchants and glancing inside the wagons.

"What do you think it means?" Eamonn asked. "Do you think the uprisings have reached Idyrria?"

Dorylss pressed his lips into a line and released a breath through his nose. "I have to think so. Or at least they expect them to. We'll find out."

*Great.* Another province where they would have to watch their every step, staying out of the way of the rebels who rioted and proclaimed their message to try to win people to their cause. These revolutionaries wanted to eliminate each province's monarchy, an institution put in place over two thousand years ago with the founding of Sarieth, when warring countries fought to keep their claim on a part of the land. While the rebels' message promoted a new way of life under a new government, all they seemed to bring to the provinces was anarchy and chaos.

The pebble that started the ripple effect came from Wolstead, on the western coast of Sarieth. About the same time Eamonn left Idyrria to start a new life with Dorylss, the Wolsteadans rose up and revolted against their king, successfully removing him from his throne and ending the centuries-old monarchy.

The unrest had started brewing some time before that, the people of Wolstead fed up with the weak monarchy that led to poverty and poor living conditions across the mining province. Eamonn first came to Wolstead with Dorylss and the caravan market as the province was trying to establish a government of representatives, mayhem ripe throughout the cities.

When Wolstead fell, whispers could be heard around Miren and Farneth about following in their footsteps, deposing their kings and removing themselves from monarchical governments. Miren, ever the antithesis of Wolstead, dispelled any such talk and continued on with their lofty way of life.

In Farneth, however, the rebels found a place to flourish, thrive, and grow. The caravan market went through Farneth a few times as the unrest grew steadily worse, but the most recent visit only months prior was the worst Eamonn had seen. The Farnish king had just died and the unrest in the province had escalated, soldiers escorting the caravan everywhere they went within cities' limits.

The slow movement of their wagon stopped any cooling breeze, making the heat feel even more stifling. Eamonn pulled a handkerchief from the pocket at his chest and wiped his face, grimacing at how wet the fabric became with one swipe.

They crested the hill, and two soldiers came toward them, sunlight glinting off their dull metal helmets.

"Good day to you, sirs," one soldier said as he reached the front of the wagon. "I'm going to ask you to step down while we search your wagon."

"What is the meaning of this?" Dorylss asked, curious rather than angry. "I've never been searched before."

"It's merely a precaution," the soldier explained. "We've had some trouble in the city, so we're trying to keep additional troublemakers out."

"What kind of trouble?" Eamonn asked as he stood from his seat.

The soldier gestured with his head for the two men to come off the wagon as the other soldier went around to the back to begin the search.

"The man from Wolstead who first sparked the rebellions there has come to Idyrria from Miren. Word is, the Mirish almost killed him." The soldier shrugged. "Better if they had."

"If you know he's here, why haven't you arrested him?" Eamonn wondered. He felt it was an obvious question, but the soldier narrowed his eyes at him as if Eamonn was an irritating child.

"He hasn't done anything illegal to warrant being arrested," the soldier answered, not hiding the condescending tone of his voice. "Not yet, at least. He's a nuisance, but he hasn't broken any of our laws. Right now, he seems more interested in recruiting."

"Hmm." Dorylss tilted his head toward the soldier. "Are many joining him?"

The soldier's expression changed as Dorylss addressed him, resuming his professional military attitude. "Some, yes. It's hard to put a number on it right now."

The other soldier exited the wagon and called, "All clear!" to his companion.

"Stay vigilant," the soldier said to Eamonn and Dorylss as he moved to the next wagon. "Things are changing quickly."

Dorylss followed Eamonn up onto the seat and took the reins. Eamonn glanced back at the soldiers who had just left them. "What do you think that means?"

"I think it means we need to stay vigilant," Dorylss said with a grin, his eyes twinkling.

Eamonn rolled his eyes and leaned back again on the wagon. "I mean, do you think they expect Idyrria to go the way of Farneth?"

"I'm not sure," Dorylss answered, and every whiff of his joking manner from moments before disappeared. "Even if they do, I don't expect it to happen quickly. But we should stay alert."

Another pair of soldiers left the wagon before them, and Eamonn and Dorylss began to move again. Eamonn studied the soldiers as they pulled away, trying to get an idea of their readiness for trouble. One soldier yawned—he clearly didn't feel a threat among the merchants—but the other soldier watched the line of wagons closely, as though he didn't trust them. The soldier's eyes passed over Dorylss and Eamonn's wagon, and Eamonn's heart nearly broke free from his chest.

It was his father.

Eamonn turned his face, sinking down into the seat and bringing his hand to cover his eyes, as though that would make him invisible. Dorylss looked over, noticing the movement, and

Eamonn shook his head, hoping it would be enough to stop Dorylss from saying or doing anything.

Once Eamonn decided they ought to be far enough away, he peeked out from under his hand. They'd passed the soldiers and now approached the city. He sat up, but held his face in his hands, rubbing his fingertips over his forehead and temples.

"Does that mean I'm allowed to speak now?"

Eamonn sighed, a deep breath that carried a heavy weight. "Yes."

"So, what happened?"

"My father was back there," Eamonn said, barely able to get the words out. He kept his eyes straight ahead, though he felt Dorylss's gaze on him. "I didn't want him to see me."

Whether Florin actually had seen him or not, Eamonn couldn't be sure. He at least hadn't wanted to make any kind of eye contact with him or even remotely acknowledge him. Eamonn's pulse still raced and he shook from somewhere deep within him. The very last thing he wanted to do in Erai, even below seeing Hadli, was to come across his father. At least this way, Eamonn knew to keep an eye out for him among their soldiers during their time in the city.

"Are you all right, lad?" Dorylss asked after a pause, catching a glimpse of the road before them before turning his concerned eyes back to Eamonn.

Eamonn's head bobbed in a slight nod, and he said, "Yes. I was just taken off guard." He sat back against the wagon again, starting to relax a little. "I haven't seen him in... crow's feathers, at least five years." He scoffed. "He hasn't changed a bit."

"He was the taller one? With the sour expression?"

Eamonn lifted and lowered his eyebrows in a flash. "That's him."

Dorylss nodded thoughtfully. "Well, I know what he looks like now. I'll let you know if I ever see him coming our way."

"Thanks," Eamonn replied with a half-hearted smile.

"Go on to the library as soon as we stop. I'll make sure the horses are taken care of."

Eamonn couldn't help but smile that time. "Thanks. I appreciate it." Dorylss knew him well. Eamonn already looked forward to the library, so it would be a good way to get his mind off his father.

The contrast between the two men had never seemed as stark as it did in this moment. Eamonn glanced at Dorylss again, who had turned his attention back to the road. A corner of Eamonn's closed mouth lifted. The man behind them didn't matter.

His father sat beside him.


Eamonn ascended the wide, shallow stairs that led up to the library, and he pulled open the heavy wooden door. It was like he had opened a page from his past. The familiar scents hit his nose and made him smile, welcoming him home.

The worn soles of his boots thudded on the tile floor, reverberating a dull sound around the tall arched entryway of the library. Eamonn passed the librarian's desk just past the entry, smiling at the familiar old man who sat there. The man smiled briefly back at Eamonn with no recognition in his eyes, and turned his attention to the stack of books in front of him.

He continued into the first room of the library, a grand, rounded two-story room completely lined with books, with staircases off to the sides to climb to the platform around the wall and reach the books on the second level. His gaze was automatically drawn upward to the murals that had been painted on the ceiling ages ago by renowned artists, scenes of people and events contained in the stories and histories within the library's walls.

In the center of the room, chairs and tables were arranged to offer individuals places to read or study comfortably, some of them occupied by students and readers. An arched window of clear glass with decorative stained-glass accents filled the wall opposite him, stretching over both levels of the room.

While Eamonn loved the splendor of the main room, he found more warmth and hominess in the library's other rooms, organized by book genre or category. He took a left and entered the room containing recent Sariethan histories. He didn't look for anything in particular, at least not yet. Eamonn was more interested in reminiscing and soaking up the atmosphere of his favorite place in Erai.

Just as he started to get lost within the library's depths, he heard shouting voices coming from the entry and he backtracked, stopping at the corridor that connected to the main room.

"Find him," he heard a silky, sinister voice call. "Spread out; he's in here."

For no reason at all, Eamonn assumed this man must be referring to him, and he ducked behind a shelf of books just as an Idyrrian man came through the corridor where he'd previously stood. Another followed him, both looking around the rooms as they darted through. Eamonn's heart leapt to his throat as he peered around the shelf, and his breath came in short gasps. No one else followed. Should he try to make a break for it? He didn't have a good place to hide. Trying to get out might be his best option.

Keeping his body low, he shot out from behind the shelf and ran through the corridor, but he stopped where it connected with the main hall to a shout from somewhere on the other side of the library.

"He's here!"

Eamonn peeked out from the corridor to see another young Idyrrian man pulling someone by the forearm into the main room: the librarian. Eamonn gasped, but clapped his hand over his mouth.

The readers in the room's chairs had risen to their feet, seemingly frozen in shock. Several new individuals had entered, other Idyrrian men and women, hooded and cloaked, who didn't appear to belong in the library.

"There you are, old man," came the first silky voice. Eamonn couldn't pinpoint who spoke. "I need to access the vaults, and you are going to open them for me."

"I won't be letting the likes of you into our vaults," the librarian, Marwan, responded. Eamonn knew him—one of the oldest librarians, but also one of the most knowledgeable.

Based on where Marwan directed his speech, Eamonn assumed the silken voice came from a raven-haired man with his back to Eamonn. Whatever the man might have worn was hidden under a black cloak, its hood hanging from his shoulders. He took calculated steps toward Marwan and spoke again, his voice bouncing off the ceiling and echoing around the room.

"You *will* let me in," the cloaked man said, his voice like a rosebush—attractive, but full of thorns, "or you will see this library burn."

If Eamonn's hand hadn't already been covering his mouth, he would have drawn the attention of everyone in the room to himself with his sharp intake of breath. *Burn the library?* The room filled with anxious murmurings of the library's patrons, some of them starting to inch toward the door.

Marwan set his jaw, scowling at the cloaked man. The younger Idyrrian who held his forearm shoved him, and Marwan led the man and a group of four who came with him to a corridor at the back of the room.

"Gather the others," the cloaked man said to one of his followers, and the follower ran down a different corridor.

The group disappeared into the passage and Eamonn's curiosity got the better of him. While the people who had been reading raced for the library's front door, Eamonn crossed them and crept into the corridor after the hooded Idyrrians and the librarian.

Eamonn followed them from a distance, careful to keep his steps light and quiet on the now stone floor. Pounding footsteps sounded behind him, and he ducked into an open room of ancient scrolls to hide. Four or five more hooded Idyrrians clambered past, catching up with the group.

They wound through a maze of passages until arriving at a part of the library unfamiliar to Eamonn. Marwan unlocked a door at the end of a corridor deep within the library, opening it and revealing a stone staircase descending into the ground. He took a torch from the wall nearby and led the way down the staircase.

Eamonn hung back until the last of the Idyrrians had disappeared from view, then he snuck along the corridor and stopped at the top of the stairs. Torches had been lit along the staircase, illuminating the path down. Eamonn's pulse thumped in his ears. Maybe he shouldn't go down, but he was too intrigued to stay put. He'd never seen the vaults, nor did he know what they contained. As a student, he'd heard them mentioned, shrouded in secrecy.

He probably shouldn't follow them.

But he did.

Careful not to make a sound, Eamonn took each footfall on the steps slowly and deliberately. The warm orange glow of torches illuminated the wide tunnel up ahead where the group convened at the end of the passage, a heavy stone door with a series of metal locks before them.

Square stone pillars lined either side of the tunnel, and Eamonn took cover behind one of the pair closest to him. He peeked out from his hiding spot and saw Marwan fiddling with his keys, all eyes on him, so he crouched low and ran ahead to the next pillar. One pair of pillars remained, but the Idyrrians stood too close to them for Eamonn to feel comfortable hiding there. He could see the door at the end of the passage well enough to stay put.

"You delay the inevitable, old man," the cloaked man said, his voice slow and smooth, his back still to Eamonn. "I will have what I seek."

Marwan stopped messing with the keys and straightened his shoulders, looking the man in the eyes. "I know who you are, Rothgard of Wolstead, torment of Sarieth. I know what you seek. And it is forbidden. There is a reason the texts are all kept under lock and key."

"Yes, and it's for that very reason I seek them," Rothgard replied, almost sounding bored. "Now, open the vaults. My threat to burn the library still stands."

Marwan scoffed. "Why would you burn what you hope to claim?"

Rothgard didn't answer, but instead crossed his arms and angled his head toward the librarian. Marwan gripped the ring of keys in his hand, not making any moves to unlock the door. Without prompt, the Idyrrian closest to Marwan lifted his hand and slapped him across the face, knocking the old man down.

"Do it!" the Idyrrian cried. His hood slid from his head with the movement, revealing his face to Eamonn.

Eamonn's legs nearly gave way beneath him, and his heart dropped to the bottom of his stomach. He couldn't believe his eyes.

"Now, Hadli, that was unnecessary," Rothgard chided calmly as Marwan struggled to get off the floor. "That's not how I like to do things. Help him up so he can open the door."

Hadli dropped his head a little at the admonishment, kneeling down to assist Marwan to his feet. Once up, Marwan pulled away from Hadli, rubbing his injured cheek with a wrinkled hand. He then spat on the floor at Rothgard's feet before sifting through his keys.

"Oh, Blessed Lady, forgive me," Marwan murmured before sliding keys into each lock, one after one, unlocking the heavy door. He stepped back to allow Rothgard to pull it open, who then reached out to Marwan for his torch.

Eamonn couldn't see inside the room well, but all he managed to glimpse were a few tattered books. It didn't matter, though. His heart hammered so loudly he felt sure it would give him away, and he couldn't seem to catch his breath. He needed to get out of there. The group would be leaving soon, and he wanted to be long gone before they turned. He especially didn't want to be seen by them now, not after seeing Hadli in their ranks.

He scurried backward up the stairs, keeping his eyes on the Idyrrians below until he couldn't see them anymore. Eamonn crept down the passage at the top of the stairs, taking quiet steps until he decided he was out of earshot, and then he ran.

Eamonn took a couple of wrong turns, but he managed to get back to a part of the library he knew. He could barely focus on where he was going, his mind so caught up in what he had just witnessed. His legs pushed until he'd burst through the front door of the library, his chest heaving and his heart tight.

Tears welled in Eamonn's eyes and blurred his vision as he tried to walk away from the library. He had to get away. He couldn't risk Hadli seeing him—Hadli, who had once been as close as a brother, had transformed from scoundrel to blackguard. Eamonn would never have imagined him treating a person the way he had Marwan, and an old man at that.

And he had joined with this Rothgard of Wolstead, who must be the man responsible for the uprisings that tore apart Wolstead and Farneth. What had driven Hadli to throw in his lot with a usurper? What had this Wolsteadan done to entice him? Perhaps he offered work, money, security—things Hadli would want. Rothgard had been mostly successful, and Eamonn could now picture Hadli jumping at the opportunity to work with him, especially if the Guild was no more. Come to think of it, a couple of the other Idyrrians in Rothgard's company had looked familiar. Could the Guild have just transitioned into some of Rothgard's rebels?

Eamonn turned a corner and stopped, leaning against the wall of a building to catch his breath. Sobs built in his throat and he held his breath to suppress them. He closed his eyes, forcing the tears not to fall. *Oh, Hadli*, he thought, *how far you've fallen.*

# EIGHT

THE MORE TIME THE caravan merchants spent in Idyrria, the more restless it became.

Rothgard and his new recruits had left Erai shortly before the caravan, paving the way for them by unsettling some of the cities on their route. Eamonn was thankful their route that trip did not include Rifillion, Idyrria's kingdom. He heard the band attempted to rile up the citizens there with desire to overthrow their king, but most Idyrrians didn't take to their message.

At least it seemed Idyrria would be safe from Rothgard's influence, but it might be too early to tell. Eamonn hoped he would finally be able to get Rothgard and Hadli off his mind as they put Idyrria behind them. He'd told Dorylss what he'd seen in the library later that day, but there was nothing for them to do. They had simply watched as Rothgard planted more seeds of rebellion and unrest in Idyrria.

But the caravan had since left the province and put the tumult behind them, their market journey complete, and Teravale awaited them promising peace and relaxation.

"How much farther is it to the city?" Eamonn asked, unscrewing his water flask to take a gulp. Being his fourth visit to Caen, the merchants' home base in Teravale, he ought to have known, but the insufferable heat prevented his brain from working properly.

"Oh, we should reach Caen in about an hour. You'll start seeing signs of civilization in thirty or forty minutes," Dorylss replied. He looked over at Eamonn as he drank the water, beads of sweat rolling down past his ears, and he laughed. "You sure can't handle Teravale in the summer."

Eamonn wiped his mouth with his sleeve. "You know I can't. The first time you brought me here in summer nearly killed me, and that was only early summer then." His eyes narrowed but the corners of his mouth started to curl.

Dorylss chuckled. "It's true, the end of summer is hotter. But it's not my fault your Idyrrian constitution is so heat-sensitive."

"I'm only *half* Idyrrian," Eamonn corrected, putting one hand on a knee and using the other to point a finger at Dorylss. "You can blame the Mirish half."

"Oh, I should? And why would I do that?" Dorylss adjusted his grip on the horses' reins. "They're both northern provinces."

"Well, Miren is farther north," Eamonn said, leaning against the wagon and shading his eyes with his hand. "So that's something. Plus, Idyrrians are just tougher."

"You think so?"

Eamonn tucked his chin toward his chest and raised his eyebrows, looking at Dorylss from the corners of his eyes. "I do now." He brought his chin back up and turned his face to Dorylss. "I'd learned all about Miren in school, but I didn't know what the people were really like until we went there. They're all so..." he shook his head and looked into the distance as he searched for the right word, "pretentious."

Dorylss said nothing, instead fighting a smirk and nodding his head. "Are they now?"

"I think so. They never offered what our goods were worth because they weren't 'Mirish-made.' And their merchants tried to make the worst deals with our people who would sell their precious goods." Eamonn didn't try to hide the mockery in his voice. "And don't even think about asking them to do something quickly, or lift anything heavier than a paintbrush. Their 'craftsman' hands aren't nearly that special."

"Mhmm, mhmm," Dorylss murmured, keeping his stare straight ahead.

Eamonn caught sight of Dorylss still trying to fight a grin and frowned. "Something you'd like to say?"

"Did my ears deceive me, or did you remind me not five minutes ago that you are, indeed, half Mirish?" Dorylss fought the smirk no longer, though he still didn't look at Eamonn.

Eamonn opened his mouth as if in retort, but snapped it shut. "Funny," he said, scowling. "Just let Eamonn make fun of himself."

The up and down movement of Dorylss's shoulders gave away his muffled laughter. Eamonn rolled his eyes.

The cover over the wagon's front seat offered some shade, but it didn't provide real relief from the heat. Maybe if Eamonn could fall asleep for the next half hour or so, he'd find himself in Teravale and on his way to a pub to have a cold ale. At least Teravale was their home base where they would take a good, long rest before starting again. Eamonn loved traveling the country and seeing the provinces, but he didn't understand how the traveling merchants had kept going in this job for decades. His few years in the business had worn him out already.

Teravalen farmsteads began to appear, white sheep dotting the hillsides around them like puffs of cloud. Eamonn released a weighty sigh, thankful that another long journey around Sarieth was drawing to a close. The dirt road before them turned into a cobbled street, and farmsteads gave way to cottages with well-stocked gardens. Not a cloud could be found to cover the blazing sun as it bathed the land in light from over Eamonn's right shoulder, now the late afternoon.

Eamonn waved back at the people of Caen who greeted the caravan arriving in the city. After years of coming to the city at the end of the caravan journey, returning to Caen finally felt like coming home. He stretched his legs out in front of him and bent his arms to lean his head back into his hands. The last eight months of cross-country travel had worn him to the bone, and only partially from a physical aspect. The turmoil they came across in the provinces wore on his heart and mind. Here in Teravale, he hoped he could get away from it all for these two months of rest.

As the caravan came into the town, people cheered to welcome them. The return of the traveling merchants was cause for celebration, many of them coming back to family and friends in Caen.

Wagons fell out of line the farther they got into the city, the merchants breaking off to return to their homes. Dorylss turned their wagon down a street bordered by individual shops on one side and overlooking the hills to the north on the other. The shops came to an end at an intersection, where Dorylss made another turn into a more residential part of town.

Houses rode the waves of the hills, the landscape allowing for larger plots of land around each one. At last, coming to a narrow lane, Dorylss guided the horses down it and to a gray and brown stone house with a sizable barn behind it. The neighbor's goats grazed around the yard, helping to keep the grass low, but the green shrubs in front of the house and the ivy that clung to its walls had grown unruly in the inhabitants' absence.

"We'll take a few days off, of course, but our first order of business when we've revived ourselves will be making this place presentable again," Dorylss said as he pulled the wagon up to the barn.

Eamonn hopped down once the wagon had come to a stop, leaning from side to side to stretch his muscles. "We *just* got back and you're already talking about more work." He reached his arms high above him, letting them fall back down with a flop. "You need to let your mind take a break, too."

"I said we'll take a few days off." Dorylss threw a finger up to point at the barn doors.

Huffing, Eamonn bounced over to the barn and swung one door open, then the other. The stale scent of horse and manure hit him, and he wrinkled his nose. Eight months of closed doors hadn't helped the usual equine odor that lingered there.

"You have to mean it, though," Eamonn called to Dorylss, stabling the horse that Dorylss had offered to him before their last voyage. The chestnut horse shook his head after Eamonn removed his bit and bridle, then he dug his nose into a bag of hay that hung before him. "There you go, Rovis, you've earned it," Eamonn murmured to the animal, rubbing his neck.

"Well, of course I mean it!" Dorylss replied with a laugh from another stall. "Have you forgotten I'm much older than you, lad? I can't keep it up the way I could in my youth, the way you can."

"Then don't even mention work! Not yet!" Eamonn poured water into a trough and Rovis started to drink. He stepped outside the stall and leaned against its wooden door, kicking one foot up on it behind him. "I think I might sleep for two days straight." His cheeks raised in a grin. "Don't even come upstairs, I want nothing to disturb me."

Leaving the other stall, Dorylss let out a single derisive laugh and shut the stable door behind him. "Not so fast, Eamonn. I won't make you work yet, but before you get any other ridiculous ideas, you should know that I'm going over to see the family of my old friend Stevyrn tomorrow. I want you to come with me."

"Ugh!" Eamonn dropped his foot from its perch and slouched his shoulders over so that his arms hung in front of him. "Already? The first full day we're back?"

"Yes." Dorylss rested a gentle hand on Eamonn's shoulder. The tenderness of the action got Eamonn's attention; he straightened again and brought his eyes up to his mentor. "Stevyrn was a good friend and a good man, and I promised to look after his family should anything happen to him. They've become like my family over the years, and, well," he tipped his head down, his eyes glistening, "you're my family now, too. You ought to be just as much a part of their lives as I am."

Eamonn couldn't argue about it now. He wouldn't. He inhaled through his nose and pressed his lips together, his heart swelling. Dorylss spoke the truth. As time had passed, Eamonn had become more son to Dorylss than apprentice. He had felt the change in relationship over the years, and he knew Dorylss had, too, but he couldn't remember a time before now that he had called Eamonn his family. If Dorylss wanted him to go visit this family tomorrow, he would be happy to go. Any natural offspring of Dorylss would be close with the family of their father's late friend, so Eamonn should be too.

"All right, I'll come with you," Eamonn said, looking back over his shoulder at his horse to hide some of the emotion seeping through his features. "But I'm still going to get plenty of sleep before we go."

"Not a problem," Dorylss replied. He crossed to the opposite side of the barn, opening the windows to create some airflow. "I'm not waking any earlier in the morning than my mind decides. I might even sleep later than you!"

"Well, I'm glad about that!" he called to Dorylss, the breeze from the open windows improving the smell already.

Eamonn followed Dorylss as he left the barn. "Come on, lad," Dorylss said, "let's go down to the pub and grab a bite and a pint. We'll stock up on food in the house tomorrow."

The mention of food and ale made Eamonn's stomach rumble. He ran down the sloped lane in a few long strides back to the empty cobbled street.

"Slow down!" Dorylss shouted from the lane. "You know I'm not about to run to the pub!"

Eamonn stopped and laughed, picturing Dorylss running down the street in quest of a pie. The lumbering footfalls, his unruly auburn hair streaming behind him, and a hungry gleam in his eye. By the time Dorylss had reached him in the street, Eamonn had pulled himself together.

"Sorry," he apologized with another chuckle. "I won't make you run. I'd never make it to the pub myself that way." He snickered. "I'd have fallen in the street laughing."

Dorylss stopped and faced Eamonn, his eyelids low over his eyes and his lips a straight line. He shook his head. "You think you're pretty funny, don't you?"

"I amuse myself, it's true," Eamonn quipped, beaming. At least Dorylss tolerated his sense of humor. Sometimes he even found Eamonn to be witty, even if he pretended otherwise.

Eamonn slowed his pace, and he and his mentor strolled down the street, following it into the city. The closer they came to the pub, the more people they encountered in the streets, finishing their business for the day. Shop owners turned signs in their windows that they had closed, and a lamplighter came down the street lighting lanterns and torches outside some of the buildings. The sun hung low over the horizon now, pulling its light and heat from the city. Eamonn took a deep breath of the fresh, cooler air. If only it could feel like this all the time.

At the end of the street, the pair could see a wooden sign hanging off the building, carved and painted with the image of a badger, signaling their destination. Eamonn and Dorylss frequented The Lonely Badger whenever they were in town, and though they initially patronized the pub because it was the closest one to their house, it earned its place as their favorite Caen haunt with its excellent food, friendly bartenders, and cold, frothy ale.

A bell jingled when Eamonn opened the door, and the pub owner looked up from behind the bar, smiling at his customers.

"Dorylss! Eamonn! Welcome back!" he greeted, spreading his arms out wide. "I heard the caravan was back in town, so I knew I'd be seeing you soon. Well, come on, come over here, have a drink!"

Eamonn and Dorylss took seats at the bar while the owner poured them two ales and set the glasses in front of them.

"Thanks, Castor," Dorylss said before picking up his mug and taking a healthy swig. He set the mug back down with a *thunk*, leaving froth on his mustache and upper lip. "There's nothing quite like a pint of Teravalen ale to revive you after a long journey."

Rather than gulping down half of his ale at once like Dorylss, Eamonn sipped on his, relishing the taste. He had to admit—Dorylss was right. He'd traveled all over the country now, tasting ale from every town in every province, and nothing beat the ale in Teravale. Maybe they grew better barley, or had perfected their fermenting process, or added a unique secret ingredient. Something made Teravalen ale perfect.

Maybe it was just that it meant he was home.

"What are you offering to eat tonight?" Dorylss asked Castor after another gulp.

"Maranie's making beef pies and mashed potatoes. Want me to call back to the kitchen an order for each of you?"

Dorylss glanced at Eamonn for confirmation, like he needed it. Eamonn's raised eyebrows were all Dorylss had to see.

"If you will, please."

Castor turned to let his wife know about the new orders as Dorylss finished his ale, setting the cup on the inside edge of the counter for a refill.

"So, Dorylss," Castor began as he filled the empty mug, "how was your journey? Did you run into much trouble in the unstable provinces?"

Dorylss cocked his head and took the mug Castor offered him. "We didn't personally, no. Wolstead and Farneth are tumultuous, I can't deny it, but the agitators there didn't really bother us. They were more interested in their own people and governments."

"That's good to hear at least." Castor wiped his hands on a towel and turned his eyes to Eamonn. "How was Idyrria when you came through? I hear it's getting rougher there."

Finishing his sip of ale, Eamonn placed his mug on the counter and wiped his mouth with the back of his hand. "It is." He made eye contact with Castor for only a moment before he dropped his gaze, wrapping both his hands around the mug. Images of the growing unrest in Idyrria filled his mind, of Rothgard, of Hadli. "Not as bad as Farneth, though. And we only caught the beginning of it."

"Hmm," Castor murmured, bringing his hand to his trimmed brown beard. "Well, I'm glad it wasn't worse than that. Who knows what things will be like in two months when you head out again?"

He leaned in closer to them, the edge of the counter poking into his round belly. "I'd steer clear of the kingdoms next go 'round. From what I hear, Swyncrest is getting rougher. It's only a matter of time before the young king is deposed. I don't think the Farnish would have sought to rid themselves of his father, but the lad just doesn't know what he's doing."

"It was an unfortunate time for King Everod to die." Dorylss shook his head. "And they said he fell ill? I never heard what with."

"Neither did I," Castor agreed. He propped a hand on his hip and raised a finger on his other hand. "I'll tell you, it's odd. He seemed perfectly well just leading up to his death, by all accounts. And he wasn't much older than you and me."

Dorylss drummed his fingers on the counter and Eamonn shifted in his seat. The tones of their voices had changed just a little, and Eamonn picked up on the new edge to them—something was not what it seemed.

Flashing his eyes around them, Dorylss added in a murmur, "I don't think the people would go so far as to kill him. He was a good king, a popular king. Before he died, I don't believe Farneth had any desire to remove the monarchy."

"Well, that's just the thing," Castor said in a matched volume, resting his forearms on the counter and leaning in close to Eamonn and Dorylss. "Some of the Farnish loyal to the monarchy have come to realize that this Wolsteadan named Rothgard appeared in the province around the same time as the king's death, the same man who was responsible for the fall of Wolstead's king."

"So, what, then?" Eamonn asked, his eyebrows knitted together and his heart rate rose. Could the man that Hadli had joined forces with be more than just a usurper? Was he a murderer too? "How could this man get close enough to the king and make it look like an illness? Poison?"

"Magic," Castor whispered. His eyes bored into Eamonn's, and Eamonn found he couldn't break the stare. "They say this man has gathered up ancient texts about magic and has been teaching himself how to practice the magic of old."

Eamonn opened his mouth to retort, thinking that Castor must be joking, when Maranie came from the kitchen carrying a tray with their food. Castor stood up and smiled at his wife, thanking her and taking the tray. Dorylss and Eamonn sat straight again and took sips of their ale. Eamonn glanced at Dorylss from the corner of his eye, trying to determine if Dorylss thought Castor's claims as incredulous as Eamonn did. Dorylss, however, gave nothing away.

"Ah, here we are." Castor set the tray down and gave Eamonn and Dorylss each a plate with a pie and mashed potatoes. "I hope you enjoy, my friends."

Another patron took a seat at the bar, drawing Castor's attention. "We'll speak again," he told them before walking away. "Let me see about this fellow here."

Dorylss dug into his beef pie, blowing on the hot dish to cool it before taking a bite, but Eamonn didn't touch his fork.

"He's not serious," Eamonn said, though it sounded more like a question.

Holding his loaded fork in the air in front of his mouth, Dorylss asked, "What do you mean?" before taking the bite of food.

Eamonn leaned over closer to Dorylss. "Magic? It's a fairy tale. It's far-fetched to say this Rothgard fellow killed the Farnish king with magic." He raised his eyebrows. "Sounds like a convenient excuse for when there's not a good explanation."

Dorylss chewed his food thoughtfully, staring down onto his plate. When he finally swallowed his food, he murmured, "I'm not so sure."

Eamonn sat back, his mouth falling open. "Not you, too."

"I'm not saying he's right, necessarily," Dorylss said, keeping his voice low enough for the rumble of conversation in the bar to cover his words, "but I wouldn't brush it off so easily."

"Dorylss, it's impossible. Magic is just a legend, a myth." Eamonn watched Dorylss take another bite of his food. "It made for good stories to tell children, so it's been passed through the generations."

"Mmm." Dorylss took a drink of his ale to wash down the potatoes. "And how do you know that? All we know is what we've been told."

Eamonn shook his head, his food still sitting untouched on the counter. "It's what I was taught. My professors at school in Idyrria—"

"Only know what they were told, too," Dorylss finished for him. He caught Eamonn's gaze, sincerity filling his eyes. "Look, lad, I don't want to argue with you about this. I know that by and large it's believed magic isn't something that's real in our world. And I could say that I fall into the category of people who believe that. But don't close yourself off to the possibility that it might exist. If it does, and if it's something this man is actually able to use, then every single one of us is at an immediate disadvantage against him."

A man in the pub came up behind Dorylss and clapped a friendly hand on his shoulder, pulling Dorylss from their conversation. Eamonn recognized him but couldn't remember his name. Dorylss turned to face the man, a smile spreading across his features, and the man welcomed him back to Caen.

Eamonn finally turned his attention to his plate of food, cool enough now to scoop into his mouth without hesitation. Oh, he needed this meal. He'd let their meaningless conversation get in the way of filling his belly.

A dull ache in his stomach pained him, but it wasn't from its emptiness. Did Dorylss actually have a point? Could there even be a possibility that the Wolsteadan was trying to teach himself magic? Eamonn might have believed in magic when he was a child, but he'd long since grown out of such juvenile thinking. Why would he change his beliefs now? What his teachers had told him made sense, that magic was nothing more than a fable. No one in their time could use magic, so where would it have gone?

He pushed the thoughts out of his mind and focused on eating his meal. It was silly, and he didn't want it to put a rift between Dorylss and himself, so he wouldn't bring it back up. He had seen no evidence anywhere in the country during his travels that magic existed, which meant this rumor must be nothing more than a rumor, and therefore nothing for Eamonn to worry about.

Hadli climbed the steep steps up the tower to the sole chamber set at the top. Rothgard had summoned him, and Hadli answered the call immediately. He'd been growing in good graces with the leader, his skills, initiative, and determination standing out among the growing group of followers and placing Hadli in a trusted position. He could see himself rising to a position of right-hand man, and he was determined to do whatever it took to cement that status.

He arrived at the top of the stairs, met with only a landing and a weathered wooden door. One of the rebels stood as a gatekeeper outside of the door, greeting Hadli with a curt nod.

"He's expecting you," the gatekeeper said, turning the handle and pushing open the heavy door.

Hadli passed over the threshold and the rebel shut the door behind him. The rounded tower room felt huge because of its high ceilings even though it filled a cozier diameter. A rectangular threadbare rug, likely once full of color but now faded to gray, covered the stone floor. Tattered paintings and tapestries hung on the walls between the tall windows. An old four-poster bed had been pushed over to one side of the room to make space for a long wooden table in the center, covered with books and scrolls. Rothgard sat at the table in the only chair beside it, his back to Hadli.

"Ah, Hadli, do come in," he said, his voice as smooth as silk. He did not sit up or even turn to face Hadli, all his attention on the book in front of him. "Here, let's have some more light, shall we?" With a flick of his left hand, the torches hung around the room instantly lit with bright flames.

"You asked for me, sir?" Hadli said, his feet planted on the floor. He wouldn't come any farther into the room until he was requested.

"Yes." Rothgard shut the book he'd been studying and pushed the chair away from the table. "You mentioned to me before an old friend of yours who possessed an interesting necklace, one that seemingly matched a description I gave you." He took slow steps away from the table toward a window, his back still to Hadli.

"Yes?"

The man stopped before reaching the window, clasping his hands behind his back. "I'm going to send you and those from your guild on a mission."

"Of course, sir," Hadli replied, energy rising within him. He'd love to get out of this dilapidated castle for a while, get outside and feel useful.

Turning on his heel to face Hadli, Rothgard's icy blue eyes pierced through him, overflowing with hunger and guile. His voice, however, remained cool and collected. "I need you to find that old friend. Find him and his necklace, and bring them to me."

Hadli swallowed, his face expressionless. What could Rothgard want with Eamonn and that necklace? He didn't need to ask questions, though.

"Yes, sir," Hadli replied, venom on his tongue. "I'll bring him to you."

# NINE

"WE'RE EXPECTED, RIGHT?" EAMONN asked Dorylss as they
trotted on their horses through the streets of Caen. "We're
not going to take them by surprise when we show up at their
door, are we?"

Dorylss chuckled, holding onto his horse's reins with one
hand while his other hand rested on his thigh, elbow out to
the side. "Oh, no. Melwyn always expects me the day after
the caravan returns. It's become a bit of a ritual now."

Eamonn squinted as the sun came out from behind a cloud
overhead. At least there were clouds, unlike the day before.
"How long have you been doing this? Visiting them at the
end of a market journey. I know it's been at least as long as
I've known you."

"Stevyrn's been gone, what, five years now?" Dorylss asked himself out loud. The hand on his thigh reached up to rub his chin. "Or close to it. The year you joined me was the second market-end I paid this visit. Stevyrn's ship wrecked about a year before that."

"I remember you telling me you had to go see this family the first year we came to Caen together, but I don't remember the circumstances," Eamonn said as he pulled on the reins to turn Rovis around a corner. "What happened?"

Dorylss released a heavy sigh, returning his hand to its resting spot on his leg. Eamonn noticed the way Dorylss's countenance drooped with the memory. "Stevyrn and I grew up together. He was the son of the farmer who took me in. He eventually became a trader overseas, and of course I traveled cross-country, but we kept in touch and would make sure to see each other when we were both in Teravale. He married and had a family, and I became close to them. We both knew the perils of the job—his especially. Stevyrn made me promise to take care of his family should anything happen to him." Dorylss didn't try to hide the grimace that overtook his features. "Then the worst happened. His ship was caught in a storm, a day out from his next destination. Debris and bodies washed up on the western shore of Marinden, and they sent word back to Teravale."

Neither spoke for a while as they came through a more crowded part of the city and into the northern residential area. Eamonn tried to imagine the pain Dorylss must feel for his friend's death. It made more sense to him now why Dorylss felt such an intense responsibility to this family, and why he wanted Eamonn to know them as well.

"I try to live up to the promise I made Stevyrn." Now that they had returned to the hills where cottages and small farmhouses stood, Dorylss spoke again. "I give his family as much of my earnings as I can part with." He patted a pouch at his waist that jingled at his touch. "Melwyn works as she is able, mending clothes and helping others with chores, but she still has three children to raise. The girls sell eggs and milk in town. It's not much, but all of it together is enough to feed them and clothe them. They don't mind living simply."

Dorylss led the way down winding streets that narrowed the farther they went out of town. The cobbled lanes faded away to roads of trampled grass, leading to homes that sat further apart from each other than the buildings in the city, each surrounded by small plots of farmland and animals.

At last, they turned toward a small stone cottage with a shingled roof perched on a hilltop, smoke puffing out of the chimney. A tree stood tall near the house, shading it with broad limbs. Well-tended pink, yellow, and white flowers bloomed in front of the house, adding a cheerful pop of color. It seemed no effort had been spared to keep the home's appearance up.

Eamonn and Dorylss brought their horses to a hitching post under the tree and tied them off. The clucking of hens drew Eamonn's eyes to behind the house, where he noticed a chicken coop and a cow that grazed in an extensive fenced area.

"Come on," Dorylss said as he looked over his shoulder at Eamonn, a joyful grin replacing the frown from before. "It's time for you to meet them."

A woman came out the front door before Eamonn and Dorylss reached it. She wiped her hands on a stained apron that hung around her waist and then put them on her hips. Her graying dark blond hair was tied up in a bun at the back of her head, and a fan of deep wrinkles popped out beside her eyes as she smiled at them. She didn't seem old, necessarily, but weary, like the last five years had added enough stress and worry to add more age than usual to her features.

"Welcome back, Dorylss!" she greeted, her tone warm and inviting.

A small redheaded boy appeared at the door's threshold. His closed lips spread wide upon seeing Dorylss, but he stayed behind his mother's skirts, peeking out at the visitors.

"It's good to be back, Melwyn," Dorylss replied as he approached the house. "My goodness, this can't be Noriden! He's a fully grown lad now!"

Melwyn looked down at the child with love, running her hand through his hair. "Six years old now. We started learning how to read and write our letters recently, didn't we?"

Noriden nodded and stepped out toward Dorylss. "I can write my name!" he announced.

Dorylss's bright, merry laugh erupted from his lips as he knelt down to Noriden's level. "Well done, lad! Now, will you come give me a hug?"

The boy bounded into Dorylss's arms and Dorylss held him tight. He met Melwyn's eyes and said, "He's looking more and more like Stevyrn every time I come."

Melwyn nodded but did not speak. Noriden broke from the hug and reached into his pocket.

"Look at these stones I've collected!" He held out his palm to Dorylss, separating the displayed rocks. "This one is my favorite."

"Noriden, love, let Dorylss come inside and have his meal, and then you can show him your things," Melwyn instructed, reaching out for her child to take her hand.

"Okay," Noriden obeyed, stuffing the rocks back into his pocket, and Melwyn ushered him inside.

"It does him so much good to have you in his life," Melwyn said to Dorylss after the boy had gone into the house. Her arms crossed and her hands clutched her elbows. "He needs a fatherly presence."

"He'll always have one," Dorylss said, his voice low and sincere.

Melwyn gave Dorylss a small, appreciative smile, her eyes starting to glisten. Dorylss nodded once, then reached his arm out behind him in Eamonn's direction.

"You haven't met properly before, but I wanted to bring my apprentice with me this time," Dorylss said, and Eamonn stepped forward. "This is Eamonn. He's been a great help to me these past few years, a quick learner and a hard worker."

"Pleased to meet you, Eamonn," Melwyn said with a slight bow of her head. "I've heard lots about you, so it's nice to finally lay eyes on you."

"It's nice to meet you, too, ma'am," Eamonn replied, imitating the head tilt.

"Come inside, both of you," Melwyn offered, stepping back into the house. "We've got a cold lunch prepared for you, but I hoped you wouldn't mind considering how hot the weather's been."

"Cold sounds perfect," Eamonn said as he followed Dorylss and Melwyn into the house.

Melwyn led them through the long, narrow front room, a couple of pairs of shoes lying on the wooden floor just inside. Empty hooks lined the walls, any cloaks or coats that might have hung on them packed away for the season.

The entry room opened up into a spacious kitchen that smelled of herbs and burning wood, a long wooden table surrounded by six chairs to their right and a stone hearth to their left. A hefty butcher's block counter stood next to the hearth, laden with food and utensils. Shelves bordered the fireplace on either side bearing dishes, bowls, and cups. Pots and pans hung from the ceiling over the butcher's block, and another shelf against the wall they passed as they entered held a variety of foodstuffs. An exterior door split the room in the middle on the back wall, two windows on either side. Two girls in simple cotton dresses, one several years older than the other, worked in the kitchen, the younger one taking a tea kettle off the fire and the older gathering plates.

"He's here," Melwyn announced to her daughters as she went to the butcher's block to retrieve the prepared food.

The younger girl spun around with the kettle in her hands and beamed at the sight of Dorylss, her reddish-brown curls bouncing with the movement. The older girl turned with a pile of plates in her arms, a grin already gracing her features, but her gaze only landed on Dorylss for a moment. She locked eyes with Eamonn, and her cheeks fell, then she flashed her eyes at her mother before finding Eamonn again.

Something in her stare sent a tingle up Eamonn's spine and he felt heat rising into his face. He didn't know exactly why, either. Yes, she was lovely, but he'd met plenty of beautiful girls before.

None of them had penetrated his very soul with a single glance, though.

She betrayed nothing of her own thoughts in her expression, but Eamonn felt a little under scrutiny. She didn't expect him, that much was already clear. But surely, she must know who he was; Melwyn said Dorylss had spoken of him before, so this girl should at least know Dorylss had an apprentice. Eamonn broke eye contact with her, hoping now that any redness in his face could simply be attributed to a horseback ride in the late summer heat.

"Dorylss!" the younger girl cried, setting the kettle on the butcher's block and running to the merchant, who wrapped her up in a hug. "I'm so glad you're here!"

"So am I, Marielle," Dorylss replied with a smile. He released her from the embrace and she returned to the kettle.

"Leyna, grab the cups and tea and I'll pour the water," Marielle requested of the older girl.

Leyna dropped her eyes, finally taking them off of Eamonn. "Right. Let me say hello first."

She didn't look at Eamonn as she set down the stack of plates and took her turn to hug Dorylss. She murmured something to him that Eamonn couldn't hear, and Dorylss smiled softly, his lips moving with a reply. Her cheeks lifted again, dimples popping up in each one.

Leyna turned from Dorylss and gathered six tea cups on a tray, scooping tea leaves into each cup before Marielle filled them with water. Leyna carried the tray over to the table and set out one cup at each place, diligently keeping her gaze focused on her work.

Eamonn had lingered in the doorway while Dorylss greeted Stevyrn's daughters, not entirely sure what to do next. He shifted on his feet and held his hands clasped together, waiting to follow Dorylss's lead.

"I've told you girls about my apprentice, Eamonn," Dorylss said as Leyna placed the teacups on the table, gesturing to Eamonn beside him. "I brought him with me this time. Eamonn, Marielle and Leyna."

Eamonn looked to Marielle first and gave her a small nod in greeting, his closed mouth turned up at the corners. She flashed a toothy grin at him and returned the nod.

He then turned to Leyna on his right. She lowered a cup gently to the table and lifted her head. Her eyes met his and his stomach constricted.

"It's nice to meet you, Eamonn." Her words sounded like a symphony.

"And you, Miss."

Sweat had formed on his palms and he felt a sudden urge to wipe his hands on his trousers. He wouldn't, though. Not till her gaze had left him.

"Marielle, grab those plates, will you?" Melwyn asked, taking a tray of cold meats and cheeses to the table. "Leyna, will you get the fruit?"

Marielle took the plates to the table and Leyna crossed her, brushing a strawberry-blonde lock off her shoulder. Her curls hung looser than her sister's, falling midway down her back like a cascade of sun rays.

Melwyn set out the food in the center of the table with serving utensils, adding the tray of fresh fruits that Leyna brought to her. Marielle arranged the plates around the table and plopped down in one of the chairs. Dorylss waited for Leyna and Melwyn to take their seats before he sat down himself on the long end of the table, and Eamonn followed suit beside him.

"Noriden!" Melwyn called out. "Oh, where has that boy gone?"

Like a flash, Noriden came through a door at the end of a hallway past the hearth, and he took his place at the table. "Sorry, Mama."

"That's all right, love," Melwyn said from her seat at the head of the table, Noriden taking the chair opposite her.

Eamonn scooped some berries onto his plate, using the movement as an excuse to glance across the table and in front of Dorylss, where Leyna sat. She held a cream jar in her hand and poured some into her tea, stirring as she set the little jar back down. She didn't look up, though; she kept her gaze on her tea.

"How was this caravan journey for you?" Melwyn asked Dorylss, picking up the cream jar after Leyna.

Dorylss cocked his head and brought it back straight in a smooth movement. "I'd like to say it was uneventful, but I'm afraid we got to see the rebellions in some of the provinces firsthand."

Melwyn wrinkled her forehead with her lifted eyebrows. "Oh no! Was it very dangerous?"

"Not dangerous, really." Dorylss shook his head. "Lots of tension and unrest, but I wouldn't call it dangerous."

Eamonn cast his eyes to their periphery toward Dorylss, not turning his head. He must not want Melwyn to worry. Sure, they hadn't personally run into any danger on their travels, but Eamonn wouldn't describe their time in some of the bigger cities of Wolstead and Farneth "not dangerous."

"Oh, thank the Lady," Melwyn said with a sigh. Now that Dorylss and Eamonn had filled their plates, she took some meat and cheese. "We've heard enough about their horrible uprisings from the chancellor here, and from the king in his monthly addresses. It sounds as though things are getting as bad in Farneth as they are in Wolstead."

Eamonn stuffed a bite of bread into his mouth. If Dorylss wanted to keep Melwyn from too much distress, Eamonn didn't want to speak and potentially say too much.

"Ever since the king of Farneth died, the people have been unhappy with his son as king. The dissenters have had more support for their position of a leader elected by the people, so things are more unstable."

*Well done, Dorylss.* He'd accurately presented information, so he didn't lie to her, but neither did he paint a full picture of the anarchy they'd faced in Swyncrest, Farneth's kingdom.

Melwyn swung her head side to side with sigh. "And now they say it's happening in Idyrria, too. It's surrounding us."

Dorylss looked at Melwyn until she brought her head up, and they locked eyes. "Don't fret. Idyrria didn't seem as susceptible to these revolts as Farneth."

Taking a deep breath, Melwyn nodded as if accepting Dorylss's words. Her countenance changed and her gaze moved to her daughters, ready to change the subject. "The girls think our cow is pregnant. So, there will be some time without milk from her, but it's a blessing, really."

Marielle stopped the hand that was about to pop a strawberry into her mouth so she could speak. "I'm certain she is! If the calf is female, then we have the potential for two dairy cows, and if the calf is male, we can sell him to a farmer and earn some money from him." She took a bite from the strawberry.

"My little optimist." Melwyn grinned down the table at Marielle, who mirrored her.

"So Eamonn, what's your favorite province?" Marielle asked, still chewing the berry. The way her eyes sparkled and the quickness to her voice gave away her eagerness to talk to him.

"Well, I have to say Idyrria, but I'm a little biased," Eamonn answered, chuckling a little at the younger girl's enthusiasm. "That's where I'm from. I've loved traveling around Sarieth and visiting all the provinces, but I don't think I'll like any of them as much as Idyrria." He released another ironic chuckle. "Not even Miren, and that's where my mother was from."

Marielle licked a finger after a bite of meat, resting her chin in her other hand with her elbow on the table, a wistful look in her eyes. "I'd like to travel one day, see the different provinces. I bet Idyrria is beautiful. I've only seen illustrations and heard stories."

"Maybe you'll have the chance to take a little trip with us when you're older," Dorylss offered. "All of you. It would be nice to see something new, wouldn't it?"

Marielle beamed as she nodded, with enthusiastic agreement from Noriden, but Leyna only lifted her eyes to Dorylss and showed her dimples for a moment. Eamonn caught the motion from the corner of his eyes. He'd been waiting for her to make a move or say something, but she'd kept to herself and eaten her food in silence.

Instead of taking her attention back down to her food, though, something about Eamonn caught her gaze, a curious expression on her face, and it was his turn to look at his plate. He could already feel the heat rising to his face again.

"Your necklace," she said, the first words she'd spoken since greeting Dorylss.

Eamonn whipped his head up to meet her cornflower blue eyes, his hand automatically reaching for the pendant.

She studied him closely, like she was trying to figure something out. Her lips parted and closed in contemplation before she said, "It's very interesting."

Realizing he'd forgotten to breathe, Eamonn sucked in a short breath before answering. "It belonged to my mother." His fingers traced the pendant's outline. "I've had it for as long as I can remember."

Leyna's stare did not leave him, and he was bound to it. He saw nothing else happening around him, knew of no one else in the room. In her gentle, quiet way, she commanded a presence.

"Where did she get it?"

Eamonn blinked a few times, his mouth agape. No one had ever asked him that before.

"I'm not sure," he replied, shaking his head and dropping his hand from the necklace. "I never knew her to ask her. I always assumed it was a family heirloom, and that's why it was given to me."

Leyna finally pulled her gaze from him, dropping her eyes to the surface of the table. She brought her right hand to her mouth, softly pressing her knuckles against her lips. "It just looks... familiar, somehow." She plucked a grape off the stem and ate it, seemingly lost in her own thoughts.

The world came shooting back to Eamonn: Dorylss tore a chunk of bread, Marielle sipped her tea across from him, and to his left, Noriden had trouble sitting still in his chair. Leyna kept her gaze down, every now and then eating another grape.

Dorylss picked up the conversation, saying something about their time in Idyrria, but Eamonn tuned everything out. He watched Leyna for a moment, wondering what was going on in her mind. She hadn't looked at the necklace in the same way as Hadli all those years ago, when Hadli had first laid eyes on it. Where there had been avarice and envy in Hadli's stare, in Leyna's, Eamonn saw fascination mingled with confusion. She said it seemed familiar; her father had been a merchant, too. Maybe it reminded her of some Mirish jewelry she'd seen long ago.

A tug in the back of Eamonn's mind told him he knew that wasn't true, but he pushed it back. He'd come to see lots of Mirish jewelry in his three years as a merchant apprentice, some of it dating back several years, and he'd found nothing that looked like his mother's necklace. He didn't have an explanation—and didn't want one—so he always pushed the thought away.

Leyna barely spoke for the rest of their meeting. Dorylss and Eamonn told them all about their caravan journey, careful to keep the details about the uprisings to a minimum, and Eamonn enjoyed getting to know the family. He could see in Dorylss's voice and behavior how much they meant to him, loving them as if they were his own kin. Dorylss had no blood relations left, with the exception of a few cousins scattered around Teravale, but he still had this family that he had chosen, Eamonn included.

The sun was well on its way toward the horizon when Dorylss and Eamonn bid them farewell. Dorylss handed Melwyn the money pouch, which she accepted with a bowed head and a quiet word of thanks.

On their way out of the house, Marielle followed, asking, "Will you come back again while you're here?"

Dorylss turned around once outside and smiled at the girl. "I will. We'll take some time to rest well, and I'll be back."

Marielle's white teeth glinted in the sunlight. "Good. Both of you?"

Eamonn looked back over his shoulder, one cheek raised in a smirk. He found Leyna lingering in the doorway, resting against the jamb with hands clasped in front of her light brown skirts. Something fluttered in his chest, and the other cheek lifted as well.

"Yes," he answered Marielle. Eamonn kept his focus on Leyna but noticed Dorylss turn to him from his peripheral vision. Maybe he imagined it, but it looked like dimples appeared on Leyna's face.

Dorylss and Eamonn unhitched their horses, mounted them, and waved at the family gathered in front of the house. Eamonn looked to each of them in turn, his eyes landing on Leyna last. She did smile this time, a full, cheerful smile, and as she waved back, Eamonn felt his stomach flip.

They set on their way, riding straight into the sun. Eamonn guided Rovis with one hand and used the other to block as much of the light as he could. Once they'd trotted far enough away from the house that the road had become cobbled again, Dorylss leaned back in the saddle and grinned.

"So, lad," he said, leaving it at that.

Eamonn waited for a moment before realizing Dorylss wanted him to acknowledge the opening. "Yes?" He could already feel the beads of sweat forming along his hairline from the sun that refused to relent.

Dorylss turned his face to Eamonn, his eyes twinkling with mirth. Eamonn tilted his head down a little and looked up at Dorylss from under his eyebrows. He had a feeling he knew what Dorylss was about to say.

"Did you have a good time this afternoon?"

Eamonn drew out his reply of "Yes." He turned his gaze back to the road in front of him, not wanting to give anything away in his expression.

"You, uh, you seemed to be a little distracted by something," Dorylss teased, looking ahead at the road as well.

"I'm not going to play your little game, you know," Eamonn replied with a shake of his head. He wouldn't give Dorylss the satisfaction.

Dorylss laughed in his merry way, apparently pleased with the result he'd produced regardless. "She's a wonderful girl, Leyna," he said, no longer beating around the bush. "It just takes her a little while to open up."

Eamonn didn't say anything for a while, riding alongside Dorylss in silence. Was Dorylss just close enough to him to pick up on his awkwardness around Leyna, or had it been obvious to everyone? Had it been obvious to Leyna?

"Will we go back soon?" he finally asked. They'd made it back into the city and slowed down around the throngs of people. A taller building momentarily blocked the sun from Eamonn's vision, a reprieve he gratefully accepted.

"I'll probably go back in a week or so," Dorylss answered, losing the jesting tone from his voice but not the glimmer in his eyes. "I don't want to occupy too much of Melwyn's time. But they don't live far away. You can go back sooner, if you like. I'm sure they'd welcome you."

Eamonn shifted on his saddle. He would like to go back, but probably not without Dorylss. He'd spent one afternoon with this family—they were only a little less than strangers so far. Besides, he felt awkward enough around Leyna as it was. He'd go back with Dorylss, whenever that might be. He would make sure to see Leyna again.

# TEN

A TWINGE OF CRISPNESS in the early morning air teased Eamonn as he strode down the mostly empty city streets toward the grocer, pushing a cart. He'd awoken earlier than usual that day to get some things he and Dorylss needed before the sun got too hot. Some cooler air had settled over the area a couple of nights before, but the sun always drove it away. Summer still hung on, especially in Teravale. Autumn wouldn't truly arrive for several more weeks.

Not only did he plan to beat the heat by going in the morning, but he also hoped he would avoid a large crowd. He spent most of his time in the caravan markets in huge crowds of people, so where he could get a little isolation, he would take it.

Only a few people milled about in the wide cobbled streets, arriving at shops just as they opened for the day. Reaching the gro-

cer on the north side of town, Eamonn parked the cart outside and pushed open the door, a little bell jingling at his
entrance. He expected a greeting from Marsenil, the grocer,
but none came. Marsenil stood behind the counter opposite
Eamonn, already engaged with a customer. Eamonn's heart
lodged itself as a lump in his throat when he recognized the
sunny tresses of the customer whose back faced him.

Marsenil spoke to Leyna in a low voice, but Eamonn managed to read his lips a little. He picked up "I wish I could,"
and "I'm sorry," before Leyna lowered her head with a downcast nod. She turned around, head still low, clutching a coin
purse in both hands.

"Morning, Eamonn," Marsenil greeted, looking past Leyna
at his new customer.

Leyna's head shot up at the mention of his name.

Eamonn pulled his eyes from her the second she looked at
him, meeting Marsenil's gaze instead.

"Morning, Marsenil." He turned his attention to her.
"Good morning, Leyna."

"Good morning, Eamonn." She sniffed and rubbed her
nose with the back of her hand.

The movement drew Eamonn's gaze to her pink nose and
glistening eyes. Something had upset her, likely something in
her conversation with Marsenil. Eamonn's heart sank to see
the tears in her eyes, tears she was too proud to let fall. If he
could help her, he would.

She moved to leave the shop, offering Eamonn a weak smile
as she came to him.

"Is everything okay?" he asked, stopping her in her tracks.

Her lips pressed together, transforming the smile into an attempt to keep her emotions at bay. She dipped her head again as she shook it, rubbing a finger under her left eye to catch a tear.

"Come on, let's go outside," Eamonn suggested. He glanced up at the shop owner to say, "I'll be back, Marsenil," before leaving with Leyna.

Once outside, Leyna shut the coin purse she had been gripping and stuck it in a pouch at her waist. She sniffed again, and Eamonn almost couldn't suppress the intense urge to reach out and touch her, to comfort her in some physical way.

"Do you want to go sit somewhere? We could go to Hathfell Park, it's nearby," Eamonn suggested.

Leyna lifted her eyes to him and studied him for a moment, as if trying to decide what his motives might be. She ended up turning her face away from him, blinking several times and tilting her chin up a little. "No, thank you," she said, and she cleared her throat of welled up sobs. "You're busy. I shouldn't keep you."

She took a step to walk away from him, and this time Eamonn didn't fight the urge to grab her hand. His body fired with electricity at the touch.

Leyna whipped back to him, her eyes wide and mouth slightly agape, looking first to their joined hands and then to his face. She didn't pull away. Maybe she'd felt it, too. Eamonn's pulse raced at the thought and he swallowed hard, trying to find his voice.

"I want to help, in any way I can," he murmured, and he released her hand. "I'm not really that busy."

Leyna held her hands loose at her sides, flexing the fingers on the hand Eamonn had just let go. Her eyes were fixed on him, but she didn't answer right away. He wondered what thoughts might be running through her mind—was she trying to figure out a way to get out of it? Perhaps she just wanted to be left alone, but now Eamonn had pushed, and she didn't know what to do.

"There's actually something I want to show you," Leyna finally said, clasping one hand over the other in front of her and rubbing them together. "Would you mind walking home with me? We can talk on the way."

Eamonn could only hope the surprise he felt didn't show on his face. "Um... uh, sure, of course," he managed, taking hold of the cart sitting outside the shop. He'd come back by the grocer on his way home. The secrecy in Leyna's words intrigued him too much to pass up.

The number of people in the streets had grown in the short time since Eamonn arrived at the shop, people coming to do business at the start of the day. A woman carried a basket into a flower shop. Two men met outside a building, shook hands, and one ushered the other inside.

Another man leaned against the shopfront of the butcher across the street, arms crossed and looking right at Eamonn. He cast his gaze down the street when Eamonn saw him, revealing a scar that trailed from his cheekbone to his jawline. Eamonn watched him for a minute as he and Leyna started the journey to her house, wondering if the man was someone he knew. When another patron exited the butcher shop, though, the man went inside. He must have been people-watching while waiting for that person to leave.

"I went to Marsenil because I thought he could help me," Leyna said as they walked, pulling Eamonn out of his thoughts and bringing his focus back to her. "He's helped us before, but I think we've run out of favors."

Eamonn's eyebrows knitted together as he listened to Leyna, her gaze straight ahead. "Help you how?"

Leyna breathed in deeply through her nose, releasing it in a huff before she spoke. "Mama's sick," she said, her voice cracking with the words. "She has been for a while. She didn't want to tell Dorylss, didn't want him to worry or keep him from the next caravan. Please don't tell him." Eamonn could see tears welling in her eyes again. "The physician says she'll recover as long as she takes a tincture of Brienroot every day for a while. It's been helping, but she ran out."

"But why did you go to the grocer? Wouldn't you get medicine from the apothecary?" Eamonn wondered. They came out from behind a line of buildings and the sun hit them, already warm.

"We can't exactly afford it, not from the apothecary," Leyna answered, her cheeks turning pink. She still didn't face Eamonn. "Marsenil has been buying it from the apothecary and selling it to us at a loss. He's absorbed it as a charity expense. He used to do a lot of business with my father, so he's tried to help us out where he can." Leyna sighed. "But the apothecary won't sell to him anymore. Maybe he thinks he's trying to make a profit off of it, I don't know. I was supposed to meet him right as he opened today to get Mama's next bottle, but he said he didn't have it and he wouldn't be able to get it anymore."

Eamonn frowned. "And the apothecary won't give you any kind of discount?"

Leyna let out a single derisive laugh. "Oh, we tried. Believe me. The man is only interested in making money. You would think someone who sells medicine would have a heart for helping people." She shook her head. "Not him."

"Is he the only apothecary in town?"

"Unfortunately. We'd have to go to another town to try another apothecary, and there's no guarantee a different one would deal with us either."

Almost out of the city proper, Eamonn stopped the cart and put it down. "I could give you some money," he said, hoping he conveyed his earnestness in his features.

The offer finally turned Leyna's gaze toward him, and she locked onto his eyes, her lips pressed together. "No," she said, though gentleness and appreciation filled her voice. "We couldn't accept any more than Dorylss has already given us."

"It could come from my personal earnings, what I'm saving to go to Nos Illni," Eamonn clarified, thinking maybe that would make a difference.

Leyna reached out and touched his arm, a motion that signaled the end of the matter. "Thank you, but no. The medicine is very expensive, and I would feel compelled to pay you back. We've just paid off all our debts to the physician with the money from Dorylss. I'd like to not be indebted for a while."

Eamonn said nothing, only partially because Leyna declined the offer so definitively. Mostly, he couldn't speak because her delicate touch had made his heart rate skyrocket once again.

They strolled in silence out of the city and onto the road that led away toward Leyna's house. There had to be a way that Eamonn could help Leyna and her family. He wouldn't tell Dorylss, but he still felt compelled to help in some way. If they wouldn't accept his own money, what could he do?

"You said you're saving your money to go to Nos Illni?" Leyna asked as they approached the house. "You intend to go to the college there?"

Eamonn shrugged, not wanting to make a big deal about going to a costly, prestigious school when her family couldn't even afford necessary medicine. "I'd like to, someday. It's been my dream for as long as I can remember."

The corners of her mouth tipped up, little dimples indenting her cheeks. "I hope that happens for you," she replied, glancing over at him. "How close are you to having all the money you need?"

"I think I can earn what I lack in one more caravan journey." He adjusted his grip on the cart as they turned off the lane to go up the hill toward Leyna's house, leaning into the cart to counteract gravity. "I'll hate to leave Dorylss, but it's been my plan all along. I never intended to be a merchant forever."

Leyna nodded, as though she'd heard it before. Of course, Dorylss had probably told her family everything there was to know about Eamonn. Well, hopefully not *everything*. He doubted Leyna would be walking or even speaking with him if she knew he'd lived several years of his life as a thief.

"I can understand that," Leyna said as they came to the top of the hill, where they stopped as Eamonn parked the cart. "It was so kind of Dorylss to give you a way to pursue your dream. He seems to have a habit of taking people in."

"Yes," Eamonn agreed with a chuckle. He didn't want to delve too far in the conversation, not entirely sure what Dorylss told Leyna and her family about how he acquired Eamonn.

Eamonn stuffed his hands in his pockets to fill the new silence. "So," he began after a moment, "you wanted to show me something?"

"Inside," Leyna said as she moved toward the front door. "Follow me."

Leyna kicked dirt off her shoes before opening the door and stepped inside the house, and Eamonn copied her. As he shut the door behind him, a voice called from somewhere in the house, "Leyna, is that you?"

"Yes, Mama," Leyna answered, turning to the right toward her mother's voice.

"Did you get the medicine?"

Leyna turned around to look at Eamonn. "I'll be right back," she murmured, then went down the hallway just past the entry and went through a doorway toward the front of the house, speaking in a low voice to her mother. Eamonn waited just past the entry room in the empty kitchen where he and Dorylss had eaten with the family. Leyna left her mother's room with the same downcast countenance from the grocer, but she covered it with an attempt at a pleasant expression by the time she returned to Eamonn.

"Over here," she said as she passed Eamonn and led him into a sitting room. Four comfortable chairs faced the lifeless fireplace, the room's only light coming from the open windows. Several bookshelves lined the walls, loaded down with books. A mending basket sat on the wooden floor next to one of the chairs, a pair of child's trousers draped over the arm of the chair.

Going over to one of the bookshelves, Leyna ran her finger along the spines until she found the book she sought, pulling it out and taking it over to Eamonn. "This is a journal my father found on one of his journeys." She opened the book and started to flip through the soft pages with frayed edges. "It had been stuck in a crate of books he took from Sarieth to Marinden. He noticed that it was actually an old personal journal of some kind, like a record of someone's adventures from centuries ago, and he kept it. He would read us some of the entries like stories and show us any sketches that the owner had made."

Leyna found what she was looking for in the journal, sticking her finger to mark the page and closing the worn leather-bound book. She stopped to inhale through her nose and held her breath for a second, as if preparing for what she was about to say.

Eamonn narrowed his eyes and tilted his head and he felt his heart quicken in anticipation. Whatever this was, she seemed to think it was important and took it seriously.

"Remember how I said your necklace seemed familiar?"

He nodded. How could he forget?

"Well, I realized why I thought so." She opened the journal at the designated page, turning the open book toward him. "I remembered it from this journal."

On the top of the right page that Leyna showed to Eamonn, a sketch had been made of the pendant that hung around Eamonn's neck. Eamonn gasped quietly when he saw the drawing. His heart beat faster, stunned to see such an accurate depiction of his mother's necklace on the aged page. In all his travels, in all his studies, he'd never found anything that resembled it so closely.

Words in a wispy hand had been scribbled beside the sketch and underneath it. Eamonn leaned in to try to read the description on the page, the handwriting tricky to decipher.

"What does that say? A relic of Avaria?" he asked, trying to make sure he was actually seeing those words written before him. He knew of Avaria—a forest realm north of Idyrria that some believed to be magical—but he couldn't fathom the necklace coming from there.

"Yes," Leyna answered, turning the open book back to her so that she could read it. "'A relic of Avaria—an ancient Avarian amulet,' it says."

"And you believe that?"

"Why wouldn't I?" Leyna asked, bewildered, drawing her eyebrows together.

Eamonn shrugged. Avaria was a forest, uninhabited and never visited. How did anything come from Avaria? "You don't know anything about the person who wrote that. You said your father found it. The whole thing might be an exaggeration of real things, or even just fleshed out figments of the imagination."

Leyna snapped the journal shut. "I believe my father."

"No, I..." Eamonn stopped himself and closed his eyes. Taking a breath, he opened them and spoke in a softened voice. "I'm not trying to discredit your father. But he didn't write it. And without knowing the source, it's impossible to verify its validity."

Her eyelids hanging low over her eyes, Leyna hugged the book close to her torso. "That's true enough. But my father had no reason not to accept the words written in this journal," she lifted her gaze to Eamonn, unflinching, "and neither do I."

Eamonn chewed on the inside of his lip. Leyna seemed like a smart, educated, practical girl, not one to hold fast to just any beliefs without good reason. He might not agree with her, but neither would he write her off as gullible or superstitious.

"You believe in magic, don't you?" he asked her, a genuine curiosity in his voice rather than an accusation.

Her head bobbed in answer.

"Does everyone around here believe in magic?" he wondered. He remembered the conversations he and Dorylss had had with Castor at the pub, and then with Dorylss himself.

She sat down in the armchair closest to her. "No," she answered. "There aren't many here who believe in magic, like everywhere else in the country, but maybe a few more do in Teravale than in other provinces."

Eamonn took a seat beside her, taking Dorylss's advice and at least opening himself up to what Leyna had to say. There had to be some kind of reasoning why Teravalens believed in magic more than other provinces. "Why is that?"

"I think it's because of all the trading we do," she replied. She tapped her fingers on the closed journal in her lap. "Our merchants go all over the country and to other parts of the world. They have for centuries. They've seen things, gathered stories, kept the memory of magic alive." A slight grin played on her lips. "If you'd heard the stories I have, you might believe in magic, too."

"I heard lots of stories about magic in school," Eamonn said, raising his shoulders and dropping them.

"You heard *about* the stories. And I'm sure you were taught that they were just stories," Leyna presumed, but she was right. "That's the difference."

Eamonn rested his chin in his hand, not saying anything for a moment as he considered what she said. Maybe he should at least give her the benefit of the doubt and see what she had to say. He had to admit, he'd been shocked to see his mother's necklace drawn in the journal, his first connection to her story in his life.

"Okay, so tell me," he began, leaning forward and sitting his elbows on his knees with clasped hands near his face, "what do you believe about magic?"

Leyna relaxed back into the chair. "I would assume I believe the same thing as anyone who believes in magic. That it's history rather than myth, and people could still use it today if properly taught."

"But what could magic do?" he pressed, surprised to find himself eager to know what she thought. "Could anyone use it if they were taught?"

"Magic is mostly a manipulation of the elements and of the physical world," Leyna explained in a voice that made Eamonn feel like he was back in school. "And anyone who was taught could use it. In ancient times, actually, *everyone* used magic in some capacity. Some people might have a stronger predisposition than others, but magic wasn't some exclusive power or uncommon practice. Farmers used magic to help grow their crops. Miners used it to cast light underground. Principles of magic could be used to create potions that would help heal the sick and wounded."

"But you said it was *mostly* a manipulation of the elements, so what else could it do?" Eamonn asked, hanging on her every word.

"Well, some of the more powerful magic-casters could cast illusions, levitate, or teleport short distances," Leyna replied, opening the journal again and looking for something. "I remember reading something in here... Oh, here it is: 'Brexa projected clones of herself that might have passed as her from a distance, but upon closer inspection were nothing but an image. I've never met another who could do this. She tells me it was difficult to learn, but she is not unique in this ability.' It's like the story of Rinner and the Bears."

Eamonn scoffed and immediately wished he hadn't. The way Leyna's entire expression fell stuck a dagger into his heart. He cleared his throat and kept his voice gentle as he spoke, hoping to mend her hurt feelings. "I've never known of Rinner and the Bears as anything other than a fairytale. A man cast multiple illusions of himself to fool the bears that had cornered him as he ran away?" He raised his shoulders and held out his hands, palms up. "I had no reason to believe it might have actually happened."

Leyna laced her fingers together and placed her clasped hands on top of the journal. "Do you, now?"

How could he answer that? The truth: no. But that didn't mean he was done listening to her. He'd never approached the concept of magic from this perspective before.

"I want to learn more," he said, sincerity flooding his tone and his features.

It seemed Leyna accepted his answer because she put her elbow on the armrest of the chair and turned her body toward him. "What do you know of Avaria?"

The question took him a little by surprise, shifting the direction of the conversation. "Uh, I know it's a forest in the northernmost part of the country that stays in an eternal summer, even though it's surrounded by ice and snow."

Leyna leaned onto her elbow toward Eamonn, her eyes sparkling. "And why do you think it stays in an eternal summer?" she asked him, her tone full of intrigue and mystery.

"I don't know. I guess something about it makes the climate different."

"Magic lingers there," she whispered, her mouth turning up at the corners. "Magic that was never entirely lost."

A shiver shot down Eamonn's spine with her words. He hadn't even necessarily changed his mind about magic, but something about what she just said drove straight into his heart and enthralled him.

"The magic of Avaria is special," Leyna continued, adding a little more volume to her voice but keeping the same captivating quality. "It can't be learned. It is only found in the race who inhabit Avaria. It's the most powerful kind of magic, giving the magic-caster the ability to control a person's will."

Eamonn frowned, the spell of Leyna's words breaking. "But Avaria is uninhabited. No one lives there."

"Have you been there to find out?" Leyna asked, unflinching.

"Of course not," Eamonn said, adjusting his position in the chair. "I'm not sure anyone has, at least not in recorded history. But I feel like we would know if an entire magical race lived there."

Leyna crossed her arms and tipped up her nose a tad, appearing triumphant. "Not if they didn't want anyone to know they existed. Some kind of magic exists there, at least." She tilted her head back down. "How else do you explain the enduring temperate climate in one of the coldest parts of the country?"

Eamonn released a breath and he dropped his head, propping his chin in his hand again. He couldn't explain it. He'd never seen Avaria himself, but he knew people had passed it by from time to time in recent years. No one ever ventured inside, though. Avaria was accepted as a strange, unidentified phenomenon. But, if what Leyna said was true, and magic filled Avaria...

"The journal said my mother's pendant was an amulet of Avaria. What does that mean?"

Eamonn noticed Leyna's right dimple appear with a crooked smile. She seemed pleased he would ask the question. "I have an idea, but I'm not sure. I'll have to do a little more digging first. We have a few books on magic that my father collected on his journeys."

Leyna stood and went back to the same bookshelf where she found the journal, leaving the leatherbound book on the chair. "He had such an interest in magic, so he always kept his eyes peeled for anything magical. He managed to recover some ancient texts from Miren and Idyrria, but he never exactly said how."

"You have magical texts from Idyrria?" Eamonn asked, hopping up from his chair and joining her by the bookshelf.

"One or two," Leyna replied, tugging out a book by the spine here and there to look at the cover, pulling out three that barely held their pages anymore. "In the ancient times, Idyrria was a prime location for magic. Miren, too. Idyrrians taught magic in their illustrious schools like any other subject." She handed him one of the ancient books, the edges of the leather worn off and the pages yellow and fragile. "Take a look."

Eamonn held the book with a delicate touch, carefully opening the soft cover and turning the frayed pages. A musty scent betraying the book's age hit Eamonn's nostrils, and he wrinkled his nose. The very first page had an inscription written in a sprawling hand, the ink having faded over the centuries.

*For the Instruction and Edification of Students*
*at the College of Nos Illni*
*A Primer on Magic for the Beginning Learner*
*Compiled in the year 723*
*Nos Illni, Idyrria*
*Sarieth*

"This can't be real," Eamonn breathed, tracing his fingers over the words. His beloved College at Nos Illni, the top center for logical and rational learning in the country, used to teach magic?

"Should I have pulled out the books earlier?" Leyna asked, hugging the volumes to her chest and watching Eamonn closely. "Do they make a difference?"

Eamonn turned a few pages carefully, noticing that the ink had faded in some parts so much it could no longer be read. There was no way this was actually an ancient magic text. Surely someone had created it years ago as a hoax, causing people to buy into the idea that magic had existed.

"I don't know," he finally replied, his eyes scanning the pages. "For someone who never gave belief in magic a second thought, it's hard to consider."

Leyna took the books she held over to the chair where she'd been sitting and stacked them on a small round table beside it. She reached out her arm to Eamonn for the book he perused, and he found himself reluctant to give it up.

"I'll take some time to go through these and see what I can find. Maybe you could come back in a few days?"

Eamonn relinquished the book, too caught up in his own thoughts to register what she said.

"Eamonn?"

He turned his head to meet her gaze.

"You'll come back?"

The expectant quality in her face made him want to smile, but Eamonn managed to suppress it. Since their encounter at the grocer, she'd transformed from the cool, quiet girl he'd met to a confident and engaging one. He'd like to think she opened up because they had begun to get to know each other, but he really believed it was their discussion of magic that brought out the true Leyna.

"Yes, I will," he answered her, his jade eyes locking onto hers.

Leyna's cheeks barely lifted, but it was enough to show her dimples. "Well, then," she said, "I'll see you in a few days."

She tore her eyes away from his and showed him out of the house, waving at him as he picked up the cart and started his trek back into the city. The chill to the air had evaporated, the sun now well on its way on its journey through the sky. So much for getting supplies before the crowds and the heat magnified.

For his entire walk back to the grocer, Eamonn mulled over what Leyna had told him about magic, about Avaria, about things he'd never seriously contemplated before in his life. He couldn't deny that she'd made some good points, and the books describing magic certainly had an ancient, realistic appearance, but was that enough to make him believe in magic?

Coupled with the rumors about this Rothgard of Wolstead using magic to spark uprisings and kill kings, the existence of magic couldn't be lightly brushed aside. Not anymore. Eamonn hoped that whatever Leyna found—or didn't find—before their next meeting would be enough to convince him of one side, but in all honesty, he didn't think anything short of seeing something magical with his own eyes would ultimately change his mind.

# ELEVEN

AFTER GETTING ALL THE foodstuffs he and Dorylss needed
and grabbing a few supplies from the hardware shop, Eamonn decided to stop by the apothecary on his way back
home. Leyna may not accept his money, but she wouldn't be
able to turn down the medicine for her mother. The money
would have been spent and Eamonn would have no use for
the tincture. He figured it was the best way he could convince
Leyna to let him help them.

Navigating the full cart through the packed streets in the
shopping district of Caen proved to be a slow-moving chore. Eamonn gladly set the cart down outside the apothecary, his arms
needing a break. He'd have to be quick getting the medicine,
not wanting to leave the cart unattended for too long. He didn't
expect any of the people of Caen to steal from him in broad

daylight, but he would rather not find out the hard way that someone was untrustworthy, so he planned to dash in and out.

The apothecary organized bottles on shelves behind the counter, making marks in a notebook as he counted. He didn't turn with Eamonn's entrance, even though a bell alerted his arrival. The man simply said, "One moment," and finished the section he was counting.

Eamonn glanced outside to his purchases, able to keep an eye on them through the front windows of the shop. His hands rested on the coin pouch strapped to his waist, ready to go whenever the man produced the medicine he needed.

After making a few more marks on the paper, the apothecary finally turned to Eamonn, adjusting his small round spectacles on his nose. "How can I help you?" he asked.

"I need to get a tincture of Brienroot, please," Eamonn requested with confidence, remembering the medicine Leyna said her mother took. "How much will it be?"

The apothecary watched Eamonn closely through his spectacles, narrowing his eyes a bit. He had no hair on the top of his head, only short cropped brown hair going around the sides and back of his head, and a mustache on his upper lip to compensate. "One vial?"

"Yes, just one." Eamonn shifted his weight on his feet, unsettled by the look the apothecary gave him.

"And why do you need it?" The apothecary crossed his right arm in front of his too-thin stomach, the elbow of the other arm resting on his wrist, and he stroked his chin with his left hand.

"I'm sorry?" Eamonn asked, stunned. He didn't know the name of the illness from which Melwyn suffered, and frankly, he hadn't thought about it before now.

A sneer spread across the apothecary's face. He didn't even attempt to conceal it. "The condition that requires treatment with a Brienroot tincture. What is the name?"

Eamonn swallowed, racking his brain. He needed a convincing lie, and fast.

"I don't remember what it's called," he said, using the sudden stress from the encounter to cause a break in his voice, which he hoped the apothecary would translate as emotion. "It's for my mother. She's sick, and she told me the physician advised the tincture of Brienroot for treatment."

A scowl replaced the sneer on the apothecary's face. "I know who you are, boy," he snarled, stepping back from the counter. "The caravan merchants aren't strangers to me. Dorylss has taken you on as his apprentice; you have no mother, no other family."

Dropping the act, Eamonn opened his coin pouch for the apothecary to see. "Look, I'm offering to pay you full price for that tincture. Does it really matter what I do with it?"

"Yes, it does," the apothecary replied gruffly, stepping back from the counter and picking up his notebook. "I have a business to run, and it's my responsibility to control what medication leaves this building. I won't have anyone dealing under the table from me. I just cut off the grocer attempting the same thing. I won't have it!"

He turned his back to Eamonn again and resumed counting his inventory. Eamonn attempted to speak again, but the apothecary held up a hand. "No more. Now go on!"

Eamonn huffed, plenty of force behind the sound to make sure the apothecary heard him, and he left the shop with heavy footsteps. He picked his cart back up and continued home, seething as he replayed the interaction in his mind. He nearly ran into people with the cart, so irritated that he didn't pay close attention to where he walked.

No wonder the apothecary wouldn't make any kind of deal with Leyna. The man was more self-serving and prideful than Eamonn had previously thought. Without some kind of official word from a physician as well as enough money to cover full price, the apothecary wouldn't be selling medicine to anyone. But Leyna's mother needed that tincture, and she had no way of getting it.

Eamonn's fiery pulse slowed when another thought came to his mind. The apothecary arranged his medicines neatly on open shelves and in easy to access cabinets. He showed Eamonn exactly how he kept his inventory. The door to the shop had a standard lock, just like ones Eamonn had picked thousands of times...

His heart rate shot right back up to where it had been moments before. What was he thinking? He'd put that life behind him years ago. He'd never even wanted to steal, and stealing always filled him with guilt, regardless of feeling like he had justifiable motives. But this could be life or death for Leyna's mother, and Leyna and her siblings had already lost their father. If Melwyn died from the sickness, where would that leave her children?

Eamonn would be doing good by stealing the tincture, more good than he'd ever done in stealing to fill his own belly. Melwyn needed this medicine, and it wasn't like they hadn't tried. Eamonn tried to buy it at full price, Marsenil had been cut off from buying it, and the apothecary wouldn't make a deal with Leyna for her mother to be treated. The apothecary almost deserved to be stolen from, not willing to supply medicine to a sick person, more concerned about making money than about healing people.

He didn't think he'd ever steal again, but Eamonn felt this theft was necessary and warranted. Forgivable. He could put his old skills to good use toward a noble cause. He wouldn't tell Leyna—she didn't even want him to give her money for the medicine. She would be angry at him to know he'd stolen it. No, he'd tell her he bought it.

Eamonn made it back to the house, pushing the cart up to the door to unload the supplies. He decided he would break into the apothecary that night. Without knowing how long Melwyn had been without the tincture, he assumed there was little time to waste.

His hands shook with adrenaline as he formulated his plans, bringing the supplies into the house in silence. He still had his old lockpicks somewhere, stashed away on the off chance he'd need them again. Eamonn knew exactly where they were, and he started to make a mental list of things to remember. A different life came flooding back to him as he planned his theft, a life of soft shoes, dark nights, stealthy movements, brothers around a fire. That felt like another age now, a life from a different world.

He wasn't going back to that life. This was a special circumstance. He wouldn't go back, because if he did, what were the past three years for? He might as well have stayed with Hadli and the Guild.

He would never go back.


Eamonn's heart pounded in his ears as he skulked through the quiet streets of Caen. Everything from his days as a thief had rushed back to him as if it was still second nature to him. Before now, he thought he'd lost it all. But with his lockpicks in his pocket, his quietest slippers on his feet, and dark clothes covering his body, he slipped through the night like a shadow, as though he'd never given it up.

He had waited until deep into the night, leaving Dorylss in a heavy slumber. No one should be about at this time, except perhaps any other burglars or miscreants, but Caen didn't have a high rate of criminal activity. Good for Eamonn, because he hadn't studied the patterns of city guards or other criminals in Caen like he had in Erai. Before he left his hometown, he'd gotten to the point where he knew the patrols like the back of his hand, knew the methods and hotspots of other thieves to stay out of their way. Eamonn was familiar with Caen, but as a citizen, not as a thief.

Only a crescent of moon hung in the sky, granting Eamonn the darkness he required to sneak through the city. A cool breeze came through and blew loose trash down the street, the sudden movement sending Eamonn to hide behind a barrel. He watched the trash float away and quickened his pace. He needed to make this operation as swift as possible and lessen the chances of running into anyone as much as he could.

A few buildings away from the apothecary, Eamonn surveyed his surroundings with as much scrutiny as he could muster in the dark. Determining no one was around, he crept past the shop faces, staying close to the shadows of the buildings. The city felt so different in the middle of the night: the streets empty, the shops vacant, everything silent. Part of Eamonn missed this world. Not the stealing, of course, and not even the rush that came with it, but the new city that appeared after everyone had gone to sleep. The city he ruled.

He came to the apothecary and glanced around him once more, just to be certain nothing had changed. Crouched low at the door, Eamonn pulled out his lockpicks and set to work, sliding the thin pieces of metal into the lock and feeling for the gears through them. Five seconds later the lock clicked and Eamonn stored his picks. He chuckled in spite of himself, pleased to discover he could still pick a lock so effortlessly.

Eamonn swung the door open and slipped his body into the shop, shutting the door quietly behind him. Everything was still, only the rhythmic ticking of a clock hanging on the wall breaking the silence.

*Now to find the Brienroot.*

He first checked the shelf behind the counter, where the apothecary had been counting the medicines earlier. He scanned over the names of the drugs, each vial clearly labeled with neat lettering. None of them said *Brienroot.*

Two cabinets framed the shelves, and Eamonn tried the one on the left first. When he opened the cabinet door, though, he sighed. While the medicines were still tidily organized, the cabinet was packed full with boxes, vials, and bottles. Eamonn didn't have a clue where to begin. Going through each and every container in the dark would take much longer than he had hoped.

A man this organized had to have a system to keep track of so much inventory.

Wait. That was it.

*Inventory.*

Eamonn turned back around to the counter and opened the drawer closest to him, taking out a notebook he found right at the top. Flipping through it, though, he realized this was only the ledger, the log of all the apothecary's transactions. Eamonn dug underneath where the ledger had sat, but didn't find the inventory notebook. He tried a couple more drawers and discovered another notebook.

A soft *clop clop* caught Eamonn's ears, and he froze. Definitely a horse, and the sound grew steadily louder, closer to Eamonn.

He dropped, hiding behind the wooden counter, dropping his head to his hands and rubbing his temples. He should have waited to do this, taken the time to plan it out before he just took off and broke into the apothecary. This was how thieves got caught: failure to learn all the necessary information and plan accordingly. Eamonn had been on that street only minutes before, picking the lock to the apothecary's front door.

His heart pulsing like a hummingbird's wings, Eamonn peeked around the edge of the counter to see the helmet of the guard pass by the shop's window as the guard patrolled on his horse. Eamonn pulled his head back around the corner and rested the back of it against the counter, releasing a relieved sigh.

He felt like a fool. In all of this, he'd neglected to consider the consequences of getting caught. A lot more hung on the line now. In Erai, the only one his bad decisions might have hurt was himself. But if he was caught stealing in Caen, where he'd built friendships, found a community, and lived with his gracious mentor, he wouldn't be the only one to suffer.

Eamonn nearly left then and there, starting to regret his decision and feeling angry at himself for falling so easily back into delinquency, but he needed to allow time for the guard to get far

away. Not to mention, if he didn't steal the medicine, Melwyn wouldn't get it. He might as well finish the job.

Retrieving the second notebook he found, Eamonn
opened the cover to find long lists of medications in a grid
with dates and numbers—the inventory. A little victory, at
least. He flipped through the pages, noticing descriptors to
mark off categories of stock. Presumably, they had corresponding sections in the shop, as well.

His heart skipped when he saw *Brienroot tincture* written
on a page. The last inventory had been taken earlier that day,
the count written in the corresponding grid as *19*. Eamonn
noticed the category and section: *Cardiac—Cabinet One,
Shelf Two, Row Four*.

Eamonn hopped to his feet, glancing through the windows
and seeing no one outside before returning to the cabinet to
the left of the counter. He assumed it was Cabinet One, but
it should be easy to figure out—if it was, he'd find Brienroot
on the second shelf in row four.

And there it sat, labeled distinctly in its specified location.
At least he could appreciate the apothecary's organization
and attention to detail.

He reached past the medicines to the back of the Brienroot
row, careful not to displace anything, and took the vial in
the very back so he wouldn't have to pull the remaining ones
to the front. Eamonn grinned at the little bottle in his hand
before stashing it in the empty pouch at his waist, his pulse
racing.

Before he could leave, though, Eamonn had to change the
inventory list. An apothecary as meticulous as this man would
without a doubt notice that his counts for Brienroot did not

match up, and after the encounter he'd had with Eamonn earlier that day, Eamonn would be the first suspect.

Eamonn returned to the first drawer where he'd found the ledger, recalling a quill in the same drawer. Laying the inventory notebook open to the page with Brienroot, Eamonn dipped the quill into a pot of ink that sat on the counter, letting it sufficiently drip so that he had only a touch of ink. He inhaled to steady his hands, then leaned over the book and turned the bottom of the number nine into an oval that transformed the number into an eight.

*That did the trick*, he thought, blowing a light, even stream of air onto the ink to dry it. Tapping the new number eight with his finger to make sure it had dried, Eamonn replaced the quill and inventory notebook in their respective locations, leaving everything exactly as he'd found it.

The tincture securely in his pouch, Eamonn crept to the door and pressed his ear against it to listen out for anything in the street. He heard nothing outside; only the sound of the clock filled his ears.

He took in a deep breath and held it, swinging the door open and poking his head out. He looked down either side of the street, not seeing anyone in the darkness. He couldn't even hear the guard's horse anymore. Hopefully, he was long gone. The problem remained, though, that Eamonn didn't know his route. He'd have to be especially alert on his way back home.

Eamonn stepped outside of the shop, staying low, and locked the door back with his picks. He kept to the same route he'd followed on the way to the apothecary, his eyes catching every wave of a banner or scurry of a rat. Soft breezes blew through the city, and with every sound caused by the wind, Eamonn froze.

His heart pounded in his ears, now keenly aware of what would happen if he was caught. He couldn't let Dorylss down like that. Even if it took a little longer to get back to the house, he'd stop at every sound and every movement in the night.

Finally, he made it to the residential district where he and Dorylss lived. The closer he got to home, the more he believed he could pass off a "couldn't sleep and went for a walk" excuse to anyone who might find him. He breathed a little easier, willing his pulse to settle down.

Small tree limbs swayed with the wind, their leaves rustling and covering Eamonn's soft steps. Creatures of the night ran from Eamonn as he approached, hiding for a moment as they scavenged in the dark. He didn't feel much above them—the badgers, the possums, the rats—darting behind buildings or trees if someone came close, using the cover of darkness to conceal themselves as they went about their business. Eamonn might as well have been a rat.

He arrived home without coming across anyone, guard or otherwise, and sneaked in the back door. Eamonn tiptoed up the stairs, but he didn't have to worry about Dorylss being awake—he could hear the burly man's heavy snores throughout the house. Eamonn unstrapped the pouch from his waist, set it delicately on a table in his room, and collapsed onto his bed, pulling his supple shoes off his feet.

Guilt washed over him, the way it always used to after he'd committed a theft. He still stood by it, though, believing it had to be done. But that didn't make him feel much better about taking someone else's property, especially since he'd turned away from that life.

What would Leyna think when he gave her the tincture? Would she actually believe the apothecary had sold to him? Would she start to suspect that he might have gotten it through unscrupulous means? Maybe he would just leave it outside her home, somewhere the family would easily find it, and they wouldn't even attach it to him.

Eamonn rolled over in his bed, forcing his eyes shut. He'd like to fall asleep before the sun rose. He heard his heart in his ears, his hands clenched in fists near his face, trying to settle his body. His stomach twisted and he groaned. He couldn't do anything like that again.

# TWELVE

EAMONN KEPT PACE WITH Dorylss's long stride as the pair walked to The Lonely Badger, meeting up with some of their friends in Caen for dinner and a pint. While they spent much of their break resting and working on things around their house, Dorylss and Eamonn did take time to catch up with friends that they only saw while in Caen.

Walking through the door to the pub, they were greeted by Bryn, Firador, and Tillrie, their local friends who waited for them at a table in the packed building. Dorylss beamed at them in return, followed by Eamonn who offered a closed smile and a nod. He'd gotten to know these people from his time in Caen, but Dorylss was the one who had grown up with them.

"Good to see you, Dorylss!" said Bryn, a tall, lean man with defined muscles from his labor as a farmer. "I hope you've been resting well."

Dorylss took a seat on a bench beside Firador, a stockier man than Bryn, shaking his hand as he replied, "Oh, yes, we're making the most of our time here."

Eamonn sat across from Dorylss next to Bryn, since he and Tillrie took up less space on the bench as Dorylss and Firador. Bryn clapped a hand on Eamonn's shoulder and grinned at him.

"Glad to hear it!" Bryn said over the low rumble of conversation in the pub. "We knew you must be close, so we already placed the order. They have fish with rice and asparagus today."

"Excellent!" Dorylss said, every ounce of his being oozing exuberance. He was clearly delighted to be back with his old friends.

Eamonn enjoyed the group, but he didn't feel at home with them as Dorylss did. For that feeling, he'd have to be back with the Thieves' Guild, but it still probably wouldn't feel the same.

The Guild had been on Eamonn's mind a lot lately, especially since he'd stolen from the apothecary four days ago. He might have stolen again, but at least he hadn't joined a usurper. He hadn't even gotten any credit for the medicine he stole, placing it outside Leyna's front door late the next evening.

After Castor had brought them their first round of pints, Firador took a sip and looked to Dorylss. "Did you come across much trouble in the other provinces on this journey?" the balding man asked. "We've heard it's gotten much worse in the last few months."

Dorylss nodded while still drinking from his mug. He set it down, wiped his mustache, and said, "I've never seen Farneth in such turmoil." Apparently, he wouldn't keep the whole truth from his friends as he had with Melwyn. "I'm afraid the kingdom is on the brink of collapse." He dropped his eyes and shook his head. "I can only assume Swyncrest will be the next to fall."

"What about Wolstead?" Tillrie asked, as lean and strong as her husband Bryn. "They've completely transitioned to a people's government. Is it chaos there?"

"It's chaotic, yes, but not as turbulent as Farneth," Dorylss replied. He gripped the mug's handle but didn't pick it up. "Most of Wolstead is in pandemonium, like chickens running around with their heads cut off. The weak government is allowing a haven for criminals, and some people are taking advantage. But Farneth is worse, at least right now. Riots happen everywhere. I don't think their king will be allowed to keep his throne much longer."

Dorylss took a drink, a heavy silence settling over the group. Eamonn lifted his own mug to his mouth, taking a healthy gulp before setting it back down with a thud. He glanced around the crowded pub, watching others laughing, jesting, and chatting merrily all around. Things were still easy in Teravale, still simple, people choosing to be unaffected by the happenings of the world outside them.

Eamonn's heartbeat quickened with the feeling that someone watched him, and he scanned back over the crowd. Alone at a table in the far corner, a man sat in the shadows, puffing on a pipe. He turned his eyes as Eamonn's gaze landed on him. Something about the man seemed peculiar, but he did nothing more than smoke his pipe as Eamonn stared at him.

"They say this Rothgard figure has left Idyrria," Bryn said, breaking the silence at their table and pulling Eamonn back to them. "I was talking to some of the soldiers I know yesterday, and they said the Idyrrians ran him and his followers out."

Eamonn straightened in his seat, surprised and relieved at the news. So Rothgard hadn't been successful there. That was what he'd expected from Idyrria. The majority of Idyrrians wouldn't take kindly to someone threatening their king.

"Where are they headed now?" Dorylss asked, drawing his eyebrows together. "Are they coming to Teravale next?"

Bryn shook his head, and Dorylss sighed. "It appears they fled Idyrria to the north. They sailed away to Nidet."

"Nidet?" Eamonn asked, making a face as though a horrible taste filled his mouth. He knew of Nidet, the largest of a cluster of islands northeast of Idyrria. Most of the islands were little more than specks of rock in the sea, but Nidet had once been inhabited.

"That's the latest report. Rothgard has holed up there in the old castle," Bryn told Eamonn.

Eamonn remembered learning about the fortress of Holoreath, built on the southern tip of the island to evacuate the king and members of the royal family during the War with Cardune. The stronghold was positioned on a cliff with a near panoramic view, a perfect place to watch for invaders. But when the war ended with an Idyrrian victory twenty years ago, the king and his family returned to Rifillion, and Holoreath was abandoned. The harsh conditions nearly year-round were too much for the island to be livable long-term, so the fortress fell into disrepair.

"What good is that doing him?" Eamonn wondered, folding his arms together on the table in front of him. "If he's trying to take down the monarchies, how on earth can he do it while hidden away?"

Bryn lowered his voice and rested his arms on the table, his hands wrapped around his mug. "He keeps from getting himself killed. He may have attracted a following, but he's gathered an even larger opposition. But no one will go after him there." Bryn looked up, noticing Castor and Maranie bringing their food to the table, and he finished his thought quickly. "I'm sure he still has his hands in Wolstead and Farneth. The rebels there are molded by him. They adopted his ideology and will do whatever he says."

The grim expressions of the group turned to smiles upon receiving their food, but they fell again after Castor and Maranie walked away. While the others all took bites of their meal, Tillrie leaned into the table. "There are rumors that Rothgard has been unearthing what ancient magical texts he could find on his push through Sarieth. They say the ones that weren't destroyed were hidden and locked away, and part of Rothgard's purpose in weakening the provinces was to get into those vaults."

Eamonn cut a bite of fish, trying not to show any piqued interest when in fact his heart hammered in his chest. The images of Rothgard outside the vaults in Erai's library came flooding back to his memory. Had he actually been uncovering magic texts there? Is that what had been locked away, what Marwan had called "forbidden"?

"Maybe so, but what is he going to do with them?" Bryn pointed out after swallowing his bite. "The reach of his hands is the bigger threat."

"I'm not saying I disagree," Tillrie clarified, shrugging her shoulders, "but enough rumors are spreading that Rothgard's goal is to learn magic to help his cause. The rumors have to come from somewhere."

"It's downright laughable," Firanor added with a chuckle. "C'mon, even if magic really *had* existed ages ago, how could he expect to teach himself magic by finding a few books?"

Eamonn had already heard that Rothgard was attempting to learn magic, but his eyewitness account of Rothgard going into the vault in Erai gave him reason to believe them.

Eamonn lifted his eyes to Dorylss, noticing that he had kept silent. Dorylss ate his food casually, seemingly unconcerned with the discussion about the rumors. He probably thought the same thing Eamonn did, but, like Eamonn, didn't think it wise to bring up.

The conversation turned, and Dorylss began to engage again, but Eamonn remained stuck in his thoughts. If the rumors were true, and if Rothgard had been searching for old magical texts to try to teach himself magic, then Rothgard must believe in magic. Eamonn had seen the lengths Rothgard had been willing to go to in order to retrieve whatever lay hidden in the vaults. If it truly was magic texts, then Rothgard must believe magic was still real in the world and that he could teach it to himself.

Something about that thought got Eamonn's heart pumping in his ears. This man was strategic, careful, and organized. He had successfully caused one monarchy to be overthrown and replaced by a government of his own followers, with another not far behind. He had attracted people as he pushed through the country, creating his own company of loyal supporters. He didn't seem like a madman or a fool, and Eamonn doubted he was taking time to uncover and steal protected, ancient magical texts on a whim, as a "just-in-case-magic-is-actually-real" approach. Rothgard had reason to believe magic was real and attainable, and if he did learn it, he was going to use it to further his power.

If Rothgard believed in magic, then maybe Eamonn needed to as well.

Eamonn ate his meal detached from the rest of the group. Talk of Rothgard and magic had been replaced with reminiscing and stories of what happened in Caen while Dorylss was gone, but Eamonn's mind was stuck in their previous conversation.

He pushed his plate away when he was finished and sat back, his eyes going straight to the man at the table in the corner. The man turned his head away this time as Eamonn caught sight of him, bringing into the light a scar that traveled from his cheekbone to his jawline.

Eamonn remembered that scar. He'd seen it on the man outside the butcher shop the day he walked Leyna home. A tremble ran through his body and he dropped his eyes, trying to appear as though he hadn't recognized the man. For some reason, the man must have been following Eamonn. Could he know something about his theft at the apothecary? Every fiber of Eamonn's being told him he needed to get out of there.

"If you'll excuse me," he said, breaking into the middle of Dorylss's conversation with his friends, "I think I'm going to head home. I'm not feeling too well."

"I noticed you weren't quite yourself this evening," Bryn said, clasping Eamonn's shoulder. "It's a shame. But we'll meet again before you go on your next journey, I'm sure."

Eamonn offered Bryn an appreciative smile and stood, his eyes falling on the man in the shadows who now brazenly met his stare. Eamonn felt his face blanche and he moved to leave the table.

"You sure you're all right, lad?" Dorylss asked, his features flooded with concern.

"I'll be fine if I can just lie down at home," Eamonn answered, casting Dorylss a reassuring glance before making his way out of the pub.

The sun had fallen and had taken most of the heat with it. Eamonn wrapped his arms around himself as he stepped into the street, wishing he'd worn another layer. He glanced over his shoulder to see if the scarred man was trailing him, but none of the people milling in the street resembled him.

A shiver went up Eamonn's spine. What could this man want with him? Eamonn doubted seeing him again was pure coincidence, not with the way the man always turned his head or moved his gaze when Eamonn looked at him.

Eamonn picked up his pace and hugged himself tighter. The quicker he could put distance between the pub and himself, the better. His stomach lurched with a sense of being watched and he looked over his shoulder again, the hairs on the back of his neck prickling. No one stood out in the dimly lit road, but Eamonn couldn't be sure the man hadn't followed him.

A sense of dread growing within him, Eamonn ducked into a narrow alley between two shops near the end of the street and hid behind a cluster of barrels. The barrels concealed his body, but Eamonn was still able to see the entrance to the alley through a slit of space between the barrels. If the scarred man was indeed following him, he might stop at the alleyway and look inside for Eamonn. Then, Eamonn would know for certain that the man wanted something from him, and Eamonn would wait till he'd passed to go out the back of the alley and run home.

But he hid, and waited, and no one came. Bugs crawled on the ground around Eamonn, and he shifted his feet to avoid them. How long should he wait? Maybe the man hadn't left the pub in pursuit of Eamonn after all.

Eamonn stayed behind the barrels for at least five minutes, allowing time for his nerves to calm down. A couple of people passed by the alley, on their way home after their dinner out, but no one stopped and looked. The alley where he hid and the passage behind the shops were not lit, so he would just use the cover of darkness to sneak out and pick up a route back home.

He listened out for a few more seconds, hearing no rustling or footsteps that would lead him to believe someone approached the alleyway, then stood up quickly and took hastened steps to the back of the alley.

Eamonn stopped short when a shadowy figure blocked his exit. Before even getting a good look at the man, Eamonn turned and ran back toward the front of the alley, but was impeded by two more menacing figures. His entire body trembled as he whipped back around to face the man at the back end, sweat forming on Eamonn's hairline despite the cool night. Eamonn's eyes flitted all around the alley, trying to plan something—anything—that might help him escape. The man approached Eamonn with strategic steps and Eamonn's heart threatened to pound right out of his chest.

"What do you want from me?" Eamonn asked in a harsh whisper.

As the man stepped forward, the little moonlight in the alley cast on his face and revealed his familiar scar. "I'm afraid you'll have to ask our master that question."

"Your master?" Eamonn threw his head over his shoulder and saw the two other men slowly closing the distance as well.

"All I know is you're valuable to him," the scarred man said, his voice rough and threatening. "I don't ask questions—I just follow orders."

Eamonn took slow steps backward, hoping to get closer to the barrels before the men behind him got there.

"I'm nobody!" Eamonn said, glancing behind him again. He could make it to the barrels in a few more steps. "You've got to have the wrong person."

The scarred man grinned wickedly, revealing a gap in his teeth on the same side of his mouth as his scar. "The master traced your magic here, and you match the description we were given."

*My magic?*

"You *definitely* have the wrong person," Eamonn insisted, the man's claim of magic nearly distracting him from his plan with the barrels. These people would probably kill him anyway, only to find out later they didn't kill the right person, but Eamonn knew they wouldn't care.

"We'll let your friends make that determination when they get here." The man sneered. He had almost reached the spot where Eamonn wanted him to enact his plan. "They're nearly here. We were just supposed to scout you out before they arrived, but when you got antsy and left the pub, we had to make sure you wouldn't get away."

*What friends?* The few friends Eamonn had lived here in Caen, and he didn't imagine any of them to be bad or want to hurt him. He didn't make a habit of forming strong bonds with the people he met on his journeys throughout the country, either, so who did this man mean?

The scarred man stepped as close as Eamonn wanted him, and with a final look over his shoulder, Eamonn was ready to put his plan into motion. The man gasped suddenly and Eamonn stopped before he reached for the barrel, turning back to see the man's eyes wide and mouth open.

"So, you do have it," he said in a breath, awe and lust pouring from his features. Eamonn followed his gaze, realizing the man stared at his mother's necklace, hanging outside of his clothes. A corner of the man's mouth tipped up momentarily in a victorious grin. "The amulet the master is searching for."

Eamonn could have taken the time to consider what the scarred man said, but he instead used the man's hesitation as an opportunity to escape. He wrapped his arms around the barrel closest to him and pushed it toward the scarred man, finding strength he didn't know he had. The barrel made contact and the man toppled backward, and Eamonn raced past him toward the back of the alley.

The men at the front of the alley had gotten too close, though, and they caught up to Eamonn before he made it out, dragging him back into the darkness. Each one had an arm, and Eamonn fought to free himself as hard as he could, nearly yanking his arms out of their sockets and kicking at the feet of his captors. They pulled Eamonn back to the scarred man, who stood up and dusted off his clothes.

"You can't get rid of us that easily," he snarled, his grotesque face only inches from Eamonn's. "We're not leaving here without you, boy." He punched Eamonn hard in the gut, causing Eamonn to slump forward and knocking the wind out of him.

Eamonn fought to catch his breath, every muscle in his body tensing as the men tried to lead him out of the alley. But Eamonn planted his feet, so solid that they might as well have been connected to the ground. He closed his eyes and clenched his fists, feeling energy draw from his hands and feet toward his chest. Eamonn felt an intense warmth at his breastbone, and then—perfect silence.

The energy had evaporated in an instant and the normal sounds of night returned. Eamonn realized the men no longer held his arms and he dropped them to his sides. Something about the alley seemed starkly different, but why? Nothing had happened.

The three men lay motionless on the ground, but that wasn't the only unexplained change. All the barrels had been pushed outside the alley, the wooden sides of the buildings had cracks and splinters from impacts, and even the dirt that had covered the cobblestones on the ground had been entirely swept away.

Eamonn felt some lingering heat at his breastbone and looked down. The stone of his mother's necklace glowed bright green, though the light faded quickly. He reached his hand up to touch the pendant and felt the warmth radiating from it.

*What just happened?*

Eamonn's breath came in short gasps and he stumbled backwards over one man's arm. He surveyed the scene again and again, trying to make sense of it. Eamonn hadn't even known that anything happened; he'd just been desperate to escape.

One of the men started to stir, and Eamonn's wits came back to him. He bolted out of the alleyway and ran, moving as fast as he could to get home. He needed his horse. He needed to talk to Leyna.

As much as he had resisted it, only one explanation came to his mind.

*Magic.*

## THIRTEEN

Rovis built up a sweat as Eamonn pushed him to a gallop. He took the longer route to Leyna's house around the city because he could go faster and because he wanted to stay as far away from those men in the alley as he could.

It was getting late now, and if Leyna was an early riser, she might already have turned in for the night. Eamonn would have to wake her up. He needed to know more. He couldn't deny the existence of magic anymore, not in ancient history and not in the present. Realizing that Rothgard must believe in magic had almost been enough to sway him, but whatever just happened in the alley left him with no excuse. His pulse hammered in his veins as he turned the final corner and rode up the hill.

Smoke still trickled from the chimney of Leyna's home, and a light was still on in at least one room. Eamonn nearly barreled

Rovis into the hitching post before sliding off the saddle and hastily tying him off. He ran to the front door, rapping on it in quick succession.

"Leyna, it's Eamonn," he called through the door. "I'm so sorry to bother you, but I have to talk to you. I need to know more about magic."

He stopped knocking, taking a step back from the door and catching his breath, his chest heaving. Seconds later, the front door opened and light flooded out into the yard. Eamonn could distinguish Leyna's silhouette against the light.

"Have you gone mad?" she asked in a sincere whisper. She stepped right up to the threshold, holding her elbows. "You know what time it is, don't you?"

"I know, I'm sorry," he said, the words spilling out in a rush. "I only came right now because it's too important."

Leyna paused, as if considering whether to let him in, then she took a step back from the threshold. "Come in. I've just been in the sitting room reading; the others have gone to bed."

Eamonn followed Leyna inside to the sitting room, where a small fire still burned in the fireplace and a book lay open face down in a chair. Leyna picked up the book, closed it, and set it on a table before sitting down, gesturing for Eamonn to take a seat as well.

"What's so important?" Leyna asked, folding her hands in her lap and leaning back in the comfortable chair.

Eamonn recounted what had happened from when he first saw the scarred man outside the butcher. He told her all about the encounter with the three men, even though he could barely describe what exactly happened in the apparent energy pulse.

Leyna's expression transformed from merely curious to thoroughly amazed as Eamonn progressed with his story.

"I knew it," she murmured, jumping up from the chair and nearly running to one of the bookshelves. She retrieved a book without looking for it, familiar with its location, and brought it back to her seat. She opened it and began to thumb through its pages.

"I've been reading through these old books my father found, trying to learn more about your mother's necklace, and I just read this today in that Idyrrian primer I showed you," Leyna said with zeal. She found the page she was looking for and sat up straighter. "Ah, here. 'The magical forest of Avaria is home to the Kaethiri, a race of immortal beings with unknown origins. These celestial creatures have a magic unlike any a human can possess, originally bestowing a less powerful magic upon humans in the old days.'"

*Kaethiri.* Eamonn hadn't heard the term in years. Something about hearing it now lit a flame within him, a flame he wanted to stoke and fuel. "I remember learning about the Kaethiri in school, but I never learned that they inhabited Avaria. They seemed much more other-worldly. A powerful, all-female race that doesn't delve into the affairs of humans, and they live right next door to Idyrria?" Eamonn shook his head. "I always thought of them more as spirits than as physical beings."

"Well, that's just the thing. They used to walk among people," Leyna said, waving her hand toward her to signal Eamonn to come beside her. "See? 'The Kaethiri are primarily separate from humans, but they occasionally travel throughout Sarieth and grace humans with their presence. They have a calming influence, oftentimes showing up in places with some form of trouble.' Some of our deities came from the Kaethiri. The Blessed Lady of the Stars is a Kaethiri—she's mentioned a few times in the passage."

Eamonn looked from the book to Leyna as he knelt next to her. The light from the fire had begun to dim, only partially illuminating Leyna's face in an orange glow. She raised her eyebrows, her eyes searching Eamonn with intensity and her lips still parted from speaking. Her fervor for magic shone through in her features, and Eamonn had to force his eyes away from her.

"This is fascinating," he admitted, turning his gaze to the fire, "but I don't understand what it has to do with what just happened to me."

Leyna took in a deep breath, as though preparing herself for what she was about to say. "Well, we already established that your mother's pendant must be Avarian." She paused, and Eamonn turned back to her to see her roll her lips together, wetting them with her tongue with her eyes on the book.

"Eamonn," she murmured, and she lifted her eyes to meet his, "have you ever considered that your mother might not be Mirish?"

He shook his head in a tiny movement. "Not really. What else would she be?"

Eamonn saw Leyna visibly swallow before she whispered, "I think your mother was a Kaethiri."

*She thinks what?* Eamonn lost all the breath in his lungs. How was that even possible?

He stood from his crouch beside Leyna, pressing his fingers to his forehead, and sat down again in a chair. He ran his hand through his sandy hair, trying to wrap his mind around the idea. His mother a Kaethiri? An all-powerful being essentially made of magic, existing since before the world as they knew it began? He put his hand over his upper lip, covering his mouth with his fingers, and set his elbow on the chair's armrest. Leyna had to be wrong. His mother could have found the pendant somewhere, or bought it from a trader who'd found it or stolen it from the Kaethiri. There had to be a logical explanation.

But the thought tugged the back of his mind. What if it *had* been possible somehow? Magic was real enough. Could the mother he never knew have been a magical being?

"Okay, so she had the pendant," Eamonn finally said, talking through his thoughts. "Why do you think that would make her a Kaethiri?"

Leyna sat stiff as a board in her chair, pressing her lips into a line as she listened to Eamonn. "For starters, I don't think the Kaethiri are in the habit of just losing their amulets. With the exception of your mother, they haven't even left Avaria in centuries. But there is another thing." She cocked her head, speaking slowly as if she chose each word carefully. She turned a page in the book, running her finger down it to a particular line. "'The amulet possessed by each Kaethiri is a powerful talisman that can only be harnessed by a Kaethiri, focusing and refining a Kaethiri's magic.'" Leyna looked back up at Eamonn and her forehead wrinkled as she drew her eyebrows together, an expression of giving difficult news. "Your amulet didn't provide the magic you used tonight; it just channeled it. The magic had to come from you."

Eamonn's mouth fell open and he fell back into the chair, losing all sense of his body. Him—Eammon, a nobody thief turned merchant from Idyrria—magical? Now *that* was really impossible.

He laughed and lowered his head, looking at his lap. The thought of Leyna's claim overwhelmed him and he began to shake inside, a deep tremor that began in his chest and stretched to every extremity, bringing the feeling back to his body.

*Half Kaethiri?* It would explain what had happened in the alleyway, but it just didn't add up. He'd never done anything magical before that in his entire life. Why would it show up now?

"I don't understand," he murmured, finding Leyna's gaze again. She still sat up straight, her hands clasped together on the book, her face a picture of concern. "I've never used magic before—ever. Why tonight?"

Leyna blinked several times as her eyes flitted around the room, as though she looked for the answer. "I assume it came from your desperation. You were caught, and scared, and you couldn't see a way out." Her eyes landed on him again and she shrugged. "So, you made one."

Eamonn ran both hands through his hair, leaving them on the top of his head. Leyna was right about him being desperate. He'd never been caught like that before, where death or some other grim fate awaited him so imminently. Not to mention, he'd been fighting his captors already. The magic might have erupted from him as just another way to fight.

As Eamonn recalled the confrontation in the alley again, one memory in particular stuck out to him. He dropped his hands and looked at Leyna. "The scarred man said something to me about 'tracing my magic.' I didn't think anything about it before, but now..." His voice trailed off. "Do you know what he meant?"

Leyna nodded, a little too enthusiastically. Maybe she was just happy to be helpful, to know that Eamonn hadn't shot down everything she said. "Magic leaves traces in the world around it, only detectable by other users of magic. It can be detected by a magic-caster over great distances, but the farther away it is, the harder it is to pinpoint."

"But there are no other magic-casters, right? Not anymore. Who else could be using magic to be able to trace the necklace's magic?" Eamonn asked, but he froze as he uttered the last syllable. He might have answered his own question.

*Rothgard.*

Eamonn stood from his chair and paced between the two chairs and the fire, one hand on his chin and the other at his waist. The rumors Tillrie had mentioned just hours ago must be true. Rothgard had found a perfect place to stay safe and hidden, giving him time to really study magic.

"What is it?" Leyna asked, watching Eamonn pace back and forth.

He stopped, dropping the hand from his chin and grasping his opposite elbow with it. "You know of the Wolsteadan who's been sparking the rebellions in the provinces, Rothgard?"

Leyna stood, nearly dropping the book from her lap before setting it on the table beside her. She pulled her eyebrows together and her lips parted as a breath escaped. "I've heard the rumors. Even if other people in the world have managed to learn magic, Rothgard seems the most likely."

Only a few inches separated Eamonn from Leyna. He noticed their closeness and his heart started to thump. Her chest rose and fell with quick, apprehensive breaths, and her parted lips moved almost imperceptibly with each breath. Eamonn's heart caught in his chest, and he fought the desire to step closer to her, instead turning away to stoke the dying fire. He couldn't get distracted right now, as much as he would like to.

"The scarred man saw my mother's necklace," Eamonn said with the poker still in the fire. "He said it's what his 'master' wanted."

"What would he want with an Avarian amulet?" Leyna asked from behind Eamonn. "I'd have a hard time believing he's half Kaethiri, too. You've got to be unique in that." She took a few steps and came beside Eamonn in front of the fire. "The amulet may contain Avarian magic, but it will do him no good."

Eamonn shrugged and put away the poker, still facing the flames that he'd brought back to life. "Maybe he doesn't know that."

"Or he knows something we don't."

Eamonn finally turned to Leyna again, hearing the deep disquiet in her voice. She looked at him with his movement, her arms wrapping around herself as her body still faced the fire. "I don't like this," she murmured.

"Neither do I," Eamonn said, pulling her gaze from the flames. His hand felt empty hanging at his side.

"What will you do now?"

Eamonn sighed, not ready to say what he knew was his only option. "I have to leave. I can't stay in Caen."

"Why?" Leyna asked, raising her voice in surprise and knitting her eyebrows together. "If those men were foolish enough to stay in town, you can identify them and turn them over to the authorities."

Eamonn dropped his eyes, staring down at the hands he wrung nervously. "It's more than that." If the scarred man referred to Rothgard, then Eamonn knew exactly which "friends" he'd mentioned as well. "There's a part of my life I haven't told you about."

Leyna turned her entire body from the fire, releasing the grip on her arms. "What's that?" she asked, her voice subdued but not accusatory.

Eamonn didn't look up. He was ashamed enough about his past as it was, but to openly admit his history of wrongdoings to Leyna... He might as well have handed her the vial of medicine he'd stolen with an explanation of exactly how he'd obtained it.

Releasing a heavy breath, he said, "I was a thief in Erai." With his eyes still cast down, he couldn't see Leyna's face to read her expression—and he didn't want to. "I stole out of need, for my own survival, and I joined with a group of boys in similar circumstances who referred to themselves as the Thieves' Guild. Dorylss actually caught me trying to steal from him, but took pity on me and offered me an apprenticeship instead of turning me in."

He inhaled deeply, his chest expanding with the breath, before exhaling and finally lifting his eyes to Leyna. The corners of her mouth turned down a little and her eyes had narrowed, but other than that, she gave nothing of her feelings away in her face.

"I've always felt guilty about stealing," he said with a shake of his head, feeling a need to explain his motives. "But I really had to. My father didn't provide for me, not well enough at least. And the Guild—I found a family in them."

Leyna rolled her lips together and lowered her eyelids, her head bobbing in a slight nod. "I see." She flicked her blue eyes back up at Eamonn. "But what does that have to do with Rothgard? I don't understand why you have to leave."

Eamonn crossed his arms, feeling a burden lifted after admitting his past to Leyna. Anything else would be easy to tell her. "I've come to the conclusion that my old friends in the Thieves' Guild were recruited by Rothgard when he came through Erai. They're some of the few people who have seen the pendant around my neck with their own eyes. I don't know how else Rothgard would even know who I am. And the man tonight—he said my 'friends' were already on their way."

Leyna gasped, fear suddenly shining through her eyes. "As long as you have the pendant, Rothgard will be able to follow you with the traces of magic it leaves, and he could send the people after you a message if he determined you'd moved. It's not likely he can pinpoint your location as far away as he is, but he could at least tell you've left Caen."

Her eyes darted back and forth, searching Eamonn's face. "Leave your necklace with me. I'll keep it hidden. They won't even know to come here to look for it, and Rothgard will think you're still somewhere in Caen."

Leave his mother's necklace? He'd never known a day without it. And whether or not Leyna would admit it, leaving the necklace with her would put her entire family in danger. The scarred man had seen Eamonn with Leyna outside the grocer's shop that day; he might remember the connection and search her out. Eamonn couldn't do that to her.

"They might know to look for it here. I'm not going to put you in harm's way."

"But the man saw you with the necklace tonight," Leyna explained, leaning toward Eamonn. "He'd have no reason to believe you came here and left it with me."

Eamonn turned halfway away from Leyna, his back to the fire, putting his hand through his hair. He didn't exactly want to leave the pendant, but if Rothgard could keep tracing its magic wherever he went, all he would be able to do was run.

"You could go through the Elaris Forest," Leyna suggested, her voice soft but firm. Eamonn felt her gaze on him, but he didn't meet it. "That will cover you most of the way to Dimrain, then you can take the ferry to Farneth. I know it's unsettled there right now, but you could get lost in the chaos."

Eamonn closed his eyes and leaned his head into his hand, his fingertips on his forehead and thumb on his cheekbone. His stomach twisted at the dark road before him, the next steps clouded and uncertain. He hoped he'd be able to hide in Farneth until the Guild gave up their search for him in Teravale, but Eamonn had a feeling it wouldn't be that simple.

Fear sprung up within him and clawed at his insides. Eamonn knew Leyna was right—he had to leave the necklace with her. *He* was Rothgard's target, not her. Maybe he could even draw Hadli and the Guild out of Caen, make sure someone saw him leaving in a hurry who could spread it as gossip.

He'd go back home first and explain everything to Dorylss before he left.

*Oh, Dorylss.*

Eamonn's heart broke to think of leaving him like this, to not know when they might meet again. At least he knew Dorylss could take care of himself.

Breaking free of his thoughts, Eamonn turned to Leyna in a sudden rush and grabbed her by her shoulders, his eyes finding hers and capturing them.

"Promise me you'll stay safe," he whispered, the intensity and emotion in his voice surprising himself a little.

The bottoms of her eyes filled with tears and she equaled his gravity. "Only as long as you promise the same thing to me."

He nodded, a miniscule movement that reflected the amount of confidence he held in his promise.

Before he stopped himself or second-guessed whether or not he should, he released Leyna's shoulders and instead wrapped her in an embrace, holding her tightly to himself. He could feel her heart beating through her chest, a steady thump that quickened as he held her.

She stunned him by winding her arms around him as well, locking him in the embrace. He released a breath and squeezed his eyes shut, feeling a tear of his own roll down his cheek.

He had to go. He couldn't stay here, though at that moment, it was all he wanted in the world.

Eamonn broke free and took his mother's necklace off for the first time in his memory. He held it out to Leyna and she took it, clasping it around her neck. Two tear trails marked her cheeks. Leyna pressed her lips together as Eamonn took one of her hands and squeezed it.

"Let me know when you get to safety, if you can," Leyna said softly, and she brought her free hand up to the pendant. "Don't worry about me or the necklace."

"Well, that's just not possible," he admitted with a chuckle, a breath of levity blown into the heavy room. "But I'll tell Dorylss everything. I know he'll look after you."

Leyna attempted a smile, keeping her lips together. The corners of Eamonn's mouth lifted for only a moment, then he dropped Leyna's hand and strode toward the exit. He only allowed himself one more glance, peering over his shoulder at Leyna, her slim frame outlined by the firelight.

When would he see her again? Would he even come back to Caen before the next market journey? Eamonn pulled his eyes away from Leyna and he let himself out of the house. The answers to those questions and more evaded him, taunted him with the fact that they could not yet be revealed. He unhitched Rovis automatically, moving through the motions as if something else controlled his body. This couldn't be his life. How had everything been flipped completely upside down in a couple of hours?

Eamonn pushed Rovis home, taking the long way around again, on guard for anyone who might seek him. By this time of night, the streets had cleared and the lights from homes began to evaporate as Eamonn passed. With a cloud covering the moon now, Eamonn had to strain to see anything other than the road ahead of him.

But he was almost home. Just a little farther, and he'd reach the lane that led to the house. He could see it there ahead of him. Eamonn dug his heels into Rovis, but right as he did, he had to force him to a stop.

A man on horseback turned off the lane ahead of Eamonn, galloping right toward him.

# FOURTEEN

EAMONN'S HEART POUNDED WILDLY, and he pulled Rovis off the road. Did the scarred man have a horse and now pursued Eamonn across the city? Where were the other two cronies then?

But the man on horseback was too big to be the scarred man and had a long, bushy beard. His eyes locked on Eamonn and he skidded his horse to a halt.

"Eamonn?" came Dorylss's voice from the other horse.

Eamonn guided Rovis back into the road, breathing a heavy sigh of relief.

"Where did you go?" Dorylss asked, the concern apparent on his face even in the dark. "You weren't at home, so I decided to go back to the pub and see if you were somewhere in between."

"I went to Leyna's," Eamonn said as loud as he dared. The night was quiet and their voices carried. "I'm going home now. A lot's happened."

Dorylss and Eamonn trotted side by side the short distance home, and Eamonn kept his eyes peeled for anything suspicious. Once safely back home, Dorylss put on a kettle for tea, the water boiling just as Eamonn finished recounting the events. Dorylss brought the kettle over to the kitchen table where they sat, pouring water over two cups of tea leaves.

"But you're not certain the Thieves' Guild is after you," Dorylss said thoughtfully, letting the steam from his cup fill his nostrils as he held it in front of his face.

"Who else could it be?" Eamonn countered, a crease forming in between his brows. "If it's Rothgard who wants the amulet, then the 'friends' *have* to be the Guild. Regardless," he added with a shrug, "someone is coming after me, so I have to leave."

Dorylss's eyelids hung low over his eyes, and he inhaled through his nose, letting the breath out through his mouth. "I suppose you do." He lifted his eyes to Eamonn. "How long will you stay away? And how will you know it's safe to return?"

Eamonn took a sip of his tea. "I'll write to you as soon as I'm settled in Farneth," Eamonn said, setting his cup back down. "I'll give you my location and stay there until you think it's safe here."

"Well, how will *I* know?"

"Watch out for a group of Idyrrians about my age in the coming days," Eamonn suggested. "I doubt you'll miss them. They might even come here looking for me. You can tell them I've left the country, that I took an opportunity to go on a ship with some merchants to Marinden and it might be months before I'm back."

Dorylss sighed, shaking his head. "The Guild will know I've lied if Rothgard sends them a message that the traces of magic are still in Teravale. They might never leave Caen."

"Well," Eamonn said, then stopped and took a deep breath. "I guess we'll figure that out when the time comes." He leaned across the table toward Dorylss, pleading with his eyes. "I just know I have to leave. As soon as possible."

Dorylss nodded. "Stay here tonight. Get a night of restful sleep," he said, a command rather than a request. "I'll keep watch for anyone that might come to the house. We can pack you up and send you off before dawn."

"Okay," Eamonn agreed, thankful that he could at least get a full night's sleep before he left everything he cared about. He swallowed the rest of his tea and stood up from the table. "You didn't seem too surprised when I told you all about what I learned from Leyna." He eyed Dorylss as a corner of his mouth turned up. "You believed what she said without question, that I'm the son of a Kaethiri."

"Oh, lad," Dorylss said with a grin, his eyes glittering with mirth despite the seriousness of Eamonn's circumstances. He stood from the table as well and walked with Eamonn to the bottom of the staircase. "I suppose I should have told you sooner."

Eamonn stopped at the stairs and crossed his arms, his eyes narrowed. "Told me what?"

Dorylss reached his hand out to the stair rail and put a little of his weight on it. "I noticed your necklace the night you broke into my wagon in Erai. Now, I didn't know what it was exactly, and I most certainly didn't know you were part Kaethiri, but I knew it was special. I knew you were special."

Eamonn felt hot pricks at the backs of his eyes, but he blinked several times to keep any tears from forming. He couldn't decide if he felt touched or deceived. "So, that's why you offered for me to come with you back then? Because I had an ancient magical relic?"

"No," Dorylss replied sincerely, his smile and eyes softening some. He crossed his arms as well. "I told you the truth. I wanted you to come with me because you reminded me of myself. I could see your true character. The necklace just intrigued me." His demeanor shifted again, back to his jolly banter. "You'll notice I haven't said a word about it in the three years we've traveled together."

Eamonn raised his eyebrows once. Well, that was true. Dorylss had never made a mention of his necklace, not if Eamonn hadn't brought it up himself.

"But why did it catch your attention? Did you know it was magical?" Eamonn asked him.

"You forget, lad, that Leyna's father, from whom you've gotten all your information, was my best friend," Dorylss answered, tilting his head toward him. "Stevyrn searched out any information on magic he could find on every journey he took. He traded, begged, and researched his way to finding those texts Leyna has now." Dorylss uncrossed one of his arms, holding it out palm up. "I just remembered Stevyrn showing me something like it from one of his books. So, I thought your pendant might be magical, but I couldn't remember the specifics."

Eamonn had cocked his head to the side as Dorylss spoke, drinking in every word. He wished Dorylss had said something before now; maybe Eamonn could have been a little more prepared for the events now unfolding. But it wasn't Dorylss's fault.

Honestly, Eamonn wouldn't have believed him if Dorylss had said anything before about Eamonn possessing magic.

"Get some rest," Dorylss said, sounding weary himself. "Don't let worry keep you awake. I'll keep watch and wake you when it's time."

Eamon nodded, taking slow steps up the stairs as Dorylss returned to the table and poured himself another cup of tea. His body dragged him down, all adrenaline worn off and fatigue pounding every muscle. He could sleep with Dorylss on guard. Eamonn trusted the man like no other.

He kicked off his boots and climbed on top of his bed, falling asleep before he'd even had the chance to pull up the covers.


"Come on, lad. It's time."

Dorylss's low voice woke Eamonn in mere minutes. No, the night had almost gone—the gray light that came before dawn filled Eamonn's room.

Eamonn rolled off the bed and planted his feet on the floor, his body stiff. He hadn't moved once from the position in which he'd fallen asleep. He rocked his neck from side to side, pushing his fingers into the tight muscles of his shoulders.

"The night was quiet?" Eamonn asked.

Dorylss nodded. "I only noticed animals and the wind. Here," he said, producing a bundle wrapped in cloth and laying it on Eamonn's bed. "I packed you some food, enough to get you to Farneth at least." Dorylss picked up a lit candle from Eamonn's bedside table. "I've already saddled Rovis, too. He's ready to ride. All you need is whatever belongings you want to take."

His belongings? Eamonn didn't want to take any, really. Something in him believed that if he took belongings, he planned to be away for an extended period of time. He hoped to be back soon enough to not need more than an extra set of clothes or two.

Eamonn stretched his back. Dorylss stayed in the room with the candle as Eamonn packed a bag of clothes, adding the bundle of food and a map to the top, and strapped a knife to his belt. Slinging the bag over his shoulder, Eamonn surveyed the room, and his heart fell to the pit of his stomach like a rock. He was really leaving. He didn't know when he would stand in this room again. Dorylss turned, leaving the room and descending the stairs, and Eamonn forced his feet to move.

Outside in the stables, Rovis whinnied and stamped his feet, as if in protest. Eamonn came to him and strapped his bag to the saddle.

"You don't want to go either, do you?" Eamonn whispered in the horse's ear as he stroked his neck. Rovis sighed in answer.

"Well, lad," Dorylss murmured, and Eamonn turned to face him, "be careful. I'll be on guard here, so don't you worry. I won't let anything happen to Leyna or the necklace."

"Thank you," Eamonn said with sincere gratitude. "And Dorylss," he continued, dropping his gaze for a moment as the warmth of tears filled his eyes, "thank you—for everything."

"Oh, Eamonn," Dorylss replied, resting a hand on Eamonn's shoulder. Eamonn thought he might have seen a glistening in the bottoms of Dorylss's eyes as well. "The last three years have been a joy." He smiled, blinking back his tears. "But this isn't the end! It's just another chapter in your story. You'll be back here soon."

Whether Dorylss meant it or only said it to be encouraging, Eamonn appreciated his hope. He needed every ounce of hope he could get. He wrapped his arms the best he could around Dorylss's burly frame, squeezing his eyes shut, and Dorylss closed the hug, making Eamonn feel small and childlike and safe all at the same time.

Eamonn pulled away, wiping a tear. He imagined it would be hard enough to leave Dorylss one day, the father he'd always wanted, but leaving him like this shredded Eamonn's heart. Dorylss may have said this wasn't the end, but in this moment, it certainly felt like the end. The end of the life he had known, at least.

He mounted Rovis and took up the reins, and Dorylss stepped back from the horse.

"I'll send word once I've found safety in Farneth," Eamonn reassured his mentor. "Stay safe."

"You too, lad," Dorylss replied. With his words, Eamonn kicked his heels into Rovis and rode out of the barn.

The sun still hid below the horizon, the morning quiet and calm, and a damp chill hung in the air. Eamonn shivered as he surveyed the lane in front of the house, checking for watchful eyes before he left. He assumed the scarred man and other two cronies would have long since regained consciousness and they likely knew where he lived. He saw no one in the lane, though, so he took a deep breath of the cool air and tried to slow the racing of his heart.

His perfectly predictable life had vanished in a night, now no idea of what lay ahead. Gathering up the courage he needed to leave his home and family behind him, Eamonn flicked Rovis' reins and galloped into the gray mist of the morning.

Leyna faced a shelf at the grocery, pretending to be mulling over what she needed to purchase.

Dorylss had sent her a message early that morning asking her to meet him at Marsenil's grocery at ten o'clock. He wrote nothing else, but Leyna had no doubt he wanted to speak with her about Eamonn.

Dorylss entered the shop with a jingle of the bell, and Leyna looked to the door. He greeted Marsenil before turning toward her, tipping his head to her.

"Good day, Leyna," he said in a particularly upbeat manner, almost as though he didn't expect to see her. She tried to mimic his smile, but her bewilderment bled through in her expression.

"Good day, Dorylss," she replied, shifting her shopping basket in her grasp. "Fancy seeing you here," she added with a sideways glance in the direction of Marsenil.

"I haven't been to visit your family in a while," Dorylss said, a little too loudly. "Is everyone well?"

"Well, actually," Leyna began, then lowered her voice under the pretense of sharing private information about her family's health. "I'm confused. What exactly is going on here?"

"I didn't want to go to your house or be seen meeting with you in public, at least not right after everything that happened," he murmured, picking up items off the shelf and turning them over in his hands. "The less connection anyone makes between you and Eamonn, the better."

Leyna looked up at Dorylss, her blue eyes wide in question. "So, he's gone?"

Dorylss nodded. "Left before dawn. He should make it to the forest soon."

Leyna released a breath, relieved that he had made it away safely while also nervous for what lay ahead. She pressed a hand to her breastbone, feeling the indentation of Eamonn's pendant under her dress. "How long do you think he'll be on the run?" she whispered.

"I really don't know," Dorylss answered with a shake of his head. "I hate to say it, but I think we might have to see an end to Rothgard before Eamonn can come out of hiding."

Leyna closed her eyes. "I was afraid of that."

The bell at the door jingled as another customer entered the shop. Leyna opened her eyes and whipped her head to the door to see an older woman come inside.

"I'll come over soon, but not yet," Dorylss said, taking a step away from Leyna. "Just go about your normal routine and let me know right away if anything happens."

Leyna nodded as Dorylss took a few more steps away, then he grinned again and said, "Good to see you. Let your mother know I'll come by sometime soon."

"Of course," Leyna replied with a weak smile. Dorylss continued to the opposite side of the store, and Leyna shoved a few items she needed into her basket. She took them to the counter, paid for them, and set out from the shop.

Somehow, the entire world felt different than it had the day before. Leyna had always believed in magic, had always been curious about magic, but she'd never held magic so close before. A magical amulet actually rested against her skin. And its owner was being hunted by someone who wished to contort magic to his nefarious purposes.

Leyna shuddered at the thought, and she strolled down the busy street. She didn't know much about Rothgard, or about how determined he was to get his hands on Eamonn's pendant, but Dorylss seemed to be taking it seriously. With Dorylss unwilling to even be seen in public with her, perhaps the threat was greater than she realized.

Leyna ambled down the cobbled street, deep in her thoughts and nowhere else to be. The people of Caen continued on as usual, as though powerful magic hadn't been performed within their midst the night before. Rothgard and his schemes had nothing to do with them, far away from their lives as well as their minds. Leyna, on the other hand, could think of nothing else.

At least the weather had begun to cool and her time outside was pleasant, the sky coated with thick gray clouds that threatened rain.

*Eamonn might be riding in the rain.*

Every time she thought of him, a pang went through her stomach. Even though she hadn't spent much time with him since he returned to Caen for his break, she'd enjoyed his company and considered him a friend. A friend she may not see again for a long time—if she saw him again.

*Don't think like that!*

Leyna chided herself for the thought. The last thing she needed to do was assume the worst would happen. None of them could predict the future, and dwelling on what might happen would only drive her mad.

Leyna's thoughts consumed her, distracting her from reality. She didn't see the man in her path until she ran into him, her shoulder connecting with his as they crossed each other in an intersection. She dropped her basket, the items scattering in the road.

"Oh, I'm so sorry!" she cried as she dropped down to the basket, reaching for the loose items before they were kicked or trampled. The man had crouched beside her, his light brown hands helping her gather her purchases.

She caught her breath and closed her mouth, standing back up slowly and raising her eyes up to the man.

He stood tall over her, at least Eamonn's height or more. Dark brown eyes met hers and a short-trimmed beard covered his jaw, the same rich brown as his hair. He'd lifted a corner of his mouth in an amused smile, seemingly unfazed by being nearly run over.

"I'm sorry," Leyna repeated, this time barely able to make a sound. Her heart thumped frantically, and she clasped the basket tighter to prevent her hands from shaking.

He had to be Idyrrian—his combination of features was rarely found in Teravale. He seemed around Eamonn's age. And his eyes—his eyes gave away a deep desire, a purpose, a goal.

Every nerve in Leyna's body came alive. She knew he hunted Eamonn.

"Not a problem," he replied pleasantly. Dark lashes framed his eyes as he gazed down at her with concern. "Are you hurt?"

"Oh, no," Leyna responded, nearly spitting out the words. She hoped to pass off her fear as awkwardness. "Just my pride. Have a good day."

He flashed her a charming smile, taking a couple steps away from her. "You, too," he said, turning to rejoin a group that had gone on without him. Leyna counted six men besides him, all a similar age, all likely foreign to Teravale.

Her own two feet wouldn't be able to get her away fast enough. She wanted to run, but that would draw attention to herself. The presence of Eamonn's necklace felt obvious, as though her dress did nothing to obscure it. If Dorylss hadn't made such a point about them not being seen together, she would have gone back to the grocery. He needed to know the Idyrrians were in Caen.

But if they were in Caen, they weren't with Eamonn, and Leyna repeated that thought to slow her heart and carry her all the way home.

# FIFTEEN

EAMONN KNEW THE WAY to the Elaris Forest, but he'd never been there before. A road led from Caen through the forest and to Dimrain on the eastern shore of Lake Elaris, where he would find the ferry to Farneth.

Rain started to fall sometime about mid-morning, or at least that was what he assumed since heavy cloud cover hid the sun. Eamonn welcomed the rain, even though it was cold and steady and soaked him to the bone. The rain limited visibility on the open road and helped to conceal him, and it likely delayed any potential pursuers. It slowed Eamonn down, to be sure, but he felt like he could afford it. Leaving as soon as he did ought to have granted him a bit of a head start.

He reached the edge of the forest and slowed Rovis, sighing as he pulled under the thick canopy of leaves that shielded him from the rain. He shook his head, flinging water out of his hair, and he wiped away the raindrops that hung to his eyelashes.

Eamonn patted Rovis on the neck as the horse trotted down the road. "Good job, fella," he murmured, surveying the dense forest ahead. "We'll take a breather in here."

As they rode farther inside, the trees stood closer together and light dissipated, the lack of sunlight overhead making the forest dark and gloomy. Trees and underbrush crowded each other on either side of the narrow dirt road, lush from a summer of plentiful rain. A shudder ran down Eamonn's spine—he found no joy or warmth in this place.

The road forked ahead, diverging into three paths. The middle path appeared the most worn, mostly likely the one that led to Dimrain and the ferry. Eamonn pulled back on the reins, and he reached into his bag for his map.

Eamonn traced the road from Caen with his finger until he reached the forest, where only one road had been drawn. *So where do the other two go?* he wondered, glancing back up at the paths before him. The one to the left cut at a sharper angle than the one to the right, which turned toward a gully. Peering along the path to the right, Eamonn saw a bridge built over the gully and a continued path on the other side. He had to assume the route led to the north, where a river branching off Lake Elaris bordered the forest. Rovis needed the water, and it might be a good place to rest off of the main road.

After packing the map away, Eamonn kicked his heels into the horse and led him down the road to the right. He wouldn't stray too far—if they didn't reach water soon, he would turn back. He couldn't lose too much time and cutting across the forest to the main road wouldn't be any quicker, not with the dense growth and frequent gullies. They would follow the path back to the fork, but even that would cost him precious minutes.

Eamonn never made it to the river, coming across a tributary within the bounds of the forest before he'd strayed too far from the main road. He allowed Rovis to have a nice rest, drinking as much water as he liked and eating his fill from a sack of grain.

He came across no signs of life in the forest save for the woodland creatures scurrying underfoot and flitting through the trees. Eamonn removed his wet clothes a piece at a time, wringing them out until they were only damp rather than drenched. He dressed and had a bite to eat, stretching his legs with a short walk along the creek.

Or, at least he thought it was short.

Between the tree cover and the overcast day, Eamonn had trouble determining exactly how much time had passed. He picked up his pace the rest of the way down the creek back to where Rovis waited, feeling an urge to get moving. He'd dallied too long.

All manner of insects took cover under logs and leaves with each footfall, the distant groan of a frog sounding a warning. Reaching Rovis, Eamonn flung himself into the saddle and turned Rovis back the way they had come, except the path didn't seem obvious anymore. Had they strayed too far down the creek?

Eamonn strained his eyes in the dim forest to find the recently trodden dirt path they'd followed there, but nothing stood out to him. He turned Rovis at a spot where dirt peeked through the underbrush, but the clearer ground did not last.

Fear tightened around Eamonn's heart for the first time since he'd left home. He'd felt he had the advantage, but that advantage started to slowly slip from his grasp the longer he looked for a way back.

Eamonn struck ahead anyway, picking the horse's way through the forest's vegetation in the least obstructed path he could make. They made slow progress, plodding through tall plants and navigating around ditches or thickets. Still, Eamonn encountered no one—perhaps the rain kept travelers at home today. Or maybe he had drifted that far from the road.

Rovis stopped at a dense thicket, and Eamonn couldn't find a way around. He hopped off the horse to get closer to the ground and see what lay ahead of them. He cursed himself for taking such a detour and getting them lost. They might have been better served to follow the creek to the river and take the long way to Dimrain around the forest's edge. It was too late now, though. He'd probably lose his way further trying to find the creek again.

Wait. In the shadow ahead of him Eamonn saw a clearing—a long clearing.

*The road!*

His heart skipped a beat and he thanked the Blessed Lady of the Stars. If he could just lead Rovis through a little more brush, they'd be there. Sudden anxiety to get back on the road sent a current to his hands and feet, and he pulled a little harder to guide Rovis forward. The horse didn't budge, shaking his head and snorting.

"Come on, fella, we're almost there," Eamonn encouraged, tugging at the reins again. Rovis pulled his head back, jerking the reins out of Eamonn's hand, and he whinnied.

Eamonn held out his hands to try to calm the horse as Rovis took a few steps backward. "Whoa, there, settle down! What's got you so nervous?"

"Must be us."

Eamonn's breath caught in his lungs and his heart plummeted. The voice came from the road, its source hidden from him by a cluster of trees, but he didn't have to see anyone to know who spoke. He knew that voice well.

Every muscle in Eamonn's body tensed, his breaths coming quick and shallow. He could mount Rovis again and try to run, but the terrain between himself and the road would be too tricky for a clean getaway. Turning around was hardly an option, as slow as they'd had to pick their way through the brush.

He longed for a weapon. A knife hung at his waist, but he couldn't take on the entire group with one short blade. If only he could summon some kind of miraculous wave of power again. He willed for it to come, but nothing happened. He had no idea how it appeared the first time, and he couldn't seem to recreate it.

Hadli emerged from the thicket on horseback, then he dropped off the saddle to his feet and crossed his arms in triumph. Six other men on horses came into view behind him as Hadli strode toward the edge of the road, approaching Eamonn.

Eamonn's heart lodged itself in his throat. Seeing Hadli in the library had been bad enough, but for him to come toward Eamonn with that much spite in his eyes... Eamonn had to force down the emotion that had already started to rise, needing his full focus on finding a way out.

"Never thought you'd see me again, did you?"

A cocky smile played on his lips. Hadli hadn't changed much in three years, still the smooth, confident leader who commanded attention. The only thing Eamonn didn't recognize was the fire in his eyes, a look reminiscent of the first time Hadli saw Eamonn's pendant, but the fire burned stronger now, unbridled and overwhelming.

"Where's that pretty necklace of yours, old friend?" Hadli continued when Eamonn didn't speak. He had the upper hand and he clearly knew it.

Hadli and the others, a couple of whom Eamonn didn't recognize, started to close in on him. Eamonn's eyes darted around the forest, searching for a way out. "How did you find me?" he asked, stalling for time as he inched back toward Rovis.

Hadli sneered. "Our contact in Caen waited outside your house last night after you attacked him. He saw you leave and followed you far enough to figure out you must be heading to this forest. He told us as soon as we arrived in Caen this morning."

Eamonn judged the crowd around Hadli. They took up the road, so he couldn't go that way. His heart thrummed like the wings of a hummingbird. His only chance would be to try to go back toward the creek. The terrain would be rough and getting Rovis through would be challenging, but that also meant the horses the Guild rode would have just as much trouble.

"How did you hide it for all those years?" Hadli asked, stepping to the edge of the road.

"I didn't," Eamonn answered, grateful that Hadli kept the conversation going. He edged closer to Rovis, hoping his movements were imperceptible. "You saw my necklace yourself."

"Not the necklace," Hadli spat, narrowing his eyes. "Your magic. You hid it so well."

Eamonn stopped and clenched his jaw. Did Hadli seriously think he'd deceived them all that time?

"I didn't even *believe* in magic until now, let alone know I had any!" Eamonn snapped back. The tone agitated Rovis and he took a few more steps away from Eamonn.

"If you say so," Hadli said, leaving the road and approaching Eamonn. "Either way, you're coming with us."

"Hmm, no, I don't think I am," Eamonn replied, his eyes fixed on Hadli.

"The only way you're leaving this forest is with us," Hadli insisted, his voice low and authoritative. "Do that, and everything will be fine."

Eamonn scoffed. "I highly doubt that."

Hadli put his hand to his heart. "I give you my word. Have I ever lied to you, Eamonn?"

Swallowing hard, Eamonn replied, "No, you never lied to me. But that was a different Hadli. I don't know you anymore."

Hadli scowled at him. Eamonn tried to close the gap between himself and the jittery horse, but he knew Hadli was on to him. He stepped into the brush, his footfalls steady and precise. Three of the other men dismounted their horses and flanked Hadli. Eamonn recognized two of them as Alithir and Joris.

"Our leader wants you. He wants your necklace." Hadli's voice became dark and menacing. "I'm not going to disappoint him."

"I don't have the necklace," Eamonn said, finally coming close enough to Rovis to try to mount him.

"Like hell you don't."

"I swear. And my word is actually still good."

Hadli clenched his jaw at the insult. "Lads," he commanded.

Eamonn gripped the reins and flung his body up on Rovis as the three men rushed at him. They yanked Eamonn down from the saddle, his body hitting the ground hard. Eamonn struggled against them, but they pulled him to his feet and held him fast, binding his hands with a rope. In the commotion, Rovis took off, leaving Eamonn with no escape.

As he fought against his captors, Eamonn tried to summon something—anything—to get him out of this mess. He felt just as desperate as the night before, but nothing happened. Why couldn't he do the same thing now? What was different?

Joris took Eamonn's knife from his belt as the two others held him by the arms. Hadli approached, pulling back the top of his tunic. He scowled at the sight of Eamonn's bare neck.

"I'm afraid we're going to need that necklace," he growled. "You're going to tell us where it is."

"I don't think so," Eamonn muttered.

Hadli threw his fist into Eamonn's stomach, and Eamonn bent over, fighting for breath. He sucked in some air and lifted his eyes to Hadli.

"You think you can get it out of me?"

Hadli's glare tore through Eamonn's heart. Never had he seen Hadli so hostile, least of all toward him. "You're going to wish you'd never uttered those words."

Hadli pulled back his fist to fire it toward the side of Eamonn's jaw, and everything went black.

# SIXTEEN

DORYLSS HAD SPENT THE three days after Eamonn left working outside, tending to the exterior of the house and the garden. He found the labor a good way to keep his hands occupied, as well as his mind. While trimming branches, pruning flower bushes, and pulling weeds, his thoughts did not stray to Eamonn. Otherwise, he began to wonder how far the lad had gotten, if he'd run into any trouble, and how he must be feeling. At this rate, by the time he eventually heard from Eamonn, Dorylss would have the garden manicured to perfection.

He stood up to stretch his back after leaning over for so long pulling weeds, and he wiped the sweat off his hairline with the side of his hand. Only a small section remained in the flowerbed where he toiled, and once he finished it, he planned to call it a day and go inside for the evening.

The whinny of a horse sounded somewhere nearby, catching Dorylss's attention. The sound came from behind the house—but not on the side of the barn, and much closer. He sighed, brushing his hands off on his trousers and plodded around the house in the direction of the noise. Somehow, his horse, Bardan, must have freed himself from the stable. Had he left the barn door open? Did he forget to close the door to Bardan's stall?

Rounding the corner, Dorylss stopped short at the sight of the horse. It was not Bardan, but Rovis, and he carried no rider.

*Eamonn.*

Dorylss's pulse raced as he scanned the open land around the house, but he saw no one. He ran to the back door of the house, swinging it open.

"Eamonn?" he called.

No answer.

He turned to the barn and saw the door was shut. "Eamonn?" he called again.

Still no answer.

Dorylss rushed to Rovis, examining the horse and his tack. Nothing appeared damaged, but Eamonn's saddlebag was still attached, full of the clothes he had packed for his journey.

Dorylss lost the breath in his lungs and his chest tightened. Something had happened. Eamonn and Rovis would not be separated willingly, and even if Eamonn had sent the horse back for some reason, he would have kept his bag.

Rovis whinnied again and Dorylss stroked his neck, murmuring soft words to him as he tried to control his own frantic heart. He led Rovis to the stable and gave him some water, then saddled Bardan. Dorylss hadn't planned on going to visit Leyna and her family so soon, but she needed to know. If the worst had happened to Eamonn, if he had been caught, then his captors would know he didn't have the pendant.

Dorylss could take it from her, spare her the danger. They could hide it away somewhere. Regardless, they had to make a plan.

He led Bardan out of the stable and mounted him, jabbing his heels into the animal's sides to spur him toward Leyna.

As the sun neared the horizon, Leyna gathered up eggs from the nests in the chicken coop, Eamonn's necklace close to her skin under her dress. She had barely been able to keep her mind from him the past few days, the pendant a constant reminder of his present situation.

After her encounter with the Idyrrians, Leyna hadn't seen another sign of them in Caen. Maybe that meant they had moved on. They could still be hanging around a part of the city that Leyna didn't frequent, but she preferred to think they'd found nothing there and had continued on to another Teravalen city.

Leyna reached down for an egg but stopped, hearing the clop of horse's hooves approach the house. A crease appeared between her eyebrows and she listened, hearing the rider on the other side of the house dismount the horse. She grabbed the egg, placed it in her basket, and walked around the side of the house. Bardan had been tied up at the hitching post, and Dorylss knocked at the front door.

"Dorylss?"

Dorylss whipped his head to Leyna at the corner of the house. The worry etched on his face sent a chill throughout Leyna's body.

"Leyna," he breathed. He strode to meet her.

"What is it?" she asked, her pulse accelerating with his anxious demeanor. She clutched the basket tighter. "You said you wouldn't visit right away."

"Things have changed," he said as he reached her, his voice barely above a murmur. "Rovis appeared at the house just before I came here. He carried no rider."

Leyna nearly dropped the basket. Her mouth fell open and the crease between her brows deepened. "We should go inside," she whispered, leading the way through the front door of the house and into the kitchen.

Her head started to throb in rhythm with her heart. Could the Idyrrians have found him? What else might have happened? She set her basket of eggs down on the kitchen table and sat down beside it, her eyes lifted to Dorylss in question as he paced the floor.

"His pack was still attached to Rovis's saddle," Dorylss continued before Leyna had a chance to speak again. "His clothes, his map, his food..."

"I saw the Idyrrians," Leyna broke in. Dorylss stopped pacing and turned to her, his expression grim. "Well, I saw some Idyrrians. I assume they were the ones coming for Eamonn."

"When?" Dorylss asked, taking a seat at the table across from her. "Where?"

"Right after I left you at the grocery. I ran into one of them in the street—literally. He helped me gather up the things that fell from my basket."

"What makes you think they were the ones from Roth-gard?"

Leyna licked her lips, rolling them together before answering. "They were about Eamonn's age. There were seven of them in total, and they seemed in a hurry." She shrugged, dropping her gaze to the table. "I don't know, they might have just been a group of travelers. But that one... the one I ran into..." Leyna kept her face tilted down but lifted her eyes back up to Dorylss. "Something about him made my skin crawl."

Dorylss frowned and leaned his forearms on the table. "How so?"

Leyna pressed her lips together and shook her head in a tiny motion. "I can't quite describe it. He seemed... sly. Like his charm is a tool and he knows how to use it. That's just the impression I got."

"Hmm." Dorylss stared at a spot on the table, deep in thought. "And you saw them yesterday morning?"

Leyna nodded. "Just that one time."

Dorylss didn't speak, apparently still considering what Leyna had told him. He ran his hand over his beard, then sat back in the chair and spread his fingers out on the table.

"What?" Leyna asked, seeing something change in Dorylss's face. She realized her knee bounced under the table, a side-effect of nerves, and she forced herself to stop.

After another pause, Dorylss inhaled through his nose and spoke. "I believe you're right," he murmured, keeping his eyes down. "I believe these are the lads from his old Thieves' Guild sent to claim the pendant. And if he'd been delayed for any reason," he met Leyna's gaze, "they would be able to catch up to him."

Leyna tried to swallow but found her throat dry as a desert, and her heart pounded like a hammer in her chest, threatening to break free. Dorylss said exactly what she'd been afraid of since the moment he said Rovis had turned up.

"What do you think they did to him?" Leyna croaked out, and she attempted to swallow again to moisten her throat.

Dorylss sighed, rubbing his hand over his mouth. "Without the pendant, I can only assume they captured him. Or at least tried to."

"Do you think he could have gotten away without Rovis?" Leyna didn't want to give herself hope with the question, but a spark lingered.

"I'd like to think he got away, somehow," Dorylss replied, "but seven against one?" He shook his head. "I doubt it."

Leyna closed her eyes and rolled her lips together. *Oh, Blessed Lady.* "So, they would take him back to Rothgard?" she asked, her eyes blazing when she opened them. A fire had been lit within her, one that would not be quenched until she'd exhausted her efforts.

"It seems the most likely assumption. Based on what Eamonn told me about the confrontation in the alleyway, that was their intention all along."

Setting her jaw and sitting up straighter, Leyna said, "Then we go rescue him. We know where to find him."

"Leyna," Dorylss interjected, his voice gentle but firm as though correcting a child, "I know you want to help, but how? Even if they did take Eamonn to him, Rothgard is holed up in Holoreath with enough followers to defend against the two of us."

"We'll get help," she countered, her heart now racing not with fear, but with anticipation. "We could find plenty of people against Rothgard in Idyrria, build a force to take him down." She stood, pushing her chair back and putting weight into her palms on the table, her gaze shooting through Dorylss. "You said yourself that Eamonn won't be truly safe until we see an end to Rothgard."

Dorylss took a deep breath, injecting some calm into the room that even helped to slow Leyna's heart. "Yes, and I still believe that's the case, but we don't even know for certain that Rothgard's followers captured Eamonn or that they are taking him to Holoreath." He sighed, his eyes kind and sorrowful at the same time. "We can't just take off across the country in pursuit of conjecture."

Leyna sat down and leaned back in the chair, crossing her arms as her eyes stung with tears. Maybe they couldn't. Maybe Dorylss had a point. But there was no way on earth she would sit there and do *nothing*.

Dorylss watched her, his expression giving away that the gears in his mind were spinning once again as he sat in silence. "I think I know how to find out what happened to Eamonn."

Leyna perked back up. "How?"

"I have an idea," was all he said as he stood. "I'll be back soon. Just promise me you won't do anything until I return."

After a slow breath, Leyna nodded and rose as well. "I promise."

Dorylss remembered seeing the scarred man in the pub the night he had waylaid Eamonn, so he knew exactly what the man looked like. In fact, it wasn't the first time he'd seen the man around Caen. Dorylss ought to have picked up on something odd about the man sooner, having noticed him often lurking around when he and Eamonn were out in the city together. By all accounts, the man seemed to be Teravalen and could even be a local. The man had stood out to Dorylss because of his recognizable scar, but Dorylss hadn't thought anything else about him.

Having ridden Bardan home, Dorylss walked back down the quiet, lamplit street to The Lonely Badger, but he didn't enter. He had seen the scarred man there on a few occasions since the merchants had returned from the market journey, and even though Eamonn was no longer in Caen for this man to stalk, Dorylss thought the pub a likely place to find him.

Dorylss peered through the front window of the pub, staying far enough away that the light inside would keep him from being seen in the darkness. He glanced around the patrons in the pub, spotting many familiar faces, and in the same corner as the other night, he found the scarred man conversing with two others.

A wave of anger rippled through Dorylss at the sight of them, no doubt the trio hired by Rothgard to scout out Eamonn. He would hold on to his rage, though. He would wait until they left and ambush them.

Dorylss lit a pipe while he waited and leaned against the building. He drew deeply on his pipe, resting his head against the wall, and he puffed out a long stream of smoke. His thoughts naturally settled on Eamonn, his entire reason for coming to The Lonely Badger. Was he hurt? Was he afraid? Was he with those old thief friends of his? Dorylss drew on his pipe again. If he'd been confronted, he would have fought, but outnumbered he wouldn't have stood a chance.

The pub's patrons slowly trickled out as the night wore on. Dorylss casually smoked his pipe not too far from the door, glancing over every time someone left. It wasn't until almost closing that the three men he awaited left the pub. Dorylss took one last puff of his pipe, still leaning against the wall, acting as though he paid no attention to the people leaving The Lonely Badger.

The men bid each other a quiet "Good night" as two turned to head down the street away from Dorylss. The third pulled his hood over his head and passed Dorylss, but not before Dorylss caught sight of the scar on the side of his face.

This would be easy.

Dorylss turned the pipe over and knocked it against the side of the building, emptying the ashes before returning the pipe to a pouch attached to his belt. The scarred man ambled away from the pub, his cloak billowing behind him, and Dorylss had to keep his pace intentionally slow to allow some distance between them. He wanted to get farther away from The Lonely Badger and its remaining patrons before he confronted the man who had tried to capture Eamonn.

The man rounded a corner, Dorylss not too far behind, and they came onto a street of sleepy shops. The few lamps and torches in front of shop faces provided only minimal light, and Dorylss saw no one else occupying the street.

*Time to move.*

Dorylss hastened his steps, closing the gap between himself and the scarred man. His footsteps sounded on the cobblestones, and the man turned around to find Dorylss nearly on top of him. Panic flashed through the man's face as Dorylss grabbed him by the shoulders, his strong hands holding the man fast. Dorylss dragged the scarred man into a dark alley between two shops, pinning him up against the wall of one building with his forearm at the man's neck, his other hand forcing down the man's right arm, and one knee pressed into his left leg. Dorylss had the advantage in both size and strength, and the man gasped for air as Dorylss pushed him against the wall.

"What do you want? I don't have anything of value. I spent all my money at the pub tonight," the scarred man whimpered with what breath he could find.

"I'm not here for your money," Dorylss growled, staring daggers at the man, their faces only inches apart. "You know who I am."

Dorylss felt the man gulp under his forearm. "No, I don't," the man replied. "You're just some criminal—"

His fury growing, Dorylss pushed his arm harder into the man's neck.

"Okay, okay, I know you," the man wheezed, and Dorylss slackened his force. "You're the merchant who took in the magical boy."

"What do you know about him?" Dorylss demanded, digging his knee into the man's thigh.

"Ah! I don't know much!" the scarred man said, his eyes wide and afraid. "My master wants him. Said the boy has magic. He wants him and the amulet he carries."

"And who is your master?"

The man narrowed his eyes and one corner of his mouth tilted up. "Rothgard of Wolstead."

Revolted by how the man seemed proud to mention Rothgard, Dorylss contorted the man's wrist, causing him to cry out.

"Where is the boy now?" he muttered, every word threatening
more pain.

"The... master... sent some of his... most trusted followers,"
the man answered, losing his breath. "Other boys. They used
to... know him."

Dorylss's stomach turned. So, Leyna *had* seen the Guild.
"Where is the boy now?" he repeated, emphasizing each word
through clenched teeth.

"They must have him," the scarred man said, stretching his
neck in an attempt to get it away from the pressure of Dorylss's
arm. "They didn't return."

The man's words made Dorylss's heart race and pump fire
through his veins. He had to hold back some of his strength to
keep from crushing the man. "Are they taking him to Rothgard?"

"That was the plan."

Dorylss's closed fist started to shake at the man's neck and his
knuckles turned white. His and Leyna's assumptions had been
correct. He didn't know what exactly Rothgard wanted with
Eamonn or his pendant, but it couldn't be anything good. And
without the pendant, he presumed Eamonn would be subjected
to questioning as to its whereabouts, and he wouldn't put this
crew past torture.

Relaxing his muscles but still pinning the man to the wall,
Dorylss murmured, "Make yourself scarce. You don't want me
to come across you in this city again."

Dorylss released the man and he didn't move at first, rubbing
his neck and watching Dorylss. "Go!" Dorylss commanded in a

harsh whisper, and the scarred man ran off like a scared child into the night.

Dorylss turned his back to the shop and leaned against it, holding his head in his hands. Eamonn was being taken by his former friends to Rothgard's newfound fortress. Rothgard had been studying magic, but what he wanted out of Eamonn remained a mystery. Eamonn's amulet was Avarian, its magic only accessible by a Kaethiri—or half-Kaethiri, in Eamonn's case. Even if he got his hands on the amulet, it would do Rothgard no good. Did he plan to turn Eamonn into his pawn, commanding him to perform heinous magic on his behalf? A shiver ran down Dorylss's spine wondering about Rothgard's nefarious purpose.

There would be no stopping Leyna now. Once Dorylss shared this knowledge with her, she would be out the door on her proposed rescue mission. Dorylss leaned his head back against the wall and sighed, closing his eyes. He had promised both Stevyrn and Eamonn to protect her to the best of his ability. If she was going to fling herself headfirst into danger, then, well, he had to do his best to keep her out of it.

# SEVENTEEN

EAMONN'S JAW THROBBED IN pain. He wanted to lift his hand to feel it, but he found that his hand seemed too heavy to raise. His eyelids, too, felt too heavy to open. What was wrong with him?

He lay on a bed, not terribly uncomfortable, but he could tell it wasn't his own. He heard voices around him, low murmurings of men's voices that spoke too quietly for him to make out words. The only thing he caught was a name.

*Hadli.*

His heart constricted as the last thing he remembered came back to his mind—Hadli and other old brothers from the Thieves' Guild surrounding him and taking him captive. Eamonn couldn't understand how Hadli still harbored enough hatred toward him to do it. Sure, he hadn't left them on good terms or with any kind of farewell, but at least Eamonn had always thought of Hadli fondly through the years. Had all the years of living and thieving side by side with Eamonn fallen from Hadli's memory, to be replaced only by a grudge against him? Eamonn didn't feel that way—well, hadn't, before Hadli agreed to take him prisoner and deliver him to Rothgard.

Eamonn's eyelids began to lose their heaviness and he peeled them apart. Yes, he lay on a bed, but he couldn't recognize where. He saw three other beds lining one wall of the room, most of the men who'd come to capture him sitting on and around the bed two away from him. They huddled close together, speaking in low voices.

They must be at an inn or some other kind of waystation. Eamonn had seen illustrations and read descriptions of Holoreath in books from the libraries in Idyrria, and this room didn't fit those pictures at all. Not overly large, clean, simple, and wooden, this room did not match the dilapidated, drafty, neglected stone of the fortress. They hadn't made it to Nidet yet.

"Hadli, he's awake," someone said, and all eyes turned to Eamonn. Hadli's back had been facing him, but now he came toward him, picking up a bottle on a table next to Eamonn's bed. He shook it and took the cap off.

"Not time to wake up yet," he jeered, pushing Eamonn's jaw down with his hand and dropping some of the bottle's contents in his mouth, closing his jaw and tilting his head back to force him to swallow.

Eamonn coughed, nearly choking on the vile, thick liquid that slid down his throat. *What the hell is that?* Hadli capped the bottle and set it back down. Eamonn tried to sit up, tried to lift a hand, but he couldn't. His eyelids dragged down again, and a fog started to descend over him. He saw Hadli's mouth moving in a malicious smirk, but Eamonn couldn't make out his words.

*That bastard.*

Leyna jumped to her feet after Dorylss told her what he learned from the scarred man. "So we go after him. Now we know!"

"Think on it for a moment, Leyna," Dorylss commanded, holding a palm out to her, remaining in his seat. "We have nothing: no resources, no allies, no weapons. All we have is the desire to help our friend."

Leyna blew a heavy breath out her nostrils, crossing her arms and stepping toward the warm fireplace. She shook her head, mostly to herself. Could they really do nothing? Would they just allow Eamonn to be doomed to whatever Rothgard had in store?

She couldn't imagine going on about her normal life while knowing that Rothgard held Eamonn in his clutches, using him for some malevolent plot to gain control of Avarian magic. If Rothgard never got information about the pendant out of him, he might decide Eamonn had reached his usefulness and dispose of him. But if he did manage to force the pendant's location out of Eamonn, then Leyna would be the next target.

Leyna didn't like either option, so their only choice was to stop Rothgard.

"Idyrria resisted Rothgard, ran him out," she said suddenly, whipping around to face Dorylss. "We'd pass through on the way to Nidet. You can't tell me we wouldn't find people who want to take him down, people with resources and allies and weapons." She stared Dorylss down, hoping her eyes reflected the fire that burned inside her. She hadn't given up on her idea from the day before. "We can't abandon Eamonn."

Dorylss didn't speak. He watched the fire behind her intently, seemingly deep in thought. Surely, he must know this was their only option.

"We at least have to try," she said, her voice softer and breaking with the words.

After seconds that dragged by in slow motion, Dorylss lifted his eyes to Leyna and spoke. "You're right."

Leyna let out a breath in relief as her open mouth curved into a slight smile. Relief, but all the troubles and obstacles they might face still lay ahead of them.

"I'll leave for Idyrria first thing in the morning and see what I can do."

Leyna's smile fell in a flash, replaced with a scowl.

"If you think I'm staying here, you're mad!"

Dorylss stood, towering over Leyna, his expression kind, but firm. "You are. There's no reason for you to go. You'd only put yourself in danger, and your mother needs you here."

"But I—"

"No, Leyna." He rested his hands on her shoulders. "I was tasked with keeping you safe, so I'll keep you safe."

The fire suddenly felt too warm. Leyna pulled herself from Dorylss's light grasp and left the room. Tears pricked the backs of her eyes as she plodded out the back door and into the sunny yard. Dorylss could let himself out. She didn't want to argue with him—it would be pointless anyway.

Leyna hugged herself tighter as a cool breeze blew past. Summer neared its end. She would need to pack warm clothes and a heavy cloak since she would be traveling north as autumn approached.

If Dorylss thought she would stay put, then he didn't know her at all.


The black night had just begun to turn gray with hazy light as Leyna reached Dorylss's house, a bag slung over her shoulder under a gray cloak. She'd made sure to leave home early to allow herself plenty of time to arrive before Dorylss left. Her family had no horse, so making the trip on foot was her only option.

Leyna had thought about leaving Eamonn's necklace behind, hidden away somewhere, knowing that Rothgard would be able to trace its magic and at least know it hadn't left Teravale. But she decided against it, keeping it around her neck instead. For one, she promised Eamonn she would keep it safe, which was harder to be sure of if she didn't have it, but neither did she know how desperately Rothgard might have his followers search Teravale while she was gone. She would do nothing that might even remotely put her family in danger. As long as she had the necklace, even though Rothgard could tell it moved north, her family should be safe.

She strode down the lane and up the slope to the house, finding the door to the barn flung open and noises coming from within. Dorylss must have been making his last preparations for the journey.

Leyna advanced toward the barn, her footfalls silent. At least, she thought they were silent.

"You're earlier than I expected," Dorylss said from inside the barn.

Leyna stopped at the open door and leaned against the doorframe, a corner of her mouth turning up. "I wanted to make sure you didn't leave without me."

Dorylss came out of a stall, leading Bardan out into the stable before guiding Eamonn's horse Rovis out of his stall as well, saddled and ready to go.

"You saddled Rovis for me?"

"Well, there's no one here to look after him if I'm going to be gone, so..." his voice trailed off and he caught Leyna's eyes in the dim light. "I knew either you would come with me, where I can keep an eye on you, or you would try to go about in your own way and land in a mess of trouble." He came toward her with reins in each hand. "So I chose the former."

Leyna bit her lip to try to suppress the smile she felt tugging at her cheeks. It seemed Dorylss knew her pretty well, after all.

She stepped toward Dorylss and the horses, and he reached out for her bag. Leyna handed it to him and he started strapping it to the saddle.

"What did your mother say?"

A lump rose in Leyna's throat and she tried to swallow it down. "I didn't tell her." Dorylss glanced up at her, his reprimanding frown visible even in the dark. "I knew what she would say and I didn't want to quarrel with her before I left. I told Marielle, and she's going to tell Mama."

Melwyn's health had improved ever since a vial of her medicine had appeared at their house one day. Leyna had an idea who was behind it, considering he'd offered to give her money for it a couple of days before, but she never brought it up. But with her mother feeling well again, Leyna felt confident she could manage Marielle, Noriden, and the house for the duration of Leyna's absence. Not like Marielle was really a child anymore. She was five years younger than Leyna at thirteen and quickly becoming a young woman. Leyna trusted Marielle to step up and help their mother while she was gone.

"And I told Marsenil yesterday evening that I was leaving and asked him to check in on them periodically," Leyna continued when Dorylss didn't respond. "He's always made sure we were all right when you were on your journeys."

Dorylss finished tightening the straps and stepped away from Rovis. "Marsenil's a good man."

Something about the way Dorylss spoke filled Leyna with encouragement, helping to ease the little bit of a guilty nag she felt in the back of her mind for running off and leaving her family.

"Are you ready?" Dorylss asked, and Leyna went to Rovis.

"Yes," she answered, forcing confidence through her voice. After all her talk yesterday, she didn't want Dorylss to hear the apprehension behind her words. She planted a foot in the stirrup closest to her and threw her body on top of the horse.

Dorylss mounted Bardan and turned his face to her. "Leyna," he said, his intent voice drawing her gaze, "you don't have to do this, you know."

Leyna found Dorylss's eyes for a moment before looking ahead, tilting her chin slightly up. "I know. But I want to."

Dorylss inhaled deeply and let out a slow, steady breath. "Stay close to me, no matter what," he instructed. "This won't be easy, and we may not be successful."

Leyna nodded, her decision set. "I know."

Picking up the reins, Dorylss reflected her nod. "All right. Let's go."

The hills were the farthest Leyna had ever ventured north of Caen. In her childhood, her father would sometimes take her and Marielle there for an afternoon spent running, playing, and rolling down the hills. Teravale's border was drawn at the northern edge of the hills, and the world beyond Leyna's province waited to be explored.

Leyna and Dorylss traveled the main road leading through Teravale and Idyrria, cresting and troughing over the grassy hills dotted with trees. The pair kept their horses at a trot despite their desire to reach Eamonn as quickly as possible. The Guild might have several days' head start, but wearing out the horses in pursuit might be more detrimental in the end.

For the first day of travel, Leyna and Dorylss never left the hills of Teravale. Dorylss led Leyna off the main road a fair distance to a small village as the sun dipped below the horizon. Though not on their route, they wouldn't reach the next town on the road until the following day.

They set off again in the morning after having breakfast. Hours passed and traffic on the road picked up, keeping their pace easy.

*This is too slow*, Leyna thought, resisting the urge to put her heels in Rovis and cover some distance. She glanced at Dorylss, who gave no indication that he disapproved of their rate. Leyna sighed and settled into the saddle.

Thin clouds veiled the sun, keeping the air chilly and as the pair traveled. As the day wore on, the veil thickened, and ominous clouds gathered in the west. Leyna studied them warily, feeling the change in the air that came ahead of a storm. A steady wind carried the clouds their way, flapping Leyna's cloak all around her.

"When do you think that will get here?" she asked Dorylss, dreading the thought of riding in the rain. She expected trouble on their journey, but she hadn't thought she'd run into it right out of the gate.

Dorylss glanced up toward the clouds, his forehead creasing. "A few hours, most likely. I don't expect it will be just a shower, either. Those clouds are dark and tall. We'll need to find shelter."

Leyna frowned. "Where are we going to find shelter out here?"

"We won't until we reach Rinfeld," he answered with a sigh. "There are a couple of other villages out here in the hills, but they're not on the road. Our best choice is to get to Rinfeld as quickly as we can."

Dorylss and Leyna pressed their horses to an easy gallop, trying to cover as much distance as they could before the storm came. The hills challenged them, though, keeping them from traveling as fast as they would like. Only a few times did they come across someone else traveling on the road, but each time they had to slow down and dodge them or leave the road altogether.

Leyna kept glimpsing the sky, watching the clouds draw near. The wind had picked up and the clouds came faster. Surely it had been a couple of hours at the very most, but the sky had already transformed into a dingy gray and the oppressive darkness to their left threatened them with occasional flashes of light and rumbles of thunder.

They left the hills behind, crossing over into the province of Idyrria. Open spaces began to diminish with the flatter land, replaced with thin pockets of trees. Leaves whipped around them, torn from the trees whose branches shook from the gusts. Thick charcoal-colored clouds pushed their way over the pair, the air warm and heavy, and the growls of thunder shook the earth.

Leyna's pulse began to race. The storm had reached them and they were completely exposed. Lightning cracked the sky, branching like bright tree roots in the gloom. Thunder boomed all around them before the light had even disappeared. Every hair on Leyna's arms stood with the electricity and her nerves lit up. That was too close.

Large, heavy raindrops splashed on Leyna, an irregular smattering that proclaimed the storm's arrival. Lighting popped again and Leyna turned her head to Dorylss.

"How much farther to Rinfeld?" she called over the thunder's roar.

"Less than two miles now!" Dorylss yelled back. "Stay close. We don't have to be in it long!"

Dorylss spurred Bardan into a full gallop and Leyna matched his pace. The rain picked up, stinging Leyna's eyes and impairing her vision. As long as she could see Dorylss, though, she was fine.

A bolt of lightning shot down and struck something about a mile northwest. The cracking thunder caused Rovis to jerk and rear back. Leyna sucked in a breath and held tight to the reins, pushing her body into Rovis's back. He dropped his front legs back down and Leyna sat back up, but Dorylss and Bardan had disappeared.

The flashes of lightning did little to improve visibility. Rain came down in a thick gray curtain, blown sideways by the wind.

Leyna heard nothing past the roar of the rain and the tremors of thunder.

At least she could make out the road. Leyna spurred Rovis onward again, bringing him to as fast of a speed as would risk in the downpour. Maybe, if she stuck to the road, she could still make it to Rinfeld soon.

The rain had soaked through Leyna's cloak in seconds, her hair framing her face in dripping wet strands. She almost couldn't feel the wetness of the rain anymore as the heavy raindrops pelted her.

A shadow came into sight ahead of her, a shapeless form darker than the gray wall of rain. She slowed Rovis as she came closer, squinting through the haziness to try to see more clearly. Her heart leapt to her throat when she realized the shadow was Dorylss atop his horse, stopped in the road facing her.

"Dorylss!" Leyna cried, and as she came up beside him, he turned Bardan back in their direction of travel.

"Are you all right?" Dorylss called to her.

"I'm fine!"

"Come on!" he said, picking up a little speed. "We're almost there!"

The rain had soaked the grassy road and the horses kicked up gobs of mud. Leyna couldn't feel the mud hitting her, but she knew at least her boots and the bottom of her clothes would be covered by the time they reached the town.

And she wouldn't have to go much further. Through the haze, Leyna made out the shadows of buildings looming before her.

# EIGHTEEN

THE GRASS IN THE road thinned and then vanished as they reached more frequently traversed areas, and Leyna and Dorylss brought their horses back down to a trot. The rain still came down in sheets, but Dorylss seemed to know exactly where he was going. He rode his horse up to a building with a stable beside it and Leyna followed him inside, sliding off Rovis in pure relief.

She still felt the phantom drumming of raindrops on her skin. Everything about her was soaked. Water ran in rivulets down her hair into her face and eyes, and she wiped it away the best she could. Her clothes dripped, creating little puddles where she stood, and she tried wringing out her clothes and hair before realizing how futile it was.

"The building beside us is an inn. We'll stay here until the storm subsides," Dorylss said, taking Rovis and leading him into a stall next to Bardan.

Leyna nodded, and Dorylss returned from the stall with her bag, water droplets rounding on the leather. At least the oil she'd treated her bag with kept it mostly dry. She could change into something else and allow her wet clothes to dry inside the inn.

The pair ducked back out into the rain for a moment as they ran from the stables to the front door of the inn. Leyna shook once she got inside, the heat in the room making her notice how cold the rain had made her.

The vibrance and liveliness of the inn warmed Leyna as much as the roaring fire in the center of the room. Men and women were packed inside, eating and drinking and chatting. Must be the thing to do on a rainy day. Raucous laughter arose at one table and drew Leyna's eyes. Her cheeks lifted with the sound, the cheer contagious. At least this inn seemed like a nice place to stop.

Leyna realized Dorylss no longer stood next to her, and she flashed her eyes over the crowd, finding him at the counter with the innkeeper. She hopped over to join him as the innkeeper welcomed him with an astonished grin.

"Dorylss! What a surprise! My, you two are soaked to the skin!" he said, friendly and spirited. "This a friend of yours?"

"Yes, a friend from Teravale," Dorylss replied, and the way he spoke with the man made Leyna think they must already be acquainted. "We're traveling to Gaulmiri and I'm afraid we got caught in that squall."

"How unfortunate! Will you be needing accommodations?"

"I think we will. It doesn't seem to be letting up any time soon."

"No, it doesn't," the innkeeper replied with a glance out the window. "Would you like adjacent rooms?"

"Yes, thank you. And we have two horses in your stable."

"All right, then," the innkeeper said, leaning under the counter to retrieve the keys, but his eyes lingered on Dorylss longer than necessary before landing on Leyna. He averted his eyes after catching her gaze, and Leyna drew her eyebrows together. Something in his studying leer turned Leyna's stomach and set her on edge. She and Dorylss looked comical, of course, as though they had fallen into a lake, but she didn't believe that was why the man scrutinized them. Whatever the reason, it made her uncomfortable.

The innkeeper found two keys and handed them to Dorylss. "Here you are," he said, his demeanor cheery and light once again. "Up the stairs, take a right, and go down the hall. You have the room on the very end and the one to its left."

Dorylss smiled at the man as he took the keys. "Most appreciated, friend."

The innkeeper tilted his head and offered a smile in return. Dorylss turned toward the staircase and Leyna fell in step, looking back to the innkeeper as they crossed the room. He didn't seem to notice her, his eyes fixed on Dorylss and his smile hardened.

Leyna plodded up the stairs after Dorylss, their clothes heavy and shoes waterlogged. They arrived at the specified rooms and Dorylss handed Leyna her key. "I'm going to check on our supplies in a minute and try to dry them. When you're ready, meet me by the fire and we'll have something to eat."

Leyna took the key with a nod. She almost said something to Dorylss about the innkeeper's strange behavior, but she decided against it. More than anything, she wanted to get her wet clothes off.

Dorylss unlocked the door before him and entered his room, giving Leyna the room at the end of the hallway. She wondered if he did that intentionally, ensuring that anyone who might come to Leyna's door passed by his own first.

Eager to get out of her wet clothes, Leyna slid the key into the lock and opened the door to her room, locking it back behind her. The room didn't surprise her in its simplicity, rather meeting her expectations for a small town's inn. A comfortable-looking bed sat next to a window with a trunk at its foot. A small table and chair were positioned on the wall opposite the bed, and a wash basin and pitcher on a tall table and a clothes rack occupied the other corners of the room.

Leyna dropped her bag on the floor near the bed, unlacing her soggy boots and unclasping her belt before continuing to the wash basin and setting the pitcher to the side. She undid the tie of her cloak and removed it, squeezing as much water as possible into the basin before hanging it on the rack. Next came her long gray tunic, then her brown trousers, and lastly her underclothes. Leyna started to shiver in the drafty room and she dug in her bag for a new set of clothes, the dry fabric a welcome change against her skin.

The bed invited her over, its plush pillow and warm-looking quilt drawing her in. Dorylss would be occupied for a little while with the supplies, and weariness from their flight in the storm was starting to catch up with her. She could take a few minutes to rest.

Leyna stretched out on the bed and settled into the covers, the warmth and comfort of the bed engulfing her. Every muscle in her body relaxed and gave into the bed as though releasing one great simultaneous yawn. She closed her eyes, her mind starting to wander, but sleep overtook her before found the subject it drifted toward.

Heavy pounding on the door startled Leyna awake. Where was she? Who was at the door? Why was she not at home?

Remembrance flooded her like the monsoon she'd just passed through. *Right.* She was in a village in Idyrria. She and Dorylss were going to Nidet to try to rescue Eamonn.

More pounding on the door. "Leyna, are you in there?"

The voice belonged to Dorylss. Leyna opened her eyes to find her room nearly dark, only a little light coming through the window. She didn't light the lamp before curling up in bed and must have slept long enough for the sun to fall.

"Yes, I'm here," she replied, sleepiness heavy on her voice. She sat up in the bed and pushed back her covers.

"You need to eat something," Dorylss said through the door. "I'm going down to order us some food."

Leyna reached her arms above her head and arched her back in a stretch. Nearly two days of riding had given her sore, stiff muscles. She reached over to the foot of the bed and grabbed her boots. Her nose wrinkled as she slid her feet into the cold, wet shoes, thankful her dry socks acted as a barrier between them and her skin.

She stood and stepped toward the door, touching her clothes that hung on the rack. Still damp. Maybe allowing them to air out overnight would dry them enough to pack up.

Unlocking the door, Leyna let herself out of the room and locked it behind her before going down the stairs to meet Dorylss. He sat at a table near the fire, his clothes still dark with water in places. The innkeeper sat across the table from him, conversing with Dorylss. Something in Leyna's gut twisted when she spotted him.

"Leyna!" Dorylss called, catching sight of her at the foot of the stairs and waving her over.

Leyna joined Dorylss and the innkeeper at the table. A hot bowl of stew sat in front of Dorylss, wisps of steam floating up from it, and Leyna's stomach rumbled loud enough for them to hear. Dorylss laughed, the vivacious sound causing Leyna's lips to curve in a grin.

"Polnir, would you get that bowl of stew for Leyna please?" Dorylss asked the innkeeper, his features merry from the laugh.

"Of course," Polnir responded with a courteous smile to Leyna. "Back in a moment."

"Thank you," Leyna said to Dorylss. "I'm famished." She watched Polnir walk away from them, making sure he was out of earshot before she turned to Dorylss and asked, "Tell me, how do you know the innkeeper?"

"Polnir? Why, I've traveled so much in my life, I get to know people I see regularly, especially the pub owners and innkeepers." He pulled his unruly eyebrows down over his eyes. "Why do you ask?"

Leyna lowered her voice, skirting her eyes around the room to make sure no one listened to them. She didn't believe the townspeople of a small village would take too kindly to an outsider speaking ill of the innkeeper. "I don't get a good feeling from him. He watched us so strangely when he was giving us the keys. I don't know what it is, but something about him makes me uncomfortable."

Dorylss stared back at Leyna, his frown more pronounced. "I don't know, Leyna," he said finally. "I've known Polnir for years, and he's given me no reason to distrust him."

The tightening in Leyna's chest didn't go away after Dorylss's reassurances, but she didn't push the matter since Polnir was returning with the stew. He handed Leyna her bowl with a smile and she took it appreciatively, though she still hadn't decided whether or not she should trust him.

Polnir returned to his seat across from them as Leyna stirred her stew, blowing on a spoonful to cool it off before she took a bite. Dorylss glanced up at Polnir as he ate another hearty bite, and maybe Leyna imagined it, but she thought she saw a scrutinizing edge in Dorylss's eyes.

"Any news from these parts, Polnir?" he asked, dipping his spoon back in the bowl for more.

Polnir shook his head. "Ever the same," he replied, folding his hands together on the table. "We haven't got much by way of travelers lately. News is slow to reach us. I'd hoped you'd have news for me."

"Teravale is quiet, for which I am thankful," Dorylss told him. A safe answer. Leyna glanced at him sideways, trying to read his expression without giving anything away.

"Come now, there must be some news!" Polnir said, his hands breaking apart in a gesture of impatience. As soon as he had, though, he leaned in close to the pair and said in a quiet voice,

"I heard some Idyrrians from the north were on their way down there. Sounds like they were looking for something."

Leyna kept her eyes fixed on her stew, afraid of giving anything away in her face. She took a small bite and Dorylss sat back, stretching, behaving as though nothing was unusual.

"Did you hear that, or did you lodge them yourself?"

Polnir smirked, a strange half-smile that betrayed secret knowledge lurking behind it. "You know me too well, Dorylss. Yes, they lodged here. Seven of them. Told me they were on their way to Teravale."

Dorylss dipped his spoon in his stew. "Why didn't you just say that before?"

Leyna didn't have to wonder if she saw suspicion in Dorylss's features anymore—it filled his face plain as day.

Shrugging, Polnir simply said, "I wanted to find out what you knew without my saying so."

Dorylss grunted, clearly not amused by his friend's secretiveness. "Well, I don't know anything about them."

"Come, Dorylss," Polnir urged, a sly grin spreading across his features, "You know nothing about them or what they were after?"

His words sounded entirely too feigned, as though he already knew the answer but wanted to hear Dorylss admit it with his own mouth. Polnir clearly had something to gain from Dorylss giving in, and Leyna wanted to spare him the interrogation.

"I saw some," she spoke up, eyes lifting in a flash to Polnir. "In Caen. I ran into an Idyrrian man in the street and saw him rejoin a group of them."

Her eyes didn't leave Polnir's: a challenge. She'd given an answer—a truthful one at that—and now it was his turn to either accept her response and be done with it or make it a real issue.

Polnir's disingenuous grin only grew wider. "I see." He stood up from the table. "If you'll excuse me, I have to make my rounds. Been lovely chatting."

Leyna watched Polnir carefully as he stopped to speak to a group at another table. She turned her face halfway to Dorylss, her eyes still on the innkeeper, and asked in a whisper, "What was that about?"

Dorylss swallowed a bite of stew. "I'm not sure," he responded, his voice a low rumble. "But it concerns me that the Guild stayed here. Polnir may be keeping a lot from us. If the Guild told him anything about their quest, or who they were looking for, then he knows why we are traveling. He would connect me to Eamonn."

The words pulled Leyna's gaze to Dorylss, her eyes widening and lips parting. "What does that mean?"

"It means," Dorylss said, lingering on the words, "we have to be careful who we trust." He didn't face her, his eyes scanning the room instead. "Rothgard attracted followers in Idyrria. He may have run off to Nidet, but he still spread his influence here. We don't know who may be loyal to him."

Leyna could feel Eamonn's pendant distinctly against her skin. She carried what he wanted. It might not be obvious to anyone now, but if those loyal to him started making connections between Eamonn and Dorylss, and herself by extension, Rothgard's target might end up on her back. She shuddered and her throat constricted, her breath coming in short gasps.

"No one can find out what we're doing."

"No," Dorylss agreed solemnly, "which means we're leaving first thing in the morning. Get a good night's sleep, and we'll leave again at dawn."

Leyna leaned over her stew and tried to focus on its warmth and comfort as it filled her belly, but her mind was trapped. How were they supposed to make allies if they didn't know who to trust? What if Rothgard discovered she possessed the pendant before they ever got there? Only one day into their journey and she already considered going back. The danger hadn't felt quite so real before she left Teravale.

But Eamonn was in very real danger as she sat there in the cozy inn, contemplating the *hows* and *what ifs* she might face. She picked up her head, set her jaw, and faced Dorylss, giving him a nod.

Departure at dawn. A full day of riding ahead. Eamonn needed them.

It was cold.

Goosebumps crawled over his skin. He wanted to peel his eyelids apart, but he couldn't. He didn't have the strength to lift his head, either. He barely felt his limbs—whether they were too weak or numb from the cold or no longer attached to his body, he couldn't tell.

Wait, he was on his knees. He tried to move a leg, but he failed. Too weak. He finally cracked his eyes open but couldn't see much, his head hanging. Darkness surrounded him; of that, he was sure. A slight breeze told him he was outside and that he was shirtless. Some feeling returned to his arms. He realized they stuck straight out on either side of him. He tried to lower them and met resistance. Something held his arms in place.

He was trapped.

Eamonn came back to the world piece by piece, as though he'd been in a deep slumber and he couldn't shake it. He fired the muscles in his neck and lifted his head to see if he could figure out where he was and what was going on.

He found himself in a ruined stone courtyard, a covered, columned pathway running along its four sides. Only a few lit torches illuminated the space, placed irregularly along the covered walkway. Broken remnants of a stone path came through the courtyard, but it had mostly disintegrated and given way to mud and weeds.

Eamonn knelt in the mud, his arms tied to two posts buried in the ground. He couldn't stand even if he wanted to, if his legs would respond to his commands. Another cold breeze swirled around him and made him shiver. His eyes were drawn upward, most of the light in the courtyard coming from the shining full moon above him. Stars twinkled through the thin clouds, a fragment of beauty in this nightmare.

He had to be at Holoreath. The Guild must have kept him drugged well enough to prevent him from waking the rest of the way to Nidet. He scowled at the memory of Hadli pouring the foul liquid down his throat. If there had been any relationship left to salvage, Hadli had sliced through it all the way to Eamonn's heart.

*What now?* Eamonn tugged at the posts to see how tightly his wrists were bound to them, and the answer discouraged him. He saw no easy way out. His breathing started to shallow and his head throbbed to the rhythm of his heart as his eyes skirted around the courtyard. No one even stood guard. Freeing himself must be considered impossible.

The slow clop of boots on stone in the distance pricked Eamonn's ears. The sound came from behind him, somewhere past the courtyard. He dropped his head, staring hopelessly at the ground with his shoulders curved and arms outstretched. The footsteps drew nearer, and if their goal was the courtyard, Eamonn wanted them to think he hadn't awoken yet.

The sound stopped as the echo diminished, and Eamonn assumed the source of the footsteps must be in the open walkway around the courtyard. He didn't dare move, forcing his breathing to slow down into a natural, relaxed rate. As long as the person couldn't hear the thumping of Eamonn's heart, they might buy his act.

The footsteps began again, one slow step, then another. Whoever had come strolled leisurely around the perimeter of the courtyard. Out of the corner of his nearly closed eyes, Eamonn saw a man's heavy black boots and black trousers, but he couldn't piece the rest of the man together without lifting his head. He didn't have to look up, though, to feel the man's gaze on him.

*Clunk. Clunk. Clunk.* The steady footsteps traveled around the courtyard back to where they had begun, and they stopped. Hanging as limp and lifeless as he could manage, Eamonn strained his ears to try to hear anything that might clue him in on what was happening, but he heard nothing. A faraway drip of water was the only sound he could place. Seconds dragged in silence before the man stepped again and the clop of the boots began to wane, leaving Eamonn alone once again.

Eamonn released a full, weighty breath, not realizing how much tension had built up within him. He wouldn't lift his head, not yet. He'd make sure the footsteps weren't coming back before he did.

The tug of the ropes on his wrists burned his skin as his body hung between the posts. Curiosity gnawed at him. He assumed the source of the footsteps had ill intent just by the way he'd promenaded around the courtyard, like a lion circling his prey. The man might have even known Eamonn was awake and used the walkaround to instill fear. If that was the intent... well, it worked.

Eamonn tried to swallow but his mouth was too dry. When was the last time he'd had water? He had a limited amount of time left to ignore his new surroundings, and when that time was up, he'd have to face whatever awaited him. Since he came to them without the pendant that Rothgard wanted, Eamonn only assumed Rothgard intended to get its location out of him. The method by which he was being held prisoner was enough to make him certain Rothgard's interrogation methods wouldn't be pleasant.

Giving up the pendant's location wasn't an option. Eamonn had to find a way out of there. That, or he'd find out exactly what measures Rothgard was willing to take to get it out of him.

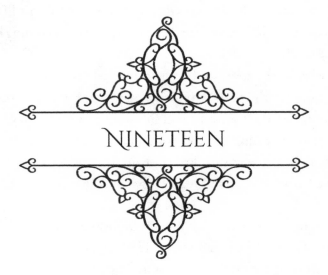

# NINETEEN

LEYNA SEALED HER EYES shut, forcing herself to try to sleep. The nap she'd accidentally taken earlier had left her wide awake well after she'd gone to bed. She needed to make the most of the night to rest and relax her aching muscles, but her mind was buzzing. Thoughts of the next steps in their journey—of the danger she faced—were keeping her wired.

It took effort to keep her eyes closed, so instead Leyna allowed them to pop open and peruse the dark room around her. The soft glow of a full moon filtered in through the window, casting weak shadows of tree limbs on the floor. Below her, the inn had fallen silent, all its patrons having either gone home or up to bed after the storm had passed.

A horse's whinny caught her ears through the silence, and she raised her head off the pillow. That was odd. She shouldn't hear a horse that clearly from the stables. It had to be close by.

A sound like a gentle breeze against the side of the building drifted to Leyna's room. The low murmur stopped and started as though the wind came through in bursts. But the shadows of leaves on the floor didn't move. The night was still.

Leyna heard the horse again, this time puffing air through its nose. Her stomach knotted and she pushed back the covers. Something wasn't right.

She eased out of the bed, crouching low and creeping to the window. Peering outside, she discerned the figures of a horse and two men just beyond the inn. The men spoke in hushed voices, one loading items into the saddlebag of the horse while the other stood by with his hands on his hips. Squinting her eyes to focus better in the dim light, Leyna realized the man away from the horse was Polnir.

Her heart rate spiked and she could feel the blood pumping in her veins. What was Polnir up to in the dead of night? Nothing good, she assumed. With a slow, steady motion, Leyna unlatched her window and pushed on the pane, opening it just enough to catch what the men were saying without drawing any attention to herself.

"...want to know about this. Can I trust you to make it there quickly and deliver the message into his hand?" Polnir murmured.

"You have my word," the other man said. His voice was deep and harder to hear from Leyna's room. His mouth still moved, but she couldn't catch what he was saying.

"No!" Polnir said in a sharp whisper. "You mustn't stop there! Of all places in Idyrria, the kingdom is the least friendly to his supporters. No, ride through and don't stop for longer than you have to till you get to the port."

The other man spoke again, his words not reaching Leyna.

"It doesn't matter," Polnir responded. "This has to make it directly to him, no delays and no interceptions. Can you do that?"

"Of course, sir," the courier replied, nodding, and he tested the straps on his saddlebag to make sure it was tight. "You can trust it will be done."

Polnir crossed his arms as the courier mounted the horse. "Very well. Now be off!"

As the courier kicked his heels into his horse, Polnir turned around the side of the building and disappeared.

Leyna tugged at the window pane to pull it back in place, her hands shaking. She stayed on the floor, her back against the wall and her heart beating wildly. Why was Polnir sending a courier in the middle of the night, and to whom? The words "his supporters" rang in Leyna's mind, and she could only think he meant Rothgard's supporters.

*So, the message...*

Did Polnir have suspicions about Dorylss's sudden appearance at his inn? Was the message he sent with the courier for Rothgard himself?

Leyna turned her palms up toward her face, realizing how clammy they'd become, and she stretched out her fingers before closing them into fists. Maybe she was jumping to conclusions. What were the chances that Polnir's courier had anything to do with Eamonn or Dorylss?

She picked herself up from the floor and slid back into bed. She needed to sleep. Leyna pressed her eyes closed, but an image of the courier flying through the night with an important message to deliver sprang into her mind. Her heart didn't slow down. She had to tell Dorylss.

Leyna threw back the covers, slipping her tunic and trousers over the underclothes she wore to sleep. She took a steadying breath as she turned the key in the lock, then she placed a gentle hand on the knob and pulled the door open with as little noise as possible.

Dorylss occupied the next room, so she didn't have far to go in the dark. He would be asleep, of course, but knocking loud enough to wake him might alert Polnir that someone was up and about.

Maybe Dorylss hadn't locked the door. It was worth a shot, at least. Leyna held her breath, as though it might bring her luck, and she turned the knob to Dorylss's room. Locked. She released the breath in a huff—she would have to knock.

Leyna scrunched her face in anticipation of the sound, almost closing her eyes, then rapped a single knuckle on the door to Dorylss's room. Three soft taps. She nearly laughed at the irony, knocking with the hope of waking someone while quiet enough so others wouldn't hear. It was useless. She might as well go back to bed and attempt to get some sleep.

As she turned back to her room, though, Leyna heard a key turning in the lock and the door to Dorylss's room opened. His looming figure filled the doorway, motioning her inside.

"What are you doing awake?" Leyna whispered, trying to keep her voice as low as she could.

Dorylss shut the door and faced her. "I've been restless and can't sleep well," he murmured at the same quiet volume. "I've had a bad feeling since our supper with Polnir."

The scant moonlight in the room was enough for Leyna to tell that Dorylss appeared troubled, his eyebrows knitted together and his mouth in a frown.

"I think you're right," she whispered, clasping her elbows in her hands. "I heard voices outside my room, so I cracked open the window and listened. Polnir sent a courier somewhere just now. He mentioned delivering a message directly to someone, and to not stop in the kingdom because the people don't like that someone's supporters." She paused briefly to give Dorylss a chance to speak. "Do you think—"

"We need to leave," Dorylss interrupted her, his voice urgent and firm. "Now. As quietly as you can, gather up your belongings. Don't light any candles."

Leyna's chest tightened as fear erupted within her. "It's that bad?" she asked.

"I'm not sure," Dorylss answered as he packed items into his bag, "but I don't want to wait around here to find out. Polnir knows something, and I—" Dorylss hesitated, his head bent over the bag, "I can't be sure he isn't a supporter himself. It could be dangerous for us to linger here."

Leyna could barely hear Dorylss over the thumping in her ears. She glided from his room back into hers without a sound, yanking down her nearly dry clothes from the rack and shoving them into her bag. She clasped her belt around her waist and slid her feet into her boots, lacing them with the quick precision of muscle memory even though her fingers trembled with adrenaline.

If Polnir knew Dorylss, he might also know Eamonn. And if he was an ally to Rothgard, the Guild might have stayed at his inn purposefully, possibly even filling him in on their purpose for traveling. Leyna tied her cloak around her neck as she considered what exactly a message from Polnir to Rothgard might say. She figured it was safe to assume Rothgard would be expecting her and Dorylss whenever they reached Nidet.

At least she knew Polnir hadn't seen Eamonn's necklace. It remained safely tucked away underneath her clothes.

Leyna stepped out of her room and nearly ran into Dorylss waiting just outside. He reached out for her bag and she handed it to him as he leaned down close to her.

"I have to saddle the horses," he whispered, clutching Leyna's bag in the crook of his arm. "Since Polnir is about and possibly near the stable, it might not be easy to leave unnoticed. Would you be able to cause a distraction?"

She rolled her lips together in thought, eyes flitting around the dark hallway. "I might have an idea," she replied. "Get the horses ready and I'll be there as quickly as I can."

Dorylss gave Leyna a sharp nod in answer and turned to tiptoe down the hallway. Leyna crept behind him, her worn boots barely making a patter on the floor. Wood creaked beneath Dorylss's steps as he descended the stairs and Leyna cringed with every sound. Polnir could be anywhere by now.

They came into the main room of the inn, empty and still. The warm glow of embers in the fireplace offered a weak light for them to navigate through the room. *Good*, Leyna thought as she caught sight of them. She needed the embers.

Dorylss continued to the front door of the inn while Leyna hung back at the round, central fireplace. She took an ashtray and broom she found nearby and swept some of the smoldering embers into the tray.

The sound of metal clanging on metal rang out somewhere in front of her and her heart jumped to her throat. Leyna jerked her head up, expecting to find Polnir in the room with them, but she only saw Dorylss unlocking the front door of the inn with the key that hung beside it.

She closed her eyes and released a breath. They were making too much noise.

Dorylss slipped into the night and Leyna followed close behind, carrying the tray of glowing embers. She took slow, deliberate steps, listening out for any noise that a person might make, but she only heard Dorylss's muted movements in the stable. Picturing the scene with Polnir and the courier in her mind again, Leyna peered toward the back corner of the inn where Polnir had disappeared from her line of sight. With any luck, he'd gone back inside.

She stopped outside the stable where chopped firewood had been stacked under an awning and surveyed the darkness around her. Nothing stirred in the night. They might not need a distraction after all. If Dorylss got the horses ready quickly enough, they could sneak away without any fuss.

A door shut somewhere behind Leyna and she froze, not even daring to breathe for fear of making a sound. She waited, listening for anything else, but she heard nothing. Once she decided it was safe, she sucked in a breath and rushed to the woodpile. Anxiety flooded her mind and made it difficult to think straight. She put the ashtray on the ground, still wet from the day's downpour, and pulled four logs off the pile before she realized how wet they were. They'd never light on their own.

Leyna's eyes darted over her surroundings, trying to settle her nerves enough to be able to use her brain. A horse in the stable whinnied and drew Leyna's panicked gaze. If Polnir was still about, he definitely would have heard that. She had to come up with something fast.

She scanned the outside of the stable, stopping on the hay that had scattered out of the entrance. The stable's floor was covered with hay. Hay would light easily and might help the logs burn.

A door closed somewhere again and Leyna jumped, her heart slamming against her ribcage. She stacked a few logs in front of the inn, far enough away to not pose an immediate threat to the building. She just needed the possibility so that Polnir's attention could go to putting out the fire.

The logs in a neat pile, Leyna raced into the stable and gathered an armful of hay. Dorylss glanced at her but right away turned his attention back to the horses. He'd finished with Bardan and Rovis looked almost ready. Her fire might help buy the little bit of time they needed.

Leyna covered the logs with the hay, stuffing it down in between and underneath them. It would light, and fast, but if the logs were too soaked, the fire might be short-lived. As long as they could get away, though, it didn't matter.

A dull, repetitive thud caught Leyna's ears and drew her attention to the back of the inn.

Footsteps.

And they were coming closer.

Leyna ran to retrieve the tray of embers and scattered them over the hay, kneeling down to blow life back into them. Their orange glow brightened and sparked, catching the hay on fire.

Leyna jumped back as the fire ripped through the hay, crackling and growing.

One cheek lifted and she sighed through the smile. *It worked.*

A horse whinnied again and Leyna whipped her head toward the stables, finding Dorylss at the entrance with the reins
to both horses in his hands. She sprinted to him, taking the
reins to Rovis and swinging her leg over his back. With a last
look at the raging blaze behind her, Leyna saw a dark figure
running toward the fire, the flames illuminating his horrified
face. Polnir didn't even seem to notice them beyond the fire,
and they spurred their horses away from the inn into the black
night.

Despite the cool air, the horses were soon glazed with sweat.
After they cleared the village and it disappeared into the darkness behind them, Dorylss slowed Bardan from his gallop and
Leyna followed his lead. They kept a swift pace, though, riding
until they came to a bridge over a rushing creek.

Dorylss led Leyna off the road and into the thin woods to
their right, following the creek until the ground sloped and
they rode down.

"We won't be as visible from the road down here," Dorylss
said when he stopped Bardan at level ground and led the horse
to the creek bank. "Just in case anyone did pursue us. We'll
water the horses and rest here a while, then continue when the
sky starts to lighten."

The horses stepped into the edge of the creek, the water level high from the storm, and dunked their noses into the cool
depths. Leyna slid off Rovis, her legs stiff and sore as she remembered how to stand. She twisted to each side and leaned forward
and backward, trying to relieve some of the pain in her back. She

hadn't yet recovered from their hard ride through the storm, and her still-sore muscles hurt afresh on top of their ache.

"I'm not sure I've ever ridden so much in a day before," she said as she rubbed particularly painful spots in her back. "I walk wherever I need to go most of the time. When I do ride, it's in a wagon or a coach."

Dorylss lowered himself to the ground at the water's edge with a grunt. "I haven't ridden that much in many a year, and I can't quite handle it as well as I could when I was a younger man," he responded, wincing. "We'll be able to get provisions at the next town. It should be Haflen, if I'm not mistaken."

Leyna sat on the leaf-strewn ground beside him, stretching her tired legs. "And where do we go from there?"

Massaging his lower back, Dorylss answered, "Rifillion. My hope is that we can find some allies in the kingdom."

Leyna tore her eyes from Dorylss and glanced down at her feet. Based on what she'd heard from Polnir's mouth earlier that night, the kingdom might be a good place to find allies. Finding people who opposed Rothgard enough to be willing to raid his fortress wasn't what troubled her, though.

"How will we find people we know we can trust?"

Dorylss released a heavy sigh. "The best we can do is try to judge their character and determine if they speak the truth." He turned his face to Leyna, eyebrows lifted. "You noticed something dishonest about Polnir right away. I believe we'll be able to trust our instincts."

Leyna chewed on her bottom lip. She hoped she could continue to trust her instincts. To her, Polnir's actions had been obvious. Not everyone might be so transparent.

# TWENTY

Morning rose over the island, though daytime wasn't much of an improvement. Sunlight filtered through the gray clouds in a murky haze, offering almost no warmth.

Eamonn's muscles had shaken and cramped to the point where he almost didn't feel them anymore. The swampy earth his knees sank into chilled him to his bones. His arms grew weary from being outstretched and his legs had all but given out, acting like supports rather than parts of his body. He couldn't leave his knees. If he even tried to stand or hinge at his hips, he pulled on his arms and they screamed until he returned to his only available position.

He wasn't just being held prisoner. This was already torture.

He'd managed a few short periods of sleep overnight as his body gave way to fatigue, but it hadn't been much. His stomach growled and twisted with hunger, and Eamonn winced at its emptiness. When was the last time he'd eaten? He couldn't recall anything about his journey there besides the time he awoke in that room with the Guild.

Eamonn hadn't seen Hadli since then. Soon after dawn, people began to appear, men and women with serious expressions who ignored Eamonn as they passed by the courtyard, but Hadli never made an appearance.

Fine with him. He only wanted to see Hadli if he could repay the gut punch from the forest.

Morning dragged on, and still, no one acknowledged Eamonn. Whether they'd been given instruction not to interact with him or they simply didn't regard him as a novelty, Eamonn couldn't tell. But he didn't mind. He didn't want to speak with anyone in this place, no matter how exhausted or hungry he was.

Most of the time, Eamonn didn't bother to look up, hanging by his arms from the post with his knees wide and his head drooped. His body felt so heavy. Sleep started to wash over him, his only escape from his pain, hunger, and thirst.

Fitful sleep led him into a dream. Eamonn stood in the courtyard, free from his prison but still stuck. He glanced down at his feet buried in the mud. Try as he might, he couldn't free them.

He found himself alone in the dream courtyard, the silence settling over him like a fog. Now was his chance to find a way out, but he couldn't pick up his feet. He crouched down, digging his hands in the mud burying his feet.

A distant *knock, knock, knock* sounded from somewhere in the castle: rhythmic, constant, irritating. Persistent. It distracted Eamonn from digging at his feet. Why didn't anyone open the door?

The sound grew louder and Eamonn pounded his hands on the soft ground before him. How long would it go on? If he could open the door and make the knocking stop himself, he would.

But the knocking wasn't only getting louder; it was coming closer. And it wasn't knocking at all, but footsteps, moving light and fast toward the courtyard. The realization jerked Eamonn awake, but he didn't move, his eyes staring into the mud where his feet had been buried. These footsteps didn't sound the same as the ones from the night before, but he'd still prefer to seem as lifeless and inconspicuous as possible.

"Stop pretending and look at me!" A clear young voice rang off the stone before the footsteps entered the courtyard, his accent Wolsteadan. "I know you're awake."

The clop of the footsteps changed to a soggy squelch as the man came into the mud. "The master wants information out of ya, scum, and I intend to get it. But you should know," he continued, now standing so close in front of Eamonn that Eamonn could feel his body heat, "if you give us the location of the amulet, you'll be moved to a much cozier dungeon room with an actual cot and dry floor. Otherwise, you stay here. It's your choice."

Eamonn didn't move, hanging his head and letting his body weight strain his shoulders. After a moment, the squelching footsteps retreated, but stopped before they reached the stone. A crack ripped through the air and fire spread across Eamonn's back. He threw his head back and screamed in agony, unable to ignore the whip. So much for thinking he might be left alone.

"We can do this the easy way, or the hard way," the voice growled. "You can tell me what you know now, or I can force it out of ya."

The man circled Eamonn, resting the handle of the whip on his shoulder. Eamonn's back burned as the man walked past him, the sick grin on his face showing the satisfaction he felt from Eamonn's pain. His head was shaved on the sides, the black hair on top of his head braided back into a ponytail, his jaw covered with a short beard.

Eamonn puffed air out of his mouth from the pain, and the man stopped in front of him, locking eyes with him. Eamonn set his jaw, determined to show his refusal to bend to this person, even with the threat of the whip looming right beside him. He wouldn't give away the pendant's location and endanger Leyna. If anyone was going to be on the front line of this nightmare, it would be him.

The man continued around, resuming his position behind Eamonn. Another crack, and the whip lashed Eamonn again. Eamonn arched his back and cried out, squeezing his eyes shut. The soreness of his limbs and the pain in his shoulders disappeared, negligible by comparison to the throbbing and stinging of his back. Slow drips slid down his back, and Eamonn knew blood flowed from his wounds. He clenched his teeth, trying to fight the pain.

He couldn't give in. He wouldn't let Leyna or his pendant fall into Rothgard's hands by his own doing.

The man chuckled. "Like I said, it's your choice," he said, then leaned close to Eamonn's ear and murmured, "Just think of me as The Scourge." He lingered long enough for the name to sink in, then he yanked his arm back for another lash.

Eamonn didn't release an anguished howl with that strike, keeping his mouth shut and burying the pain within him. The Scourge might try to break him, but Eamonn would endure his torture.

He opened his eyes as another show of his resolve, but when he did, his gaze was drawn to the second story of the castle overlooking the courtyard. A dark figure loomed by a window, watching them. The pulse in Eamonn's temples blurred his vision, and he couldn't make out any details. He shivered, the hair on the back of his neck standing on end. Eamonn knew who watched them, who supervised his torture. The master himself hung behind the scenes, ever present. The Scourge cracked the whip again.

Dorylss had agreed with Leyna that they needed to take the time to sleep after they reached Haflen, so they ate a hearty breakfast at the local inn and paid for two rooms to get a few hours of sleep. Leyna was grateful for a break and a bed, her exhaustion catching up with her as they arrived in Haflen with the sun. Dorylss awoke her at midday, and after another meal, they rode on to a village for an uneventful night of sleep that prepared them for the ride to Idyrria's kingdom of Rifillion the next day.

The main road that ran through Teravale and Idyrria, though little more than packed, grassless earth nestled among trees, would lead them directly to Rifillion, for which Leyna was thankful. Staying on the main road felt safer, as they frequently passed other travelers and could stay attuned to the type of traffic on the primary thoroughfare. Nothing seemed amiss as they traversed Idyrria, helping Leyna to feel at ease as they approached the kingdom.

Another long day of travel almost behind them, Dorylss and Leyna rode in silence as the sun sank to their left. Blue sky turned to orange, and they pushed the horses a little faster, hoping to reach the kingdom before nightfall.

Leyna's head pounded with an intensifying ache, each thud of Rovis's hooves on the well-trod path accentuating the pain. She needed to drink some water. Once they stopped at the gate to the city, she'd grab her water flask and gulp down whatever she had left. If they could get a meal soon, that might help, too.

A cool breeze swept through the trees and Leyna shivered under her cloak. Had it been so cold the night before? She added a warm fire to the list of things she needed.

"See the break in the trees up ahead?" Dorylss asked, breaking the silence for the first time in at least an hour. "That's the path that leads to the kingdom. We'll turn there."

Leyna nodded, not sure she could find her voice to speak in reply. She turned with Dorylss at the path he'd pointed out, the thumping of the horses' hooves transforming to a loud *click-ety-clack* as the dirt road changed to cobblestone. The trees on either side of the road were well-tended and the brush underneath them mostly clear, indicating that they neared the city.

They rounded a corner and the walls of the kingdom stood before them, proud and secure. As Leyna and Dorylss rode out from under the cover of trees, they were greeted with a fuller picture of Rifillion, and Leyna gasped.

The whole city sat on a hill, elevated from the world around it. Inside, they could see the roofs of homes, shops, and other buildings, and beyond it all, on the highest point, sat the palace.

Gold spires shot up from tall turrets, with blue and gold banners bearing Idyrria's crest flapping in the wind. Its doorways and windows were trimmed in gold, boasting the opulence and wealth of the kingdom.

But what captured Leyna's attention the most was the color of the walls. The entire palace was constructed out of nearly white stone, a far cry even from Teravale's grandest wooden buildings. She couldn't take her wide eyes off the palace, admiring its beauty and opulence. Her heart twisted, home feeling far behind her.

Leyna realized her mouth had fallen open and she snapped it shut, glancing out of the corner of her eye to see if Dorylss had noticed. These sights must be perfectly normal to him, but for Leyna, who'd never so much as ventured out of Teravale, she'd crossed into a whole new world.

A tributary separated them from the kingdom, and crossing the bridge officially put them in the territory of Idyrria's capital. Leyna could see the gate ahead of them, a broad wooden structure with intricate detailing carved into its planks. Guards stood at either side, sheathed swords hanging from their belts. Leyna looked over at Dorylss, their horses now slowed to a trot. As if reading her mind, Dorylss spoke.

"They'll ask our business, so our story will be that you have a sick cousin," he said, only loud enough for Leyna to hear over the clop of horses' hooves. "We are on our way to Braedel for you to visit him. Many people here know me and know of my relationship with your family, so my accompanying you should be easy to explain."

"Right," Leyna said, ironing out the details of their story in her mind. "Does 'my cousin' have a name? We clearly can't use Eamonn."

"No," Dorylss agreed. "Call him Renn. That's generic enough for Idyrria."

"Easy to remember, too."

"All right, so here it is. Your cousin Renn is sick in Braedel. We received word a few days ago, and because of my closeness with your family, I agreed to travel with you," Dorylss recited as they drew closer to the gate and the guards. "Don't worry, you don't have to say a word."

Leyna nodded and they trotted up to the gate, grabbing her water flask and finishing it off. Dorylss smiled in his natural jovial manner and addressed the guards as they approached.

"A fine evening, is it not gentlemen?"

"Very fine!" one of the guards responded. "What brings you this way Dorylss, coming from the south and with no caravan?"

"Ah, well, this trip isn't for business, but I'm afraid it's not quite for pleasure either," Dorylss answered, his tone easy and casual. "I'm escorting my old friend here, Leyna, to Braedel. Her cousin is sick, and she hopes to visit him in case he takes a turn for the worse." His face fell with the story, giving the impression of a grim outlook. "We're just passing through, I'm afraid."

The guard turned to Leyna. "In that case, I offer my sincerest hopes that your cousin improves, miss."

Leyna smiled politely, keeping her eyes dishonestly sad.

"Well, please enjoy your stay here, though it be brief," the guard continued. "And Dorylss, good to see you again. A kind thing to do in your free weeks."

Dorylss nodded to the guard in appreciation as the gate opened before them, ushering them into a land beyond Leyna's imagination. She'd seen illustrations and read descriptions of Idyrria's kingdom, of course, but she could never accurately picture a city so different from any in Teravale.

The narrow stone street wound around buildings that sat close together and close to the street, making the city feel tight and crowded. Multiple homes or shops were connected in a single white stone structure, the same white as the palace but less ornate, standing three or sometimes four stories high with long rectangular windows.

The simple block architecture and plain facades were made up for by the intricacy of the city design. Paths crossed above their heads, as many in the air as on the ground where they walked, connecting lower rooftops to higher ones. More people traveled on foot along the rooftop paths, though a few still maneuvered around the horses and occasional wagons that squeezed through the street below.

Leyna marveled at the design, gawking at the complexity of the maze and the way the locals navigated so effortlessly. She wondered if the rooftop paths had always been part of the city design, or if they came about as a way to decrease congestion on the streets.

Dorylss and Leyna led the horses up the city's gentle slope and arrived in an open circle, the most spacious area of the city that Leyna had seen so far. Steps built into the sides of buildings offered a way from the rooftops into the round space, and roads led away from the center like rays beaming off the sun.

"This is the plaza," Dorylss said to Leyna, pulling her attention from the fascinating city. "We set up our caravan market here." He pointed across from them. "We'll take the horses to a stable over there and walk to the inn."

They rode toward the stable, passing a crowd that had gathered around a man on a raised platform who spoke in an impassioned voice. People filtered in and out of the throng around him, several shaking their heads and murmuring to each other as they left.

Leyna caught a few of his words as they passed: *Rothgard*, *threat*, and *act*.

She wanted to hang back and hear what the man had to say, but Dorylss continued toward the stable. He'd looked in the man's direction, but he didn't seem as eager as Leyna to listen to him.

"What's that about?" Leyna asked, hoping to pull Dorylss back toward the speaker.

"I'm not sure," Dorylss replied. "Doesn't seem to be anything bad, at least. The crowd is peaceful."

Leyna nearly stopped Rovis. "I want to go listen."

"We will. But we need to tend to the horses first."

With a sigh, Leyna followed Dorylss into the stable and settled Rovis in, removing his tack, brushing him down, and ensuring he had hay and water. Leyna nearly ran out of the stable after finishing the horses, joining the thinning crowd around the speaker.

"Surely you want to keep Rothgard's influence out of your province," he said, his voice deep and rich. "You don't want the same things that happened in my province of Farneth to happen here."

"Rothgard's come through Idyrria and was run out," someone in the crowd called. "He isn't a threat to us."

"He lies in wait on Nidet, in Idyrria's territory, growing stronger every day," the speaker continued, lines appearing on his dark forehead as he raised his eyebrows. "We have the advantage, but not for long. The time to act is now!"

Grunts and grumbles filtered through the crowd. Apparently, most of the Idyrrians weren't convinced of the speaker's arguments. Several turned to leave as the light in the plaza started to fade.

Dorylss stepped forward and Leyna's heart jumped. Was he thinking the same thing she was?

"Do you have the means to raid Nidet?" Dorylss asked, keeping his voice low for only the speaker to hear.

The man's eyes widened at Dorylss's interest and he came closer. "We have a small force, mostly from Farneth, but some from Wolstead and Idyrria as well. We've been trying to gather as many as we can."

"And do you plan to attack?"

"We do," the man replied, "but I can't tell you when. We hope to build our force and learn the island before we make a move. Our estimates put Rothgard's numbers far above ours."

"How do you know?"

The speaker watched the crowd around the platform evaporate, and he stepped down next to Dorylss. "Would you be interested in going somewhere to talk?"

"We'll be staying at The Golden Shield Inn just over there," Dorylss replied, pointing across the plaza. "Should we go there and discuss over a meal?"

The man nodded. "I'll be there momentarily. Let me find my lieutenant." The man lifted his hand and placed his palm on his chest. "I am Kinrid te Oberron of Farneth. And you are?"

"Dorylss Roan of Teravale," Dorylss answered, and he gestured to Leyna just behind him. "This is my friend, Leyna Perth."

Kinrid tilted his shaved head to Leyna in acknowledgement. "We'll be there shortly."

Dorylss directed Leyna across the plaza to the inn he'd mentioned to Kinrid.

"Do you know the innkeeper here?" she asked, the memory of Polnir's sly smile coming to her mind.

"I do," Dorylss said, stopping at the door to the inn. "I chose this inn because I believe he is trustworthy. You'll let me know if you notice anything unusual, of course."

"Of course," Leyna repeated, and Dorylss opened the door for her.

Leyna chose a table, one close to the inn's fireplace since she had been feeling chilly as the sun dropped, while Dorylss got keys to their rooms and ordered them some food and drink. He came back with two mugs—ale for himself and water for Leyna, as she had requested—and he sat down beside her at the table.

"Are you feeling well?" he asked, a crease forming between his eyebrows. "You look a bit pale."

Leyna took the water and gulped it greedily. "I'm just worn out," she replied as she set her mug down. "And I'm hungry. I think I'll be better once I've eaten and rested."

Dorylss nodded, but he still pulled his eyebrows together and he studied Leyna. She turned her face from him, feeling like a weakling. She knew Dorylss's scrutiny came from a place of care and concern, but it only made her feel like a burden to him. He'd planned to go on this mission alone, and maybe he should have. What would she actually do when they made it to Nidet and attempted to free Eamonn? She couldn't wield a sword; she had no magic. Yes, she'd discerned Polnir's cunning and overheard his betrayal of Dorylss, but so far, that was all she had been good for.

If she believed she could make it on her own, Leyna might have gone back home. It would free up Dorylss and likely keep her out of danger. But then she thought of Eamonn, held prisoner in a cold, decrepit castle, possibly undergoing some kind of torture. She shut her eyes to try to clear the images from her mind.

Eamonn wouldn't stop until she was safe if their positions were reversed. She'd learned that much about his character. She had to find some kind of strength within her, some determination that she would not back down in the face of danger.

Leyna opened her eyes. She didn't want to admit her misgivings to Dorylss after her stubbornness to join him, so instead, she'd have to search herself for that same resolve and embrace it. If for nothing else, she would do it for Eamonn.

# TWENTY-ONE

KINRID ENTERED THE INN with a tall Farnish woman before
Dorylss and Leyna had received their food. He stopped at their
table and extended his hand toward the woman to introduce her
before they sat down.

"This is Gilleth, my lieutenant and second-in-command of
our force."

Gilleth offered a pleasant, toothless smile before she and Kinrid took their seats opposite Leyna and Dorylss. The food Dorylss had ordered arrived, and Kinrid and Gilleth placed orders
for their own.

"You're military?" Dorylss asked as he stirred his stew.

"Former military," Kinrid replied. "Gilleth and I left after
it became clear Farneth's military wouldn't make any kind of
advance against Rothgard, even though he uprooted our entire

way of life." He and Gilleth shared a look that mixed anger with heartbreak. "Some others from the Farnish military left with us, and we recruited anyone in Farneth who was willing to fight for our province. After that, we went to Wolstead, and have since ended up in Idyrria."

"So, what's your plan?" Leyna asked with a small shake of her head, and she immediately regretted the question. Impertinence aside, these people were complete strangers. They probably didn't want to divulge any kind of plan or strategy with people they had just met.

Gilleth's dark brown eyes landed on Leyna, her gaze soft and welcoming. "We've been sending scouts to the island of Nidet where Rothgard has set up his headquarters. They've been able to come back with estimates of his numbers and resources." She inhaled, then puffed the breath out of her nose. "We want to ensure our success, and as of now we don't have the numbers ourselves to guarantee a victory," she said as she shook her head, the twisted black locks of her hair dancing in the arrangement at the back of her head.

"What is your interest in our pursuit?" Kinrid asked, his narrowed eyes flitting between Dorylss and Leyna. "For all we know, you could be Rothgard's spies."

In spite of herself, a smile broke across Leyna's features and a laugh escaped her lips. Them? Really?

"You think us foolish for being cautious?" Kinrid continued, his voice quiet and severe as he leaned in toward them over the table. "Rothgard has attracted every kind of person with his ideas, from simple farm girls to chancellors. Not all of his supporters accompanied him to Nidet."

Leyna opened her mouth to speak, but found it dry. She tried to swallow, her throat scraping against itself, and only managed, "I'm sorry," before clearing her throat and picking up her water for a drink.

"Don't let Kinrid frighten you," Gilleth said with a slight curve to her lips. "He's just trying to do his due diligence. Unless, of course, you *are* spies," she added, her eyes glittering.

"We are no spies," Dorylss said, his voice easy and sincere. "We've traveled from Teravale to go to Nidet ourselves. Rothgard has taken our friend captive."

Leyna swung her head to Dorylss, surprised that he decided to reveal so much to these strangers. He must have decided that he trusted them.

"And you're hoping to rescue your friend, just the two of you?" Kinrid scoffed. He didn't try to hide the disbelief in his voice.

"We hoped we would find allies," Dorylss replied, holding Kinrid's gaze. "We know we can't do it alone."

Kinrid and Gilleth shared another look, conversing with each other through their eyes. When they turned back to Dorylss and Leyna, Gilleth spoke. "We would help to free your friend, but as we said before, we don't have the numbers to mount an attack against Rothgard. It might not happen any time soon."

Leyna's heart sank to the bottom of her stomach. These people and their band of fighters seemed like the perfect opportunity to raid Holoreath and defeat Rothgard, but Leyna doubted Eamonn had long to wait for help to arrive.

"What about Idyrria's military?" she wondered. "If Rothgard has taken over an island in Idyrria's territory, why hasn't the king sent an army?"

The muscles in Kinrid's jaw clenched. "We met with King Trinfast yesterday and asked him to send his military to Nidet, but to no avail. He opposes Rothgard and would rouse the military if Idyrria were directly threatened, but he is not interested in sending his soldiers to war in the north." Kinrid scowled. "Says he doesn't want to lose them unnecessarily. As long as Rothgard remains quiet, the king sees no reason to attack."

"But this is the opportune time to attack," Gilleth added, "when Rothgard feels safe. When we have the advantage." Gilleth sighed, her eyes falling as she shook her head. "The king couldn't be persuaded."

Kinrid and Gilleth's food arrived and the party ate in silence. Dorylss had invited the soldiers for a meal, so Leyna assumed he was following through with his request and they would then go their separate ways. Leyna turned her attention to her stew, welcoming each bite that filled her empty belly, the smooth heat soothing to her throat as it went down.

"Have you been through Mareldon yet?" Dorylss asked after taking a swig of his ale.

"No, not yet," Kinrid replied. "But we plan to. We'll touch every corner of the country in search of anyone willing to fight."

"Well, you might want to save yourself the trouble of recruiting in Teravale. The few people you might find to go with you wouldn't be worth the amount of time you lose in the province. But if you go to Mareldon soon," Dorylss continued, leaning in closer to Kinrid, "I have some contacts there that I believe would join your cause."

Kinrid and Gilleth both sat straighter and zeroed in on Dorylss. Leyna, too, tore her eyes from her stew to look at him, intrigued.

"What kind of contacts?" Gilleth asked, her dark eyes eager. "How many?"

"Mercenaries. I don't know their current number, but it should be between thirty and fifty," Dorylss said. "Many are ex-military like yourselves, mercenaries hired from across Sarieth to fight for Idyrria in the war against Cardune. The ones I know settled in Mareldon at the end of the war."

Dorylss had the Farnish soldiers' rapt attention.

"If they're mercenaries, won't they expect payment?" Gilleth pointed out. "We can't pay them."

"Surely Rothgard has some kind of plunder," Leyna suggested. She was fully invested now that Dorylss had given Kinrid and Gilleth a solution to the hindrance preventing them from attacking Holoreath. "Offer the mercenaries first pick of the spoils. You're not in it for the loot, anyway."

"You're right," Kinrid mused in his rich, deep voice. "Seeing Rothgard defeated is all the plunder we need."

"I know these mercenaries are against Rothgard," Dorylss added. "With the right incentive and more soldiers to fight alongside, I feel confident they would join you."

The corners of Kinrid's mouth lifted, the first time Leyna recalled seeing him smile. "I sincerely hope you're right. It would be the best news we've received in some time. We'll leave for Mareldon tomorrow."

Dorylss called for the innkeeper and asked him to bring a quill, ink, and paper. He wrote down the names and locations of his mercenary contacts and handed the note to Kinrid, who touched the paper as if it were pure gold.

Leyna glanced from Kinrid to Gilleth, both of their demeanors transformed. But just how much of a difference would these mercenaries make?

"If—if their numbers match what Dorylss estimates, and if they agree to fight for you, would that be enough for you to attack?" She fought to get the words out, afraid she was setting herself up for disappointment.

Kinrid nodded slowly, his eyes softening from the stern gaze he'd held almost their whole meeting. "I believe so. The fact that they are former soldiers is significant as well. They've had training, they've fought before, they understand strategy." His lips curved across his face. "That is an incredible asset."

Leyna reflected his smile and released a weighty breath. She had reason to hope again.

"We'll continue to Braedel and wait for you there," Dorylss told the soldiers, then looked at Leyna. "Both of us would like to personally go to Nidet to rescue our friend."

Kinrid's brow furrowed and he grunted. Gilleth caught his reaction and turned back to Dorylss and Leyna.

"It may not be wise, but we won't stop you," she said, her eyes kind. "You are always welcome to fight for us if you choose."

Gilleth and Kinrid stood, leaving money on the table for their meal.

"We'll be in Braedel in ten days' time," Kinrid said. "Then we sail for Nidet."

The soldiers tilted their heads toward Leyna and Dorylss in a farewell and departed the inn. Leyna leaned an arm on the table, resting her head in her hand and facing Dorylss.

"I take it you decided we can trust them."

"I did. Do you disagree?"

She shook her head. "No. In fact, I think they're our best chance at freeing Eamonn."

"Likewise." Dorylss met Leyna's gaze with a soft smile. "Are you feeling better now that you've eaten?"

Her head still ached a little and her limbs felt weak, but Leyna imagined it was only a matter of time before the food helped. She could have used a full night of good rest, though.

"Somewhat. Why do you ask?"

Dorylss's eyes twinkled, and Leyna knew he had something up his sleeve. "We still have a good hour or so in the day. Idyrrians often stay out and continue their business after sunset."

Leyna cocked her head, waiting. She knew he was leading up to something.

"I noticed you admiring the palace when we rode up to the city gates," he said, his cheeks lifting. "The Grand Hall of the palace is open to the public if you'd like to see it."

Eyes wide, Leyna downed the rest of her water and pushed her mug back into the table. She'd manage another hour of exhaustion if it meant seeing the palace up close. "Let's go!"

Dorylss chuckled and handed the passing innkeeper the payment for their meal. "I thought you might be interested."

Leyna and Dorylss left the inn and stepped into the plaza, as bright and lively as it had been when they arrived before sunset. Dorylss led the way to one of the sun-ray streets off the plaza, where they climbed one of the stone staircases built into an outer wall of a white building.

They entered the maze of rooftop pathways, still bustling with people. Leyna stuck close to Dorylss among the throng. If she lost sight of him, she'd have no idea how to get to the palace or even remember the way back to the plaza. How did people manage to not get lost in this city?

Flickering lanterns hung close together along both the lower streets and upper paths, flooding the maze with plenty of light. Dorylss guided Leyna through the city with the confidence of one familiar with a place, pointing out different shops or homes of people he knew well.

The paths connected to higher rooftops with intermittent sets of steps, leading up toward the golden domes and spires of the palace. Leyna's breath came in heavy gasps the further she walked, the gradual climb getting the best of her fatigue. Thankfully, they reached the palace and Dorylss led her to steps going down, and they met the road directly in front of open golden gates.

Leyna forgot her breathlessness as her eyes landed on the palace in all its splendor. She'd never seen anything remotely like it in her entire life. A large golden dome in the center was surrounded by several smaller domes, their spires reaching into the sky. Tall windows filled the arched designs of the palace's walls, and intricate mosaic designs surrounded the main entryway. Leyna and Dorylss passed through the massive, shining gates and entered into a courtyard garden filled with ponds, statues, and fountains, and surrounded by a pillared portico.

As they approached the ornate gilded front doors, a guard opened one for them and welcomed them to the palace's Grand Hall. The huge rotunda drew Leyna's eyes upward to the dome, the ceiling even higher than she imagined from the outside. The underside of the dome had been inlaid with gold and painted with blue, red, and yellow in a beautiful design. Leyna walked in a slow circle, her head thrown back to take in each exquisite detail.

While the most eye-catching, the dome wasn't the only magnificent aspect of the room. Ivory columns surrounded the rotunda, and squares of a shiny, light-colored tile made up the floor. The hall continued past the rotunda, where the ceiling dropped from its astronomical height and the room extended in a long rectangle.

A several-meters-long table stretched down the center of the hall, lined with chairs and topped with multiple candelabras. Huge paintings and tapestries hung on the walls all the way down the hall, pulling Leyna further into the room while Dorylss remained under the dome, circling the grand entrance.

At the end of the hall on a dais sat an ornate golden throne with blue velvet cushions, two banners bearing the Idyrrian crest hanging on either side. Leyna approached the empty throne, thinking she might even dare to sit on it, but just as she reached out to touch the gold filigree detailing the throne's arm, a voice rang out and made her jump.

She yanked her hand back and froze. She had thought she and Dorylss were alone in the Grand Hall. Leyna looked over her shoulder at Dorylss who examined a painting near the rotunda, giving no indication he'd heard anything.

The voice sounded again, quieter, pulling Leyna's eyes in its direction. Past the throne and to her right, a dark wooden door stood ajar, and she saw the back of a tall man in ornate clothing with a gold crown atop his head—King Trinfast, no doubt. Leyna could tell from his impassioned movements that he spoke to someone else with intensity, but she couldn't see the other person. She took a deep breath and stepped closer, curiosity getting the better of her. What was Idyrria's king like? What kinds of things did he discuss? As Leyna neared the door, Dorylss still far behind her, the voices became clearer and words more distinct.

"...next shipment of supplies exactly on schedule, not sooner."

"But I told you, Trinfast, we're nearly out. We need the next shipment now!"

The other male voice sounded frustrated, concerned... almost angry. He clearly didn't like what the king had to say.

"These are the terms we set forth and signed upon," King Trinfast countered. "I will not break it. One crack in our agreement and it might start to fall apart. I will not be responsible for that."

"This is serious, though! We need more food! You agreed to provide us with supply shipments and not bother us on the island. If you can't hold true to that, then we might not hold up our end of the agreement. An advancement of supplies seems a small price to pay for us to leave Idyrria alone and not try to depose *you* of *your* crown!"

"The shipments have a schedule. If I start to make exceptions now, where will the exceptions end?" The king scoffed. "Besides, I don't see how you could have possibly run out already. I provided the same amount as always."

The other voice grew softer, and Leyna took a few more soundless steps toward the door. "We have new recruits, and the numbers keep growing. You need to either increase the number of supplies in the shipments or change the frequency of schedule. We'll sign a new contract, if necessary, but it has to change."

Silence ensued. Leyna chewed on her bottom lip, debating sneaking away in case the men left the room through the hall, but somehow, she couldn't move her feet. Her limbs froze in place as she realized the nature of the conversation on which she eavesdropped. The hair on the back of her neck stood up and an icy chill ran down her back.

"Very well," Trinfast declared. "An addendum to the contract. We will increase the frequency of shipments, but everything else remains the same. You still do not attack Idyrria."

"We wouldn't think of it," the other voice said with obvious relief, and Leyna heard the sound of rustling parchment. Holding her breath as if it would make herself invisible, she took a single step closer to try to get a look at the other man in the room. The king bent over a table, quill in hand, and another Idyrrian man watched the words appear on the parchment. His face was angled away from Leyna enough that he wouldn't see her, but she didn't need to see his whole face to know exactly who he was.

Her heart stopped. He was the same Idyrrian she had run into in Teravale after Eamonn had left, one of Rothgard's followers who had been sent to find him.

Leyna covered her mouth with her hand to cover the rising sound of her shaky breath. Every nerve in her body on high alert, she inched noiselessly away from the door until she had to be out of their earshot, then hurried to Dorylss with soft footfalls. She grabbed his elbow, prompting an expression of surprise from him, and dragged him toward the door.

Dorylss didn't resist, following Leyna without question outside of the palace. They passed through the courtyard and the gates, climbed the steps back to the rooftop paths, and Leyna didn't stop. She didn't know where she was going, but she slipped through the mass of people in hopes of putting some distance between themselves and the palace. Dorylss took Leyna's wrist and gently tugged her to a halt.

"What happened?" he asked, turning Leyna to face him, his eyebrows drawn together in concern.

"I saw the Idyrrian," she whispered, her voice shaking, "the same one I encountered in Caen. He's one of the Guild, one of Rothgard's men."

"In the palace?" Dorylss asked, alarm pervading his features.

Leyna nodded vigorously. "Speaking to the king in a room off the hall. I caught part of their conversation."

Dorylss's eyes widened and he pulled Leyna off the main pathway. "What did they say?"

"They have some sort of contract," Leyna responded, glancing all around them to make sure they hadn't caught anyone's attention. "King Trinfast provides them supplies and doesn't attack them, and in return, they don't attempt to overthrow Idyrria."

Dorylss swallowed visibly, lifting his eyes from Leyna. "So the king lied to Kinrid and Gilleth. That's why he was so adamant against sending the military to attack."

Leyna crossed her arms, holding them close to her chest, and wrinkled her forehead. "There's more. The Idyrrian wanted the king to move up their next shipment of supplies. They were running out ahead of schedule because they have so many new recruits." She waited until Dorylss met her eyes, her voice gravelly and quiet when she spoke again. "Rothgard's force on Nidet is still growing. And quickly."

Dorylss's lips parted, but he didn't speak. Leyna watched his eyes dart over the world around them as if searching for the words to respond. Leyna knew how he felt, like the ground had been snatched out from under her feet. Somehow, from the remote island of Nidet, Rothgard was still building his following. He was building an army.

Dorylss and Leyna had kept a sharp eye out for any pursuers on their way back to the inn, but neither noticed anything out of the ordinary. They decided to remain in Rifillion for the night, Leyna especially needing a good night's sleep, and planned to depart right away in the morning.

Leyna barely had time to unlace her boots and kick them off her feet before collapsing on the bed in her room and falling asleep. She dreamed of being in the palace, only this time, the Idyrrian saw her and recognized her. He rushed toward her, catching her by the arm and grabbing at the chain around her neck. The panic that arose within her as the Idyrrian clutched Eamonn's necklace lurched her awake, and she sat up in the bed panting.

Her heart raced with her shallow breaths, so she shut her mouth and inhaled deeply through her nose, her eyes closed. Nothing threatened her. At least, not yet. She raised her hand to the pendant around her neck, finding it safely tucked away.

Leyna opened her eyes to find soft morning light coming through the window. She winced, realizing her head still throbbed, and her hand continued up to rest on her forehead, glistening with sweat. She'd hoped a full night of sleep would have healed her headache, but if anything, it had gotten worse. She huffed, bringing her legs over the edge of the bed and dropping her head forward, her palms on the mattress. How was she going to ride for a full day feeling like this?

Dorylss had already ordered them a hearty breakfast by the time she came down. Even though she didn't have much of an appetite, she ate as much of the eggs, bread, and sausage as she could stomach. They wouldn't have many opportunities to eat, so she needed to fill her belly while she could.

The morning passed by in a blur. Leyna moved automatically, saddling Rovis and falling in step with Dorylss and Bardan without much thought. Her mind was shrouded in a fog. All she wanted was to close her eyes and go back to sleep, but they needed to keep moving.

The sun shone down on them from a cloudless sky, offering warmth that didn't seem to penetrate Leyna's skin. Even under her wool cloak, Leyna shivered as they rode.

After a few hours of travel, Dorylss suggested they take a short respite at a creek to water the horses and allow them a chance to rest. Leyna sat at the base of a broad tree and closed her eyes, leaning into the trunk.

"Leyna," she heard Dorylss say with a note of panic in his voice, "are you unwell?"

Leyna didn't open her eyes. She swallowed and felt the urge to drink, but she didn't want to lift her arm to reach for her water flask. "I'm all right," she lied. "I'm just tired."

Dorylss eyed her skeptically. "Can you ride?" he asked.

Leyna took a deep breath to muster some strength. "I can ride." Another lie. When no strength came to lift her off the ground, she admitted, "But I'd like to stay here and rest a minute."

"We can take a little longer if you need to," Dorylss said, his voice kind but wary. In an instant, though, his tone changed as he called out her name.

"Leyna?"

*Yes?* Oh, she hadn't spoken. Where was her voice?

"Leyna!"

She felt her back slide from the tree trunk and she landed hard on the ground on her right arm. It didn't hurt. In fact, she couldn't feel her limbs at all.

Dorylss's voice came from far away, maybe even from somewhere underwater. Someone might have grabbed her and lifted her body from the ground, but she wasn't sure. Her head rolled back like a dead weight and the world pulled away from her.

# TWENTY-TWO

EAMONN LET HIS BODY hang. He'd gotten a few hours of sleep, at least. The Scourge had blindfolded him and taken him to a cell in the dungeon, where he said Eamonn would stay between lashings. At least that way, Eamonn's muscles had a chance to stretch and move, not that he noticed the stiffness of his muscles much over his flogging wounds. The searing pain had kept him awake deep into the night; he'd finally passed out when his mind gave up.

His back didn't feel much better with the passing of time; it just became a different sort of pain. The fire caused by the whip had dulled to an ache—relentless, consuming, and brutal. The skin around the open wounds pulled tight as it tried to heal, and if Eamonn so much as moved the wrong way, he risked tearing the thin skin and adding another trail of blood down his back.

As his head drooped and he tried to ignore the throbbing of his back, he found some solace in the thought that through it all, he'd given nothing away. It made the scars worth it.

Eamonn heard voices and movements around the courtyard. People in the castle went about their day. Eamonn didn't lift his head. These supporters of Rothgard spoke to each other and carried on business as if nothing out of the ordinary had occurred in the courtyard the day before. As if they didn't pass a man hanging by his arms tied to posts, his knees buried in the mud, crusted blood coating dark lines all over his back.

"Awake at last!" cried out a grating voice from behind him, and Eamonn's whole body tensed.

The Scourge.

"Y'know, you really look a lot worse in the light," he mocked, his same light and fast footsteps growing ever closer until at last he reached Eamonn. "Today's going to be an interesting day. Would you like to know why?"

Eamonn raised his head, finding The Scourge in front of him and glaring at him from under his matted curls.

The Scourge held out a leather flask and Eamonn opened his mouth for the cool water to pour down his throat. He almost hadn't trusted The Scourge to actually give him water and decent food, but he'd been surprised by the meager meal he'd been given in the dungeon. They must want to keep him alive.

"Someone arrived at the island just now with some interesting information," The Scourge continued, pulling the flask back. "A courier, carrying a letter from a loyalist in Southern Idyrria. It would seem," he said slowly, forming each word deliberately, "two people came through a village there just a few days ago. One, a traveling merchant named Dorylss, your mentor and friend with whom you live and work. The other, a girl about your age and a friend of your mentor."

Eamonn wouldn't betray his thoughts and emotions on his face. He could tell The Scourge looked for any kind of response in his expression or body language, so Eamonn kept his countenance blank. His heart, however, had jumped to his throat and his mind buzzed.

"They claimed to be traveling to Gaulmiri, but did not give a reason why. Our loyalist described their actions as 'suspicious.'" The Scourge fought a smile, the corners of his mouth twitching. "Now, Eamonn, can you tell me why they would be going to Gaulmiri?"

Eamonn refused to respond.

"Your silence is the answer this time," The Scourge continued, bending over to put his hands on his knees in front of Eamonn. Face to face, he said, "They aren't going to Gaulmiri at all, are they? They're on their way here. Their plan is to rescue you."

Still, Eamonn did nothing. He only allowed himself to glare as he stared into the murky grey pools of The Scourge's eyes.

The Scourge didn't move, narrowing his eyes in response to Eamonn's glare. He lowered his voice to a menacing murmur. "Of course, you know they will fail. Our force here is too great. Even if they managed to sneak into this fortress, they'd never make it out alive. So, now," he snarled, standing up and taking a step back from Eamonn, "the master has decided to make you a new offer. You tell us what you know, and your friends will survive. They will come to no harm in their rescue attempt. If, however, you continue to withhold the information we need, the master will ensure their deaths to be as slow and painful as he can make them."

The Scourge started to pace in a circle around Eamonn. "Obviously you have a short time to consider the offer, but the sooner the better. Wouldn't want to risk them getting here before they're expected, eh? I doubt you would let anything happen to your mentor if it was within your power to stop it. And the girl—your sister? Or a lover, perhaps? I know the last thing you want is for her to suffer on your behalf."

He paused behind Eamonn, letting the weight of his words hang over the courtyard for a moment. In the silence, Eamonn felt a rush of heat pour over his back, and he flung his head as far over his shoulder as he could, expecting to see The Scourge drenching him with some hot, heavy substance, like mud or even tar. But The Scourge stood several feet behind him, motionless.

Eamonn couldn't see what was happening to his back, but a deep shiver overtook him as the lines on his back from the whip prickled, and he felt his gaze pulled to the second story of the courtyard. Rothgard occupied the same window, his body hidden in the shadows and a pale hand extended in front of him, his fingers in a peculiar position.

The hand fell and the sensation on Eamonn's back evaporated. Eamonn turned his head again, finding only ragged pink welts where his open wounds had been. Only a dull ache in his back remained.

Rothgard had healed him with magic.

The Scourge departed with his trademark swift footsteps and Eamonn dropped his head. The relief from pain was a lifted burden, but in its place, a heavy panic settled in Eamonn. Rothgard had learned magic. Without knowing how much he had taught himself or his skill, Eamonn had no idea what to expect about his future at Holoreath, about Leyna and Dorylss coming to him.

Rothgard could use all sorts of twisted magic to accomplish his goals.

Eamonn dropped his head again, his heart tearing in two. He wished he could warn his friends and tell them not to come. Of course they would try to rescue him, no matter how foolhardy. How did they even find out he had been captured and taken to Nidet?

It didn't matter. Eamonn had to decide between giving the enemy information or risking the lives of people he cared about. And now, he knew Rothgard had mastered at least some magic.

If Leyna still carried his pendant, Eamonn couldn't give Rothgard that information. He'd put the key to Avarian magic in Rothgard's hands. But giving him wrong information or no information put Dorylss's and Leyna's lives in jeopardy.

Eamonn squeezed his eyes shut, needing a third option to appear before him. All he could see, though, was Leyna's face, her blue eyes full of tears before he left. A lump rose to his throat.

Her blood would be on his hands.

A fire crackled. The sweet scent of a fragrant herb hung in the air. Leyna could tell she was inside, but she hadn't the slightest idea where. Her eyelids were still too heavy to open, but her ears listened to everything. Voices—unfamiliar voices—surrounded her.

"It would have been worse if they'd waited," a male voice said.

"It might have gotten better," said a female voice.

"I don't know how you can possibly think that," the male voice countered. "See, she's awake."

Leyna's heart fluttered. How did these people know she was awake? She hadn't moved, she hadn't opened her eyes. Did her breathing pattern change? More importantly, who were these people? Could she trust them? Where was Dorylss?

"She's better," the male voice continued. "Your concoction worked. How did you know the Aranthum would do it?"

"Aranthum is nearly the same as Isifia, but only grows near water."

"Right, so that would increase its healing properties."

"Exactly."

Leyna cracked her eyelids open to find two figures hanging low over her, backlit by bright orange firelight that bounced off the walls of the room and cast a warm glow around them. She blinked a few times, breaking apart the haze of sleep that still clung to her. She lay on a bed in a spacious, multifunctional room, the walls constructed of the same white stone she'd seen throughout Rifillion. An orange cat sat on a window sill, watching them with sleepy eyes, its tail twitching.

Both people before her were Idyrrian with warm, tan skin and complementary dark brown hair, their deep brown eyes framed by dark lashes. A man and woman, not much older than Leyna herself, who held their mouths with the same jovial curiosity, and their eyes turned upward at an identical soft angle.

"She's probably frightened," the young man said.

"Of course she's frightened," responded the woman.

"But at least she's awake."

"What good is it to be awake and frightened?"

"Awake and anything is better, compared to her previous condition."

The two ricocheted off each other almost as if they anticipated the words before they left the other's mouth. Leyna's eyes flipped back and forth between them as they spoke, attempting to find an ounce of comprehension.

"Who are you?" Leyna finally croaked out after finding her voice, although it didn't sound like her voice at all, rough and dry and deep. In fact, she didn't necessarily believe it even came out of her own mouth.

"I'm Taran," said the man.

"I'm Teiyn," said the woman.

"I was starting to wonder when you were going to wake up," Taran said.

"I was afraid you wouldn't," Teiyn countered.

Leyna furrowed her brow, trying to put the pieces together from what she last remembered. "What happened?"

Teiyn spoke first. "You were sick."

"Terribly so," Taran continued.

"Something you had picked up in a village, no doubt."

"A virus that attacks fast—"

"—and is sometimes fatal."

"We've seen it before."

"I knew just what to treat you with," Teiyn said.

"I'm glad she did. I would've tried Dramweed," Taran told her.

Teiyn's gaze shot from Leyna to Taran. "Dramweed? Are you trying to kill her?"

"No! Dramweed reduces fever and would help open up her airways," Taran argued, staring back at Teiyn.

"But you need the fever with survalet to kill the virus. Reducing the fever would have caused her to succumb to the virus and ultimately die."

"We're not sure she had survalet," Taran noted.

"I'm almost positive that's what it was. And look, the Aranthum treated it. So, it was either survalet or something in that family."

Taran turned back to Leyna, a half-smile lighting up his face. "She can win this one. She's better with healing and medicine than me anyway. I beat her on inventions and crafty solutions to problems."

"I am just as clever as you are when it comes to solving problems," Teiyn said, then turned her eyes to Leyna. "And we really do best when we solve problems together. It's part of our twinness."

"You're twins?" Leyna asked, but she didn't need confirmation from them to believe it.

"Yes," they answered simultaneously, then Teiyn added, "But I'm four minutes older."

"That doesn't give you any kind of edge over me," Taran declared with a sigh, as if for the hundredth time.

"It gives me the edge that I'm older."

Taran rolled his eyes, his mouth still curved. "You hold on to those precious four minutes, sister."

Leyna had been wondering when they might take a breath. She took the opportunity to try to shed some light on her situation. "Where am I? And where is Dorylss?"

Teiyn smiled at her with closed lips, her glittering eyes kind. "You're in Braedel, at our home. Your companion went out to get some supplies. He knew you would be safe with us."

"How... how long have I been out, exactly?" Leyna wondered, sitting up on her elbows.

"No, lie down," Teiyn insisted, placing a gentle hand on Leyna's shoulder. "You need to recover your strength. As soon as you do, Dorylss says you will be off on your journey again. And you have been unconscious for three days."

*Three days!* Leyna's heart started to race, her eyes wide and her mouth agape. "We've wasted so much time! We need to be off as soon as Dorylss is back!"

"No, rest," Teiyn said, her hand returning to her shoulder with soft pressure to keep Leyna down. "You are in no condition to go yet. Trying to save your friend now would end with a terrible outcome. Besides, you are supposed to wait here till Kinrid's army gets back from Mareldon."

Lines creased Leyna's forehead as she lifted her eyebrows. What had Dorylss told these two strangers? After he'd made such a big deal about keeping their mission quiet and not knowing who they could trust, had he spilled it all to these eccentric twins? Three days passed out with a deadly virus sure had set Leyna back a bit.

"Did Dorylss already know you?" Leyna didn't know what else to say. Why else would he have divulged so much to them?

"Yes," said Teiyn.

"No," said Taran.

Leyna cocked her head to one side, her lips parted and curled in annoyance, flicking her eyes back and forth between them. "Okay, it has to be one or the other."

"We've met him before, when he came through with the caravan," Teiyn explained.

"But we didn't get to know him very well," Taran added.

"You see, we're kind of outcasts," Teiyn told her with a shrug. "A few generations ago, our ancestors uncovered knowledge about magic, and it has been passed down since. But we can't use it, at least not openly. Most people don't believe magic was ever real, and they think we've tapped into some kind of dark arts. They're afraid of it."

"We spent a lot of time bouncing around from city to city after completing our standard education," Taran expounded. "We wanted to see how we could use our education and a little bit of magic in the world around us without sticking in one place for too long. But people never accepted us, so we came back to Braedel and set up a small home base."

"We still travel when we can."

"But we had to find a way to earn money."

"I work alongside an apothecary, and Taran is an artificer for the city."

"Wait," Leyna interjected, sitting up on the bed and throwing a hand in the air. Teiyn didn't try to push her back down. "You can use magic?"

"To an extent, yes," Teiyn answered, her mouth turning up at both corners.

"Not quite to the level of magic in the ancient days," Taran pointed out.

Leyna felt a cheek rise in spite of herself. She'd always believed in magic, that it could still be accessed even in her time, but she'd come face-to-face with it more in the past couple of weeks than she'd ever dreamed possible.

She dropped her smile and crossed her arms. "This doesn't tell me anything about how you know Dorylss."

"Oh, we got sidetracked," Teiyn admitted.

"Tends to happen," Taran added.

Leyna tucked her chin to her chest and looked at them from underneath her eyebrows. Nothing about that surprised her.

Teiyn straightened her shoulders, her brown waves falling down her back. "We met Dorylss many years ago when we were still children. His caravan was coming through a more remote part of Idyrria, where we'd happened to set up camp for the night. One of Dorylss's horses fell off an embankment and had a nasty injury. We saw it happen and ran to help."

"I helped Dorylss get the horse out of the ditch and Teiyn made a salve for its injury. Then, when Dorylss wasn't paying attention, we used a little healing spell to speed up the salve's work. The caravan ended up making camp there to let the horse rest, and by morning, the horse was nearly healed."

"Dorylss was amazed," Teiyn said. "When we told him what we did, he didn't cry 'witchcraft' or 'sorcery.' He thanked us." She smiled, glancing at her brother, who mirrored her expression.

"Fate led us to you on the road to Braedel," Teiyn continued, bringing her gaze to Leyna again. "Dorylss was trying to load you, unconscious, on his horse to take you back to Rifillion when we passed by. We offered to help and he let us, remembering our previous encounter. After he saw how much you improved the first day, he decided to trust in us and told us everything about your journey."

"We want to help you any way we can," Taran said. "We hate the way Rothgard is twisting the use of magic into something evil. He will do nothing but perpetuate the stereotype among people that magic is bad, magic is witchcraft, when actually it can be used for good."

The door to the room burst open and the orange cat, who had closed its eyes and drifted off to sleep as they talked, leapt from his place on the windowsill. Dorylss came through the open door, his travel bag heavy with supplies. A smile spread from one ear to the other when his eyes landed on Leyna.

"Leyna!" he cried, shutting the door behind him with his foot. "You're awake!" He lowered the bag to the floor and strode to the bed, reaching out for her hands. "I was so worried about you, but Taran and Teiyn have kept you here with us."

Leyna couldn't help but reflect Dorylss's contagious grin. "I'm feeling quite well, actually." She turned to find Teiyn, who knelt by the fire, mixing some herbs into a steaming liquid in a tankard. "I'm very grateful."

"We're not entirely out of the woods yet," Teiyn pointed out, bringing Leyna the tankard, a sweet aroma drifting out of it. "I have a tonic for you. Drink the whole thing when I make them for you, and you'll be yourself again in no time."

"Yes, hopefully tomorrow we can all set out for Avaria," Taran added, packing some items from around the house in a little bag as though he hadn't suggested something utterly outrageous.

Leyna choked on her elixir and spat some back into the tankard. "Avaria?" she repeated, wide eyes flitting from Taran to Teiyn before landing on Dorylss. "Why on earth would we go to Avaria?"

Taran spoke first, turning away from the bag he packed to face Leyna. "Dorylss told us about your pendant."

"Well, Eamonn's pendant," Teiyn interjected, standing from the fire.

"We know it's an Avarian relic."

"And obviously what Rothgard is looking for."

"The best way to learn more about it is to go to Avaria and speak with the magical beings who live there."

Teiyn nodded in agreement, turning to Leyna and crossing her arms. "You have several days to wait for Kinrid, so the best use of that time would be to travel to Avaria."

"But I don't need to learn about it," Leyna asserted, setting the still-full tankard aside. "I already know what it can do and why Rothgard wants it. The pendant can harness the power of Avaria, the only magic known to bend will."

"But you don't know how it does that," Taran objected.

"Or how strong it is," Teiyn noted, with a glance toward Taran.

"Or why Rothgard might want it when he isn't a Kaethiri and can't access its magic."

"These are things that Rothgard has likely already learned."

"And if he hasn't, then you learning them puts you at an advantage."

Undaunted, Taran and Teiyn stood with arms crossed, their gazes pinned on Leyna, apparently ready to tackle whatever argument she might put up. Leyna found herself at a loss, no further defense to offer.

It didn't make sense to her to go out of their way to Avaria on the off chance they might be able to interview ancient magical beings who hadn't made themselves known for centuries. Gilleth and Kinrid expected to meet them there, in Braedel. *That* was real, something tangible in their crusade against Rothgard. Leyna lifted her bewildered eyes to Dorylss with her mouth agape, and he met her gaze with a shrug as one cheek tugged at his mouth.

"We have some time to spare. The worst that could happen is that we find nothing and we come back empty handed."

Leyna's mouth only fell further open, her eyebrows halfway up her forehead. She studied each of the three non-chalant people in the room with her, flabbergasted that they considered the idea a real plan. Was she the one going mad?

"Has everyone just forgotten that *no one* has been to Avaria—ever—in recorded history?" she asked as she raised herself from the bed. Leyna brought her eyebrows down, knitting them together and narrowing her eyes. "No one actually knows what lurks there. Magic, absolutely, but the ancient race who is said to live there?" She shook her head. "They haven't meddled in human affairs in centuries. Clearly, they want nothing to do with humans. It might be a death wish just to step foot in the forest!"

Teiyn's eyes lifted at the corners with the soft rise in her cheeks. "The Kaethiri have always been regarded as a peaceful people. Magical and set apart, yes, but never violent."

"They withdrew from the world of humans because they are too powerful and too much greater," Taran said with an identical subdued smile. "When they took the knowledge of magic from humans, they had no reason to mingle with us."

Blinking as she searched for words, Leyna plopped back down onto the bed, her legs giving way beneath her. It was clear she'd lost. These twins seemed disconnected from reality, but Dorylss was the real surprise. What about these two near strangers made him so willing to essentially turn over the decision making of their mission to them? Or did he really believe they needed to go to Avaria?

"So that's it?" Leyna asked, throwing her hands in the air before slapping her palms back down on her thighs. "If I'm doing better by tomorrow, we're just going traipsing into Avaria?"

Taran and Teiyn mirrored each other with an identical nod. Leyna turned to Dorylss again, hoping to get some kind of support from him. Instead, he tilted his head toward her and locked her eyes with a gentle but firm gaze. He agreed with the twins.

The orange cat appeared out of nowhere to jump onto Leyna's lap, and she flinched. He purred and rubbed his head against her hand, as though trying to win her over on the twins' behalf. She couldn't resist his affection, stroking him down his back and scratching between his ears.

"All right, then," she conceded, "I guess we're going to Avaria."

# TWENTY-THREE

FOR THE FIRST TIME since Eamonn had arrived, the sun shone bright and clear over Nidet. The clouds had parted at last, the hazy veil was scattered, and a fraction of the sun's warmth reached Eamonn in the middle of the courtyard. He leaned his head back and soaked up the weak rays, a welcome change from the cold, miserable, soggy days he'd known there.

Exactly how many days had passed since he awoke in the fortress, Eamonn didn't know. He'd lost touch with reality, dim days blending into dark nights and sleep coming at irregular intervals. His previous life felt long gone, belonging to a different world and time.

Every day, The Scourge dragged Eamonn from the dungeon and flogged him, turning his back into a mutilated mess of blood and torn flesh. But, after The Scourge stopped the whip, a hand would extend from the same dark figure hidden in the shadows, and magic would knit up Eamonn's back for the next session.

How long would the cycle go on? Eamonn hadn't decided whether or not to give Rothgard the pendant's location. If Leyna and Dorylss never made it, perhaps deciding to turn back or getting held up on their way before Eamonn found a chance to escape, it wouldn't make a difference. Regardless, he still couldn't determine if saving his friends' lives was a nobler goal than keeping Avarian magic out of Rothgard's hands for the good of the entire country.

Light footsteps clicked into earshot and Eamonn tensed, shutting his eyes and drawing his fingers in to form fists.

"Oi! Pretty boy!"

The Scourge's voice resounded through the silence in the courtyard. "The master is feeling generous!" he announced as he approached Eamonn. "You'll be getting a change of scenery."

Eamonn brought his head back down and rolled his eyes. Generous, hardly. Removing him from the only sun he'd seen since he was taken prisoner was exactly the opposite of generous.

Besides, based on the treatment he'd received and the fact that they'd been unable to get him to talk, Eamonn doubted this "change of scenery" was anywhere he wanted to be.

"Can't have you getting any ideas," The Scourge said as he pulled out a piece of black fabric from his belt and tied it around Eamonn's eyes. He cut the ropes that tied Eamonn's wrists to the posts, pulling his wrists behind his back and tying them together.

"Come on then, get those legs working!" he ordered, hoisting Eamonn to his feet. The Scourge had to support most of Eamonn's bodyweight, Eamonn's legs stiff and weak from lack of use.

His joints ached and his tight muscles throbbed with pain, but Eamonn found a little bit of strength and started putting one foot in front of the other on the soft, wet earth. Little by little, the steps became easier to take.

The ground under Eamonn's feet changed to stone and he found more stability in his legs. The Scourge led him through passageways and around corners, eventually descending a long staircase. The light filtering through his blindfold almost entirely petered out and the dank, stale smell of the dungeon met his nose. Once they stopped, a loud metal clanking sounded before Eamonn, and The Scourge tugged at him to take a few more steps before removing his blindfold.

Eamonn found himself in a dark stone room, the only light coming from torches in sconces from somewhere outside the room. To his left stood a heavy iron door with a small barred window at the top. To his right sat a rectangular table-like device, something he'd never seen before. Roller bars occupied both ends of the table, with handles on the flat sides of the rollers and two ropes wrapped around the circumference of each.

All the air flew from Eamonn's lungs and his chest caved in as his mind put the pieces together. The ropes would be tied to a victim's wrists and ankles and the handles would turn the rollers. At best, it would dislocate limbs. At the worst, it would rip them off entirely.

Eamonn sucked in a loud breath through his open mouth, his body starting to shake. Flogging, he could force himself to bear, even if it did tear his skin and muscles to shreds. But this...

This was meant to break him.

A pink glow on the horizon signaled the rising of the sun. Frost clung to the grass and a misty fog hung in the air. Leyna shivered. Even with her warm layers, she still felt a chill on her skin.

Leyna couldn't believe she was going along with this. She had done nothing but improve the day before, likely due to Teiyn's elixirs, and everyone had deemed her fit for travel. Part of her had hoped she wouldn't have recovered well enough to allow time for a trip to Avaria, but Teiyn clearly knew what she was doing with the potion-making. So Leyna gave up, helping get the horses ready for travel in the cold, but she waited to mount Rovis until the others were ready to go.

"Coming, Leyna?" Dorylss called, as Taran and Teiyn started ahead of him. Leyna yawned as she nodded and spurred the horse in their direction.

She raised a hand to touch the pendant hanging around her neck. If a journey to Avaria would help Eamonn, then she was happy to go.

Her mind drifted to Eamonn, wondering what he might be going through at the hands of Rothgard. Every thought unsettled her stomach and put her heart in her throat, and she tried to push them from her mind. Getting bogged down by questions that couldn't be answered and images that weren't real didn't help either her or Eamonn. She needed to stay present in the moment and focus on what she could actually do to save him.

They passed a few villages along the road, but they didn't stop for longer than a short rest to water the horses and have a bite to eat. The farther north they rode, though, the fewer towns and villages they came across. As night began to fall around them, the twins scouted out a good spot for them to set up camp.

Taran and Teiyn got to work building a fire in a more open area of the sparse forest through which they traveled. Leyna guided Rovis to a stop near them and tried to dismount, but she found herself weaker and stiffer than she expected, and her head had begun to ache again. Teiyn's tonic must have been wearing off.

"Here, let me help you," Dorylss said, going to Leyna. He gripped her waist and she pressed her hands onto his shoulders for support as he lowered her to the ground.

"Thanks," Leyna said, trying to smile but forming something similar to a grimace instead. "I don't think I'm completely well yet." She turned to the growing fire and said to Teiyn, "I could use another one of those elixirs, I think."

"I'll get to boiling some water for one as soon as the fire is hot enough," Teiyn responded with a grin, the bright flames casting light onto her face.

Taran gathered wood for the fire, taking three similar sized sticks to make a cooking stand: two sticks with branches that made a V at the top on either side with the third resting across them. Teiyn hung her pot full of water from the stand and got it boiling for Leyna's tonic.

Dorylss busied himself tying the four horses to nearby trees and Leyna took a seat on the ground beside Teiyn. She stuck out her hands to the fire, stretching her cold, stiff fingers.

"You two definitely know what you're doing," Leyna said, glancing from the fire to Taran, who worked at creating a simple shelter by tying a broad canvas sheet to trees.

"We've had a lot of practice," Teiyn replied, her eyes dropping a little as she stared into the fire. Leyna noticed the touch of sadness in her voice, but Teiyn said nothing else as she prodded the fire. Leyna decided to leave it alone. They sat side by side and watched the flames lick the air, the only sound the crackle of the burning wood.

Leyna tried to think of something to say, something to make the silence less obvious, but she came up short. She knew nothing about Teiyn or her brother, not really. They said they could use magic, but she had yet to see it. Leyna glimpsed Teiyn from her peripheral vision before casting her eyes at Taran across the fire. She trusted Dorylss, which had landed her in the northern Idyrrian woods with two complete strangers. Time would tell if they could earn her trust, too.

Dorylss helped Taran lay out bed rolls underneath the shelter before joining Leyna and Teiyn by the fire. Placing his pack on the ground next to him, Dorylss dug out some bread and wrapped cheese, handing out portions to each of them for their meager supper. He chatted with the twins, but Leyna had zoned out. Her eyes didn't leave the fire as she placed bites of food in her mouth. All she wanted was to go to sleep.

"Here," she heard Teiyn say next to her, drawing Leyna from her reverie. She held out a mug full of the same sweet-smelling elixir. "I added a little something extra to help you sleep. You'll feel better again when you wake in the morning."

Leyna offered Teiyn a small, appreciative smile as she took the mug. "Thanks."

She downed a hefty swig, and this time the tonic burned her mouth, her throat, and all the way down inside of her. But the burn wasn't the kind from a high temperature—it was more like a hot spice, almost, or a strong alcohol. The heat trickled into her bloodstream and sent warmth through her whole body.

Leyna welcomed the heat and gulped down the rest of the liquid. She'd only had time to hand the tankard back to Teiyn before her vision began to cloud. Teiyn spoke, saying something like "too fast" and "watch out." Someone supported Leyna's back as her eyelids drooped and her limbs became heavy. Voices mumbled, and someone laughed. Strong arms scooped her up, and she felt like she was flying through the cold night air before she touched the ground and drifted off.

One thing Eamonn had learned about Rothgard during his time as a prisoner was that the man did nothing hastily. Everything was calculated and methodical. Rothgard had weakened Eamonn before having him removed from the posts in the courtyard and taken to a new location within the castle, preventing an escape attempt. He used his friends' safety as a bargaining chip, and either way Eamonn chose, Rothgard would win.

For his next move, Rothgard had The Scourge strap Eamonn to his next source of agony for an entire night, building his anxiety and dread at what awaited him. Eamonn got no more than a few minutes of sleep all night long, unable to relax with his ankles and wrists tied down on either end of the rigid rack and his mind swirling with the possibilities that lay in his future.

Leyna and Dorylss might be close now. Eamonn had no idea how quickly they were traveling or how much time had passed since they were spotted in southern Idyrria, but each minute that passed was another that brought them closer to Nidet.

Eamonn no longer knew what he thought was the better of the two choices Rothgard had given him. He might have had a preference before, but the lines had become so blurred the longer he waited and the more torture he endured. Why was he holding back? If information kept Leyna and Dorylss safe, then he'd give them information.

Oh, right. The whole "putting magic right into Rothgard's hands" bit. The future of the world as they knew it was potentially at stake. That would be on him if he gave up the pendant's location.

But Rothgard couldn't even use the pendant. And if Leyna arrived on the island with the pendant, she was as good as dead, *and* Rothgard would have exactly what he wanted.

A clang resounded at the iron door and a key rattled in the lock. Eamonn's heart started to hammer against his ribcage as the door to his dungeon room swung open. Against all reason, he hoped maybe someone brought him some food or water and it wasn't yet time to see what the machine could do.

"Sleep well?" asked The Scourge.

No, not food. Eamonn stared straight ahead at the ceiling, his pulse throbbing in his ears and his body starting to tremble. He wouldn't say anything—he couldn't. His voice had vanished in anticipation of his suffering.

"I figured as much," The Scourge said, coming to the rack. "You've had plenty of time to consider the offer the master has given you," he murmured, leaning in close to Eamonn's ear. "This might just be your last chance to take it."

The pounding of Eamonn's heart intensified. What did that mean? Were Leyna and Dorylss close? Or did Rothgard plan to torture him to death? Surely not; they needed him alive to find the pendant.

*Right?*

"Well," said The Scourge, stepping back and grasping the handle attached to the roller by Eamonn's head, "time to get cracking." He spoke the last word with an ugly sneer, reveling in the double meaning.

The Scourge started turning the handle and the rollers began to rotate, pulling Eamonn's arms and legs in opposite directions. At first, the stretch felt surprisingly nice, decompressing Eamonn's spine and loosening his joints. But The Scourge continued to turn the handle, his pace slow and steady, the ropes wrapping around the rollers and tugging at his limbs.

The stretch became uncomfortable. Eamonn already wanted it to stop. He balled his hands into fists and clenched his jaw, trying to pull his arms and legs back toward his body. Of course, it did nothing. He opened his mouth and let out a grunt as the bones in his limbs started to loosen from the joints.

Pain surged down Eamonn's arms and legs.

*Leyna's on her way here.*

His skin stretched, covering his body too tightly.

*I have to protect her. I won't let anything bad happen to her.*

His limbs pulled farther away, begging to come free and end the strain.

He had no certainty of keeping her safe. Nothing guaranteed they wouldn't all die. Only one thing might save her.

His left shoulder popped, sending a lightning bolt of pain down his arm. Eamonn cried out in anguish, no relief to be found as the rack kept him held tight.

"I'LL TALK!" he shrieked. "I'LL TELL YOU!"

At once, The Scourge turned the handle in the opposite direction and returned Eamonn's limbs to his body. His left shoulder seared in pain, and Eamonn half expected his arm to be ripped off. He glanced to his left and saw his arm still attached, but hanging off his body at a distorted angle.

"You're a hard one to break, you know," The Scourge said, and Eamonn could hear the sick smile on his lips. "Most people would have caved long before now. But you," he said, backing away from the rack, "you were stubborn. It's good you've finally seen reason."

"The offer," Eamonn choked out, slow tears falling from the corners of his eyes.

"Yes, the offer is good," The Scourge confirmed. "Your friends will be spared should they make it into the fortress."

"Your word."

"My word isn't the one y'need," The Scourge uttered, and the silhouette of a man stepped into the room, lingering in the shadows of the cell. Eamonn turned to look, the closest he had ever been to his captor, but he couldn't get a good look in the darkness.

The Scourge turned to face the man before returning his gaze to Eamonn.

"You have his word," he said, and silence fell in the dungeon room as they waited for Eamonn to reveal his secret.

"She has it," he murmured, barely able to find his voice. "The girl on her way here. Leyna. She has it."

More silence. Did they not believe him? Would they keep torturing him?

"She's bringing it right to me," said a new voice, as smooth as silk, rich as earth, and slippery as ice. He'd heard it before, in the library in Erai. Even then, Eamonn had only seen Rothgard's back. The figure stepped into view beside The Scourge, and for the first time, Eamonn had a face to put with a name.

Something in the glint of Rothgard's icy blue eyes and his malicious smile made Eamonn forget his pain for a moment, his calm assurance sending a chill down Eamonn's spine.

"You could have spared yourself much pain with those few words." Rothgard turned on his heel and strode out of the cell, his footsteps the same slow, heavy clop from Eamonn's first night on the island.

Eamonn released a breath. He came back to the world, feeling his pain again, but worse; his heart thrummed without a pause and he felt sick to his stomach. Nothing about Rothgard seemed honest or trustworthy. Leyna was his new target.

*What have I done?*

# TWENTY-FOUR

THE SNOWFALL BEGAN HALFWAY through their second day of travel, off and on without accumulating more than a dusting on the ground. The wind picked up and the temperature dropped overnight, and on the third day, snow came down steadily, covering the land around them in a blanket of white. The snow slowed their progress, so they had to camp one more night before reaching Avaria.

Leyna never knew she could be so cold. Taran and Teiyn built fires where they would set up camp, clearing the snow around them. They managed to keep the fires going overnight, but the constant cold penetrated Leyna's core. She rubbed her hands together and massaged the blood back to her toes as often as she could, but she could only do so much, especially when away from the fire.

Dorylss didn't seem bothered by the weather. "It's only autumn," he had said to Leyna as they traveled through the snow. "This will melt after a couple of days." He'd glanced over at her as she shivered and he offered her his cloak to go over her own. "It's a good thing we're going now. I wouldn't advise a trip like this in the winter unless we were prepared."

Teiyn continued to make Leyna's tonics—not always with the special sleeping ingredient—which warmed her better than any fire could. They all crowded together under the shelter at night to utilize their body heat, but Leyna still couldn't get warm. For someone who hadn't even wanted to make the trek to Avaria in the first place, the weather only soured her mood even more.

*This had better be worth it.*

The sun rose high in the clear sky on their fourth day of travel, too small and distant to provide real warmth. The group had left the woods behind that morning, traveling up and down over hilly, rocky terrain where the snow had started to melt in spots.

Dorylss stopped his horse at the edge of a cliff, Leyna bringing up the rear. She stopped behind the others, squinting with the bright reflection of sunlight off the snow. Had they gone the wrong way? She leaned forward on Rovis with a sigh, wishing they'd never taken this trip. They'd have to go all the way back now completely empty handed.

"Leyna," Dorylss called from the cliff's edge, "come here."

Huffing, Leyna sat up and guided Rovis around the other horses. She opened her eyes despite the bright sun and gasped.

She'd heard stories of Avaria throughout her childhood, about the magical forest of eternal summer in the far northern reaches of the continent. She'd always believed it existed despite the impossibility, but to see it with her eyes... she couldn't find the words.

"That," Dorylss said, "is Avaria."

The short cliff stood about ten or fifteen feet over a lush green forest beneath them, stretching as far as they could see. Snow still covered the land behind them, but not a single snowflake touched the bright green of Avaria's trees.

"How do we get down there?" Taran asked, peering over the edge of the cliff.

Dorylss studied the rocky crag and the landscape around them. "The earth slopes this way," he said, pointing to his left. "We might find a way down."

Dorylss led the crew along the cliff's edge until the bluff became a ridge they could guide the horses over. Leyna kept her eyes on the forest as she rode, her uneasiness about their journey abated after its appearance. Maybe this hadn't been such a bad idea after all.

They stopped once they were at the level of the forest, where frozen earth and snow gave way to rich dirt and grass just about a meter from the forest's edge.

"I can't believe I'm seeing Avaria with my own eyes," Teiyn breathed, her eyes wide with awe.

"It's kind of incredible that people don't come out here much," Taran murmured. "It's truly a sight to behold."

Leyna stepped Rovis a couple of paces ahead of the group, bringing his hooves to the line of white on the ground. A soft glow, the color of the sun in the late afternoon, hung within the trees, bathing the inside of the forest in gentle light. Leyna slipped off of Rovis's back, feeling drawn into the forest from somewhere deep within her.

"Wait, Leyna!" Dorylss cried.

"Stop!" Taran and Teiyn proclaimed in unison.

Leyna turned around to face them, still sitting on their horses. "What?"

The three others shot glances at each other before landing their eyes on Leyna.

"Maybe this isn't the best idea after all," Dorylss remarked.

"I agree," Teiyn admitted, swallowing at the awe in her expression transformed to fear. "It doesn't exactly feel safe anymore."

Leyna frowned. Was this a joke? "So, what, we rode all the way out here in the freezing cold for nothing? To turn around?" She put her hands on her hips. "Might I remind you, this was *your* idea."

"Yes, it was, but now—" Taran searched for words, his eyes flitting over the trees ahead of him. "The forest feels... foreboding."

"I'm dreading going in there," Teiyn added.

"This was a bad idea."

"We should just go back."

"No!" Leyna replied, a crease forming in between her eyebrows. "We've traveled for days through the coldest weather I have ever experienced just to get right here. We made it. We're not going back. Besides," she added, turning back to face the forest, "it doesn't feel like that to me. It seems rather lovely, actually. Inviting."

"Leyna, you shouldn't go in there," Dorylss called, but Leyna ignored him.

She took a few more steps as her companions tried to convince her to turn around, but she kept going until she could no longer hear them. What were they so afraid of? All three of them had been so eager to go, so what had changed?

Leyna didn't stop, unable to resist the forest's pull. Trees with dark green leaves closed in around her, the underbrush minimal and tidy. Rays of golden light intensified as she delved into the forest, as though a bright, low sun hung just above the treetops and filtered its light down through the leaves. A faint tintinnabulation floated through the air from every direction, like the soft ringing of chimes.

Energy filled the forest. Leyna could feel it coursing through her, like the forest was alive and vibrant. She extended a hand in front of her briefly before closing it into a soft fist, feeling a tingle over her palm.

Leyna lifted her face up toward the treetops as leaves fluttered in a gentle breeze and glimmering flecks of light floated around her. She'd left the cold outside, the forest warm like the end of spring. A force she couldn't identify drew her deeper into its depths, and she didn't resist. The music of a trickling brook pricked her ears, but before Leyna could spot it, a melodic female voice spoke.

"Do not be afraid, Leyna of Teravale."

Leyna stopped and glanced around, searching for the source of the sound. "I'm not afraid," she replied.

"Come further," the echoing voice commanded.

Leyna obeyed, strolling over the leaves and brush on the forest floor. Her eyes wandered all around the forest and above her to the treetops again, but she found nothing. When she brought her face back down, she inhaled a sharp breath at the sight of a figure before her.

A beautiful woman, though not a human woman, had appeared in front of her. A faint light surrounded her as though her milky skin glowed, illuminating her sharp features. Her hair was a silvery-white, flowing in gentle curls down to her waist and adorned with long strings of pearlescent jewels. She wore a gauzy dress the color of moonlight, cinched at the shoulders and waist with white flowers seemingly woven into the fabric.

Leyna closed her mouth and let the breath out slowly through her nose. If everything around her hadn't buzzed with energy, if every nerve in her body didn't prickle with life, she might have thought she'd strayed into a dream. Nothing about this place, about this woman, made rational sense. But Leyna knew, without a shadow of a doubt, that she stood in the presence of a Kaethiri.

"We have been expecting you," the woman murmured, her voice like a song.

"You have?" Leyna asked, only a little surprised. She tried to take another step, but she couldn't move her feet. Leyna dropped her eyes to her boots, but nothing about her feet looked unusual.

"You can't expect the presence of a Réalta in your world to go unnoticed."

Leyna met the woman's lavender eyes again and knitted her eyebrows together. "A Réalta?"

"The amulet you wear," the Kaethiri responded, and placed her hand over an identical pendant adorning her neck. "One of our stars."

Leyna brought her hand to Eamonn's necklace and pulled it out from under her shirt. The green jewel in the center glowed faintly and Leyna's heart jumped.

"What exactly can it do?"

A soft smile spread across the Kaethiri's face. "Let's not get ahead of ourselves. We should begin with an introduction." She let the hand at her amulet fall and held it, palm up, at the level of her chest. "My name is Imrilieth, and I am Queen of the Kaethiri."

Leyna's cheek lifted for a moment in disbelief. *The queen?* Her eyes wandered past Imrilieth, looking for any others that might be lingering in the distance. "How many of you are there?"

"Our number is ninety-nine, after the one we exiled."

"Exiled?" Leyna repeated.

"Yes." Imrilieth took a few silent steps in a half-circle around Leyna, her bare feet poking out from underneath her clean garments. "We exiled one of our own. But first, you must understand the nature of the Kaethiri."

Imrilieth stopped, clasping her hands in front of her in a delicate grip and her eyes changed to a light blue. "The Kaethiri are magic made into form, the only true source of magic in this world. We first offered it to humans many ages ago as a gift. For humans to use magic, it has to be drawn from the energy in the world—wind, water, flame, and such. But, after years of peaceful magic, some humans began to draw energy for magic from life.

"We knew then humans could no longer be trusted with magic. But magic, once bestowed, cannot be withdrawn entirely. The Kaethiri left the company of humans, taking our strong source magic back into our realm. We removed the desire to practice magic from humans' wills. After a few generations, magic among humans died out."

"Then how can someone learn to use magic now?" Leyna asked, thinking of Taran and Teiyn beyond the forest's edge.

"With the proper instruction, one can still learn how to pull from the energy of the world to cast magic," Imrilieth answered, retracing her steps in the half circle and coming to a stop by a tree. "The Evil One from Wolstead is learning magic, it is true. We cannot prevent that."

The hairs on Leyna's arms stood up. "You know of Rothgard?" If they did, maybe they could help.

"Of course we do," Imrilieth replied, reaching her hand out to the tree and idly running her fingertips over the bark. "We know much more about the workings of humans than you realize. Though we are no longer among you, we are still very aware of the happenings of the human world."

"So you know what he seeks?" Leyna's heart started to thump.

"He seeks Kaethiri magic. He seeks the Réalta you wear." Imrilieth brought her hands back together as she turned her gaze back toward Leyna, her golden eyes piercing into Leyna from under stern brows. "A piece of Avarian magic should never have ended up in your world, but it has, and you must never allow him to take hold of it."

All of Leyna's breath left her lungs with the intensity of Imrilieth's expression, and her shoulders shook despite the warm air. "What would happen if it did?" she asked after taking a breath. When Imrilieth didn't answer, Leyna tried a different question. "How exactly did the amulet end up in our world?"

Imrilieth tilted her chin up and her gaze left Leyna. "This Réalta found its way into your world because one of our own fell prey to the wiles of humans."

Leyna waited, silent, as Imrilieth resumed pacing in her half-circle, the jewels in her hair tinkling with each step. She reached the end of her path in one direction and turned back before she spoke.

"Though we no longer dwell among humans, we have remained involved with human affairs from within our realm. Now, you must understand," Imrilieth stopped and faced Leyna again, her eyes blue, "the Kaethiri do not love as humans do. We need only each other. But, two decades ago, a human man caught the attention of a Kaethiri called Laielle. Even now, the wisest of us do not understand what caused her to feel the pull toward a human.

"Laielle fell in love with the man, leaving the forest and concealing her true nature to be with him. In doing so, she broke the laws of our people. She was exiled and stripped of her magical abilities, though she begged for forgiveness and to not be banished."

Leyna saw Imrilieth's eyes change to gray before she cast them down to the ground in front of her. "But it was too late. She had made her decisions, and there was no going back. So, she stayed with the man. She became pregnant by him and bore a son, but the birth killed her. It was a blow to us all."

Imrilieth's glow faded. She kept her gaze on the ground, clasping her hands in front of her again. "For thousands of years, the one hundred Kaethiri lived together as the embodiment of magic," Imrilieth continued, her voice softer and melancholy. "Exiling Laielle brought pain upon us, but when she died, we felt the loss of a part of ourselves."

The Kaethiri Queen paused for a moment with her head lowered, and when she lifted it again, her glow returned. She strolled to the other side of Leyna, looking straight ahead into the forest. "We kept her son here for the first few years of his life. None of the Kaethiri had ever borne offspring, and we had no way of knowing if he would develop the magical abilities of his mother. We returned him to the care of his father when we determined that any magic he might have possessed had not manifested itself."

"The son," Leyna interrupted, her eyes wide as her cheeks tugged up the corners of her mouth. "His name is Eamonn, isn't it?"

Imrilieth dipped her head in a low nod. "Your friend Eamonn is Laielle's child. The amulet hanging around your neck is connected with Laielle, and, therefore, Eamonn."

Leyna looked down to her chest and touched the glowing pendant with light fingertips. "So, if the magic is connected with Eamonn," she asked, returning her gaze to Imrilieth, "does that mean Rothgard can't use it?"

"No, Rothgard cannot wield it any more than you or I can," Imrilieth answered, and relief replaced worry in Leyna's heart. But Imrilieth's eyes changed to brown, and she took three slow steps in Leyna's direction, the first time she'd walked toward Leyna during their meeting. Leyna held her breath, anxiety creeping back in.

"He would know this, yet he still seeks it," Imrilieth murmured. "I fear for Laielle's son."

Panic rose up in Leyna, but her feet remained locked in place. "Why? Is Rothgard going to... do something to him?" The word "kill" wouldn't form on her lips.

"We cannot speak to that which we do not know," Imrilieth replied, taking back her three steps. "The Evil One has not yet revealed his plan."

"Well, what does he want with Avarian magic? Surely you at least know that."

Imrilieth did not pace around Leyna again, instead locking eyes with Leyna. "When we gave humans the gift of magic, we kept it limited. We did not give them a share of all of our abilities.

"Kaethiri have a unique power over humans. We can control a human's will with as little as a thought. The subject would never know they were being controlled. We seldom used this power, and we did not bestow it on humans for apparent reasons.

"It would appear that when the Evil One learned of the Kaethiri's ability to bend the wills of humans, he put all his energy into finding a way to obtain it. He came to Avaria on his way to Idyrria, but he never ventured inside, of course. The magic within the forest fills the hearts of those who reach our borders with trepidation so that none dare to enter."

"What about me?" Leyna wondered, too curious to care that she cut Imrilieth off. "I'd been dreading everything about the journey, but it all changed once we reached the forest. I was the only one of my companions who wanted to enter."

A smile spread across Imrilieth's face and her eyes turned purple. "You bear Laielle's Réalta, the magic of which belongs here. The magic of the Kaethiri drew you inside."

Leyna pressed her lips together in a slight grin, thankful more than ever that she had kept Eamonn's pendant with her. She would have never made it inside Avaria without it.

"So, when Rothgard came to Avaria, he hoped to take one of your amulets?" Leyna asked, returning to the previous conversation.

"We do not know the details of his plan," Imrilieth told her as her eyes darkened, "only that he intended to seek out a way to obtain our magic. He needs it to accomplish his goal of bringing Sarieth under his rule."

Leyna swallowed. If Rothgard had gone to Avaria in search of their magic, he was serious. Few people ventured to Avaria, and those who did were usually either dared to go, curious to a fault, or lost.

"Though we do not know what it is, we believe he has found a way to use our magic," Imrilieth continued. "One possibility is through Laielle's son. The Evil One would not be able to command a Kaethiri, but the boy's magic has only now made an appearance. It is weak and untrained. It's unlikely he would resist The Evil One's demands, compelled to be a source of magic for him."

Leyna's heart lodged itself in her throat. "What does that mean?"

Imrilieth released herself from Leyna's stare and resumed her slow stride. "It could mean a number of things."

Imrilieth clearly intended to be cryptic with her words, but did she mean to be so irritating, too? Even after an audience with the Queen of the Kaethiri, this trip might be worthless after all.

"If you're right, and Rothgard used Eamonn to access Kaethiri magic, he could control minds?" Leyna said, though it came out like a question. She hoped it was still hypothetical. "Anyone he wanted to control, he could just make them do whatever he wished?"

"Yes." Imrilieth stopped and turned to stroll in the other direction. "Initially, only people near him would fall prey. As he becomes more familiar with the magic, his power could traverse greater distances. He might even be able to get into the minds of people just by envisioning them."

Leyna took a faltering step back. "He could do whatever he wanted," she breathed.

"Which is why he must be stopped," Imrilieth said, her tone earnest and firm. "He could use our magic to build armies, make people love him, or even have the kings abdicate. That might only be the beginning. If he is able to unlock Avarian magic, there is not much he would be unable to do. The Réalta is the key to his success."

All of Leyna's breath left her lungs and her chest caved in. She brought her hand up to her breastbone as her heart dropped, and her fingers found the pendant hanging from her neck. She had promised Eamonn she would keep it safe, but instead, she was carrying it straight to Nidet. She and Dorylss had started on this quest to save Eamonn, only entertaining the idea of trying to defeat Rothgard because otherwise Eamonn would stay on the run.

Now, if she failed, she could potentially facilitate the demise of the world as they knew it. Her chest heaved with shaky breaths. She was certifiably in over her head.

No. This wasn't her responsibility, and neither would it be her fault. Leyna shot her eyes to the Kaethiri Queen. "This is *your* power," she accused, almost angry. "*You* are the ones who have the power to control wills. You are more powerful than Rothgard could ever be! Why don't you stop him? Why don't you use your power to intervene and change his will?"

Imrilieth tensed her jaw and tilted her chin upward once more. "We will not."

"Why not? You have the power!" Leyna cried. "You could end this!"

Imrilieth's eyes returned to a golden color, and she stiffened her shoulders. "Humans must bear the weight of others' decisions, for good or for evil. We cannot interfere."

Leyna stared at Imrilieth, her mouth hanging open. "You *have* to!"

"No," Imrilieth replied, and the force of the word rippled through the forest like thunder. "We must not. The events of the world must play out as intended. What has been set in motion must not be stopped by any outside force."

"How can you even say that?" Leyna exclaimed. Heat rose to her face as her temper flared. She couldn't believe what she was hearing. "Don't you feel any obligation to the rest of us? Why can't you step in and use your powers for the good of the world?"

"It is not our place." Imrilieth's features remained composed, but her resounding voice caused the earth below Leyna's feet to tremble. "You want us to intervene now, and surely humankind would want our help again in the future.

"But where does one draw the line? What is too far? Bending a person's will is an immense violation of that person's humanity, whether it be for good or for evil. Human volition is each individual's right. You would begin to hate us, to resent our power. You would beg us to leave you alone. We do not meddle in human affairs for a reason."

Defeated, Leyna slumped her shoulders and she stared at her feet. Maybe Imrilieth was right. Ironically enough, the Kaethiri might be too powerful to get involved.

"Do not be so disheartened, Leyna." Imrilieth's gentle voice drew Leyna's gaze back up to her now-blue eyes. "There is a time the Kaethiri would intervene. We will not sit by and let the world crumble." She gave Leyna a small smile. "We aren't ruthless."

Leyna inhaled and tried to reflect the smile. Imrilieth seemed to offer hope, but how much would the world go through before the Kaethiri decided to step in?

"Do you think..." Leyna began, then licked her lips as she planned her words. They came out in a breath. "Can we at least save Eamonn?"

Imrilieth began to move, closing the gap between them with carefully placed steps until she stood right in front of her. Leyna had to lift her face to Imrilieth towering over her, almost unable to breathe with the magical being so close. The glow of her flawless skin seemed to touch Leyna, and the air around them hummed with energy.

"You are the only one who can." The Kaethiri laid a gentle hand on Leyna's cheek and closed her eyes for a brief moment. A tingling sensation erupted on Leyna's face and spread throughout her body. If her feet had been released, she might have pulled away from Imrilieth's touch. As it was, Leyna had no choice but to accept her magic.

Imrilieth released Leyna's face and took two steps back, rejoining her hands together in front of her ethereal gown. Leyna lifted her fingers to feel the cheek where Imrilieth's hand had pressed, the tingling of her magic gone.

"How?" Leyna asked. Something had happened, but she had no idea what.

Imrilieth grinned and her eyes changed again to lavender. "A gift. You will know when the time is right."

A crease formed between Leyna's eyebrows, but she knew she would get no further explanation from the Kaethiri. The pressure at her feet released. Their meeting had ended, and Leyna turned to go. Before she took a step, though, one more question came to her mind.

"I'm curious," she said, meeting Imrilieth's gaze one final time, "if there are ninety-nine of you, where are the others?"

"All around us," she replied, opening her arms with her palms up. "They simply chose to not reveal themselves."

A dimple showed in Leyna's right cheek with a last glance at the seemingly empty forest around them. The thrumming of energy in the air—it matched the hum that had emanated from Imrilieth, only at a lower intensity. The entire company of Kaethiri had surrounded her from the moment she'd stepped foot into Avaria.

Before her, a path had appeared to guide her back out of the forest. Leyna glanced back over her shoulder, but Imrilieth had vanished.

If someone told her so, Leyna might have believed the whole thing had been a dream. She couldn't prove to her companions that she'd actually seen or spoken to anyone. Leyna replayed the meeting in her mind as she strolled down the earthen path, determined to remember everything.

She could see the forest's edge. Beyond it, she spotted the rocky cliff-face as tall as a house, and in between waited the friends she'd left behind. Dorylss had dismounted Bardan, holding both his and Rovis's reins as he spoke to Taran and Teiyn atop their horses. No one noticed Leyna's approach till stepped past the trees.

"Leyna!" all three cried out at once.

Dorylss handed the reins to the twins and ran to Leyna, catching her in a tight embrace.

"We've been so worried!" he told her, holding her close as if he'd thought he'd never see her again. "You've been gone for so long, and something about the forest feels so unsafe. We were certain something had happened to you in there!"

"I'm fine!" Leyna reassured, grinning as Dorylss released her.

"We were just debating who would go in after you," Taran said, his clear voice bouncing off the side of the cliff. "Of course, I had volunteered."

"You liar!" Teiyn accused, turning to Taran with her eyes narrowed. "You did no such thing! You had nominated Dorylss to go into the forest."

"Well, I considered volunteering," Taran admitted, "but I thought Dorylss was better suited to the task."

Teiyn rolled her eyes. "Right. That's it." She faced Leyna and handed her the reins of Eamonn's horse. "What was it like in there? Why were you gone so long?"

Leyna's cheeks lifted, the memory of Avaria's magic fresh in her mind. "I met the Queen of the Kaethiri."

Teiyn gasped and leaned back on her horse, eyes wide. Shouts of "No!" and "Impossible!" came from the men to her right.

"It's true!" Leyna promised, putting her foot in a stirrup and swinging the other leg over Rovis. "Let's ride and I'll tell you all about it."

They retraced their steps up to the cliff's edge and Leyna started recounting the events in detail. The farther from Avaria they rode, the more the encounter felt like a dream. The others expressed no reservation in believing her, though. They listened with rapt attention, sometimes asking questions or commenting with awe.

Leyna only wished Eamonn had been there to experience it himself.

# TWENTY-FIVE

AFTER EAMONN'S CONFESSION, IT seemed Rothgard and
The Scourge had forgotten him. Well, perhaps not forgotten,
but had turned their attention to more important things.

The Scourge had twisted his hurt arm and jammed it back
into his shoulder, causing an agonized scream to erupt from
Eamonn. Afterward, though, the pain shooting from his
shoulder diminished to a throb.

Eamonn had then been led from the torture chamber to
a simple cell in the dungeon with a barred door and small
cot. Rothgard hadn't left him to die or finished the job, so he
must still want Eamonn alive. But why? Would there be more
questioning? Maybe Rothgard wanted to wait until Dorylss
and Leyna arrived and made sure Eamonn had spoken the
truth.

He lay on the cot, staring at the ceiling and trying to figure out if he had done the right thing by telling Rothgard about Leyna and the pendant. He wished more than anything that he could warn Leyna and Dorylss, tell them not to come. He wasn't worth it.

Eamonn did them no good locked away in a cell. If he could manage a way out, his friends would have no need to come after him anymore. With any luck, he'd find them around the same time they arrived on the island, and they could all turn around and go back together. It was wishful thinking, more than anything, but it got Eamonn's heart pumping.

He'd been left alone for so long, aside from the delivery of food and water. This might be his chance.

Where was his supposed magic when he needed it? After its unexpected appearance in Caen when it helped him get away from Rothgard's men, Eamonn hadn't remotely felt it again. He'd gone back to being the perfectly ordinary thief-turned-merchant he'd always been.

But even a perfectly ordinary thief-turned-merchant could pick a lock.

Eamonn studied the barred door at the entrance to his cell. It wasn't thick and heavy like the leaden door to the torture chamber with an exterior padlock. The barred door was comparatively light and simple, its lock probably similar to common locks on regular doors: the types of locks Eamonn had picked hundreds of times.

He sat up on the cot as his pulse raced, considering escape as a real possibility. All he needed were lockpicks, or at least some metal he could fashion into lockpicks. He scanned his eyes over his cell, landing on his plate and spoon from his meal earlier.

The spoon.

Eamonn's stomach flipped and he left the cot, picking up the spoon and examining it in the firelight from the dungeon's torches. A thin handle attached to the shallow, round bowl of the spoon. It might actually work.

He would need all the strength he could muster, though, to bend and manipulate the spoon. A week or more of meager meals and regular beatings had debilitated him, so finding enough strength to break the spoon wouldn't be easy.

Wait—the metal bars of the door. They were sturdy enough for him to push the spoon against and supply significant resistance.

Eamonn took one deep breath and glanced outside the cell. He saw no guards posted anywhere in his field of view. The little noise he'd make shouldn't attract anyone farther off than inside the dungeon, so he crouched beside the cell door, spoon in hand.

He pressed the spoon against one of the metal bars of his cell door, bending it around the bar where the handle and spoon met. Eamonn flipped the spoon around and bent it at the joint the other way, repeating it over and over until the handle snapped off.

Eamonn held the handle up at eye level and examined it. The end was rough, but it should be thin enough for the large lock on the cell door. All right, he had one lockpick. He needed one more.

Where could he get another slender piece of metal? He didn't have another spoon. All that remained in the cell was a wooden plate, a bucket for his waste, and the cot.

The wooden cot would be held together by nails. He might be able to ease one out and use it as his other pick.

Bounding to the cot, Eamonn searched the planks for a nail he could try to pull from the wood, and he found one at the foot of the little bed. The wood had expanded around the head of a nail and the nail had begun to protrude.

Eamonn took the bowl part of the broken spoon and tried to tuck it between the nail and the plank, hoping to use it as leverage to work the nail out, but he couldn't quite fit the spoon behind the nail.

He sat back with a huff. Now that he had escape on his mind, he couldn't shake the idea. He had to figure out something to get the nail out.

Eamonn's first makeshift lockpick caught his eye, lying on the cold dirt floor. It was no thinner than the bowl of the spoon, but it was sharper. He could use it to scrape away at the soft, weathered wood of the bed and expose the nail head a little more.

The wood around the nail crumbled to dust as Eamonn chipped away at it with the spoon handle. He bit his bottom lip as he wedged the spoon's bowl underneath the nail, but he couldn't get the nail to come out. He didn't have the proper leverage. What he needed was an opposite force to give him greater pull on the nail, but that would mean putting pressure on his left arm and injured shoulder.

Eamonn gritted his teeth and put his hand to the wood of the cot, anticipating the pain in his shoulder. But it would be fleeting, and it might give him a way out of the dungeon.

He pressed his left hand against the cot and winced, a sharp pain instantly shooting through his shoulder, but it gave him the leverage he needed to work the nail the rest of the way out.

He let his arm drop, his shoulder burning. He had the nail.

Eamonn's heart felt lighter and his body started to tremble with excitement. He wouldn't allow himself to celebrate yet, though. He wouldn't do that until he was long gone from this place.

He pushed the side of the nail against the cell's stone wall and used the spoon handle to help bend the tip of the nail into a slight hook. He licked his lips as he held the two picks in front of him, pleased with his ingenuity. Now, to see if they actually worked.

Crouching by the cell door, Eamonn surveyed the dungeon again to make sure no one had entered. No, still empty. He closed his eyes as he filled his lungs with a deep breath and drew out its release, hoping to steady his shaking hands. The nervous anticipation of his escape attempt coupled with lack of proper nourishment made his hands quiver, and he needed them as steady as possible.

Eamonn took another deep breath and held it, pressing his lips together to keep from accidentally releasing it. His heart slammed against his ribcage and he heard it thumping in his ears. He slid the picks into the lock on the inside of the door, feeling the tools and imagining the inner workings of the lock in his mind. He maneuvered the picks, making slight adjustments as he felt and heard slight changes with the lock, until he felt the mechanism give and he turned the picks all the way.

Eamonn opened his mouth and his pent-up breath burst out. It actually worked. He pushed on the barred door, the metal hinges squeaking with the movement. Eamonn froze, cringing with the sharp noise that had to have filled the dungeon.

But nothing happened. No one came. Eamonn pushed the door further, the squeaking stopping after he'd opened it a little more, and he slipped his body out of the cell.

His mind raced as he took silent, crouched steps through the dungeon. He'd made it out, but he wasn't free. He wouldn't be free until he found his way out of the castle.

Except he'd never traveled through the castle without a blindfold. In the times The Scourge had brought him to and from the dungeon between his floggings, Eamonn had mapped out the part of the fortress that connected the dungeon to the courtyard. It probably wouldn't help him that much, but it was all he had to go on.

A stone staircase that led out sat on the opposite side of the dungeon, and Eamonn climbed the steps up to a wooden door at the landing. He almost pulled out his picks again to unlock the door before he even tried opening it, but he changed his mind, lifting the door's handle in a quiet motion. Eamonn raised his eyebrows as the door unlatched.

No guards and an unlocked dungeon door. His insides knotted together. Would they really leave him that unguarded? He couldn't help but feel like something wasn't right.

The door to the dungeon opened into a small torchlit antechamber, the only way out another staircase, curving in a tight corridor. Eamonn crept up the stairs, taking slow, quiet steps as he listened out for any kind of noise. He might as well have been a thief again—except he was trying to break out rather than in.

Eamonn almost chuckled with the thought. He never imagined his skills from being a thief would come into play in a good way.

He clung to the shadows of the wall as he approached the top of the staircase, light from another source growing brighter as he got closer. Stopping before the corridor opened into a broader passage, he strained his ears for any sound. Distant footsteps died out and a door shut somewhere far away. Nothing else.

Taking the last few steps, Eamonn stuck his head out of the opening and studied the wide, empty passage. Old, faded paintings hung on the walls, and a tattered runner covered part of the floor. Lanterns hung from the ceiling, but some of the light filling the corridor was sunlight.

The sunlight pulled him down the passage into another corridor, flooded with light from windows spaced along the wall. He'd found an exterior wall, which meant he had a greater chance of finding a door to the outside.

The clop of footsteps on stone hit his ears. Eamonn's heart rate spiked and he ducked behind a column on the other side of the sound. The footsteps became clearer, continuing with purpose at the end of the passage before becoming muffled again.

Eamonn poked his head out from behind the pillar once the sound had dissipated, finding the corridor empty once again. He picked up his pace, staying low and keeping his steps silent. With freedom so close, he couldn't get caught now.

Turning a corner, Eamonn's heart leapt to his throat and he rejoiced. A massive wooden door awaited him at the end of the passage, indisputably a door that opened to the outside world. With a quick glance all around him to make sure he was alone, he started to run toward the door, ready to end this nightmare.

His sprint was cut short when a door along one wall opened and a man stepped out. Eamonn stopped in the middle of the passage, his pulse pounding, nowhere to hide. He might have turned to run in the other direction, hoping to hide around the corner, if he hadn't locked eyes with the man as soon as he'd stepped into the corridor. The sight of the familiar face had frozen Eamonn where he stood.

Hadli closed the door behind him, but stopped just beyond, as motionless as Eamonn. Eamonn's options ran through his mind, but he still couldn't move. He watched as Hadli studied him, waiting to see what he would do. Something passed quickly over Hadli's face—was it pity?—before he crossed his arms and wetted his lips.

"You look terrible."

Striking up a conversation was at the bottom of the list of things Eamonn expected from Hadli. What should he say to that? Should he say anything at all, or just run for it? Finally, he mustered, "Funny, because I feel great."

Hadli smirked at Eamonn's sarcasm and shifted on his feet. "I never thought I'd see you again, you know," he said, his eyes never leaving Eamonn. "One night, you just disappeared without a trace. I was stunned. We all were."

Eamonn swallowed, the apple of his throat raising and lowering. This could be a ploy by Hadli, distracting him and keeping him there until someone else came around. But in his eyes, Eamonn could see the Hadli from his past, not the Hadli who had captured him in the woods.

"I never thought I'd see you again, either," Eamonn replied in a hushed voice. Maybe he should run, but something about the moment held him there. "I didn't want to leave you, but I needed something different."

Hadli nodded, releasing Eamonn's gaze. He uncrossed his arms and took slow steps down the corridor the way Eamonn had just come, looking straight ahead. Eamonn followed him with his eyes, expecting Hadli to rush and grab him or call for aid. He did neither. He simply continued down the corridor, not turning back, until he'd reached the next passage and left Eamonn's sight.

Eamonn felt life return to his muscles and he ran the rest of the way to the wooden door. Using strength from his good shoulder, he pulled it wide and it revealed the world beyond, cold air blasting him in the face. He couldn't help but smile.

A path led away from the door but was lost quickly in the mud and weeds. Eamonn assumed he hadn't come out the main entrance of the fortress, considering the lackluster passageway he'd left behind and the stone storehouses ahead of him. He couldn't see far beyond the stone structures due to the steep downward slope of the muddy ground. Pockets of trees studded the landscape here and there, and gray ice had started to cover parts of the mire that was Nidet. If nothing else, one thing was clear: Eamonn had no idea which way to go.

The sun shone behind a haze of thin clouds, hanging in the sky on Eamonn's left side, but whether that was east or west he could not say. He had been trapped inside the dungeon for so long, he had no way of knowing if the sun was rising or setting.

Eamonn assumed the best thing he could do would be to continue around Holoreath until a path or direction became apparent. He kept close to the castle walls, hoping it would prevent him being spotted by anyone within the fortress, but he soon realized he'd have to come up with another plan. The castle was situated on a cliff. He crept along the walls as long as he had ground to stand on, but soon there was nothing on the other side of him except a drop.

He made it far enough around the side of the castle to see a different part of the island. That was something, at least. Eamonn could see the shore far below in the distance, where several empty ships were anchored at some docks. That was his goal, but he'd have to find a different way down.

Eamonn hurried to retrace his steps until more ground separated him from the sharp drop. He decided to follow the edge of the cliff, hoping to find a place where it sloped less severely and he could make it down to the shore.

A rumbling resounded deep within the earth, quiet at first, but growing until it became a roar and the ground beneath his feet shook.

*That can't be anything good.*

He started to run, heading away from the castle along the cliff's edge, but he never left the rumbling behind. It only grew, the reverberation filling his body. His heart pounded in a rhythm separate from the steady roar. He knew this escape had been too easy.

The icy ground cracked and split before him, and Eamonn skidded to a stop, gasping for breath. Pointed spikes of hard ice sprouted out of the ground in front of him, pushing their way up thick and tall into the air. Eamonn turned to run the other way, but ice spikes had appeared to his right and behind him as well, the drop-off to his left.

The growth of the spikes stopped, at least two heads taller than Eamonn and each as thick as a tree trunk. Eamonn glanced over the cliff—he would never survive that fall. His rapid pulse filled his ears as panic started to set in. He was trapped.

In an instant, the ground where Eamonn stood turned to ice and his feet lost their grip, sending him sliding closer toward the cliff's edge. He knew better than to struggle—instead, he dropped to the ground to lower his center of gravity, the ice freezing the bare skin of his arms and torso.

This was no act of nature. Even before Eamonn heard the heavy, steady footsteps approaching him, he knew who was responsible and how. The spikes that held him cornered against a fall to his death could only be produced by magic.

From his prone posture on the ice, Eamonn lifted his eyes to the dark clad figure that approached him. He looked different in the misty sunlight than he had in the dungeon, the sharp contrast between his black hair and pale skin shocking. His eyes hadn't changed, though; the piercing blue that still shone with malice was exactly the same.

Rothgard closed the distance between himself and Eamonn, lowering two of the ice spikes with a wave of his hand so that he might stand in their place. Hadli must have tipped him off after all. Anger rippled through Eamonn at the thought.

"You have two options," Rothgard said, as if he was conversing with a friend over tea rather than his prisoner. "You can come with me, where you will find a less hospitable environment than the one you left, or you can plummet to your death here and now. The choice is yours alone."

Eamonn glanced past Rothgard at the empty space in the spike cage, searching for option number three, even though he knew it was foolish.

"Don't even think about trying to escape again," Rothgard warned, only a touch of a menacing quality to his voice. "You don't want to find out what I'm capable of."

Jaw clenched, Eamonn's narrowed eyes met Rothgard's. He had to admit defeat. He could sacrifice himself and plunge over the cliff to his death, but to what purpose? There was no question: he had to return with Rothgard.

Eamonn lifted himself to his knees with a scowl, no attempt at holding back his contempt. "You win."

Rothgard shook his head, saying, "No, not yet. But soon."

He strode over the ice patch where Eamonn was trapped as though it was rock, took Eamonn by the wrist, and held his fingers in an odd position before waving his hand. Eamonn felt a lurch and a pull inside his body and the world flashed around him. The next moment, he and Rothgard stood outside the castle door from which Eamonn had escaped.

"Wha—" Eamonn tried to get out, but his mind spun and he couldn't form words. "Did—"

"Teleportation *is* a strange feeling the first time," Rothgard remarked, his tone still calm, as though nothing was out of the ordinary.

Rothgard dragged Eamonn down the castle's corridors on the route Eamonn took from the dungeon, and they passed Hadli speaking with another man. Eamonn caught a glimpse of Hadli, expecting to see either smug triumph or guilt in his expression, but instead, he saw Hadli's mouth fall open as he passed, his eyes wide. Had he not been involved after all?

"I do hope you've learned your lesson," Rothgard uttered when they had reached the dungeon, as if he was a parent reprimanding a child. He led Eamonn to a cell with an iron door like the torture chamber, though it had no torture device inside. In fact, it was completely empty. "You may withstand physical torture well, but I can find more effective ways to punish you."

Rothgard shoved Eamonn inside and slammed the heavy door shut, the impact reverberating throughout the dungeon. Eamonn crumpled to the floor, infuriated and disheartened at the same time. The wooden door to the dungeon slammed and Eamonn was alone once again. Sobs formed from deep within him, shaking his whole body as he wept in a heap on the floor.

He had been so foolish for trying to escape. He should have known he would never get far. Rothgard might have even set the stage for him as a test to see what Eamonn might do, and Eamonn had fallen right into the trap.

The demonstration of Rothgard's abilities struck fear deep within Eamonn's heart. He didn't stand a chance against Rothgard, and neither did Leyna and Dorylss. Eamonn assumed Rothgard's new threats had something to do with them, even though Rothgard had promised to send them back safely if Eamonn gave up the location of his pendant. He felt less and less that Rothgard was a man of his word, and more that he was a man of loopholes.

# TWENTY-SIX

THE SNOW MELTED UNDER clear skies and the air warmed back to a tolerable autumn cool, making the trip back to Braedel easier and quicker. Leyna barely spoke to her companions, staying in her own thoughts for most of the journey, burning every detail of her meeting with the Queen of the Kaethiri into her mind.

She wished Imrilieth hadn't been as cryptic about the things that really mattered. They hadn't learned what Rothgard wanted with Eamonn or what he planned to do with the amulet if he got his hands on it. And then, Imrilieth had said only Leyna could save Eamonn without any kind of elaboration. Regardless, Leyna didn't think the trip a waste—she had actually stepped foot into Avaria and met with the magical beings that had become myth. In all honesty, she had a hard time believing the whole encounter hadn't been a dream.

The company had made it back to the well-traveled road that ran from Nos Illni to Braedel, now only a few hours from their destination. They kept a brisk pace, ready to be back and hoping to have time to rest before setting off for Nidet with Kinrid and Gilleth.

"If Rothgard can trace the magic of the Réalta and know when we're coming to Nidet, then we should just hide it somewhere safe in Braedel," Teiyn said, breaking the silence that had fallen among the group as they passed other travelers. "That way, he wouldn't be able to track us and there is no chance of the Réalta falling into his hands."

"That's where you're wrong, dear sister," Taran disagreed, making eye contact with his twin. "Leaving the Réalta behind makes it vulnerable. Those loyal to him are everywhere, and anyone could find it, especially once they tied it to us."

"We don't have to worry about that," Dorylss replied with a shake of his head. "All we have to do is wait in Braedel for Gilleth and Kinrid and their army. They should be arriving soon, hopefully with a strong enough force to take Rothgard down. He won't even have the chance to get it."

Leyna didn't offer an opinion. She agreed with them all. Taking the Réalta right to Rothgard wasn't a good idea since he would know exactly when they were coming, but leaving it behind would be too risky. Waiting for the mercenary army seemed to be the best option, but they'd heard nothing from them. They could only assume Kinrid and Gilleth had found the mercenaries Dorylss knew and had almost reached Braedel.

"We have plenty of hiding places to keep it at home, all of them safe and secure," Teiyn argued, ignoring what the others had said. "The enemy wouldn't be able to get their hands on it."

"All right, then," Taran countered, tilting his head and gesturing with the hand not holding the reins, "take this, for example. If, perhaps, we were captured on Nidet and found to not have the Réalta, what would happen to us? Torture? Death? At the very least, we would have to give up its location, and then we're no better off."

"You're just assuming we're going to get captured."

"There's a terribly high possibility."

"For you, maybe."

"I'm just trying to keep us all safe."

"Shh!" Leyna interrupted, stopping Rovis and holding a hand in the air. Rovis snorted and took a few steps underneath himself. "Did you hear that?"

Her companions slowed their horses, their eyes all turning to Leyna.

"What are we listening for?" Teiyn asked in a whisper.

"I thought I heard something in the woods," Leyna explained, eyes peeled as she searched through the trees that surrounded them. "Dorylss, is there a town nearby?"

Dorylss shook his head. "Not close enough for people to be wandering."

The group came to a stop, following Leyna's lead. She listened with bated breath, but she didn't hear anything out of the ordinary. The woods were still, the only sounds coming from a few birds calling to each other. Leyna sighed, feeling uneasy about the woods but deciding they'd better keep going. She had just grasped Rovis's reins again when she heard a soft crunch in the trees.

Goosebumps covered Leyna's skin as she shot a glance to Dorylss, hoping he'd heard it too. The sound could have come from an animal, but it sounded controlled and heavier than a creature along the ground.

Dorylss's wide eyes met Leyna's. He must have heard it. Leyna's heart raced and her knuckles turned white as she gripped the reins. She waited for Dorylss's lead.

Before he'd given a direction, though, Leyna heard the *thunk* of a crossbow and an arrow whizzed by Taran's face.

"GO!" Dorylss yelled, and all four of them spurred on their horses.

A volley of arrows came flying from the woods to their right as they rode, narrowly missing them but striking both of the twins' horses. The creatures screamed and groaned as their legs buckled and they dropped. Rovis reared at the two fallen horses in front of him and Leyna lost her grip, sliding off his back and hitting the ground with a thud as he tore off down the road.

"Rovis!" Leyna screamed, completely exposed in the middle of the road.

Teiyn waved her over from behind her fallen horse and Leyna ran to take cover with her and Taran as another volley flew toward them. Leyna crouched as low as she could behind the dying horse, hearing the dull clatter of the arrows that landed on the road and in the woods to their rear.

"What do we do?" Leyna croaked out, panic etched onto her face.

Before Teiyn could answer, Leyna saw Dorylss charging into the trees, unsheathing a long knife from his belt. Had he lost his mind? They didn't even know how many attackers there were.

Leyna started to stand, planning to run to Dorylss and stop him from rushing into the ambush, but Teiyn grabbed her arm and yanked her back down. More arrows came, and one hit

Dorylss in the bicep. Leyna screamed as Dorylss fell to a knee, overcome with the urge to go to him. Teiyn would hold her back, though. Leyna turned to face Teiyn, about to beg her to let her help Dorylss, but the twins had turned their attention to the trees.

From their hiding spot behind the horses, Taran and Teiyn extended their hands to the trees ahead of them, holding their fingers in an identical peculiar position. Their eyes didn't leave the woods.

Leyna was about to cry out and ask what they were doing, but loud cracking sounds coming from the woods pulled her gaze and her mouth fell open.

Dry tree limbs started breaking and falling, coming from high up in the trees and gaining momentum on their way down. Screams echoed around them as limbs fell harder and faster, coming to deadly stops on the ground below. No storm had appeared, no wind tore the limbs from the trees. Leyna looked back at the twins, both deep in concentration, and she almost smiled. So they *could* use magic.

Arrows no longer zoomed toward them, and after another moment, no more voices came from the woods. Leyna still huddled behind the horse, but Taran and Teiyn stood up, tall and confident. They glanced at each other, speaking with their eyes, and as soon as they broke eye contact, Taran delved into the woods and Teiyn grabbed her pack from her horse to tend to Dorylss.

"What *was* that?" Leyna wondered aloud, finally feeling safe enough to leave her hiding spot. She hurried over to where Dorylss sat on the ground, Teiyn squatting beside him.

"It could have been a band of highwaymen who intended to rob us," Dorylss replied, wincing with the pain in his arm, "or it could have been Rothgard's men, looking for us."

Leyna's face fell with her heart. "It couldn't be," she breathed. She didn't want to believe it. As she started to recover from the stress of the attack, her hands began to tremble and she could feel her heart almost vibrating in her chest.

Dorylss groaned as Teiyn broke the arrow and extracted it from his arm. She dug around in her satchel and pulled out a few herbs as well as her mortar and pestle, grinding the herbs before adding water from her flask. Satisfied with the consistency of the mixture, Teiyn applied some of it onto Dorylss's wound. Dorylss closed his eyes and sucked in a breath through clenched teeth, and Teiyn began to bandage him.

"Four of them," Taran called as he strode out of the woods. "Two Idyrrians and two Wolsteadans."

Leyna looked at Dorylss, and he caught her gaze from the corners of his eyes. Two Wolsteadans? Leyna tried to swallow, but a lump had lodged itself in her throat.

"They're dead," Taran said when he reached them, keeping his voice low, "but they were definitely Rothgard's men. One of them carried this."

He held out a piece of worn paper for them to see. It bore a crude illustration of the Réalta.

Dorylss sighed, lifting his right hand to his forehead and running his fingers across it. "They must have been sent to kill us and obtain the pendant," Dorylss said.

Leyna could hardly draw a breath. They were being hunted. Potential danger had become imminent danger. Rothgard knew they carried Eamonn's pendant. "How did they find us?" she asked, staring blankly at the broken trees.

Teiyn shrugged as she packed away her tools and ingredients. "Hard to say. Rothgard might have known we traveled to Avaria from tracing the pendant's magic, assuming we would come back to Braedel as it's the best way from the mainland to Nidet. He might have sent these people days ago and they've been lying in wait."

"But how did they know us? How would they know what we look like?" Leyna wondered, standing up and helping Teiyn lift Dorylss to his feet.

No one had an answer, then Dorylss's expression changed. He lifted his eyebrows and his lips parted as if he'd realized something. "The courier," he murmured, looking at Leyna. "The courier Polnir sent. You were right." Dorylss dropped his head and shook it. "Polnir assumed we were traveling to Nidet and warned Rothgard."

"But the pendant?" Leyna continued with a furrowed brow, still trying to put the pieces together. "Even if he knew we were coming, how would he—"

She snapped her mouth shut. Leyna figured out the answer to her own question and it turned her heart to lead.

Rothgard knew they carried the pendant because he had gotten it out of Eamonn.

Leyna's knees buckled underneath her, but Taran caught her before she hit the ground. She heard the others speaking, but a hum from somewhere within her filled her ears and she couldn't make out their words. Leyna only heard the beating of her own heart and her thoughts screaming in her mind.

*Eamonn's been tortured! He's been tortured to the point of breaking! What has he undergone to try to keep you safe?*

"Leyna. Leyna!"

Dorylss called her name and pulled her back to the world around her. She lifted her eyes to him, but he was blurred by the tears obscuring her vision.

"We must keep moving," he said, picking up her hand and squeezing it. "We aren't safe anymore."

Leyna blinked and the tears fell. Dorylss helped her to her feet, and Leyna noticed the pools in the bottoms of his own eyes. So he'd figured it out, too.

She turned away from him, feeling the heat of tears again, and she saw the two dead horses lying in the road. *Oh, right,* she thought, her heart sinking. Rovis had taken off in the scuffle and was nowhere to be found. Only Bardan remained, standing a short distance down the road away from the action. Dorylss went to him, talking to him in a gentle voice as the horse shook his head and picked up his feet with agitation.

Taran had returned to his horse and Teiyn joined him. They collected what they could carry before speaking soft words over the lifeless animals and stroking their necks. Leyna took a few steps toward them, not sure what else to do. She didn't have a horse to attend to, nothing to occupy herself with. She felt so lost, the world she'd been living in suddenly replaced with one she didn't know.

"What do we do now?" she asked anyone, trying to suppress the panic she could tell was rising in her voice.

"We travel as quickly as we can by foot," Dorylss said as he led a calmed down Bardan to them. "The remainder of our journey to Braedel will take longer now, and we don't need to stop until we get there. You can ride on Bardan and we'll keep pace with you."

"No," Leyna replied firmly, facing Dorylss and frowning. "You're hurt. You ride on Bardan; I'll be fine walking."

Dorylss didn't argue. He sighed and nodded before pulling himself into the saddle with his good arm.

"There's no questioning what our best move is now," Teiyn said, slinging the strap of her pack over her shoulder. "We go straight from Braedel to Nidet. No lingering. And no hiding the Réalta."

No one argued, and Leyna might have been surprised since they had all seemed set in their opinions a few minutes before. Things had changed in those few minutes, though. Their time had run out.

Taran and Teiyn set out side by side, leading the party down the road. Leyna strode alongside Dorylss to keep him company and make sure he didn't need anything for his arm. The twins set the pace at a brisk walk, and Leyna almost had to jog to keep up with them. A stitch formed in her side within minutes and she groaned internally, wishing she'd taken up Dorylss's offer to ride.

They met few travelers, but every time they passed someone, Leyna imagined what they might do when they found the dead horses on the side of the road. Hopefully, none of them would make the connection between the horses and the travelers on foot. If they did, what would they do? Leyna pushed herself to keep walking at the twins' pace, wanting to reach Braedel as soon as possible.

The group barely spoke as they traveled, and Leyna lost herself in thought. Teiyn had been the one to suggest hiding the pendant in the first place, but she'd doubled back on her plan after the ambush. The more Leyna thought about it, the more she wondered why.

"Teiyn," Leyna said as the sun dipped below the horizon and they were alone on the road. "Why did you change your mind about hiding the pendant? If Rothgard knows we have it, wouldn't we be safer if we hid it somewhere?"

Teiyn looked back at Leyna over her shoulder before answering. "We know he has people looking for it," she said, barely above a whisper. "There are people in Braedel who would connect you to us, so hiding it at our home isn't safe anymore. I can't trust stashing it anywhere else."

"He's made it clear he's desperate for it," Taran added. "He would tear Idyrria apart until he found it, and then we would be no better off than if we'd kept track of it the whole time."

"You keep it in your hands—"

"—and out of his."

Leyna huffed. None of their plans were good ones. "So, we just take it to him?" she grumbled. "There's got to be someplace where it will be safer than *on me.*" Memories of Imrilieth's words flooded her mind, examples of what Rothgard could do if he harnessed Avarian magic through the Réalta.

"I agree with Teiyn," Dorylss said, his voice heavy with wisdom. "Rothgard has loyalists all throughout Idyrria and an entire force on Nidet he could send to look as well. The pendant wouldn't be safe."

With a sigh, Leyna conceded. "At least we'll have Kinrid and Gilleth's army. If they're able to make short work of Rothgard, we might be okay after all."

It was Taran's turn to glance over his shoulder before sharing another knowing look with his sister.

"Actually, about that..." Teiyn began.

"We said we're going straight to Nidet, and we mean it," Taran finished. "We can't linger in Braedel at all."

"The closer we get to Braedel, the more danger we're in."

"Rothgard knows we have to go there for the harbor."

"He will likely have people all over looking for you."

"That means we can't wait for Kinrid. The longer we stay there, the greater chance we'll be found before we even leave for Nidet. We have to go ahead," Taran said, ending the matter.

Leyna faced Dorylss again, hoping for some backup this time. He'd met with Kinrid and Gilleth along with her, he knew what they had said about Rothgard's force on Nidet, and he knew they couldn't go in alone. But when Leyna looked at him, Dorylss simply shook his head.

Leyna's mouth fell open and a scoff left her lips. She pulled her eyes from Dorylss, even though he wouldn't be able to see the tears welling in the dim light.

None of them understood, and they wouldn't. *She* was the one who could doom the whole country. *She* was the one at the top of Rothgard's list now. The attack on the road proved he would kill her for the Réalta. Her heart pounded and a tightness expanded in her chest. Rothgard would know when they were on Nidet. He would hunt her down. There wouldn't be a place to hide or a way to run.

For the first time, Leyna came face to face with a possibility she hadn't considered since setting out on this mission.

There may not be a journey home.

# TWENTY-SEVEN

IT MIGHT HAVE BEEN nighttime. Eamonn didn't know. He'd scraped up hay that littered the floor into one of the corners and curled up on it, losing himself to sleep. It was the only way he could escape his nightmare.

The clang of the heavy door to his cell and the clatter of a wooden plate on the floor had awoken him, but he left his food untouched. What was the point of continuing to eat? If Rothgard fed him, it meant he wanted him alive. Since trying to escape hadn't worked, Eamonn could at least keep Rothgard from getting whatever he wanted with him. He saw no way out. It would be his final act of rebellion.

Eamonn heard a noise in the dungeon, a distant thud like the dungeon's door had been opened and shut. He didn't move. He'd been given a meal already, so he had no idea what this might be about. Maybe Rothgard had come for him, ready to use his "more effective" ways to punish him.

Faint footsteps came toward the cell door, unlike those of either Rothgard or The Scourge, as though the person approaching had spent most of their life sneaking around. Eamonn turned one of his ears toward the door to hear better.

"Hey."

Hadli spoke quietly, his voice heavy with familiarity. He sounded like the Hadli Eamonn had encountered in the passage earlier that day, more like the Hadli from his past.

Eamonn said nothing. What was he supposed to say? *Hey, good to see you, thanks for taking the time to visit me?* He curled himself tighter into the corner and hoped that if he didn't engage, Hadli would leave him alone.

"I want you to know that I didn't tip them off."

Could Hadli fake that much compassion in his voice? Eamonn didn't know him anymore, so anything was possible. Either way, it drew something out of Eamonn, something small and childlike and trusting that he thought had vanished long ago. He sighed and picked himself up from the corner, turning to face the little window in the cell door where Hadli stood, still lingering in the shadows.

"I know."

Hadli's lips parted and a crease formed between his dark eyebrows. "You do? How?"

"I can just tell."

A corner of Hadli's mouth twitched. "I'm almost surprised you'd even let yourself believe it was true."

Eamonn shrugged. "I guess I just like to see the good in people." He swallowed and took a few steps toward the cell door, barely able to find his voice to croak out, "We were brothers, Hadli."

Hadli pressed his lips together and the apple of his throat bobbed. "I came here to tell you something."

Keeping silent, Eamonn watched Hadli through the bars, waiting for him to speak.

"When you left the Guild, I felt betrayed," he began, meeting Eamonn's eyes. "Rothgard sent me to find you and I went willingly. I didn't care what he might do to you. His success was mine by extension." Hadli swallowed again, and Eamonn saw the muscles in his jaw tense. "But then I saw what he's done to you." He shook his head in a small movement. "You didn't deserve that, and I'm sorry for my part in it."

Eamonn kept his face blank, refusing to give Hadli any satisfaction by revealing his shock at Hadli's apology. Eamonn's heart tore in two, feeling like he'd finally reunited with Hadli while knowing a gulf still lay between them. They'd never be able to go back to how they were before. He sucked a deep breath through his nose to steady his voice before he responded.

"I saw you in the library at Erai with Rothgard." Eamonn crossed his arms and held them tightly across his chest. "I was there when your crew came in, and I followed you down to the vaults. I saw you strike old Marwan." Eamonn clenched his teeth, feeling the warm prick of tears behind his eyes and pushing it away. "I couldn't believe it." His voice came out thick with emotion and he cleared his throat. "I knew then you'd changed. You weren't the person I'd known."

Hadli didn't break eye contact. "You're right. I'm not."

Eamonn thought he might have seen a glistening in Hadli's eyes before he blinked and it was gone.

"This is my life now," Hadli continued, straightening his shoulders. "Those of us left in the Guild couldn't go on like that forever, and Rothgard offered us what we needed."

Eamonn didn't reply, but he knew what he wanted to say. Hadli's eyes searched his face for a moment, and when he didn't speak, Hadli said, "Well, there you go."

He turned to leave and Eamonn squeezed his eyes shut. He had to say it. He had to see if there was any hope.

"It's not too late for you, Hadli."

Hadli's face reappeared at the barred window. "Not too late for what?"

"For you to have an honest life. For you to start over." *For you to be my friend again.* He kept that to himself, knowing deep within his soul it would never be the same.

Hadli took a single step backward, his expression hardening as his chin tipped slightly up. "Rothgard has well-laid plans and is close to succeeding. Soon, he'll be the ruler of all of Sarieth, and his wealth and power will be endless. I won't need to start over."

He didn't wait for a response. Hadli turned on his heel and strode back toward the stairs that led out of the dungeon, leaving Eamonn alone in the dim cell once more. Eamonn brought his hands to his face and pressed his fingers to his forehead. Maybe there wasn't any hope for Hadli after all.

Leyna and her companions arrived in Braedel late into the night, exhausted and sore. They crept through the sleeping city back to Taran and Teiyn's little home, thankfully coming in contact with no one.

Teiyn got a fire going in the stone hearth and Leyna crashed down on the bed in the main room where she had lain sick. Everything about her ached. She ripped off her boots, almost certain she had worn holes in them, and massaged her feet before lying flat on the bed, reaching her arms above her head to stretch out her back.

"We'll sleep here tonight to regain our strength, and then we'll be off at first light," Dorylss told the others as he untied his boots. "Any of Rothgard's followers in the city will soon learn that the attackers sent to ambush us are dead, if they haven't already, and will likely assume we're back here. We make for the port at dawn."

Leyna shut her eyes and sighed. Dawn? They'd only get a few hours of sleep, barely enough to fully rest after the day they'd had. Besides, she wasn't quite ready to plunge into the peril that awaited them.

"I'll make a broth," Teiyn said, filling a pot with water to boil. "It'll help us recover faster."

"And we can replenish our supplies," Taran added, "but we shouldn't take much, only the necessities."

Still lying supine on the bed, Leyna did nothing. She could hardly move, let alone figure out what she needed to do to prepare for their final voyage. The minute Teiyn had that broth ready, Leyna planned to eat it and fall asleep.

Taran picked up his bag and poked around the house, looking for things they would need on their journey. He picked up items here and there, sometimes dropping them into the bag and other times putting them back. Dorylss busied himself laying out cushions and blankets, setting up a spot for him to sleep on the floor. The orange cat appeared out of nowhere to investigate what he was doing, sniffing at the blankets with immense curiosity.

"Dorylss," Leyna said, propping herself up on her elbows, "do we have any kind of plan?"

Dorylss lifted his head from the pallet to look at Leyna. "Not much of one, no," he replied, running his fingers through his bushy red beard. "I have never been to Nidet nor seen Holoreath, so I don't know what to expect on the island."

Leyna turned to face Teiyn. "Have you and Taran ever been there?"

Stirring the broth over a low flame, Teiyn nodded. "We have. It was several years ago."

"Before any of this nonsense," Taran piped up.

"The island is known for a special plant called Siran that only grows in the harsh cold and heavy humidity."

"In the past, after the fortress was abandoned, Idyrrians used to travel there every winter to gather it," Taran added, joining his sister at the hearth.

"Its flower has unique healing properties and it only blooms once a season, right before spring begins."

"The journey to retrieve it can be treacherous, both on sea and on land."

"Making it precious," Teiyn said, ladling bowlfuls of the broth.

"We went once," Taran continued, taking bowls from his sister and handing them to Leyna and Dorylss. "We wanted some Siran for our own supply."

"But it wasn't easy. We haven't been back since."

A silence hung in the air as Leyna waited to see if the twins had any more to say, flicking her gaze back and forth between them.

"Well," she finally said, "does that mean you know the island? Have you seen the castle?"

The twins nodded together. "The port is on the southwest side of the island, the easiest part of the island to reach from the mainland," Taran said.

"The shore there is sandy and is met with high cliffs," added Teiyn.

"The castle is situated on the cliffs."

"And it overlooks the shore, giving anyone there an advantage."

Taran's mouth twisted and Teiyn furrowed her eyebrows, their expressions divulging what they hadn't said.

Leyna sat up on the bed and turned to Dorylss before returning her gaze to the twins. She filled in the rest. "So Rothgard will see us coming."

They nodded again.

"Undoubtedly," Teiyn admitted.

"The cliffs are impossible to scale," Taran said.

"So, you have to take the long way 'round."

"By then, he will definitely have seen the boat and know we're coming, if he didn't have sentries see us land to begin with."

Leyna groaned and dropped her head into her hands. Even the topography was against them. No wonder Rothgard had taken up residence at Holoreath. He was untouchable.

"Do you have any suggestions, then, for how we approach the fortress?" Dorylss asked. Leyna heard the sigh in his voice, the same weariness that plagued them all.

Taran spoke first. "Don't pull in at the port. No one will be there anyway. Sail to the west of the island and pull the boat onto the shore."

Leyna's head shot back up. Wrinkles appeared on her forehead and her lips parted as her pulse started to quicken.

"It's rockier there, of course," Teiyn noted, "so it would be more of a challenge to sail those waters and beach the boat."

"But he wouldn't see us coming?" Leyna asked, a shred of hope rising within her.

Teiyn shook her head. "I wouldn't think so. There's always a possibility he has sentries on that side of the island, but they wouldn't have as much of an advantage as they do from the cliffs. There's an incline, but it's not too steep and it wouldn't take as long to get to the fortress."

"Then that's our plan." Leyna said, straightening her shoulders and holding her hands out in front of her with her palms up. "We sail to the western side of the island."

Dorylss rested a hand on Leyna's shoulder. "So it is. Once we get there and have a better idea of what we're up against, we'll determine our next steps."

Leyna nodded, releasing a tense breath. Her broth still sat on the table beside her, untouched. She hadn't paid any attention when Taran had handed it to her, but now, her stomach growled and she picked it up.

If they could figure out a way onto the island away from Rothgard's eyes, perhaps they could come up with a decent strategy once they got there as well. The mercenary army should follow them anyway, according to Kinrid's timeline, and they might not have to come up with a plan without them at all.

Leyna slurped down the broth and lay on the bed, nestling herself in the covers. The little bed in a warm home was a welcome change to the several nights they camped out in the cold. She took a deep breath and settled into the bed, allowing herself to relax and hope. She'd cling to every fragment of hope she could find.

Dawn came much sooner than Leyna wanted. She woke on her own to the sounds of the others stirring about the room, but she didn't open her eyes. The heat of a fire reached her, and she wondered how long everyone else had been awake. Not that it made a difference. With no idea when she might rest this comfortably again, she took advantage of her final moments of calm and comfort.

Whether due to a special ingredient in Teiyn's broth or the fact that she'd slept in a real bed, Leyna awoke feeling refreshed, but that didn't mean she was ready to get up. Her dread of the mission that lay before them had paralyzed her, keeping her bound to the bed.

Before she'd had time to really savor the cocoon she had made, Dorylss laid a hand on her shoulder and shook it gently.

"Time to get up, Leyna," he murmured.

Leyna groaned. She stretched before pushing back the covers and sitting up, reaching for her boots at the foot of the bed.

Taran and Teiyn stood by their packs, naming off items as they seemed to go through a final count of their supplies. Leyna's bag—and all the possessions she'd brought—had vanished with Rovis. They hadn't come across him the rest of the way to

Braedel, but Leyna still hoped he was all right and would manage to find his way back to them.

A knot formed in Leyna's stomach as she fastened her belt at her waist and tied her cloak around her neck. The plan they'd come up with the night before made her feel better about their chances of making it to Nidet unnoticed, but then what? They ran from people who hunted them in Braedel to the very island where their enemy had plenty of followers at his disposal and no resistance. Despite the warmth in the room, Leyna shivered.

"Tea?" Teiyn asked, pulling Leyna from her thoughts.

Leyna searched for her voice. "Yes, please."

Teiyn took a kettle near the fire and poured some water into a cup on the table. Handing it to Leyna, she murmured, "There's a little something extra, for strength and for stress."

Leyna tried to smile as she took the cup, but she came up short. Though she hadn't hidden her misgivings about their upcoming expedition from the others, she didn't like for them to view her as anxious and afraid. Dorylss and the twins seemed ready to meet the danger head on. She wished to be as bold as them, as confident as she'd felt when she and Dorylss had first set off from Teravale. Leyna had seen that girl less and less the closer they got to their destination.

Leyna sipped on her tea for a little while as Teiyn doused the fire and Taran made the last additions to their packs. Dorylss turned to Leyna and slung his bag over his shoulder.

"Ready?"

After taking a final sip, Leyna put down her cup and bobbed her head in a quick, shallow nod.

"Taran and Teiyn will go first to prepare their boat at the harbor. We'll follow a few minutes later," Dorylss directed. "If we move quickly enough, we should be able to avoid coming across many people."

Taran gripped his bag and Teiyn pulled the edges of her cloak tightly around her. "We'll see you there," Taran said, and he and his sister stepped out the door into the cold, empty streets.

Leyna swallowed hard and gripped at her own cloak, her eyes still on the door where the twins had just exited.

"You're smart to be scared," Dorylss said, his gentle voice pulling Leyna's eyes to him.

She took a shaky breath as her eyes filled with tears. "I'd rather be brave," she said, strangling the emotion she felt welling to the surface. A slow tear rolled from the corner of her eye.

Dorylss took Leyna by both shoulders, tilting his head down to look her square in the face. "But you *are*. You are brave to have left Teravale, brave to have already faced dangers and not turn back. You are an example of bravery by going forward even now, when you know what awaits you."

Leyna's chin quivered, and she was grateful the twins had already left. "I'm not ready to die," she whispered, blinking through her tears and avoiding Dorylss's gaze.

"Nothing says you will," Dorylss murmured, searching her face until she met his gaze again. "That isn't certain. What's certain is your willingness to sacrifice yourself for someone you care about, and that is the truest love there is. That is valor." His mouth tipped up slightly at the corners. "Don't sell yourself short, Leyna. You are a force to be reckoned with."

A small smile tugged across Leyna's face, and she sniffed as she wiped her wet eyes. Dorylss squeezed her shoulders before releasing her, and they both went to the door to wait. Leyna felt like she was in a trance, as though she inhabited someone else's body. How could this be her own life?

The minutes that separated them from the final leg of their journey sped past. Without the fire, a chill settled in the air, but Leyna hardly noticed it. She already trembled from deep within her core, a side effect of the anxiety that had taken up residence in her heart.

Dorylss turned to Leyna, though she didn't look at him. "It's time to go."

Leyna inhaled a deep breath of the cool air, awakening her heart and mind, and she pulled the hood of the cloak over her head before following Dorylss out of the house.

# TWENTY-EIGHT

DORYLSS LED LEYNA THROUGH the foggy city streets, arriving at the harbor as the sky began to lighten with the imminent rising of the sun. Unlike the rest of the city, the harbor bustled with life as fishermen returned after a night on the sea, mooring their boats and bringing in their haul.

"Over here," he murmured to Leyna, leading her to a small cog ship with its square sail unfurled. Dorylss helped her across the gangplank that separated the boat from the dock, and Teiyn met her on deck.

"There are two beds in the hold at the back of the ship," Teiyn said, gesturing to the cabin's door. "It will take over a day to reach the island, so we'll take turns resting."

They may have time to rest, but Leyna didn't know that she could. Every nerve ending in her body fired, awake and alert to everything around her.

Dorylss helped Taran get ready to make way while Leyna wandered to the starboard side of the ship and leaned on the railing, staring out at the dark waters beyond. Teiyn positioned herself at the helm, guiding the ship out of the harbor.

Wind filled the sail and pushed the boat out to sea. Leyna closed her eyes and breathed in the nostalgic scent of salty air. She hadn't been on a ship in years. Her father used to take their family on his merchant vessel when she was young, sailing around off the Teravalen coast for fun before he would set off for another trading journey.

Unexpected memories of happier times came flooding back. They mixed with the thick emotions that already coursed through her and created sobs in her throat that she fought to hold back. She sniffed and bit her lips together, two tears trickling down her cheeks.

Leyna opened her eyes again and looked over her shoulder at the city as it faded away into the fog. No one followed them, it seemed, but it was hard to tell in the thick haze. Getting onto the ship had been easy enough, so maybe they'd made it out without attracting the attention of anyone looking for them.

Taran and Teiyn manned the ship and Dorylss came to the railing beside Leyna. She looked out over the sea again and sighed. Diffuse light from the sun appeared over the horizon in front of her, cold and bleak in the mist. Leyna wound her cloak tightly around her shivering frame.

"Why don't you go in the cabin for a while?" Dorylss suggested. "There's nothing to see out here."

Without a word, Leyna nodded and headed toward the cabin automatically. She doubted there would be anything to see in the cabin either. Her body wouldn't relax to go to sleep, but at least she would be out of the wind. No matter where she was, though, her anxious anticipation accompanied her. Over a day at sea with nothing to occupy her mind meant Leyna would live in her thoughts—the very last place she wanted to be.

Eamonn awoke from a dreamless sleep to his cell door slamming open. He couldn't get his eyes open before he was grabbed by the arm and lifted from the floor where he slept. Someone held his arms behind his back, clapping irons around his wrists.

"The master is ready for you," came The Scourge's voice from behind Eamonn.

Eamonn blinked, trying to wipe the haze of sleep from his vision as he was pushed out of the cell and through the dungeon.

"Ready for what?" he asked, tripping over his own feet as his muscles lagged.

"The next step," The Scourge answered, shoving him up the narrow staircase. "Your friends will be here with the pendant soon."

Eamonn's chest tightened and squeezed the breath out of his lungs. Rothgard must still be tracing his pendant's magic. The assumption was that Leyna still had it—but if she didn't, someone loyal to Rothgard might be the one bringing it to him. Eamonn didn't know which option was worse.

The Scourge hadn't bothered to blindfold Eamonn this time as he led him from the dungeon through the castle. They must believe Rothgard's threats enough to keep him from trying to escape again. They weren't wrong.

"What does he even want with me?" Eamonn dared to ask. It didn't matter much what he said anymore. This was all about to be over soon, with Rothgard as the victor, so he might as well see if they would quell his curiosity.

"You'll have to ask the master," The Scourge replied, a sinister note in his voice as though he knew the answer but chose to keep it to himself.

They continued down passageways and up stairs into an entirely different wing of the fortress, arriving at a winding spiral staircase that presumably led up a tower. The Scourge dragged Eamonn up the stairs by his elbow, the space too tight for them to stand two abreast. Eamonn struggled to climb, his legs weak and his breath coming in ragged gasps. He stumbled up after The Scourge, relying on him to practically pull him up the steps the farther they went.

At last, they reached a landing with a single wooden door, and The Scourge opened it with his free hand. Rothgard waited beyond the door in a circular room, standing with another man beside an empty table in the center.

"Bring him here," Rothgard ordered, his malice not lost in the silkiness of his voice.

The Scourge tugged Eamonn's elbow and pulled him into the room, forcing him up onto the table. He picked up some leather straps attached to the underside of the table and fastened them around Eamonn's ankles.

Eamonn's heart rate jumped and he started to fight against
The Scourge, but a strong hand gripped his upper arm and
held him back. Rothgard's fingernails dug into Eamonn's skin
as The Scourge unlocked the restraints at his wrists. He grasped
Eamonn's other arm and they pushed him on his back, wrapping
two leather straps across his body—one at his chest and the other
below his hips.

Rothgard made a motion with his hand and the straps across
his body pulled tighter, pressing Eamonn firmly against the
rough wood of the table and restricting his movement. He rolled
his head to the left, finding The Scourge close to the table, his
arms crossed, and then to the right, where Rothgard had joined
the third man in the room at a smaller table. The man opened a
long, shallow box and spoke to Rothgard in low tones, gesturing
from the contents of the box to Eamonn.

"What's that?" Eamonn croaked, hardly able to speak past
the lump in his throat. His heart hammered in his chest and he
trembled under his restraints.

Rothgard faced Eamonn and took a few deliberate steps in
his direction. A cunning smile spread across his features, his
cold blue eyes piercing Eamonn. "You may not be aware, but
the amulet you possess is tied to your magic," Rothgard said,
coming to a stop a couple of feet away from him. "When I obtain
the amulet, it will be useless to me without your specific magic.
*This*," he said with a flourish of his arm toward the box, "is how
I take your power."

The man Eamonn didn't know came to him, lifting the hem
of Eamonn's shirt and tugging the waistband of his trousers
down enough to expose his prominent hip bone. He rubbed a
cloth soaked in an icy cold liquid against his skin before return-

ing to the box, removing an item and taking it to the roaring fire
before coming over to Eamonn with it.

Eamonn's breaths came quick and shallow, and he could feel
his pulse throbbing in his veins. His stomach twisted with the
sickening thought that something terrible was on its way. He
kept his eyes fixed on the unknown man, on his balding head
and his hollow face, as the man came closer to him with the item
from the box. Eamonn got a good look at it, a fat cylinder with
a long, pointed, narrower cylinder on one end and a plunger on
the other.

Too late, Eamonn figured out what was about to happen. He
tried to fight against his restraints, but they kept him strapped
down, magically tugging tighter as he struggled.

"No!" he cried as the man approached him and examined his
hip bone.

The man sighed and rolled his eyes, turning back to Rothgard.
"I need him to be still. Are you sure we can't give him something
to sleep?"

Rothgard tilted his head down, steepling his fingertips in front
of his chest. "No. I want him to feel it."

"Well, do what you can with these restraints, then," the other
man grumbled, and the heavy leather straps dented into Eamonn's flesh. He could wriggle, but nothing more.

"NO!" he yelled again as the man directed the pointed end
of the tool toward his hip bone. He placed his other hand on
Eamonn's stomach between his hips to brace himself as he stuck
the thick, hollow needle into Eamonn's skin.

The stab tore a cry from Eamonn's lips. The man pushed hard
and jabbed the needle into Eamonn's hip, and Eamonn howled
until his voice left him. He felt a crunch and a fiery jab as the

needle punctured his bone and lodged itself deep within his hip. Eamonn writhed in agony as much as his restraints would allow, his mouth still hanging open though no sound came out, and he took shuddering breaths to try to manage the pain.

The man pulled back on the plunger and Eamonn sucked in a breath, tears springing to his eyes. A deep burning came over his hip with an intense sucking sensation from inside his bone, and Eamonn couldn't hold back the sobs that arose in his throat. He pressed his eyes closed, wishing he had something between his teeth to bite down on. Tears streamed down from the corners of his eyes as his body shook with sobs.

Would the torture never end?

Eamonn rolled his head to the side and he found Rothgard again, an evil smile playing on his lips, more than a sick satisfaction to seeing Eamonn in agony. The triumphant gleam in Rothgard's eyes told a different story, frightening Eamonn to his core.

The pain didn't stop and Eamonn's weak body couldn't take it anymore. He'd been through too much with too little food and rest. The pain diminished until it evaporated, and Eamonn felt the room slipping away. Everything around him fell silent, and for a moment, as the edges of his vision filled with black, Eamonn found peace. In a limbo between awake and asleep, between living and dying, a melodic voice filled his mind.

*"You are not finished, Son of Avaria."*

Taran and Dorylss hopped out of the boat into the shallow water, using all their strength to pull the boat onto the rocky shore. Teiyn guided the boat at the helm, watching out for the larger rocks in their way.

On the boat with Teiyn, Leyna lifted her face to the sky. The late morning sun provided no warmth through the hazy cloud cover. She shivered under her cloak and sighed, the puff of her breath appearing as a mist before her.

They'd taken longer to arrive than they'd wanted, navigating carefully after dark through the massive rocks nestled in the water. Leyna didn't mind. She wasn't exactly in a hurry, unlike the others, and it might give Kinrid and Gilleth time to catch up.

Dorylss and Taran beached the small cog well up onto the rocky shore, heaving with all their strength to get the boat up onto the beach. They'd pulled in at the flattest, sandiest part of the beach they could find, the gray shore covered with rocks and surrounded by cliffs. The men tied the boat off as Teiyn and Leyna made their way down.

"So, we're on the western side of the island?" Leyna asked when her feet met the rough, pebbly sand.

Taran cocked his head to the side. "Well, we're low on the western side. Not too far from Holoreath, but we went around the long way so we shouldn't have been seen."

Leyna thought she might sigh with relief, but her breath came out with a shudder instead. *Except the closer we get to Rothgard, the better he can pinpoint the location of the pendant I'm wearing around my neck.*

"This way," Teiyn said, leading the group up a stony slope and into a leafless forest. Low clouds hung on the tops of the trees, shielding the sun and shrouding the forest in a cold blanket.

Taran stuck close to his twin, and Dorylss tried to bring up the rear, but Leyna lingered behind them.

"We have a bit of a trek before we reach the fortress," Dorylss said, kind eyes looking down at Leyna. "There's still hope Kinrid and Gilleth will be here before we have to make any decisions."

Leyna nodded, an acknowledgement rather than an agreement, and followed Dorylss up the hill into the woods.

"Be careful of your footing," Taran warned, looking back at the three behind him. "The ground may be icy in places."

Leyna turned her face toward the cold, mushy earth beneath her feet. Some of the mud had frozen over into almost invisible ice patches in their path. Leyna grunted, keeping her eyes on the ground in front of her as they hiked.

After hiking for about an hour, Leyna could feel the sweat forming on her body underneath her clothes. Even though a perpetual chill hung in the air and the sun didn't reach them, the uphill climb had her heart pumping and her muscles burning.

Taran stopped up ahead, taking his bag off and retrieving his water flask. "Let's take a break."

*Oh, thank the Lady.* Leyna almost fell down onto a fallen tree beside her, groaning as muscles relaxed. She grabbed her own water flask and tilted it up to her mouth, sucking the water down.

"Leyna."

Leyna nearly spit out the water as she threw her head behind her in search of the weak voice. She might be exhausted, but she hadn't imagined that. Someone had said her name.

She turned her head back to look at her company. Dorylss had sat with the twins to discuss what sounded like the topography they might expect on the back side of the castle. None of them looked in her direction as though they had called her.

"Leyna."

A little louder, and definitely behind her. Leyna stood, turning back toward the foggy woods behind her. Through the mist, she could see nothing. She stepped around the fallen tree, hoping that a few feet closer to the sound she might find its source.

"Help me."

A breath caught in Leyna's throat and her heart jumped. Could it be...?

Then she saw a mop of short dirty blonde curls come out from behind a tree. The face that followed underneath sent a dagger through Leyna's heart.

"Eamonn," she whispered.

He looked so different—hollow, pained, weak. He leaned on the tree as though he didn't have the strength to stand. Filthy clothes hung from his frame and the color had left his skin.

"Help me," he croaked as his knees buckled beneath him and he fell behind the tree.

"Eamonn!" Leyna cried, bounding over the wet leaves and soggy earth to reach him. She threw a glance back at her companions, shouting, "It's Eamonn!" to their bewildered faces. Diving around trees and under branches, she reached the tree Eamonn had clung to and found him lifeless on the ground.

Tears ran down her cheeks and sobs rose to her throat as she knelt down to him.

*Please don't let us be too late.*

She heard the commotion of Dorylss and the twins rushing toward them, but before they reached them, Eamonn sat up like a bolt and wrapped his hand around Leyna's wrist.

The illusion fell, and Eamonn no longer sat before her. Leyna gasped at the pale man with black hair and piercing blue eyes that appeared in his place. She didn't have the chance to gawk, though. Without warning, Leyna felt a tug from inside her and her vision blurred like she was spinning in an impossibly fast circle.

Her feet landed on stone and her legs gave way. If not for the man holding her at the wrist, she would have fallen flat on the ground.

The man flung open a wooden door in front of them and pulled Leyna inside the crumbling castle. It had to be Holoreath. He led her down corridors and through passageways in a flash, causing her to stumble over her feet and barely giving her time to collect her thoughts.

Eamonn had never been in the woods. This man must have cast some kind of illusion spell to draw Leyna in and then teleported them both to the fortress. To be able to cast both of those spells, he had to be strong in both knowledge and practice of magic.

Leyna lifted her gaze to the side of his face as she lumbered along beside him. Younger than middle age, with a dark beard along his jawline, and maybe handsome if not for the malevolence etched onto his face. Skilled with magic. She didn't have to guess this man's identity.

Rothgard already had her within his clutches.

Her heart plummeted to the bottom of her stomach at the realization. She'd been on Nidet just over an hour and she'd already failed. Rothgard would take the Réalta and the power of the Kaethiri would be in his grasp. Leyna's stomach twisted and she nearly vomited right there.

Rothgard opened a narrow door and pushed Leyna in front of him, forcing her up a spiral stone staircase. She could try to resist, try to get away, but to what point and purpose? He'd be able to overpower her, with either magic or his own strength, and the Réalta would be lost anyway.

A guard at the top of the stairs opened another narrow door and Rothgard shoved Leyna into a circular room with a long, bloodied table in the center and a fire blazing in a fireplace to her right. As she stepped onto the tattered, faded rug covering the floor, movement from somewhere to her left caught her attention.

"Don't you dare touch her!" a rough voice called, and Leyna turned to see Eamonn—the real Eamonn—crouched by the wall but trying hard to stand. He couldn't seem to put weight on his right leg, and his clothes at his right hip were stained with something dark. Other than that, he exactly matched Rothgard's illusion of him. Shackles lay on the floor beside him, open and useless, as though Rothgard didn't believe Eamonn was a threat to him. Which didn't seem too far-fetched, based on his appearance.

"I'm afraid it's too late for that," Rothgard replied, his voice a sweet symphony of evil.

Eamonn started to lunge toward Rothgard, clenching his jaw as he stepped on his right leg, but Rothgard lifted a hand in the air and Eamonn shrieked and fell to the floor, the dark stains on his clothes spreading.

Leyna's heart leapt to her throat and she took a step toward Eamonn, but an invisible force stopped her and held her back. She fought to move her feet, to rip herself from the magic's grasp, but it was useless.

Eamonn writhed on the floor, pained grunts and cries escaping his lips. Rothgard still held his hand out and Leyna saw a corner of his mouth twitch as he watched Eamonn.

"Stop it!" she screamed, her voice echoing off the high ceiling of the room. "What are you doing to him?"

"Eamonn is simply discovering that if he tests my patience, he will be met with pain," Rothgard said in his sickly smooth voice. "I suggest he not test me."

Eamonn scowled at Rothgard, baring his teeth and tensing the muscles in his jaw. He fell back against the wall as Rothgard released the magic that caused his pain, taking deep breaths and staring daggers at Rothgard. Leyna watched the rise and fall of his chest, grateful that she had at least found him alive.

"You gave me your word," Eamonn grumbled, his eyebrows knitted together in a frown. "You promised to release her unharmed!"

"Is she harmed?" Rothgard asked, casting a quick glance at Leyna. "My apologies if I was a bit rough leading you here."

"You promised to send her back," Eamonn said, anger and disdain bleeding through his features. Leyna had never seen him so full of hate. "She is to be set on course back to Idyrria!"

"She will be, in due time," Rothgard said, dropping his hand and taking away the invisible wall that bound Leyna. He took calculated steps toward her, his eyes boring into her. Leyna wouldn't be surprised if he could see into her soul. "You see, I have yet to gain what I seek from her. Besides, I never specified *when* she would be returned."

"You bastard!" Eamonn yelled, rising to his knees but immediately falling back down with a grimace and a sharp intake of breath.

"Now, now, Eamonn, I thought you had learned," Rothgard said, his hand in the air again. He didn't turn from Leyna, though, closing the distance between them until he stood inches from her. Rothgard brought his hands together in front of him, resting them against his black tunic.

"I believe you have something for me, Leyna," he continued, tilting his head down toward her and ripping her to shreds with his icy gaze. "That's what Eamonn told me, at least."

Leyna rolled her lips together, wondering what kind of torment this man had put Eamonn through to cause him to give up Leyna and his mother's pendant. She knew Eamonn wouldn't give them up willingly.

"Did he lie?" Rothgard asked after no response from Leyna. "If so, I might not feel compelled to keep either of you alive."

Leyna challenged Rothgard's fiery gaze, mimicking his posture by lowering her head and narrowing her eyes.

"He didn't lie."

Rothgard lifted a hand, palm up, and held it out in front of Leyna. "Give it to me."

Leyna's eyes flashed to Eamonn again, and he met them. She read the defeat in his eyes, his hopelessness, his pain. They had no choice. The Réalta was Rothgard's.

Leyna's chest rose with a deep breath as she dipped her hand underneath her layers of clothing and found the pendant, pulling it out into view. The moment it appeared, Leyna felt the chain yank from her neck and the necklace left her hand, flying into Rothgard's grip.

A single corner of his mouth raised in triumph. He fastened the chain around his own neck and closed his eyes, apparently in some kind of meditation.

Leyna gasped in disbelief as the green stone in the center of the pendant began to glow, growing brighter as the seconds passed until a powerful light emanated from Rothgard's chest, casting his face in a wicked green glow.

He opened his eyes and a devilish grin spread across his face.

# TWENTY-NINE

DORYLSS STOPPED IN HIS tracks when Leyna disappeared before their eyes. He and the twins had almost reached her right as her form vanished from view, evaporating into thin air in the snap of a finger.

"What on earth?" Dorylss murmured, gaping at the spot where Leyna had stood.

"It wasn't Eamonn," Taran said, breathless, the first to have arrived at the tree. "I saw the illusion drop just before they disappeared."

Teiyn faced her brother, wide eyed. They had another one of those wordless conversations, a glance to each other enough to speak volumes. Teiyn released a weighty breath and said, "We underestimated Rothgard's ability to trace the magic of the Réalta. He knew exactly where to find us."

Dorylss closed his eyes, dipping his head down and shaking it as he ran his fingers and thumb across his eyebrows. "How could we be so foolish?"

The pendant had turned Leyna into a walking target as they'd come closer to Nidet, but none of them had accounted for it. Dorylss couldn't help but feel responsible. Everyone except Leyna had agreed on the plan to leave Braedel as quickly as possible, but as the oldest of the group by many years, he should have approached their options with more wisdom.

He had tasked himself with Leyna's safety. This was *his* mission, but he'd let her come along to keep an eye on her. Now he'd lost Leyna as well as Eamonn, and a tightness filled his chest that refused to let go.

"Do you hear that?" Teiyn jumped several paces past them, her attention drawn far into the distance.

"Hear what?" Taran asked, following her.

"I hear voices," she replied, hopping down the slope toward the southern tip of the island.

"Teiyn, wait," Dorylss called, and Teiyn froze to look over her shoulder at him. He wouldn't lose everyone today. "It's probably Rothgard's people."

"I don't think so. The docks are that way. If that army of yours is here, they would have to pull in at the docks."

Teiyn turned away from Dorylss and took careful steps down the slope, Taran on her heels. Dorylss strained his ears to listen for the voices Teiyn had heard, but he couldn't hear anything over the squelch and crunch of the twins' footsteps. If they were determined to go, though, he would go with them.

They held onto thin trunked trees as they descended the slick slope, crossing the terrain in the direction of the docks. Dorylss kept his eyes on the rippling gray water, waiting for the docks to come into view.

The sound of voices carried over the air and reached his ears. His heart skipped, hope rising within him. Teiyn might be right.

The group came past a ridge and a better picture of the sea opened before them. Several large ships with billowing white sails sat in the water, anchored off the shore, and crews of people rowed toward the docks in smaller boats.

A surge of emotion rushed through Dorylss and tears pricked his eyes, though he blinked them away. It had to be Kinrid and Gilleth's people. They must have sailed through the night.

They had a chance.

"Is that them?" Teiyn asked, grinning.

Dorylss nodded, his cheeks rising. "It has to be. Let's go."

"How?" Leyna asked in a breath, her lifted eyebrows wrinkling her forehead. "How is this possible?"

Eamonn had a guess. His right hip throbbed and ached even worse at the memory of the procedure. He'd passed out from the pain as the man drew marrow from his bone, and when he came to, he saw Rothgard sitting in a chair as the man injected Rothgard's veins with Eamonn's marrow.

So that's why they hadn't killed him. Rothgard needed his blood—the blood of a Kaethiri—to use the amulet.

But now that Rothgard had what he needed from Eamonn, did he have a reason to keep him alive?

"Victory is not always found in having the greatest numbers or the strongest in battle," Rothgard said in apparent response to Leyna's question, though he walked toward the table in the center, away from both of them. He thrummed his fingers on the tabletop. "You have to have the right minds, as well. Artists, physicians, alchemists... they're helping me to achieve things I once thought impossible."

Eamonn rested his eyes on Leyna, who watched Rothgard with puzzled horror. He would go to her, if he didn't believe Rothgard would press the rough bandages into his wound again, or worse. He had Eamonn's pendant now, Avarian magic at his disposal. His options were endless.

Leyna's feet remained locked in place as her face followed Rothgard. Whether fear or magic kept her there, Eamonn couldn't tell. His heart sank to see the terror in her expression, her sweet face drained of color.

Rothgard traced his fingers over the glowing amulet hanging from his neck. He turned away from the table to face Leyna, glancing from her to Eamonn, his lips curved in a sneer. "Now," he said, "let's see what this can do."

Eamonn summoned all his strength to stand again and put weight on his right leg, ready to protect Leyna in any way possible. If Rothgard really could channel Avarian magic through the pendant, what Eamonn did wouldn't make a difference, but he still had to try. He wouldn't let Leyna come to harm while he still drew breath.

As Eamonn stood, Rothgard lifted his hand toward him, but an urgent rapping at the door pulled Rothgard's attention. Even without an answer from inside, the door swung open.

"Several ships have just dropped anchor off the southern shore, and scores of soldiers are unloading from the ships at the docks," the man at the door said.

Eamonn knew that voice. It touched the oldest part of his memory and gripped like a hand around his heart. He whipped his head toward the door, gaping at the soldier who had entered the room.

"Ah, excellent," Rothgard said, the words rolling off his tongue. "The perfect opportunity for a demonstration. Thank you, Florin."

After tilting his head toward Rothgard, Florin's eyes landed briefly on Leyna and then turned to Eamonn as he took a step backward and grabbed the door handle. He dropped his eyes from Eamonn for an instant before doing a double-take and stopping in the doorway.

Eamonn locked eyes with his father for the first time in over five years. He closed his mouth and swallowed, trying to dislodge the lump that had risen in his throat.

Florin stood in the doorway and stared at Eamonn, recognition sweeping over his features. Eamonn's heart pounded faster every second that passed. Would he say something to Eamonn? Would he say something to Rothgard? Was there any chance on earth that he would do something to help?

"*Thank you*, Florin," Rothgard repeated.

Florin broke Eamonn's gaze, tilted his head in Rothgard's direction once more, and backed out of the room without another glance at his son.

Eamonn felt like the wind had been knocked out of his lungs. He knew Florin recognized him, yet he chose to do nothing. Five years later and nothing had changed.

Eamonn's eyes burned, but he didn't exactly know why. He had no emotional attachment to the man anymore, or so he believed. His reaction most likely had nothing to do with Florin himself and everything to do with the direness of Eamonn's circumstances. Even with Eamonn facing death, Florin wouldn't help his own son.

Rothgard strode across the room to one of the windows, motioning for Eamonn and Leyna to follow him. "Come," he ordered.

Eamonn caught Leyna's questioning gaze, but all he could do was raise his eyebrows and shrug. If they didn't obey Rothgard themselves, he could use the amulet to make them do what he said anyway.

Limping on his right leg and pressing against the room's stone wall for support, Eamonn hobbled toward the window. Leyna came to him instead of Rothgard, helping him up and resting his right arm across her shoulders, her left arm around his back.

They hadn't touched since he hugged her in the sitting room of her house before he'd left for the Elaris Forest. He wanted to hug her then, wrap her up in his arms and feel her warmth. She turned her face to him, her cornflower blue eyes inches away from him, and for a moment, the nightmare faded away. He focused on the support of her shoulders, the compassion in her eyes, the embrace of her arm around his waist—the things that mattered.

They reached the window where Rothgard waited and looked out at the world beyond. From their vantage point, they saw an endless sea punctuated by the ships Florin had mentioned. People gathered on the beach at the docks, outfitted in armor and armed with swords and bows. Had Leyna come with them? Had she and Dorylss managed to find an army to attack Rothgard?

Eamonn glimpsed Rothgard out of the corner of his eye, the sinister smile on Rothgard's face dashing every sliver of optimism. He must have no doubts about his ability to use his new magic.

"It looks as though you have some aid," Rothgard sneered, watching the army unload on the beach. "But not for long."

The swarming soldiers on the beach formed clean, orderly lines as they marched toward the sloping forest. Eamonn saw the leaders and those following right behind them disappear into the trees. The glow from the pendant intensified and the soldiers remaining on the beach abruptly stopped. Chaos erupted and the lines broke as the soldiers started to fight each other. It could only be described as a free-for-all. Streaks of red appeared as weapons drew blood, and a few bodies fell lifeless onto the sand.

Eamonn turned his eyes to Leyna, her gaze glued to the beach as she took shuddering breaths and lifted her hand to cover her mouth. She didn't try to hide the panic exuding from her features.

Rothgard's eyes flicked through the crowd, his mouth slightly open and its corners upturned. Eamonn's gaze fell on the amulet at Rothgard's neck, squinting at the powerful green light. He could reach out and rip it from his neck right then. He could end it.

"Brilliant, isn't it?" Rothgard asked, pulling his eyes from the force that was tearing itself apart. Eamonn released a breath, losing his nerve. "They're just puppets. They do whatever I command," he murmured. "I can have them fight each other down to the last man, and your resistance will evaporate. Or," he said, one corner of his mouth lifting in a snarl, "I could have them all join me."

In an instant, the soldiers stopped fighting and faced the castle, still as statues.

"It's a perfect plan, really," Rothgard continued, clasping his hands behind his back and stepping away from Eamonn and Leyna. Eamonn had lost his chance. "No one will be able to withstand my power. I can have every province in this country under my control. People across Sarieth will bow to me, obey me, love me, and be none the wiser."

Eamonn reached out and found Leyna's hand, gripping it with his own. She faced him as she drew a shaky breath, her eyes welling with tears. The hopelessness in her eyes shattered his heart.

"Shall I bring them inside?" Rothgard asked, turning back around to face the window. "They certainly have traveled a long way. I should show them some hospitality."

The moment Rothgard finished speaking, the army began to march toward the woods where the others before them had gone. Leyna squeezed Eamonn's hand and his pulse shot up. They both knew their fight was over.

Their chance at defeating Rothgard had vanished before their eyes.

Rothgard took a deep breath through his nose and tilted his chin up. "Unstoppable," he muttered, almost to himself. "The world at my fingertips." His lips curled. "It's quite a feeling."

Eamonn held onto Leyna's hand, if nothing else, to remind her that she was not alone. Whatever Rothgard's plans for them, Eamonn would stay beside her as long as he could, as long as he belonged to himself. Nothing stopped Rothgard from taking control of Eamonn's will, or, for that matter, Leyna's.

The thought sent shivers down his spine.

"There's Kinrid," Dorylss murmured to Taran and Teiyn as the broad, dark-skinned man stepped down from his ship. "And the woman with him is Gilleth. They're commanding this army."

"They're so exposed," Teiyn whispered.

"There's no way they haven't been spotted," Taran added.

Dorylss held his breath, waiting for Rothgard's people to spring into action at any moment. It could be a volley of arrows from the castle, or a quiet ambush coming down the hill where they hid. Dorylss studied the woods behind them, his eyes peeled for movement, but saw nothing and returned his gaze to the docks. The army continued to unload, unhindered. There was no attack, no ambush. The castle was silent.

"I don't understand," Teiyn murmured under her breath. "Nothing's happening."

Dorylss swallowed and his blood ran cold. Rothgard must have found a way to harness Avarian magic with Eamonn's pendant. "He might not need to send his soldiers."

He didn't have to say what he meant out loud. Taran and Teiyn shared a look, and Dorylss knew they understood. If Rothgard had unlocked the potential of the Réalta, the army encroaching on his fortress posed little threat to him.

"Well then, Kinrid and Gilleth's army is our best chance," Taran whispered, easing up from his crouched position. "There come your people now—let's go meet them."

The Farnish leaders crossed the tree line as Taran spoke, along with the first couple boats' worth of soldiers. Taran started down the hillside, but he slid to a halt when the soldiers still on the beach all stopped marching at the exact same time. Without prompting, they all drew their weapons and started to fight each other, no sides taken.

Kinrid, Gilleth, and the soldiers with them in the woods turned back and drew their weapons, but Kinrid lifted his hand in the air, as if telling them to hold their position. They watched the madness unfold on the beach, not making a move, presumably waiting to see if the soldiers on the beach would attack them in the woods.

Taran ducked behind a tree and Teiyn huddled in the shadow of the ridge beside Dorylss. She lifted her eyes to him, a crease between her eyebrows. "This is Rothgard."

Dorylss's heart dropped like lead. Their entire army, minus the small band within the boundary of the woods, belonged to Rothgard in the blink of an eye. The army had been Dorylss's last hope. Without a force to attack Holoreath right then and there, before Rothgard became too skilled with the Réalta and therefore untouchable, they lost any chance of defeating him.

He needed to let Kinrid and Gilleth know what they were up against.

"Stay here," he whispered to Teiyn as he crept down the slope toward the soldiers who faced the beach, away from him. He didn't want to sneak up on them or startle them with their weapons drawn, so he positioned himself within earshot but out of their swords' reach.

"Kinrid!" he called, and he stepped forward a few more paces. "Gilleth! Kinrid!"

Kinrid and Gilleth turned around to face Dorylss, swords at the ready. The bewildered panic in their eyes was met with relief upon seeing Dorylss, and they lowered their weapons.

"Dorylss! You're here!" Kinrid said, closing the distance remaining between them. Gilleth and the rest of the soldiers with them followed. "I thought you had changed your mind when I didn't find you in Braedel." He sheathed his sword and held out his arm to Dorylss, and they grasped each other's arm near the elbow in greeting, their free hands clasping each other's shoulders.

"We had to come on ahead of you," Dorylss murmured. "Idyrria became too dangerous for us to linger there."

On the beach, the clatter of swords and armor fell silent as the soldiers sheathed their weapons and all turned to stand in the same direction. Dorylss and Kinrid broke apart, Kinrid drawing his sword again and taking command of his people, all standing at the ready.

Seconds dragged out as they waited to see what the rest of the army would do. Dorylss rested his hand on the dagger at his waist, the only form of weapon he had. Taran and Teiyn had no steel, but they had magic, which might prove to be a better weapon.

A cool breeze blew and a few soft snowflakes filtered through the trees. Dorylss let his hand fall from his dagger and lifted his foot to take a step in Kinrid's direction when the army turned as a single unit toward them and marched into the woods.

"Hide!" Dorylss called in a harsh whisper. He didn't know what these mind-controlled soldiers might do if they saw them free of Rothgard's control, but he didn't want to find out.

The army entered the woods beyond them and trekked up a route through the trees as if they'd traveled it for years. The unaffected soldiers had taken cover behind boulders and trees, none of them moving without direction from Kinrid. Gilleth had her back pressed against a tree, using hand motions to speak to Kinrid where he had taken cover across from her. Dorylss glanced at the spots where he'd asked Taran and Teiyn to wait, but he couldn't see them, hopefully because they kept themselves hidden.

When the last of the soldiers had made it well up the slope toward the fortress, Kinrid motioned to his crew and left his hiding spot. Gilleth joined him, speaking to him in a low voice.

"Rothgard has Avarian magic," Dorylss said, approaching Kinrid and Gilleth and interrupting their discussion. Whatever plans they tried to make, they needed to know what they were up against. "He's in control of those soldiers' wills."

"Avarian magic?" Gilleth repeated, drawing her eyebrows together. "How is that possible?"

"The friend we came here to rescue—it's his. But Leyna had his pendant."

"Where is she now?" Gilleth asked, scanning her eyes over the woods behind Dorylss.

Dorylss cleared his throat, trying to rid his voice of the emotion that arose. "Rothgard captured Leyna soon after we arrived."

Kinrid's eyes followed the path his mind-controlled soldiers had just hiked. "I'm not sure I would believe it if I hadn't seen it for myself."

Gilleth crossed her arms, looking over her shoulder at the path as well. "Why weren't we affected?"

"It's likely he was only able to control those he could see," Teiyn said, appearing at Dorylss's right. Dorylss jumped at her voice, whipping his head down to her.

"You and the soldiers with you must have entered the woods and left his sight before he used the magic," Taran added, hopping over a downed tree and landing on Dorylss's left.

"Who are they?" Kinrid asked, glancing from Teiyn to Taran before meeting Dorylss's gaze.

"Some friends from Braedel," Dorylss answered, gesturing to each twin in turn. "Teiyn, Taran. They're magic-casters, and they have extensive knowledge about all kinds of magic."

"Okay, then," Kinrid said, resting a hand on the sword at his hip, probably an old habit. "Where did our army go?"

"To the castle," Teiyn answered.

"To become part of Rothgard's army, most likely," Taran added.

Gilleth huffed and released her arms, letting them swing at her sides. "Do we even have a fight here? This sounds like it's over before it even begins."

Taran and Teiyn shared a look, their mouths in the same less-than-optimistic twist.

"We could still manage to get into the castle," Taran said, lifting his hands in front of him, palms up.

Kinrid's eyebrows furrowed under his bald head. "How?"

"We pretend to be as controlled as the army," Teiyn said with a shrug. "It gets us in the door, at least."

"And then what?" Dorylss asked. Their band numbered below twenty. Against Rothgard's own forces and his newly acquired army, they didn't have a shot.

"We can find him and try to take back the amulet," Taran suggested.

Teiyn nodded with a glance at her brother. "We'd be able to trace his magic and find him within the fortress, just as he found Leyna."

"But we'd have limited time once we located him," Taran pointed out. "He'll be able to control us the minute he lays eyes on us."

Dorylss raised his eyebrows briefly, thoughtfully running a hand over his beard. It wasn't the worst plan, especially considering their options. Or, lack of options, rather.

Gilleth crossed her arms again and made eye contact with Kinrid. "I don't know what other choice we have."

Kinrid chewed on his lip in thought before turning to the twins. "We take this amulet from him, we get our army back?"

Taran and Teiyn nodded, and Kinrid looked back at Gilleth.

"Gather our people," he ordered. "We have to make this count."

# THIRTY

LEYNA AND EAMONN WATCHED at the window with clasped hands until the last of the soldiers under Rothgard's control disappeared into the forest. Leyna could hardly breathe. She had no reason to think Dorylss, Taran, and Teiyn might be among the soldiers that Rothgard led to the fortress as his own, but she couldn't stop herself wondering if they were. If they'd managed to avoid it somehow, did they at least realize what had happened? Would they know they'd lost the entire army they depended on?

Leyna felt Eamonn's gaze on her and she turned to meet it. His bloodshot eyes studied her face, as though he tried to soak up every moment he could see her as himself.

The realization stung her and she inhaled a sharp breath.

"Eamonn," she whispered, her voice breaking.

Before either one of them could say another word, Rothgard pulled them by their arms away from the window toward the center of the room. He leaned against the bloody table and crossed one of his ankles over the other, his palms behind him on the tabletop.

"So now you see what it can do. What *I* can do," he said, lifting one corner of his mouth. "Nothing can stop me now. I'll be able to remove kings, turn the people to my side, and become ruler of all of Sarieth." He pushed himself away from the table, his hands meeting in front of him and his fingers lacing together. "I can create a better world for all the people of Sarieth—for the pushed aside and forgotten."

Rothgard clasped his hands behind his back and took a few steps toward Eamonn. "You should be thankful to see me as Overlord. You lived a life of scrounging and scraping, of keeping to the shadows. My rule will raise up people like you." He shrugged. "Until now, people have resisted me. They're afraid of change. No one is willing to do what is necessary. But soon," he added, a wicked gleam in his eyes, "everyone will be willing."

Eamonn scoffed. "I hardly consider manipulating someone's will the same as them being willing."

Waving a hand in the air dismissively, Rothgard said, "No matter. Either way, the world will soon do as I command. Now," he snarled, raising his chin and looking down his nose at Eamonn, the Réalta's green glow pulsing, "bow to me."

But Eamonn did not bow. Instead, he spat on the floor.

Rothgard scowled and crossed his arms. "Your Kaethiri blood will not save you. I said, *bow*."

Leyna's eyes didn't leave Eamonn as she watched him struggle to resist Rothgard's magic. He clenched his jaw and the muscles in his neck tensed. Maybe he had enough Kaethiri in him to be outside of Rothgard's control. He clearly fought a battle within himself, pressing his eyes closed and curling his hands into fists as muscles throughout his body twitched. Lowering his head, Eamonn gritted his teeth and grunted, drawing his balled fists up toward his chest.

Leyna's jaw trembled and her teary eyes never left Eamonn. He fought, but he was losing.

The veins in Eamonn's neck and arms bulged out and he threw his head back as a cry tore from his lips. The moment the sound dissipated, Eamonn released all his tensed muscles and brought his head upright, then bent graciously at the waist, dipping his head in Rothgard's direction.

"My lord," he said, raising himself back up. His face had lost any expression other than attention, his lips closed and his eyes staring straight ahead.

With a shuddering breath, Leyna closed her eyes and sent tears rolling down her cheeks. Eamonn was gone. She dropped her head, her hands trembling at her sides as her heart plunged into despair.

"And you," Rothgard commanded, but she refused to look at him. She wouldn't give him the satisfaction while she still belonged to herself.

Leyna took slow, steady breaths, waiting to feel some sort of change. Maybe she wouldn't. Maybe it didn't work like that. She might retain her sense of self but take on different beliefs and motivations.

But her attitude toward Rothgard hadn't changed. She chose not to bow to him. She chose to stand there with her eyes shut and ignore him. Leyna opened her eyes and stared at her feet, wiggling her toes within her boots. When Rothgard had taken hold of the soldiers, their actions had changed immediately. So why hadn't she fallen victim in the same way?

Something was wrong.

Leyna lifted her face to Rothgard, her mouth agape and her brow furrowed in disbelief. She saw her confusion reflected in Rothgard's face, neither of them understanding why his magic wasn't working on her. Rothgard closed his eyes and sucked in a deep breath, as though he tried to focus more intensely on what he tried to do.

Still, Leyna felt nothing. Eamonn had battled himself to resist the magic but had succumbed, and he was even half-Kaethiri. What made Leyna different?

Rothgard growled in frustration, raising his hands to his head and clenching them into fists. "What's happening?"

Leyna gasped, the realization almost knocking her off her feet.

*Imrilieth's gift.*

The Queen of the Kaethiri had given her immunity to the power of the Réalta. Leyna was the only human person who could resist the Réalta's magic, which meant she was the only person who could retrieve it.

Leyna's eyes fell on the glowing amulet around Rothgard's neck. She knew her purpose. She had to get it back.

Time was of the essence. Once she moved, Rothgard would likely stop trying to use the Réalta to control her, but he could still use practical magic or sheer brute force against her. Leyna scanned her eyes over the room, searching for something she could use to help her get close to Rothgard, and her eyes landed on the fireplace and the tools that sat beside it.

Leyna bit her bottom lip. Fire was unpredictable; she might end up trapping herself and Eamonn in a burning room, but it was worth the risk.

She heard Rothgard gasp as she lunged toward the fire, grabbing the fireplace shovel and plunging it into the burning logs. The shovel flew from her grasp as Rothgard pulled it through the air with magic, sending sparks and embers shooting through the room. Leyna jumped back and brushed off sparks that had landed on her clothes, and Rothgard magically pushed away embers soaring in his direction. Some of the embers landed on the tattered rug and threadbare tapestries, and new flames sprung up around the room.

Rothgard turned his attention to the little fires, pushing down the flames with magic, and Leyna dove behind a chair close to him. Her heart raced and she heard her pulse throbbing in her ears. This was her chance. She allowed herself one second to take a deep breath of air tinged with smoke, and then she charged at him.

The surprise of the blow helped Leyna tackle Rothgard to the ground with just her body weight. The Réalta hung limply from his neck, touching the wooden floor. Leyna and Rothgard locked eyes for a fraction of a second, and the unadulterated malice in his stare stopped Leyna's heart for that moment.

If she failed, the world was doomed.

She met his malevolence with fierce, steely eyes and a set jaw. Leyna threw her hand to the floor and wrapped her fingers around the pendant, pulling the chain free from Rothgard's neck.

Rothgard reached for her, but Leyna jumped to her feet before he could grab her and kicked some nearby embers toward his face. He cried out as the burning embers met his skin, rolling away from the fire. Leyna stepped back, her breaths shallow as she watched him writhe on the floor.

"Leyna!"

The sound of her name brought her back to reality and she turned her head in the direction of the voice. Eamonn staggered toward her, as quickly as he could with a limp in his right leg. Leyna glanced down at the pendant in her hand—it had lost its green glow. The spell had been broken when she ripped the Réalta from Rothgard's neck. Leyna rushed to Eamonn who held out his hand to her with urgency, his forehead wrinkling with his raised eyebrows and his mouth hanging open.

"Give it to me!" he ordered, holding out his hand. "I need it! The necklace, give it to me!"

The edge to Eamonn's voice unnerved Leyna, and for a moment she held back, wondering if he might still be under Rothgard's control and this was a way for him to reclaim it. But the light from the pendant had faded, and the look in Eamonn's eyes was passionate and familiar.

Leyna didn't have time to mull over the possibilities, though. She heard Rothgard coming to his feet and extended her open hand to Eamonn, the necklace resting in the center of her palm.

The old, brittle furnishings in the room caught fire as the flames spread and smoke poured into the air. Eamonn took the Réalta and attached it around his neck, the stone in the center of the pendant glowing the minute Eamonn connected with it. Coming from Eamonn, though, the light it cast seemed vibrant rather than evil.

Leyna's mouth fell open with a gasp and she took a faltering step back. Her heart leapt, pounding faster against her ribs, and the corners of her mouth turned upward.

Eamonn harnessed the power of the Réalta.

"The necklace, give it to me!"

Eamonn didn't bother trying to make sense of the pull within him. As soon as Leyna retrieved the pendant from Rothgard and he came back to his own mind, he felt an inexplicable compulsion to get it back. He had no idea how to use the amulet, but the force drawing him to it couldn't be ignored.

Leyna offered him the necklace and he grasped it, returning it to his neck for the first time since he'd left it with her in Teravale. At once, he felt a change surge through him. The pain in his hip and shoulder disappeared. Power pulsated through his body from head to toe, a feeling he'd never known before. He'd had a taste of it once, when he used magic against Rothgard's men in Caen. This time, energy filled him, ran through him, emanated from him. He felt unstoppable.

Eamonn found Rothgard behind Leyna, his face red and splotchy from the embers Leyna had kicked at him.

"You are mine," Eamonn muttered through clenched teeth, taking a step in Rothgard's direction.

Eamonn did nothing special to use his magic; it simply emerged from him like an extension of himself. The spite and hatred in Rothgard's expression transformed to stone-faced attention, and a touch of a smile played on Eamonn's lips.

*Finally.*

He had the upper hand, no longer subject to Rothgard's torment. Eamonn's hands trembled as he relished the power that flowed through him like electricity. He could do whatever he wanted to this man who had mistreated him. The possibilities were endless.

Eamonn's gaze drifted to Leyna between himself and Rothgard, realizing her eyes were fixed on him, and his stomach lurched. Her presence held him back. A thousand horrible ideas about what he could do to Rothgard ran through his mind, but Eamonn wouldn't let Leyna witness him become a monster.

The flames lapped at the paintings and tapestries on the walls, stretching up to the wooden beams in the high ceiling. It wouldn't be long before the ceiling collapsed into the room, crushing everything below. Leyna coughed, the smoke stifling her. Unless Eamonn wanted to take Rothgard with them—which he didn't—he wouldn't have time to spend torturing him anyway. As much as he would like Rothgard to pay for his abuse, Eamonn decided to let the fire take him.

"You're staying here," he snarled, speaking to Rothgard with his head tilted down and glaring at him with narrowed eyes. "You don't leave this room, no matter what happens."

Rothgard stood in the same spot, motionless, his face blank. "Of course," he said in his silky voice, clasping his hands behind his back.

Eamonn knew from his brief experience moments ago that Rothgard would follow Eamonn's command as if it was his own idea. He would be aware of the fire, of the danger, but would believe he had chosen to stay in the room and be consumed.

Eamonn felt no guilt or remorse keeping him there. Rothgard deserved that and more.

Leyna coughed again, and Eamonn reached out a hand to her. "Let's go!" he cried over the crackling of wood underneath the flames. She took his hand and they hurried toward the door.

"Do you need help?" she asked, and he turned back to see her looking him up and down with confusion in her eyes. "You couldn't walk."

"It's the magic," he answered, hoping she would accept a brief explanation. "I'm fine."

Eamonn opened the door and led Leyna out, nearly stumbling down the steep, winding steps as he raced down. He ought to remember the way out of the fortress. Rothgard had dragged him through the castle up to the tower after his escape attempt only a few days before. And if they ran into anyone, he could use his newfound magic to turn them away.

As they came near the bottom of the staircase, a rumble of noises reached them. Eamonn could hear shouting voices, the clanging of metal, and the thundering of footsteps filtering into the staircase. Leyna tugged at Eamonn's hand and he stopped before they reached the staircase's entrance.

"What do you think is going on?" Leyna asked, holding Eamonn back from the bottom of the stairs.

Eamonn listened for anything that might give him a better idea, but the noisy clanging drowned out the words being shouted. He crept down the stairs, Leyna on his heels, ready for the moment the opening appeared to poke his head out.

"I have an idea," he murmured on his way down. "When you took the pendant from Rothgard, it broke his control over me."

Leyna gasped. "The soldiers. They were already here when the magic was broken."

Before they reached the bottom of the stairs, Eamonn heard quick footsteps approaching and entering the stairwell. He put a foot back up on the step behind him, but he knew they couldn't go back that way. He spread out his arms to shield Leyna from whomever raced into the stone staircase, his heart thumping in his ears.

Rounding the tight corner jumping two steps at a time, Hadli nearly smacked face first into Eamonn, stopping himself and catching his momentum by pressing his hands out to the stone walls on either side of them.

"Hadli," Eamonn murmured, lifting his eyebrows. Unsure if Hadli was friend or foe at the moment, Eamonn kept his arms out to protect Leyna behind him.

"You made it out," Hadli said, flicking his gaze to Leyna before returning to Eamonn, his eyes landing on the glowing pendant at his chest. "I was on my way to help you. One of the Idyrrians sent me; he told me you were in trouble."

*I've* been *in trouble*. Eamonn wanted to say that and more to Hadli, but now wasn't the time. "We have to get out of here, the..." Eamonn let his sentence trail off, pausing to meet Hadli's dark brown eyes and dropping his arms. "What Idyrrian?"

Hadli drew his eyebrows together. "A soldier from Erai, Florin." Hadli searched Eamonn's face, apparently trying to figure out why Eamonn cared.

Eamonn couldn't speak. He blinked over and over and dropped his eyes from Hadli, his heart in his throat. His father had sent Hadli to help him, and Hadli came. The emotions welling within him blindsided him, but he pushed them back down. He couldn't unpack them yet, not until he'd gotten out of this place.

"The tower is on fire," Eamonn said, meeting Hadli's eyes again. "We have to get out, and fast."

"On fire?" Hadli repeated, turning and heading back down the stairs. "How did that happen?"

"It was how we got away, basically," Eamonn replied, intentionally keeping the details vague. Hadli reached the passageway at the bottom of the staircase and Eamonn and Leyna filed out behind him.

They found themselves in the midst of a full-scale battle, the soldiers from the beach fighting Rothgard's people throughout the castle. Eamonn and Leyna stuck close to Hadli, running past people fighting each other and ducking around swinging weapons. The smells of blood and sweat filled the air, and Eamonn wrinkled his nose in disgust. They turned a corner, entering a corridor that Eamonn recognized, and Hadli led them behind a wide pillar for cover.

"The door is that way," Hadli told them, pointing from their hiding spot. "You shouldn't have trouble getting out now."

Eamonn frowned. "You're not coming?"

The muscles in Hadli's jaw tensed momentarily. "I got you out. That's all I wanted to do."

"Hadli," Eamonn said, gripping Hadli's upper arm, "come with us. There's nothing for you here anymore."

Hadli pulled his arm out of Eamonn's grasp, taking a step back with a new arrogance on his face. "You underestimate Rothgard."

He didn't give Eamonn the chance to respond, turning his back on them and leaving the corridor.

Leyna pulled at Eamonn's arm. "Come on."

Eamonn realized he was still watching the spot where Hadli had left them, almost waiting for him to come back. Hadli had made it clear where his loyalty lay. Eamonn pulled his eyes from the empty corridor, ignoring the twisting of his stomach, and he dashed with Leyna to the door at the end of the passageway. She reached up for the iron handle as the door opened before them, forcing them to jump back out of the way. A group of soldiers waited on the other side of the door, silhouetted by the daylight behind them.

Eamonn's stomach dropped like a rock. So much for their way out.

The largest soldier in the group pushed through the others and came straight for Eamonn. Eamonn held his breath, waiting for something horrible to happen, but once the man stepped into the light inside the castle, all of Eamonn's fears vanished.

"Dorylss!" Eamonn cried, throwing himself into his mentor's embrace. Sobs caught in his throat, overcome at the sight of his friend.

"It's good to see you, lad," Dorylss said with a smile, tears pooling in his eyes. He laid a hand on Eamonn's shoulder and squeezed it gently.

"You, too," Eamonn responded, unable to stop the grin that spread across his face.

"You got the Réalta back," said a girl in the group he didn't recognize, her brown eyes wide and locked on the illuminated pendant.

"The what?" Eamonn asked, stepping away from Dorylss with a furrowed brow. "Who are you?"

Leyna gestured to the girl. "Eamonn, this is Teiyn, and her twin brother, Taran," she added, moving her hand to a man with the same brown skin and twinkling eyes as the girl. "Your pendant is called a Réalta. But we'll have more time to get into everything later."

Taran and Teiyn offered the same toothless grin with the introduction, and Eamonn nodded once in acknowledgement.

"We've trapped Rothgard in the tower and set it on fire," Eamonn said, his focus on Dorylss. He brought his fingers to the pendant. "I have him under my control."

"If you've taken care of Rothgard, we'll spread the word among our soldiers and call for a surrender from his followers," said a Farnish woman with sharp features. She looked up at Dorylss and added, "Go. You've accomplished your mission; this is our battle now."

Dorylss smiled at the woman, then at a broad Farnish man beside her. "We can never offer you enough thanks."

"You don't have to. We had a common goal," the man said, leading the rest of the company behind them into the castle alongside the woman. "We'll meet again in Braedel. I believe you can answer some questions we have."

Dorylss tilted his head toward the man and the small force dove into the castle, leaving Dorylss, Taran, and Teiyn with Eamonn and Leyna.

"We have a boat beached on the shore, away from the docks," Taran said, his eyes on Eamonn. "We'll show you the way."

Taran and Teiyn led the group away from the castle, a gentle snow falling and covering the earth in a dusting of white. They hadn't gone far when a low rumbling sound filled the air.

Eamonn's stomach turned at the sound, too eerily similar to the sound he heard when Rothgard shot ice spikes out of the ground.

The rumble came from behind them. Taran and Teiyn were the first to turn and look for the source of the noise. Eamonn followed their eyes to a tower at the front of the castle, its turreted roof giving way as smoke and flames billowed out. The collapsing roof toppled the stone walls of the tower, sending crumbling rock cascading down the cliff on which the fortress was perched. Eamonn watched in awe as the rumble grew to a roar, and the tower where he and Leyna had fought Rothgard minutes before became a thing of the past.

The others turned and headed for the tree line, and Eamonn tore his eyes from the spectacle to join them. Rothgard's body must have tumbled with the rubble down the cliff. It might even be unrecognizable by the time it came to rest.

Eamonn's train of thought was cut short. A figure fell purposefully out of the sky in front of them, landing with bent knees on two feet with a thud that made the earth around them quake. The figure stood and blocked their path, his skin red and blistered and his clothes blackened, tattered, and smoking.

If not for the gasps and exclamations from those with him, Eamonn might have believed he'd strayed into a nightmare. He dipped his head down to look at his pendant, the green stone dull. When had it stopped glowing? He didn't realize he'd lost the connection. Eamonn tried to find it again, tried to summon the magic he'd used before, but nothing happened. His head shot back up in horror as the demon Rothgard approached them.

"Where do you think you're going with *my* amulet?" he growled, raising his hands in the air. He may have lacked the amulet to control their wills, but he could still attack them with practical magic.

"Get behind us!" Teiyn yelled as she and Taran took positions opposite Rothgard.

Teiyn began quickly rotating her fists in a tight circle before pulling her hands apart, palms out, and casting a forcefield in front of them as Rothgard flung sharp ice spikes at the group. Taran opened his palms to the sky and raised them in the air, then turned his hands toward Rothgard and sent a burst of wind to push the ice spikes back.

"Hide in the rock!" Taran shouted.

Eamonn grabbed Leyna and pushed her to safety behind a nearby boulder. Dorylss crouched beside her, hidden by the rock, but Eamonn stood on Dorylss's other side, keeping his eyes on the fight. He kept trying to connect with the pendant again, hoping to step up and end this. Sweat formed on his forehead despite the cold air as Eamonn fought to find the magic he knew lived inside of him.

The twins held their own against Rothgard's magic, all their backup inside the castle. Teiyn released her forcefield and Taran turned the ground under Rothgard's feet to an ice patch, causing him to lose his footing. The distraction granted Teiyn a moment to pass a hand across her chest and turn it palm up in front of her, sending dozens of illusions of herself all around them. Rothgard's eyes flitted among the identical copies of Teiyn, then he grunted and shot another volley of ice spikes into the illusion.

Taran rounded up loose rocks in a whirlwind and sent the cyclone zooming at Rothgard. He flung it away, but not quickly enough to avoid being hit by some of the outer stones, and he shrieked as the stones came in contact with his burned skin. With curved fingers pointed to the sky, Rothgard lifted ice spikes out of the ground in front of him, destroying Teiyn's illusion. She cast another forcefield while Taran copied Rothgard's flying ice spikes, but Rothgard whisked them away like they were snow.

"Why don't they just push him off the cliff?" Leyna asked Dorylss and Eamonn, fear bleeding through her features.

"It's pointless," Eamonn responded, taking a moment to duck behind the boulder. "He can teleport, he can hover, he can do a number of tricks with magic to keep from plummeting to his death."

Eamonn glanced back out at Taran and Teiyn, and he could tell they were beginning to lose steam. They were their last line of defense against Rothgard and quickly getting overwhelmed.

Resting his back against the boulder, Eamonn closed his eyes and searched for his magic. He recalled the voice that came to him as he fainted in the tower room, the voice that sounded like a song in his mind. Stilling his heart and his mind, he reached into the deep recesses of his spirit and spoke from within.

"I need my magic."

Eamonn waited and listened, and a soft hum filled his ears.

*It's right here, within you*, the same melodic voice said.

The hum spread throughout his body and he opened his eyes to find the pendant glowing once again.

*But it is not refined*, the voice continued, fading as he reentered the world. *It will not last.*

Eamonn took a deep breath and stepped out from behind the rock. Whatever he did, he had to make it quick and make it count.

*Stop fighting,* he commanded Rothgard in his mind.

Immediately, Rothgard lowered his hands and stood at attention again as Eamonn's magic wrapped around his mind. Eamonn left the boulder and passed Taran and Teiyn, looking over his shoulder to call, "Get behind the rocks!"

The twins shared a glance before dropping their magic and joining Dorylss and Leyna behind the shield of the boulder.

Eamonn rushed toward Rothgard, already feeling the power within him dwindling. He had to do something before he lost the magic again and Rothgard returned to himself.

*Why don't they just push him off the cliff?* Leyna's words rang in his head. Rothgard couldn't do anything about it now.

Eamonn positioned himself so that Rothgard was between him and the cliff's edge, and he closed his eyes. He recalled the day he'd first used magic in Teravale and tried to recreate that feeling. He focused his mind on the thrum of power deep within himself, and he felt energy pulling from all around him through his hands and feet toward his chest. This time, aware of what he hoped to accomplish, he felt the warm shockwave shoot from his body, and he opened his eyes in time to see Rothgard's helpless form go flying off the edge of the cliff.

Eamonn released a heavy breath and fell to his knees, his face falling to his chest. His pendant still glowed, but its light had started to dim.

He heard footsteps approaching, and someone lifted him to his feet. Eamonn looked up to see Dorylss smiling down at him. A weight fell off of Eamonn's shoulders and he couldn't help but grin in return.

Rothgard was gone.

Eamonn fell into Dorylss's embrace, sighing into his comforting closeness. His body started to tremble as he hugged Dorylss as though he withdrew from a drug. He hadn't felt so free in his life.

He closed his eyes and pressed his face into Dorylss for a moment, the man's shirt catching the few tears that had pooled in Eamonn's eyes.

"That was incredible!" Taran said, running with Teiyn from their hiding spot. Eamonn pulled away from Dorylss and faced the twins.

"Well done, Eamonn," Teiyn added, her eyes wide with awe and her cheeks lifted in a cheerful smile.

He tilted his head in thanks and stepped past them to the only one who still hung back.

Leyna kept her head down, examining the ground that Eamonn had cleared of loose rubble. Eamonn ambled over to her. He had an idea what she must be feeling—trying to comprehend victory when defeat had been so certain.

He reached out and took her hand, and she brought her eyes to his. Tears pooled in the bottoms of them.

"I can't believe it," Leyna whispered, so quietly that Eamonn had trouble hearing her.

Eamonn lifted his other hand to her face and rested his thumb on her cheek. He finally had the chance to experience her presence again, to feel the warmth of her soft skin. She filled him with a power different from his magic, but just as great.

"Me neither," he murmured back. "It's like a dream. I woke up from the nightmare, but I'm still dreaming."

Leyna's closed lips spread across her face and she blinked back her tears. "I promise you, you're not dreaming. You're here. I'm here. It's over."

Eamon's lips curved in a smile and he let his hand fall from her face. "It's over."

She let a breath out through her mouth and squeezed his hand at her side. Eamonn saw relief sweep over her features like a wave coming upon the shore. When the wave pulled back into the sea, he saw the Leyna he remembered, the Leyna who had sat in the sitting room of her house with him and had shown him sketches of a pendant like his.

It felt like another lifetime.

Dorylss had come up behind them, stopping a few paces away. "Come on, lad," he said, motioning for them to follow. "Let's get you on the boat."

Eamonn dropped Leyna's hand, and they both fell in step behind Dorylss.

"So, what do we do now?" Eamonn asked his mentor. He didn't live in the same world he'd left anymore, and he wasn't sure how to navigate it.

"We'll go back to Teravale," Dorylss replied, helping Eamonn down the slope through the woods. "You need some time to rest and gather your strength. Then," he said, casting a glance at Leyna, "I think you'll be expected in Avaria."

Eamonn's brow furrowed, but a small smile played on his lips. He turned to look at Leyna behind him, her blue eyes bright.

"The Kaethiri will want to see you again."

# EPILOGUE

THEY SAID IT WAS ready, so he descended the stairs to their laboratories to find out if their claims were true.

He'd given his artists and alchemists the task of constructing an amulet months ago, when he still didn't know if obtaining a Réalta was possible. They'd studied all the information he'd gathered about the Réalta and had collaborated to create something similar, but it still lacked an element they couldn't identify.

The life-matter obtained from a Kaethiri—even a half-Kaethiri—seemed to offer the solution they sought. The alchemists had injected the amulet with the same marrow that filled Rothgard's veins, and now it was ready for him to test.

It had taken all the physicians he'd acquired in his push across Sarieth, as well as all the healing magic he could conjure, but

Rothgard had managed to reconstruct his appearance with minimal scarring in spite of his burns.

The boy had shown his inability at wielding the amulet both times he'd held his mind—he'd failed to account for Rothgard's use of protective magic in dire circumstances. He'd stayed in the burning tower and had fallen into the sea, but on both instances, he'd still had the faculties to use magic to save himself.

If the boy had known better, he would have commanded him to not use magic.

Rothgard entered the laboratories, and one of the alchemists called him over to his table. A pendant lay before him, a deep red translucent stone inlaid in a gold casing. Rothgard lifted the amulet from the table and hung it around his neck.

The stone shone bright red, and Rothgard's mouth twisted into a smile.

When saving the world means losing himself,
Eamonn will risk everything to see evil defeated
and exact his revenge

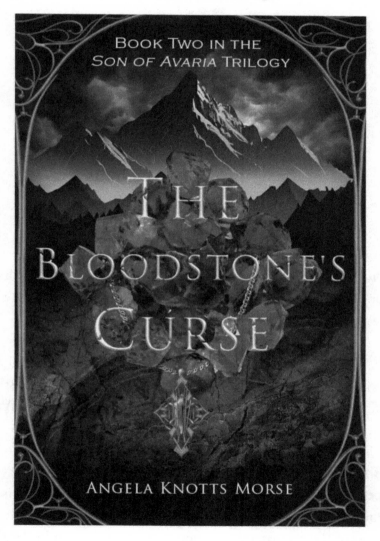

BOOK TWO IN THE
*SON OF AVARIA* TRILOGY

THE
BLOODSTONE'S
CURSE

ANGELA KNOTTS MORSE

Eamonn travels to Avaria and
beyond to defeat Rothgard in

# THE BLOODSTONE'S CURSE

# ONE

THE WOUNDS WOULD HEAL, but the scars would remain. Each long, ragged gash on his back would forever remind him of a time he only wanted to forget.

A mere two weeks had passed since Eamonn was rescued from the crumbling fortress of Holoreath, where he had endured endless torture at Rothgard's hands. Two weeks separated his past life from his present one. Because that was what it was, now. A past life.

The entire world felt different to Eamonn. Heavier, but also somehow lighter. The torture he'd endured changed his perspective, but at the same time, the threat of Rothgard had been eliminated from their country of Sarieth. Eamonn had left the island of Nidet a changed man, hoping he'd be able to find a place for himself in the world before him.

"We'd best get going, lad, if we're to arrive in Rifillion by nightfall."

The voice of Eamonn's mentor, Dorylss, broke through his reverie in the stables after Eamonn's hands had stilled in his work to saddle Rovis, who had returned to Braedel after running off in an ambush. Eamonn craned his neck over his shoulder to see Dorylss's eyes turn up at the corners, a fan of lines spreading out beside them. Even though an unruly auburn beard largely hid his mouth, Eamonn knew Dorylss smiled. Layered under the man's features was another, more subtle emotion: relief. To see Eamonn strong. To see him well. To have his honorary son returned to him, whole.

Of course, Eamonn didn't feel entirely whole.

Eamonn pulled the straps tight against his new leather bag, its rich scent filling his nose. Dorylss and Leyna had shopped for him during their stay with Taran and Teiyn in Braedel, purchasing new clothes as well as the bag. The old clothes he'd been wearing upon his rescue—bloodied, sweat-stained, and ragged—had been burned.

The thought of Leyna, who lingered in the inn eating her breakfast, gripped Eamonn's heart. Something about her had changed as well. She'd risked her own life to save Eamonn by invading Rothgard's hideaway with Dorylss and the twin magic-casters, Taran and Teiyn, so Eamonn wasn't surprised she'd been affected, but he hated himself for it and took the entirety of the blame for the weight she now carried.

Every now and then, she'd had a conversation with Dorylss or one of the twins, but then she would go back to quietly tending Eamonn's wounds or reading one of the books in the house. She hadn't been entirely closed off, though; sometimes Eamonn would notice her eyes on him—kind, compassionate, and caring—but when she met his gaze, she would look away.

Was it because he had betrayed her? Leyna had traveled across provinces and through clear danger for the sole purpose of rescuing him, only for Eamonn to give her up to the enemy, but neither brought that up.

A horse snorted, and Eamonn worked faster. He was getting too lost in his thoughts.

"There's no way Leyna can ride this mare the rest of the way. She can barely support her own weight, much less Leyna's." Dorylss shook his head as he stroked the horse's nose. "That fall was too much for this old girl."

They'd purchased the senior cream-colored mare in Braedel for Leyna to ride, only able to afford her because of her age. Right after they entered the village of Dorca, the horse had twisted her ankle in a muddy divet in the road concealed by recent rain.

"What will we do?" Eamonn dropped his hands from Rovis's saddle as Dorylss turned to his own horse to work on his tack.

With a hopeless shrug, Dorylss said, "Leave her here. Sell her for what we can. Someone in the village might be willing to nurse her back to health for the right price."

"We can't afford another horse."

"No, we can't."

Leyna was again without a horse. A rippling warmth nestled in Eamonn's stomach as he considered how Leyna might travel.

*Leyna.* There she was again in his mind. His heart ached with the thought that she might be angry at him. Maybe Dorylss knew something he didn't. He hadn't had the opportunity before to ask if Dorylss knew of something bothering her, and the lack of her presence in the stable had Eamonn itching to bring her up.

"Uh... Dorylss," he started, his voice low, "how's Leyna doing?"

Dorylss caught Eamonn's gaze briefly, his narrowed eyes curious. "I believe she's all right, given the circumstances."

The word "circumstances" hit Eamonn's gut like a rock. So something *was* wrong.

"What do you mean?"

"She was determined to save you but had no idea what she was walking into on that island. Capture may have meant imprisonment or torture or... death." A softness washed over Dorylss's features. "She carried your pendant, and with it, the weight of what would happen should it fall into the wrong hands."

*Which it did.* The rock in Eamonn's gut dropped, heavy and horrible. It was because of him. Eamonn had condemned her before she'd set foot on the island.

"Does she... does she resent me for it?" The words barely managed to scrape out. He kept his eyes on Rovis's saddle, ensuring the straps were secure.

Eamonn thought back to the last time he'd carried on a conversation with Leyna shortly after they'd arrived in Braedel. He'd told Leyna he saw his father in the tower and that Florin had sent Hadli to help Eamonn, explaining the significance without going into detail.

He'd also briefly described what he'd undergone at Rothgard's hand. Though he kept the specifics of his torture to himself, he did confess to breaking under duress and giving her up to Rothgard as the one who carried his pendant.

Eamonn had betrayed her. He'd broken her trust to save his own skin and make the torture stop. Granted, he had hoped it would also save Leyna's life, but he should have guessed Rothgard was not a man of his word. It only made sense that Leyna should resent him.

"Lad." Dorylss's voice was authoritative, pulling Eamonn's gaze upward. "Why don't you talk to her? It would do much more good than asking me."

Eamonn looked to the saddle again, still fiddling with the straps even though he didn't need to tighten them any more. "I guess I think coming from you, it'll hurt less."

"Give her the benefit of the doubt. She might not know what to say either. Maybe she's waiting for you to say something first."

Dorylss was probably right. He usually was, about most things.

"And I don't think someone who resented you would put as much time and effort as she did into helping you heal." Dorylss gave the mare another gentle pat. "I'm going to speak to the stable master and see if he'd be interested in buying the old girl here and finding a new owner."

Dorylss exited the stall, his last words about Leyna on repeat in Eamonn's mind. Although more reserved, Leyna had been by his side ceaselessly the last two weeks, which had to be a good sign. He hoped he hadn't done something to create a rift between them or ruin their friendship. Maybe it was selfish of him after all she'd been through for his sake, but he couldn't deny his growing affection for her. It was true he'd already been attracted to her, but her determination to save him from Rothgard, and then her kindness and attentive care after his rescue, had rooted those feelings.

Once Dorylss returned with a small sum from the sale of the mare, they led their horses out into the open air to find Leyna leaning against the stable wall, her arms wrapped around herself as her breath appeared in short-lived puffs. A lightning bolt shot upward through Eamonn's core. He expected her to wait for them inside the warm inn.

"Ah, there you are," Dorylss said, stopping in front of Leyna. "I'm afraid your mare isn't fit to ride after her fall. The stable master knows someone who will buy her, so we at least have some money back for her." He offered the reins to his own horse out to her. "You can ride on Bardan."

"No, don't." Eamonn heard the sudden urgency in his tone and cleared his throat. Trying again, he spoke more evenly. "There's no reason we can't all ride. You can sit in front of me on Rovis."

Leyna's lips parted and her eyes flicked between Eamonn and Dorylss. Eamonn's heart sped up and his stomach twisted. Did she not want to be close to him that badly?

"I can just ride on Bardan, if Dorylss is offering."

"Dorylss is being overly generous. He can't walk all the way to Teravale."

"Give me some credit!" Dorylss interrupted with a chuckle. "I'm not as old and brittle as you seem to think I am."

Leyna pressed her lips together and asked Dorylss a wordless question with her eyes.

"It's up to you," Dorylss replied with a shrug. "I don't mind walking, but Eamonn is right. We could all ride."

Leyna's chest rose with a slow inhale. "Dorylss, you can take Bardan. I'll ride with Eamonn."

The way she'd said it only made Eamonn's stomach knot tighter. Riding with her would be a good time to talk to her, as Dorylss had suggested. But even then, Eamonn knew the words wouldn't be easy to find.

Eamonn held out his hand to take Leyna's bag, attaching it to Rovis's saddle opposite his. She mounted first, settling herself at the front of the saddle. Eamonn grasped the pommel in front of her, his thumb unintentionally brushing her knee and sending his pulse into a frenzy.

In a swift movement, he swung his leg over the horse and tucked into the saddle behind her. His chest pressed into her back for a fleeting moment before he pulled away, allowing a hand's breadth of space between them.

The warmth of Leyna's body banished the cold in front of Eamonn. She reached to her bound strawberry-blonde hair and pulled it over her shoulder, revealing the pale flesh of her neck. Leyna took the reins and Eamonn rested his hands on his legs, conscious of her personal space and respecting it how he could. He was conscious of everything about her.

The morning sun peeked over the bustling city, spreading across the tall buildings enclosing narrow, muddy streets. Thin clouds drifted through the sky, a cold breeze pushing them along with the scents of cookfires that warmed the crisp air. Idyrrians, bundled to their necks in clothes of bright colors, filtered into the streets as they began their day.

As the group set off on the road south, Leyna sat ahead of Eamonn as stiff as a board, holding the reins and guiding Rovis down the road. Her natural flowery scent drifted to Eamonn's nose, and he lost himself in the comfort and familiarity of her presence. She was safety. She was home.

In the midst of Leyna's soothing closeness, something decidedly unnerving touched the back of Eamonn's mind. It was foreign and unwelcome and dark. Where it had come from, he couldn't fathom, so he pushed it away until only the peace from Leyna remained.

The trip back home to Teravale would take several days, especially if they kept a slow pace to keep Eamonn's nearly-healed injuries from regressing. Eamonn was eager to return, but he didn't mind the prolonged travel time as much if Leyna would be riding with him the rest of the way.

Dorylss had suggested that Eamonn stay home in Caen as he went off with the caravan market for their next months-long journey, allowing his body to fully heal and letting him spend some time with Leyna, but Eamonn had resisted. As much as Eamonn liked the idea of several months of rest with Leyna, he knew how restless he would get if Dorylss and the other merchants they worked with left him behind. He needed to be out there, traveling through the country, getting his life back to normal.

Not to mention, Eamonn hoped to stop by Avaria as the caravan traveled through Idyrria. Leyna had recounted her interaction with the Queen of the Kaethiri—the magical beings who dwelled in the forest realm, one of whom had been Eamonn's mother—to him on the boat ride back to Braedel. In his previous life, Eamonn would have had trouble believing her, but after everything he'd seen, none of it came as a surprise. He wished he'd had the chance to meet with Imrilieth himself. He had so many questions to ask about his mother, about his magic, and he wanted to use the caravan journey as an excuse to visit Avaria himself.

Leyna's back curved against Eamonn's chest as she relaxed in the saddle. He sucked in a breath that caught in his throat, and his heart jumped to meet it. He prayed she couldn't feel the rapid hammering against his ribcage.

Movement to his right pulled Eamonn's gaze, and he saw Dorylss watching them, the glimmer of a smile playing on his lips. It confirmed to Eamonn that his offer for Leyna to ride Bardan had been intentional in order to spur Eamonn into sharing his horse.

That man knew exactly what he was doing.

"Doing all right over there?"

Leyna's head turned to the sound and her spine straightened slightly in response, separating her from Eamonn.

"Yes."

Eamonn could glean nothing from Leyna's single-word response. At least she didn't say no.

"So far, so good," he replied, catching the twinkle in Dorylss's eye. Eamonn's eyelids fell low over his eyes as he spoke through them to Dorylss. He knew the man would pick up on his meaning. *I'm on to you.*

Dorylss no longer suppressed a grin, but, with any luck, Leyna wouldn't grasp its true meaning. "Good, good. We have quite a way to go before we arrive at the kingdom."

Rifillion, Idyrria's kingdom, was their only lengthy stop between Braedel and Caen. They would take the time to rest well, refresh their supplies, and help spread the news about Rothgard's defeat. After two weeks, Dorylss hoped word had started to make its way through Idyrria and beyond. Kinrid and Gilleth—the Farnish ex-soldiers who had led a small force against Rothgard's followers on Nidet—should have long since left the island and sent their fighters home to their corners of the country with the news. The people needed to know Rothgard would no longer be a threat to their provinces, monarchies, or families, and hopefully, things across the cities he'd influenced would return to how they were.

Eamonn had expected Kinrid and Gilleth to be right behind them leaving Nidet. They had said they had questions to ask Eamonn and would meet up with them in Braedel, but they never showed. Weeks ago, it would have made Eamonn uneasy, but with their common enemy vanquished, nothing should pose a threat to them. Perhaps they had other business to attend to after taking care of Rothgard's supporters that delayed them.

The sun crept up the sky, like it was in no rush to carry on with the day. Eamonn needed it to go faster. At least Leyna's proximity helped keep his mind off thoughts that always seemed to drift in when Eamonn was otherwise unoccupied: thoughts of his father and Hadli and the events on Nidet that still haunted him. He closed his eyes and breathed in deeply the sharp air tinged with Leyna's sweetness, willing those images away. They plagued his nights enough as it was, his nightmares forcing him to relive his torture; he didn't need them encroaching on his days.

Unbidden, the same unease from before crept back into his mind, heavy and foreboding. Eamonn wanted to believe it was the memory of his trauma, but no. This was new. Dread washed over him as the unease spread from his mind to his core and settled there, sending a low rush of warmth through his veins.

Fear curled in his gut, but Eamonn didn't know why. Nothing was amiss. Leyna sat in front of him. Dorylss rode beside him. Rothgard was defeated. There was no obvious reason for the apprehension that caused sweat to bead on the back of his neck.

His whole body shook—which he could pass off as the cold—and his fingers curled into fists on his thighs as he attempted to bury the fear deep within him. But instead of him controlling the dread, it took root inside him, dragging him down into the darkness of his trauma.

# NOTE TO THE READER

Thank you, reader, for taking the time to read my book. I hope it whisked you away to a different world for a time, and you got to know and love these characters as much as I do. One of the best things about writing is sharing with readers these stories that grow so near and dear to my heart.

Reviews are immensely valuable to me, as they help other ideal readers find my books. If you enjoyed *The Thief's Relic*, I would so greatly appreciate for you to write a review or even just leave a star rating on as many review sites as you would like. Amazon and Goodreads are the two big ones that people see. It really goes a long way to getting my book in the hands of others who will love it.

Stay tuned for the next book in the trilogy, *The Bloodstone's Curse*, and continue the adventure with Eamonn and Leyna.

-Angela

Review on Amazon

Review on Goodreads

# ACKNOWLEDGMENTS

Wow. Just wow. This has been the definition of a dream come true. If you're reading this, you might already know that this is my debut novel. I've dreamed of becoming a published author since I was a young girl, and to find myself at this point is overwhelming, to say the least.

This book was written over the course of five years, but not consistently. I put it to the side and picked it back up again more times that I even remember. I originally planned for it to be a standalone, but with the help of my husband (we'll get to him) it's been expanded into a trilogy, and I'm so excited to continue the story.

Having this book published wouldn't be possible without a number of people, and I want to take the time to thank them for their help in bringing it about.

My cover art team is Etheric Tales, and the leader of the team, Aamna Shahid, is the greatest delight to work with. She and her team have gone above and beyond to create such beautiful art for me, from the cover to my logo to the chapter headers and breaks, and I couldn't be more thankful that I found them.

I wanted to say thank you to my editor, Sara-Jean Englert, and critique partners who helped in a variety of capacities, Izzy, Rae, and Ashley. You pointed out so many (often different) things that helped tighten the story or make my words flow better, and I appreciate your input so much.

The pendant on the cover and the inside title page were created by a friend of mine, Laura Parker, who is such an incredible artist. She has made lots of original art for this book, going all the way back to 2018 when I just wanted a visual representation of Eamonn. She makes beautiful art and she's a beautiful person and I just love working with her. You can find her on Instagram @theludap.

Thank you, the readers, for taking the time to actually read my book. I hope you enjoyed it and if you did, I would love if you would take the time to write a review. Reviews are so important for indie authors, and they are a fantastic show of support for your author friends!

I also want to thank my family: my parents, my brother, my in-laws. Thank you all for being so encouraging and supportive, and for being excited with me! I'm so thankful for the interest you show in my dreams, and I love you all.

Now, to my husband. The one without whom this book in its current form would not be here. He helped me brainstorm, discussing different plot and character possibilities and actually coming up with a lot of the events you just read. He's read so much in this genre (he's a scary fast reader) that he was always ready with a new idea when I got stuck. He's such a creative person and has come up with great ideas that really transformed this story.

More than that, though, he has encouraged me every step of the way. He stayed up with me when I had to write into the wee hours of the morning (on MULTIPLE occasions), he never really complained about how much this book took over my life, he took on extra duties taking care of our daughter to allow me the opportunities to get this book finished, and he always, *always* picked me up when I was down. Getting this book publication ready has been one heck of a challenging journey, and hubs has been there for me to lean on through it all. I am so blessed by him and can never thank him enough.

Lastly, but most importantly, I want to thank my Lord and Savior Jesus Christ for giving me dreams to pursue and passions to explore, as well as the hard work ethic and determination to see them through. All Glory to God!

Angela Knotts Morse is the author of *The Thief's Relic* and *The Bloodstone's Curse*, the first two books in the *Son of Avaria* trilogy. Her love of fantasy began with *The Lord of the Rings*, and fantasy continues to be her favorite genre to both read and write.

When not writing, you can find Angela reading, snacking, binge watching a TV show, or (most likely) wrangling her two small children. She has a special place in her heart for musical theatre, performing in and attending shows when she can. *The Phantom of the Opera* is her favorite.

Angela currently resides in Birmingham, Alabama with her husband, daughter, son, and cat.

You can keep up with Angela on social media and through her newsletter at www.angelamorse.com

Instagram: @angelakmorseauthor • Facebook: Angela Knotts Morse - Author • Twitter: @angelakmorse • Goodreads: Angela Knotts Morse

Printed in the USA
CPSIA information can be obtained
at www.ICGtesting.com
LVHW041801290923
759430LV00003B/44